Finny

Finny

A Novel

Justin Kramon

RANDOM HOUSE TRADE PAPERBACKS

NEW YORK

A Random House Trade Paperback Original

Copyright © 2010 by Justin Kramon

Published in the United States by Random House
Trade Paperbacks, an imprint of The Random House
Publishing Group, a division of Random House, Inc.,
New York.

RANDOM HOUSE TRADE PAPERBACKS and colophon are
trademarks of Random House, Inc.

LIBRARY OF CONGRESS CATALOGING-IN-PUBLICATION DATA

Kramon, Justin.
Finny: a novel / Justin Kramon.
p. cm.
ISBN 978-0-8129-8023-3 (trade pbk.)
eBook ISBN 978-0-679-60367-2
1. Teenage girls—Fiction. 2. Boarding school
students—Fiction. 3. Boarding schools—Fiction.
4. Adolescence—Fiction. 5. Parent and child—Fiction.
6. Friendship—Fiction. I. Title.
PS3611.R365F56 2010
813'.6—dc22 2009034297

Printed in the United States of America

www.atrandom.com

1 2 3 4 5 6 7 8 9

Book design by Rebecca Aidlin

For Lynn

Contents

Book One
Growing Up

Book Two
Reunions and New Friends

Book Three
From Here On Out

Book One

Growing Up

Chapter 1

Finny Meets a Boy

She started out life as Delphine, named by her father for the city where the Greek oracle was from, but she'd always had an independent mind about things like names, so she'd gone by Finny ever since she was old enough to choose. It sounded Irish, which went with her dashing red hair, and in any case Finny always liked everything Irish, for no reason she could say. She had an older brother named Sylvan, probably because her father, Stanley Short, wanted to carry on the tradition of the S.S. initials, which always gave Finny the expectation that the name of a ship was to follow. She thought it was dumb to let someone else decide what you'd be called for the rest of your life—what if they named you Pooh Bear or Dishrag?—so she went ahead and made that decision herself.

Finny was a tough, rascally kid, with a plucky assurance, hair as red as a ripe tomato, a spray of freckles across her nose and cheeks like she'd been splashed with mud—cheeks that were puffed up like bread starting to rise, the kind of cheeks old aunties like to pinch. Sometimes when they did that, Finny pinched back. She wasn't the type of kid to be ogled and fondled all day, to go oogly-googly when people told her how adorable she was. Once when she was four and her aunt Louise gave her a pinch on the cheek, Finny pinched the woman right back on the breast, so hard that Aunt Louise howled in pain and dropped Finny on the floor. It was a linoleum floor, and when Finny crashed down, everyone thought she was dead. Then Finny started to laugh. The reason she was laughing was that she'd plucked the button from Aunt Louise's breast pocket clean off her blouse. She had it balled in her sweaty fist.

Finny's mother, Laura, was a tall woman with a bony frame, a small mouth, a sharp little nose. She wouldn't have been anything special to look at, but she put herself together in an appealing way. Hairpins and colorful sweaters and elegant black skirts. Laura had a warm smile, a shy, flirtatious way of speaking to you, and adults tended to talk to her the way they talked to Finny: in a slightly higher voice, with a practiced gentleness, a simple vocabulary. Finny saw the way her mother transformed herself for guests into a pleased, curious child—and Finny didn't like it. All the posturing, the willed submission, the need to grab up people's attention in greedy handfuls. As a girl Finny wore old soccer shirts and jeans cut off so the strings hung down over her knees. She always had a skinned elbow or a bruised calf muscle from roughhousing after school. She liked kick ball, and for a while could take down most of the boys in her class in a wrestling game they played at recess.

Laura was adamant about proper bathing and grooming, looking neat and tidy whenever you went out of the house. *It is unfortunate but true that people judge you on your looks,* Laura once told her. She had a way of imparting her own beliefs as if they were objective facts about the world.

So Finny responded, "How can I dress if I want to look like an orphan?"

Finny avoided baths, saying she'd bathed the day before and that was enough. Or else she'd get in the bath and neglect to use the soap. Or use it only on her legs but not her arms.

Put the shampoo on her feet. Anything to throw her mother off, show her in what little regard Finny held all those careful preparations and disguisings. She came out of the tub sopping wet, dirt under her fingernails, mud on her cheeks, hair as tangled as a bowl of spaghetti. Finny was supposed to comb her hair after she got out of the bath, but for a while, when she was seven or eight, she stopped doing that. She would just comb the front, and then flip it in a way so that it looked neat when Laura saw it before bed, but the back got so knotted her brother, Sylvan, started calling it the rat's nest.

Finny liked that. She modeled it in the mirror, in front of Sylvan, posing with her arms behind her head, or tilting her chin in an imitation of the coquettish poses she'd seen women striking in magazines. "My beautiful rat's nest," she'd say, stroking it like she was in an ad for shampoo. There was a thrill in this, in so brazenly tossing aside her mother's notions. Like parading around with Laura's underwear on her head. It made Sylvan nervous, Finny knew—he tried to do everything the right way—but he wasn't going to tell anyone about it. Her brother wasn't a snitch.

In the mornings and evenings Finny began to wear her hair up, just to hide it. One night she wore a hat—an old beret from a Halloween costume—when she couldn't find a way to gather it up in any kind of decent shape. Laura asked her to take the hat off, and when she saw what was beneath it, she yelled at Finny and made her go to the Hair Cuttery and get it all combed out. It took four hours, and Finny's mother had to pay triple because they needed three hairdressers working at the same time. Sylvan sat in the empty barber's chair next to where the young women were grooming Finny like a prize poodle, and he told her how adorable she looked.

"Shut up," Finny said. *"Ouch."*

"You look like a strawberry shortcake," he said.

That made her mad, the image of herself as a cute little dessert. "You look like something that gets flushed down the toilet when I'm sick!" Finny yelled in the middle of the hair salon. It was the most disgusting thing she could think of, and one of the young women dropped her comb.

"I'm sorry," Laura said, shooting Finny a cautioning look.

Finny's dad was a lawyer, the managing partner of a small firm in Baltimore, though the family lived far out in the suburbs. All her father ever talked about at the dinner table was "great men." It was his favorite subject, and when they had dinner guests, he liked to sound people out on the issue. He even talked about writing a book one day if he could ever get his ideas in order. He loved to apply quotations by great men to whatever people were discussing. "Good artists borrow; great artists steal," Stanley would offer during any discussion even mildly related to the subject of art. Then he would say, in a more sober tone, "Picasso." Just the name. Never *Picasso said that* or *That was Picasso's idea.* "God does not play dice," was another of his favorites, and to Finny it sounded like a warning, as if God were telling you not to mess with Him. Then Stanley would say, "Einstein," in the way other people say *Amen* at the end of prayers. The name was enough to command respect, dropped like a punctuation mark at the end of whatever point he was making.

Stanley was a shortish man, with red-brown hair, perfectly round wire-rimmed glasses, and a nose that looked slightly too large for his face. He had a finicky stomach, and he chewed Pepto-Bismol tablets like they were after-dinner mints. He didn't like to announce trips to the bathroom, so when he had to get up from the table to attend to his stomach, he would always say he was going to brush his teeth, and then click his top and bottom teeth together, as if to illustrate what he meant. Sometimes he brushed his teeth three or four times over the course of an evening. Because of the Pepto, his breath had a milky, minty smell, like peppermint ice cream, which Finny would always remember waking to on Sunday mornings, when her dad got her out of bed.

Sylvan, who was a year older than Finny, seemed to gobble up everything Stanley said. Or at least he saw no reason to fight against it. When Stanley talked about his theories at the dinner table—about how and why these great men were such geniuses—Sylvan nodded, or asked little questions to spur his father on. He liked the show of it more than anything else, Finny thought later, the sight of his father so engaged, so dynamic. "Look at Jefferson," Stanley would say. "Rousseau. Spinoza." And when she was very young, Finny used to actually turn and look around the room, half-expecting these great men to be found crouching beneath the floral tablecloth, or beside the marble buffet where Finny's mother kept the cracked teal candy plate, the birthday and holiday cards they'd received that season. "They all believed in the rational self-sufficiency of man, the potential of people to do good. Even if it's rarely the case that they do."

Sylvan nodded vigorously, then asked, "What's 'rash on all selfs'?"

Finny laughed. "It's what you have," she told Sylvan.

"Be serious," Sylvan said.

"Be normal," Finny shot back.

"Be quiet," Laura said, "and let your father finish his point."

Then Finny began to feed the dog, Raskal (after Raskolnikov; *Crime and Punishment* was the book that had turned Stanley on to Dostoyevsky), under the table. She liked to pinch little morsels of fish and potatoes off her plate, then slip them like secret messages into Raskal's mouth. Like Stanley, Raskal had a sensitive stomach. He was a loafing, overweight golden retriever with asthma, and when he ate human food, he passed gas noticeably. As soon as Finny began to smell something funny, she heard her father say, "Fiiinnny," his voice gradually rising through her name, like the volume being turned up on a stereo.

"What?" Finny said.

"Goddammit," Stanley said. "Can't you just sit still and listen?"

"I am listening."

"Don't feed the dog people food."

"I don't feed him people food. I feed him doggy food."

"Food at the table is people food, and the doggy food is in the doggy room."

"Sometimes people eat people food in the doggy room when the dog is eating doggy food," Finny said.

"The point is, don't feed him the food we're eating, Finny."

"How could I feed him what we're already eating, Daddy?" Finny said, holding her palms up like it was the craziest question in the world. She knew it would get Stanley riled up. It was great men and mediocre men he wanted to make distinctions between, not people food and doggy food.

"Get up to your room," he told her.

"But—"

"I said get up there!" He was red, and he glared at her. It wasn't that she liked teasing her father, getting him steamed; she just felt like he wasn't speaking to her when he talked about his great men, like everything he said was offered with a wink in Sylvan's direction.

One time, when Sylvan and Finny were much older and they were talking on the phone about their father, Sylvan said, "It's the dinners I always remember. The way Dad held court."

"The thing was," Finny said, "he always seemed to be talking to you, don't you think?"

"I think it's only because I was listening. Really, you were a lot smarter than me. He knew you saw through it."

It was like Sylvan to do this, jumble up all the pieces and rearrange them in a pleasing way, make everyone seem earnest and well-intentioned. She had never thought of the situation that way before, and she wasn't sure if her brother was saying these things now only to make her feel better about what she couldn't change.

"But that time I made fun of him?" she said, trying to pull their conversation back to surer ground, a silly story they could both laugh at.

That was the time her dad had yelled at her for feeding Raskal under the table, and from some perverse motivation, when he was done yelling, Finny had said, "Aristotle." Just that one word, but in a voice that was clearly an imitation of the way Stanley quoted great men.

"What did you say?" Stanley asked.

"Nothing."

"I heard you."

"It wasn't *anything*."

"Don't mock me, Finny."

"I don't mock," she said, unable to resist the opening. "I steal."

Stanley's eyes lit up. *"Get out!"* he screamed, jostling the table so the plates clattered.

On the phone, Sylvan said to Finny, "I'd never seen him so angry before."

"Me neither," she said. "To tell the truth, I was a little frightened."

"I don't think you were ever frightened, Fin."

"You're wrong about that, Syl. I was more frightened than any of you ever knew."

Finny grew up in northern Maryland, in the area of rolling farmland just west of Interstate 83, just south of the Pennsylvania line. The Shorts' home sat on a hill, and from the back windows you could see the whole scoop of the valley where they lived: cornfields, clusters of trees, horse pastures, all threaded with fences and gravel driveways, dotted with big manorish houses. It looked to Finny, from her bedroom window, like a huge gaudy quilt. The air outside their house smelled like grass and dirt, honeysuckles in the late spring, horse manure when the farmers were planting. One lap around the block was eleven miles long, by the car's odometer. (It had been Stanley who'd measured, on a Sunday, with Sylvan in the passenger seat: they'd reported their findings as soon as they'd walked in the door. "Eleven point two," Stanley said. And Sylvan nodded.)

Finny's childhood memories were a clutter of impressions: dried-out fence posts, the feeling of wet grass slapping her feet and the swishing sound it made when she walked in it, swampy summer air, dandelion dust, snow days where everything was bleached white, bright cool fall afternoons turning to silver evenings, hills like a great green sea rolling into the distance. Only at the farthest edge of her vision did the land appear to flatten out. At the horizon there was a kind of green-gray ribbon, which could have been trees or even mountains, some sort of border. It was too far away to tell. But when she was very young, Finny always imagined going there, and in her mind that far-off and magical place got mixed up with ideas she had about her future, about what lay beyond this house.

Another thing Finny remembered: Sunday mornings. It was the only day Stanley didn't go into work at the law firm, and he spent it with the family. He was very adoring of Finny's mother. It showed in his formality in social situations, holding doors and pulling out chairs. Then, at least one Sunday every month he made breakfast in bed for Laura. He was an awful cook, and managed to impart the flavor of five-alarm chili into any dish he prepared. Even when he made French toast, he was able through a combination of seasoning and cooking techniques to capture the essence of five-alarm chili. Some avant-garde New York restaurants would have appreciated his secrets.

The kids would jump into bed with Laura, and since Stanley always made too much food, they'd help her eat it.

Finny's mother ate happily, saying, "You spoil me, Stanley.

You're too good." Every time. Sylvan and Finny would lie in bed with her, sampling the charred remains of Laura's breakfast, as Stanley beamed at his family from the couch in their bedroom.

Only Finny once said, "How could you possibly eat this?"

"Because to me it's the best meal in the world," Laura said.

"Do you get out much, Mom?" Finny asked.

Stanley broke in. "Did you know that Henry James went to a hundred and ten dinner parties in one year alone in England?"

"Really?" Sylvan said.

"Yes. Or maybe he had a hundred and ten invitations. In any case, it was some kind of record. And all that time he was writing *The Portrait of a Lady*. The only way I can make sense of it is that he was gathering material, observing the decadence and waste of a dying society so that he could write about the great unfulfilled potential of man."

"Isn't *Portrait of a Lady* about a lady?" Finny asked.

"Yes," Stanley said, looking confused. "What's your point?"

"You said the 'potential of *man*.' "

"Ah," Stanley said. "When I say 'man,' " he explained in his most professorial voice, "I mean it in the broadest sense. I am talking about all of us, collectively. I'm saying it in the way that a great man once said, 'The effect of the law is to make men good.' " He paused long enough to give weight to this remark, then said, "Aquinas."

"Then why don't you say *people*?" Finny asked. She knew it was just the way you said it. But still. It irked her.

"Because it's simpler," Sylvan said, then looked at his father, who nodded.

"But it's wrong," Finny said, her voice breaking, betraying anger. She knew it didn't matter, but the comment stuck in her somehow.

"Right or wrong," Stanley said, "that is the convention."

"The convention is stupid," Finny said, wanting to say

more, to fight about it, to make clear how ridiculous she thought all his conventions were. She felt her family's eyes on her, her mother's smile like a barrier pushing her back.

"Speaking of ladies," Laura said, giving Finny a meaningful look, "I'm not sure you're acting like one right now."

"Mom, if you had a penis, you would act like a lady." Finny wasn't sure what it meant, but she was so agitated that the words just spilled from her, like water from a cracked glass.

"That's disgusting talk," Laura said, and Finny noticed she was sucking in little breaths, about to cry. "And we—we were having such a nice breakfast," Laura sputtered. "Why can't you ever just let it be when things are going nicely?"

"Sweetheart," Stanley said, getting up from the couch, walking over to her. "She's nothing."

What he actually said was, "It's nothing," but for some reason Finny heard him wrong.

Stanley put his hand on Laura's shoulder. "Don't you think it's enough, Finny?" he said, holding his wife like a demonstration of all Finny had screwed up.

"This food tastes like burnt!" Finny screamed, and stomped out of the room.

"It doesn't really," she heard her brother telling her father as she walked down the hall.

There seemed to be something about her family that Finny couldn't take in. Or maybe it was her family who couldn't take *her* in. All their agreements and rules, rituals and defenses and bargains, it was all wrapped in a fog of mystery, a haze that Finny wasn't sure would burn off in the light of experience.

Finny spent that afternoon in her bedroom, trying not to cry, then giving herself over to it in short, maudlin bursts. She stuffed her face into her pillow and howled, shook with tears. The thought of it, of how she looked, made her sick. If one of her parents or her brother had walked in during these brief concessions to grief, Finny probably would have hopped out the window, or pretended she was trying to suffocate herself. Anything to not be seen like this, so vulnerable, so compromised. She thought of herself like the white birch tree in her parents' yard, which grew far away from all the other trees because it would wither in their shade. On its own, though, it flourished. She wanted to be like that, so odd and lonely and strong.

She thought of things she could do to get them. She could stick a knife in her shirt and spill some ketchup on it, so it would look like she'd stabbed herself. Or she could take one of her mom's earrings and hide it and pretend Raskal ate it. Or stick pictures of women inside her dad's great men books. But all these ideas seemed silly, a little clumsy. She could see them shaking their heads at her, like she'd tripped over her shoelace, or accidentally put her underwear on over her pants. She was hopeless, they'd think, a bum toaster or a wobbly table, something they'd just have to live with because they'd already shelled out the cash.

So she did the only thing that made sense to her. She ran away.

She headed for the sliding glass doors in the back of the house. She thought it might be tricky to get out without anyone seeing her, that her mother might ask her where she was going, or her brother would stop her to see if she'd been crying and she would have to make up some story about her allergies, or how she'd just gotten up from a nap. But the house was quiet. They were tucked into some rooms, somewhere, watching movies or reading or doing work. Sometimes Finny imagined her dad with his great men like a kid with his toy soldiers, lining them up and having them fight, making little machine gun noises with his mouth.

She slid the door open, stepped out, closed it behind her.

This was in the fall. She walked down the hill to the split-rail fence that surrounded the horse pastures behind her house. She started walking along the fence, in the high grass.

Some horses trailed alongside her. It was cool outside, and she hadn't brought a coat, just a little green sweatshirt she liked to wear, with a hood she sometimes tied so that only her nose and eyes stuck out. She called the sweatshirt "the green reaper." The sun was low and bright in her eyes, and the air had that smoky fall smell. A breeze carried the musky scent of the horses to her every now and again, and also the smells of crackly leaves and dirt and grass and manure.

At the end of the fence Finny turned up the dirt path through the old vineyard that had been out of commission for years. On both sides of her some leafy vines wrapped a wire trellis, making a green wall that was just taller than Finny's head. Plants sprouted from cracks in the hard soil, winding in with the vines. Finny loved coming here when she was by herself; this place had a magical feeling to her, like those hills she could just barely make out from her bedroom window. She kicked rocks and listened to the sound of her shoe soles scraping the dusty ground. She liked the noise of it, the bite of cold air on her face, her hands plunged warmly in the green reaper's pockets.

She thought of her mother. *It's almost dinner*, Laura said. *Where's Finny?*

I don't know, Stanley said. *Sylvan! Do you know where your sister is?*

She left the vineyard, walking away from her house. She went up the dirt road that snaked through some hills where cows grazed in the afternoons. This was as far up as she'd ever gone. But she kept walking. Past a decrepit horse barn with a sagging roof, the rails in front of its entrance collapsed so that they made an X. Past a little pond with a fountain in it that someone had made on his property. Finny could hear the water splashing. Inside the pond there were some exotic-looking birds the man must have also bought. They had long, pointy beaks, and black lines around their eyes. Their feathers were streaked with bright colors, purple and gold and green. They looked at Finny through their lined eyes, with serious, arrogant expressions, like the women in fur coats with big leather purses whom Finny had seen on Madison Avenue when she'd gone to New York. She spotted one of their feathers—a blue and silver one—on the grass beside the pond, and picked it up, put it in her pocket.

She walked up a steep hill that was covered in onion grass so it smelled like cooking. When she got near the top, where it flattened out, she saw a pasture on the other side of another split-rail fence. But this fence was in bad shape, bending under Finny's weight when she tried to climb it. She was almost over when one of the boards cracked beneath her foot, and she let out a little scream and fell back.

Only she didn't fall. Something stopped her. Held her. Eased her down onto the grass.

"Thanks," Finny said, before she even saw who had saved her.

"It's okay," the voice said back, and when she turned around, she saw that it belonged to a boy. He was shorter than she was, and a little chubby in the face. His body was like none Finny had ever seen. It looked like a man's, with broad shoulders and strong arms—but smaller, and with shorter legs. Like the kind of pictures you can mix and match—a man's top half on a child's legs.

"I just saw you coming towards that fence," he said, "and I know it's bad. I got hurt on it once. I was going to say something, but you were already on it." He had a high voice, a slightly embarrassed way of speaking, that didn't go with his man's body at all. She noticed his cheeks got a little color when he talked to her.

"Thanks," Finny said again, not knowing what else to say. She wasn't sure if he was fishing for compliments.

But he just said, "Come on. I'll show you the easiest way to get up there."

They walked along the fence a little, and he showed her a

place where two boards had cracked, so that all they had to do was duck a little to get under the top one.

"Easier to go under than over," the boy said.

"Especially for you," Finny said, not knowing why she'd said it. The words had just popped out—it was the way she liked to challenge people, to press a little and see if they pressed back. It seemed mean, though, and she wanted to say she was sorry. After all, he'd saved her life.

But he just laughed. "Yeah," he said. "I can fit in tight places."

She still wanted to apologize, but he just walked on to the middle of the pasture, as if he'd forgotten what she'd said.

The middle of the pasture was also the top of a hill that overlooked the valley. The sun was almost down behind the trees now, and the sky was a crystal gray-blue color. They sat down without saying anything. The valley looked like a giant checkerboard of cornfields, forests, and fields. The land was spotted with barns and farmhouses, sectioned by dirt paths and meandering roads. Finny heard the distant shout of a farmer calling in his horses from the fields, and also some birds tweeting and the buzzing of insects.

"How do you know about this?" she asked the boy.

"I come up here a lot," he said. "When my dad's giving lessons. He teaches piano. We live down there." He pointed at a little brown house, which looked from where they sat to be hardly bigger than Finny's living room. "It's kind of small," the boy said, "so I like getting out if he has people."

"Do you have brothers and sisters?"

"No. Just my dad."

"No mom?" Finny said.

"No," the boy said, and left it at that.

"My name is Finny."

"I'm Earl."

"It's nice to meet you, Earl," Finny said, and held out her

hand to shake. It was an imitation of the jokey, flirtatious way her mother sometimes introduced herself to men. But it was all she had.

He took her hand, though, and shook firmly. She noticed his palm was slick. And his round cheeks were still flushed.

"How old are you?" Finny asked.

"Fifteen," Earl said. "I just turned."

"I'm fourteen," Finny said. "But I'd say I act at least sixteen."

"How do you know?"

"Because there's no one I like who's under seventeen. Except my brother. Sometimes. When he's not being a kiss-ass."

"How old's your brother?"

"Sixteen. We live way over there." She pointed in the direction of her house.

"That's probably nice. He's in high school with you?"

"Yup. But he doesn't like it. He thinks the work is too easy. He's a nerd."

Earl laughed. "I'm glad you like him, then," he said.

"Why?"

He didn't answer the question. He stood and walked a few steps away, a breeze pushing his hair off his face. Finny thought he looked better like that, without his hair hanging down on his forehead. She watched his boxy silhouette against the sky.

"My dad's done," he said, and pointed down to his house. Finny could see a car pulling away from it, a tiny spark of light from the setting sun reflected on its hood. There was another car in the driveway, a brown station wagon. Earl's dad's car.

"That was his last lesson," Earl said. "I better go."

Finny wanted to say something about how she'd had a nice time sitting with him, but she didn't know how to do it without sounding foolish, like she was trying to get him to invite her over or something. She never wanted to seem needy, like she couldn't make her own meal without the scraps of praise other people offered.

Then she remembered the feather—the blue and silver one she'd nabbed from beside the bird pond. She took it out of her pocket. "Here," she said, and handed it to Earl. "I found it while I was walking. Have a good evening."

Earl looked at it, then put it in his pocket. "Thanks," he said. "I'll treasure it always." He took her hand, and helped her out of the grass. When she was up, he did something unexpected. He brought her hand toward his face. She was afraid he was going to kiss it, and she almost screamed to stop him. She hated the thought of some saccharine scene, a romantic farewell.

But all Earl did was brush the backs of her fingers quickly over his chin. She felt the scratch of his stubble. It was a strange gesture, a cross between a dog's nuzzling and something a very old man would do.

Then he was off, headed back down the hill to his house. Finny went down the other side of the hill, under the fence in the place Earl had shown her. The crickets were chirping now. She went back through the hills, through the old vineyard, where she tried to find her scuff marks from walking before. But in the dim light she couldn't find them.

When she was out of the vineyard, she started to run, back along the fence to her house. *What the heck were you doing?* she imagined her father saying. *We were worried sick. I almost called the police.*

It was getting cold. A dog barked—maybe Raskal—and then let out a long howl. Lights were coming on across the valley, speckling the countryside like stars. She ran toward her house, its windows aglow in the gathering dusk.

Inside, her mother was carrying a casserole dish to the dining room. "Wash your hands, Finny," she said. "I was just going to get you."

Chapter 2

An Important Introduction

She woke up with a tingly feeling on the backs of her fingers. His chin, she realized. All night she'd dreamed about it, the sandpapery feeling of his stubble against her hand. Again and again, she'd found herself stroking his face, like she was calming a young child. She couldn't understand why that moment, that sensation, had made such an impression on her. She got out of bed, laughing a little at herself.

And as she waded into her morning, the day before did seem more and more like a dream. There was breakfast with her mother and brother. Finny didn't like to eat in the mornings, but Laura always said, "If there is one meal that people expect you to eat, it's breakfast." So Finny force-fed herself a few mouthfuls of granola, toast with peanut butter. At the kitchen table her brother was reading a book of short stories by women writers for English class. When Laura asked him how it was, he said, "Good but not great."

Then the ride to school with her father. Before they got out of the driveway, Stanley stopped the car.

"Oh," he said, like he'd just remembered something. "I forgot to brush my teeth." He clicked his top and bottom teeth together, then bolted out of the car.

Stanley came back in ten minutes, his suit jacket making

crinkling sounds from the Pepto wrappers he'd stuffed in his pockets, his breath smelling like peppermint ice cream. They started driving. Sylvan was in the front, as always. He was reading his book of short stories.

"What are you reading?" Stanley asked him.

"Some stories for English," Sylvan said. "All by women writers. They're pretty boring."

" 'There are no dull subjects,' " Stanley quoted. " 'There are only dull writers.' " He nodded at the book. "Mencken."

"Are there dull car rides?" Finny asked.

When she got home from school, she walked back to the field where she'd met Earl. She passed the pond with the fountain in it, but this time the birds didn't look so stridently colorful—just the usual blues and grays. She wondered if maybe she'd exaggerated to herself. The afternoon was overcast, and she had the hood of the green reaper over her head. Not tied tight. She didn't want to look scary. When she got to the pasture where she'd met Earl, he wasn't there. She looked down at his house, and there were no cars in the driveway. Not even the brown station wagon.

She felt suddenly depressed. Hugely, embarrassingly so. She had expected—irrationally, she realized—that he would be here, waiting for her, whenever she arrived. That she didn't need to call or make a date. That, like in a book, he would know she was coming. But the world was never like the world in books. There were always these snags and bumps, these unexpected turns and abrupt disappointments.

She could have gone to his house. She could have knocked. But it seemed so far away. She felt foolish for all her misplaced hopes and expectations, like she'd gussied herself up for a party that was on another day. He'd probably forgotten all about their meeting already.

Walking back home, she felt as if she'd been holding a full basket and something had dropped out of it. She didn't know what or where, but she knew it was important, weighty. She wasn't sure she'd ever get it back.

She promised herself she wouldn't go back the next afternoon. And in school she did a pretty good job of forgetting about Earl. She took notes in history class. Worked on a diorama about Ancient Greek theater during her lunch hour. In biology they dissected an owl's pellet, which was a wad of hair an owl throws up after digesting its food. Hers had the skeleton of a mouse tangled in it, the tiny bones brittle as matchsticks. She wondered if the owl needed to swallow some Pepto after it ate that. She thought of joking to her teacher that she'd found some Cheetos and half a doughnut in hers. But there wouldn't have been much point. Mrs. Alston would have just looked confused, read the package the pellets came in to see if there'd been a mistake.

"What are you going to do this afternoon?" Laura said when they got back home from school.

"Go for a walk," Finny said.

She was just going to walk around their yard, by the horse fence, and maybe into the vineyard. But then when she was in the vineyard, she couldn't resist going a little farther.

Up the road. Past the fountain. Over the hill.

The brown station wagon was there.

She thought of going down and knocking on the door of the little brown house. *Hi. I'm Finny. Is your son home?* Then Earl coming to the door. *Oh, hi.* But if he wasn't every bit as excited as she was, it would kill her. She would literally drop dead in his doorway. Just to show him. *There, now you clean up this mess.* It would be embarrassing, but it wouldn't matter because she'd be dead.

She decided it was too risky. She turned away. Headed back down the hill.

But then she heard something behind her. A voice. She didn't turn around, though.

She heard it again: "Finny!"

Now she turned around, and he was standing there, just behind the fence, waving his arms over his head as if flagging down an aircraft. She laughed. Relief more than anything else. She wasn't sure if she would have come back a third time.

"Earl!" Finny shouted, waving her arms like his. It would have seemed too playful, too familiar, with anyone else.

"I thought it was you," he said when she got back up to the top of the hill. "I'm so glad you came today. I was worried all yesterday that you were going to come and I wasn't going to be there." His cheeks were flushed. "On Mondays my dad travels for lessons, and I usually go with him after school."

Finny was about to tell him she did come yesterday, how she felt when she saw he wasn't there. She could have told Earl that. But instead she said, "You're lucky I didn't."

Earl smiled. He had a way, she'd learn, of softening under her pressure, offering up his belly the way a puppy would. When she kidded him or spoke sharply, he just laughed and went on. He seemed to trust in her good intentions. When Finny teased her mother, Laura puckered up her mouth like she'd eaten something sour. But here was this funny little half-man, the best audience she'd ever had.

"You wanna see my house?" Earl said.

"Sure," Finny said.

When they got close to the house, Finny could hear the piano music. She didn't recognize the piece, but she knew it was beautiful. Or thought it was. Something about the way it swirled and tumbled at you. She understood that her feelings about Earl might have influenced her reaction to the music. But she still allowed herself to believe this was the most beautiful music she'd ever heard. Much later, when she and Earl had to be apart for some time, she would go to a library and

try to find the piece in their music collection. It was a senti-
mental gesture, but she knew that no one would ask her why
she was doing it. She didn't know anything about classical
music or composers. She listened to dozens of albums. She
tried to describe the piece to the music librarian: "It's this cas-
cade of notes. All piano. Just really full and happy, but with an
edge of something sad." And then she realized she was describing her own feelings, and stopped.

Now, though, she asked Earl, "Is your dad giving a lesson?"
She hadn't seen another car.

"He's just practicing," Earl said.

When Earl opened the door, the piano immediately went
quiet. The instrument was enormous, probably eight or nine
feet long, and it took up half the living room. It was kept
against the shadowy wall opposite where Finny stood. In fact,
the whole house was shadowy. Only a couple of little peep-
hole windows punctured the wall to her right, and then one
window in each of the two bedrooms, the doors of which
were open. The house was decorated in dark colors, a brown
and gold rug on the floor of the living room, beige shades,
wood on the walls and floor, giving the place the look of a
cabin. The light was dim, too, flickery like candlelight. In the
kitchen there was a stove with some pots stacked on it, and
the sink was full of dirty dishes. (*It's a sad but true fact that
guests to your home will lose their appetites if they see a sink
full of dishes,* Finny's mother once told her.) There was another door that presumably led to a bathroom. And that was
the whole house.

"Dad?" Earl said.

"Yes," the man sitting at the piano said.

"I have a guest."

"No," Finny said, "don't stop because of m—"

But the man was already turning around. He was a short
man, and when he sat up fully on the piano bench, facing
Finny as he did now, his feet dangled just off the ground. (In

order to play, he'd had to sit on the very edge of the bench.) He had a paunch, and the top half of his body was shaped like a summer squash. He'd combed a flap of wispy walnut-colored hair over his astoundingly pale scalp. His head was round as a basketball, and his lips pouted a little when he closed them, so that he seemed to have an expression of mock-seriousness or concentration on his face.

"Menalcus Henckel," he said to Finny, and at first she thought he was casting a spell on her, the words sounded so crazy. His voice was high like Earl's, though not as gentle. He had a touch more impatience in him. After he spoke, he did an odd thing with the corners of his mouth, moving them up and down, like he was switching between a smile and a frown.

Finny realized he had said his name, so she said, "Finny."

She stood there, then, for maybe five seconds, in absolute silence, until Earl said, "We met outside up there." He pointed in the direction of the hill above his house. "Finny lives in the neighborhood."

"Very good," Mr. Henckel said, like he was commenting on a piano exercise Earl had just finished, and then he performed three of his smile-frowns.

"So, Dad, we're going to spend some time here, okay? You can just go on practicing if you want."

"Actually, I'd love that," Finny said.

Finny had trouble seeing Mr. Henckel in the dim light, but it looked like he was nodding. It also looked like he had his eyes closed. He was very still. And then all of a sudden his mouth dropped open.

"Earl?" Finny said. "Is your dad okay?"

"Yeah. You just need to give him one minute," Earl said. "Let's sit down and wait for him."

They sat in the beige-cushioned chairs across from the piano in the living room. Mr. Henckel was slumped over on the piano bench. His flap of hair had come loose and was dangling over his ear. He breathed noisily, the air whistling in his nose.

"I hope you don't mind," Earl said, and Finny knew he was talking about his father.

"I'm having fun," she said. Because she was. Entering into this family's house was exciting for her, like peeping in the windows of a place she was told never to look. She'd been to other girls' houses before, but they were always so neat, and everyone was so polite, and she could nearly hear Laura saying *I told you so* in the background. The friendships never stuck.

All of a sudden Mr. Henckel made a loud snorting sound. Finny let out a little yelp, but clapped her hand over her mouth in time to stop herself from making too much noise.

"So sorry, my dear," Mr. Henckel muttered when he was awake, his hand darting to smooth the flap of hair back over his scalp. "You have to understand," he told her in an almost pleading way, "it just comes upon me."

She was delighted that Mr. Henckel had called her "my dear." She said it was fine, that she needed a rest, too.

"Thank you for being so kind," he said with four smile-frowns. "A lovely young lady." She loved his formal way of speaking, calling her "my dear" or "young lady."

"My dad was a professional piano player a while ago," Earl said. "He played one time at Carnegie Hall."

"Not a soloist, mind you," Mr. Henckel said, correcting his son. "Just a kind of exhibition."

"And he was once in the Tchaikovsky competition," Earl said.

"And that, my dear, was very sadly the end of it all," Mr. Henckel reported.

"Why?" Finny asked. It sounded like he wanted to talk about it.

"I fell asleep," Mr. Henckel said. "During a rest in the piece. I couldn't help myself. It just comes upon me." Finny noticed his forehead shining. He took out a handkerchief and swiped at his brow. It turned out Mr. Henckel always sweated when he talked about himself.

"The judges didn't know what to do," he went on. "They thought I was in a very deep concentration. But then it just kept going and going. It was the first time it had happened in the history of the competition. After thirty seconds, they realized I was asleep and disqualified me. A pity. They said my performance was top-notch until then."

"I'm sorry," Finny said.

"Very kind, my dear," Mr. Henckel said, and concluded his story with a smile-frown.

He then offered everyone coffee. It was his favorite drink, and he dosed himself with it constantly. His breath smelled strongly of coffee, and he treated the drink as if it were some vital drug.

"I sleep better when I have a cup before bed," he confided at the kitchen table, where they sat next to the pile of dirty dishes in the sink. Mr. Henckel mopped at his forehead with the yellowed handkerchief, which Finny was afraid might touch her, so she scooted back.

Earl served the coffee out of a silver pot, into white china cups. Despite the indifferent housekeeping, there were these odd flourishes in the house—a fancy coffee set, a piano that must have cost a fortune, some antique-looking furniture.

"My mother's," Mr. Henckel said about the coffee set.

"It's very nice," Finny said.

"I have decaf normally," Earl said. "But since it's a special occasion."

"I've never drunk coffee before," Finny said.

Mr. Henckel raised his cup and proposed a toast. "To our lovely young lady friend," he said. And then seemed unable to help going on: "Who has every bright prospect in front of her, and appears more than wise enough not to squander them in the manner of some of her elders."

They all clinked cups and drank. Finny nearly spit her first mouthful out, the taste was so bitter. But she swallowed it down, then asked if she could have some sugar.

"Of course," Mr. Henckel said, and brought out a little silver dish of sugar from the cabinet, and a silver pitcher of cream from the refrigerator. "Forgive my rudeness, my dear." He offered a smile-frown with his apology.

"It's fine," Finny said. "My mom says I act like I live in a barnyard."

"Well, you live *next* to one," Earl said, and Finny laughed.

"May I ask what distinguished family you come from?" Mr. Henckel asked.

"The Shorts," Finny said. "But I'm not sure they're distinguished. My dad quotes a lot of famous people."

"So he is a man who knows history."

"I guess."

"Finny has an older brother," Earl said.

"And what is this young fellow's name?"

"Sylvan."

"Perhaps you could bring him by one afternoon, and we could increase our eminent party by one."

"Maybe," Finny said. Though she knew what her brother would say about her new friends. *Misfits*. It was a word he'd picked up from Stanley, and he used it to describe anyone he didn't approve of. But Finny had grown to like the word, and thought it was a pretty good description of how she saw herself. As someone who just didn't fit. A square peg in a world of round holes. Earl and his father were the same.

"I'd like to meet Sylvan sometime," Earl said, his cheeks glowing a little, "but it doesn't have to be soon."

"Okay," Finny said.

Mr. Henckel had fallen asleep again. Finny heard his breath whistling in his nose.

"It's usually not this bad," Earl said about his dad. "I think he just got excited that you were over and it made him tired.

I think he likes you. You're very nice and interesting to talk to."

"Thank you."

Earl had a way, Finny saw, of building up the people around him. He'd done it before with his dad, when he'd talked about his piano playing, and now he'd turned his attention to Finny. It was a way of making people feel accomplished and important, and they immediately became comfortable in his presence.

"I think I should go soon," Finny said, as she watched Mr. Henckel's comb-over flop back down over his ear. "But I wanted to say bye to your dad."

"It's okay," Earl said. "I'll tell him. But you'll definitely come back, right?"

"Of course," Finny said. She hesitated. "But I was thinking. My parents might not like it if I'm coming over too much."

"Why not?"

"It's just how they are. They have to approve everything. But maybe there's a way I can get over more."

"What were you thinking?"

She told him her idea. It was as bold as she'd ever been with a boy, but something about Earl made her that way.

When she was done, Earl said, "It sounds great."

Back at home Finny felt jittery from the coffee, and from the excitement of her afternoon, the plan she and Earl had hatched.

"Where were *you*?" Laura asked her.

"Just walking," Finny said.

Chapter 3

Lessons

Stanley loved Bach. He'd been to the Tanglewood festival once and heard the Mass in B-Minor in a church, and since then he'd thought Bach was the greatest composer who ever lived. He had Bach records lined up in his study, a poster of the first page of the cello suites on his wall, and he talked about Glenn Gould, the Bach pianist, like he was a family friend. "Gould is tough," he would say whenever the subject came up. "You have to take time to get to know him." Sometimes he would play a brief recording for Sylvan and Finny, and they would have to sit there and pretend they were listening. Stanley would do a little conducting as the record played, working himself up feverishly in the crescendos. When the recording was done, Stanley would say "Bach" and nod.

He'd wanted Sylvan and Finny to be musical. They'd obliged by joining chorus. But Finny hated singing. She thought her voice sounded like a creaky gate, and her high notes were enough to make Raskal whimper. She hated being stuck up there, in the white turtleneck and black slacks they made them wear, howling out her part. The boy next to her used to stick his finger in his ear on the side Finny was on. "Am I that awful?" she asked him. "It helps me hear myself," he said.

"I was wondering if maybe I could take piano lessons,"

Finny said to her father at dinner on the evening she'd visited Earl's house.

"Of course," Stanley said, and she thought she saw his mouth tremble with pleasure. Sylvan stopped eating.

"If you practice enough," Stanley said, "you might be able to play the Well-Tempered Clavier. Or at least the Inventions."

"That would be great," Finny said.

"Maybe the Goldberg Variations!"

"There's a teacher I heard was pretty good. He actually lives near here."

Sylvan was watching Finny, a little crease denting the skin between his eyes.

"How did you hear about him?" Stanley said.

"Through some people at school. He was in the Tchaikovsky competition."

"Tchaikovsky," Stanley said.

"I think he charges very reasonable prices, too."

"Money is no issue in art," Stanley said.

"It would be lovely if you learned to play a little for guests," Laura said. "There is nothing in the world a party guest enjoys more than a recital."

"Are there any more potatoes?" Sylvan asked. He was shaking his head at Finny, like she had suddenly decided to perform a jig on top of the dining room table.

"'I don't like to think much about my playing,'" Stanley began. "'It would be like a centipede considering in which order to move its legs.'"

Nobody knew quite what to make of this, and they all just watched Stanley. In the silence, Raskal let out a small fart.

"Gould," Stanley finally said, and for some reason this seemed to settle the matter.

So Finny began a routine of piano lessons. She went to Mr. Henckel's house twice a week because, she told Stanley, she needed to get a good grounding. The lessons were supposed to be an hour, though with all they had to cover, they often lasted longer than that.

Usually the lessons began with a nap. Maybe five minutes or so. Finny sat at attention on the piano bench, and listened to Mr. Henckel breathe. Sometimes he snored. He had a deviated septum, he'd confided to Finny with a large number of smile-frowns. "It's very unpleasant," he'd told her, "but of course we all must accept the fates we are dealt." He'd always come awake from his nap with a giant snort, and if Finny wasn't ready for it, the shock of it might knock her off the piano bench. "Whoa!" Finny said when he did it. Sometimes she clapped. Then Mr. Henckel's hand would dart to his head to fix his comb-over, and he would say, "So sorry, my dear. It just comes upon me."

After this part of the lesson was done, there was usually a period in which Mr. Henckel told a story about his past. This was Finny's favorite part of the lesson. The stories Mr. Henckel told usually centered on some embarrassing revelation about himself. In the first few weeks of lessons, Finny had already learned that Mr. Henckel had been born to a very wealthy family in Massachusetts, but was effectively disinherited when his parents learned that he was responsible for "the offspring of a nontraditional pairing," as he'd put it. She'd also been informed that Mr. Henckel sometimes "salivated excessively" while he slept, and that he could never drive anywhere without Earl because if he fell asleep at the wheel, Earl would have to take control of the car and steer it to a safe resting spot— something Earl had become expert at doing. Mr. Henckel sweated so copiously when he told his stories that he had to continuously mop his face with the yellow handkerchief, and sometimes still a droplet would escape and roll down his cheek, fall to the floor. "So kind of you to listen, my dear," he told Finny, though she could never say that she really had a choice. Mr. Henckel seemed compelled to confess.

After the story portion of the lesson it was usually time for Finny to play what she'd practiced since the previous lesson on her family's upright Yamaha piano. Her father always said that their little piano had "good tone," but it was nothing compared to the way Mr. Henckel's grand piano reverberated in the tiny space of his house. It was magnificent, the sound of it. Yet it was like a magnifying glass on Finny's technique, blowing up the tiniest faults until they were mammoth. Finny was not a good player. She knew it. She crossed her fingers and bungled melodies, missing notes or hitting two at once. Earl usually stayed in his room with the door closed, mercifully, during her lessons. Finny had a terrible time counting out rhythms, too. Nothing sounded the way it did when Mr. Henckel played it, and Finny had an uncanny ability to get a ragtime beat into any piece. She could make the Moonlight Sonata sound like a Scott Joplin composition.

When she was done, though, Mr. Henckel would say things like, "Very fine work, my dear. Just a little practice. That's all it takes. A little practice and you'll be performing Shostakovich at Carnegie Hall. It is not hard to ascend in life with the proper discipline."

Finny thanked him for his kindness and gave him the check Stanley had written for thirty dollars. "A pittance," Stanley always said about Mr. Henckel's fee, which Finny suspected had been lowered for her.

Then they would break for coffee, which Earl would pour out into the china cups. He made regular for Mr. Henckel, and decaf for himself and Finny. Finny began to like the taste of the coffee, probably because her cup was filled mostly with milk and sugar. At some point Mr. Henckel would fall into a nap, and Earl and Finny would clear the cups away, then go into Earl's room to hang out, or into the fields outside his house. They got to the point where they just went through these stages without asking each other; they'd grown comfortable that way, accustomed to their routine.

Once, walking in the hills, Earl said to Finny, "It must be nice having dinner with your whole family." It was December, sunny and cold, a day after Finny's school had let out for winter break. They were walking behind Earl's house, by a little stream that trickled through some rocks. There were brittle shelves of ice over the water, which Finny liked to crunch with her feet as she walked.

"Sometimes," Finny said. "But not as much as you'd think." She felt bad the moment the words left her mouth.

But Earl didn't seem to mind. "Why?" he asked.

The valley was quiet, and only the wind whistled in her ears. She thought Earl seemed down, and she felt the need— as would often be the case in their lives—to make him feel better.

"Because I always feel like I'm doing the wrong thing," Finny finally said. It was something she had never tried to put into words. "I feel like I'm not the person my parents want me to be." She felt a sharp pain behind her eyes, and realized she could have cried.

"I'm sure that's not true," Earl said.

They walked on, up the hill to the pasture where they had sat together that first afternoon when they'd met. It felt like such a long time ago to Finny, though it had only been a couple months. Now Earl led the way. He had a silly shuffling walk when he climbed hills, because his legs were so short. Finny always laughed a little when he was in front of her, but she never let him see her doing it. It wasn't out of meanness she was laughing. It wasn't like the way she laughed when she fed Raskal under the table and her dad got angry. It was more like the way parents laugh at young children, or the way her aunt Louise laughed at her cats when they batted their toys around the living room. There was something warm and protective about it, tender actually, though Finny hated words like *tender*. She could never explain the feeling to Earl, so she kept it to herself.

It was getting dark. The sky was rolling to reveal its silver belly. Already, lights were coming on in the houses. These were the shortest days of the year, when night arrived at five o'clock and you woke up in the same darkness you went to bed in. Finny had to leave Earl's house earlier and earlier so that she didn't break her mother's rule of getting home before dark.

"Are you cold?" Earl said.

"Not really," Finny said. "We can stay out a little longer."

They walked over the top of the hill and kept going, into a copse of trees that cast long shadows in the low sun. Finny's face stung from the wind, and she sniffed a little because the cold was making her eyes tear up. She heard a twig snap under her foot, and Earl turned to see if she was okay.

"Nothing," Finny said about the twig, though she'd felt a twinge of nervousness when Earl had turned around, as if he were going to say something important.

They kept on, feet rustling the tall grass. In the distance Finny saw some horses with blankets on their backs, walking toward a barn. Everything was quiet now. Earl stopped and turned toward her.

"I think anyone would like you," he said.

"That's nice," Finny said, wanting to say more, but not knowing what.

"You must think my dad and I are strange."

Finny was shaking her head, but all she could get out was the word "No."

"I just want you to know how nice it's been having you come over."

"Earl," Finny said.

Then he kissed her. It was the first time Finny had been

kissed, and she felt his mouth like a warm fruit bursting on her tongue.

"I love you," Earl said.

"I love you, too," Finny said.

Then they walked back to his house.

Chapter **4**

Harsh Consequences

That evening, when Finny got back to her house, her mother was at the sliding door in back. The sun had just set, and the purple sky was reflected in the glass. Laura's shape looked like an apparition behind it.

Laura opened the door. "You're late," she said.

"I'm sorry," Finny said. "After my lesson I had to—"

"I don't want to hear it."

"But—"

"The first thing any person judges you on is punctuality," Laura said with a severe expression on her face. Finny's mother rarely got angry with Finny. She was more the type to sigh and leave a room than to yell at or hit her children. It was as if she didn't want to risk getting tangled up with them, so she kept a careful distance. Several times, though, when some point of honor had been violated, when shame drifted like a storm cloud over the family, Finny had seen Laura furious. Her anger was much sharper and more enduring than Stanley's bursts of temper, which went off like firecrackers and disappeared just as quickly. Laura got a sour, disgusted look on her face when she was mad, and she squinted up her eyes at you. It was how she looked now.

"It won't happen again," Finny said as she slid past Laura, into the house.

"No, it certainly won't," her mother said, speaking in a low voice, through her teeth, as if trying to hold something back behind them.

"I'm going to wash up for dinner."

"Just wait, just wait," Laura said, grabbing Finny's arm and yanking it so hard Finny felt her shoulder nudging out and back into the socket.

They were in the mudroom, where Raskal slept and ate his meals. There was a smell like sawdust from his food. It always felt cold in this room, because of the tiles and the drafty door, and now Finny shivered. They faced each other.

"Listen to me," Laura said. "You're not having dinner with us tonight. You can eat in your room."

"Why?"

"Because you need time to think about what you did."

"What are you talking about?" Finny said.

"Your behavior," Laura said. "This *trickery*." She pronounced the word like someone in old Salem might have pronounced *witchcraft*. "Maybe a little consideration will make a difference." Finny had heard grown-ups talk in this righteous way before, when they wanted to make it clear they were inconveniencing themselves for your sake.

"A difference in what?"

"Your morals," Laura said.

"What's wrong with my morals?" Finny asked.

And then something surprising happened. She saw her mother's stern expression buckle, the way a very large and imposing building might buckle under certain strains. Almost instantly it collapsed. Her mother was in tears. Laura had a silly, hiccuping way of crying, and Finny had the impulse to pat her on the back.

"To think," Laura said through her sobbing. "To think you were fooling us all this time."

"Fooling you about what?"

"All your lessons. The freedom we gave you. It was our mistake, and now we must suffer for it."

If she hadn't been so angry at her mother, Finny might have felt sorry for Laura, who made it seem as if she had no part in the decisions that were made, as if the world simply tilted in certain directions, and she was a ball that rolled however the ground sloped.

"The worst part was what you did to your father," Laura went on. "Getting his hopes up and toying with him that way. You could see how happy you were making him. All he ever wanted was for you to play *Bach*."

"He liked my Bach."

"And the whole time you were doing it just so you could go off and kiss that boy. He looks like he's ten years older than you, Finny. I've seen him. He probably has a wife and child somewhere."

Finny couldn't imagine how her mother knew she had been kissing Earl. It happened less than an hour ago—she'd hardly become accustomed to the fact herself. And now it was being yanked from her, that memory, that moment, torn from her hands and trampled on.

"Earl is fifteen, Mom. *Relax*."

"We let you come and go from this house, day after day. We didn't ask any questions, because we trusted you. We thought you had our best interests in mind, the way a child should with her parents. But you didn't care about anyone but yourself."

"Who told you?" Finny asked.

"That's not important. You lied to us."

"I didn't lie. I was taking lessons from Mr. Henckel."

"You were taking lessons from that sexual predator. I can't have you sneaking around already. It's too early for that. Not that any time would have been good. But you're fourteen years old, Finny. It's not right. You're lucky we found out.

You're going to be grounded for the rest of your vacation. No one could ever become a lady the way you're going."

"Mom, I want to be a lady about as much as you'd like to stick your head up Raskal's ass."

Laura let out a gasp like she'd been socked in the stomach. Her forehead was wrinkled, and Finny saw she was ready to start crying again. "What you don't seem to understand, Finny," Laura said, "is that I'm not doing this to torture you. I love you and I want the best for you." Her voice caught when she said that, and then she did begin to cry.

When Stanley came home, Finny pleaded with him. She caught him in the upstairs hallway, between their bedrooms. Stanley had his suit jacket tossed over his shoulder, and was clearly on the way to "brush his teeth."

"We can't have you sneaking around," he told Finny. "That's the bottom line." And then he quoted, " 'Happiness is a working of the soul in the way of excellence or virtue.' " He paused to allow the idea to penetrate, and seemed to contemplate whether to attribute the quotation. In the end he held off, probably because of the solemnity of the occasion.

"You have to understand," Finny said. "I wasn't lying to you. Please. Listen to me, Dad. I wanted to take lessons. I want to take them."

But Stanley shook his head. "You can take lessons with someone else. And you won't have the distraction of that deviant."

"He's not a deviant," Finny snapped back. To hear Earl talked of that way was like having her hand slammed in a door. "And anyway, I'd rather be fondled by a deviant than have to listen to another one of your lectures."

Stanley's face colored, but he just shook his head. She could see he'd resolved to stay calm.

"Well you might just have your wish," Stanley said. "You might not have to listen to me for a very long time."

"What do you mean?"

"You need to go back to your room now."

"Please, Dad," Finny said, and felt her voice catch in her throat. She began to cry. There was no way to stop it. The tears just streamed from her, like she'd been slit open. "Please, please," she kept saying.

And Stanley stood there, shaking his head, in a way that was now more sad than stubborn. She saw him through her tears, the hall lights like sunbursts in her bleary vision.

She spent the week and a half of her vacation at home, watching television and movies, flipping through mystery novels and comic books, trying to find a gap of time she could squeeze a call to Earl into. As long as she stayed inside, her parents let her be; they seemed busy with their own plans and discussions. Once, when Stanley was at work and Laura was out getting groceries, Finny dialed Earl's number, and listened to the phone thrill once, twice, three times on the other end. An image of Earl's house, the day the brown station wagon wasn't there, flashed in her mind.

Then someone picked up. "Hello?" It was Earl's voice, distant and awash in a tide of static. But still him. Earl. Happiness flooded her heart.

"Earl, it's me. Finny."

"Finny!" he said. He never held back with her. It was something she'd loved about him from the moment they'd met, the way he opened himself to her. She felt as if she could curl up in the space he'd given her. "I was so worried about you. When your mom called and said you couldn't take lessons anymore. I didn't know what happened."

"My mom caught us kissing."

"How?"

"I don't know," Finny said.

"When am I going to see you?" Earl asked. It was a question each would ask the other many times over the years.

"Soon, I hope," Finny said. "But we're going to need a new plan. I'm grounded now. They think I was sneaking around to get to spend time with you."

"Well, you sort of were."

"I know. But they have the idea that you're a lot older and taking advantage of me."

"Oh," Earl said, and Finny could tell by how his voice sounded that he was blushing. He would always be reserved, and a little formal, about sex. She wished that she could reach through the telephone wire now and touch his face.

"But it's okay," Finny said. "They don't understand that I like being taken advantage of." It sounded like the kind of sexy thing a woman might say in a movie, and Finny laughed at the role she was straining toward: a heroine, some breezy beauty. It wasn't her. She was just Finny.

"Listen, Earl," Finny said, "I have to get off the phone soon. My mom is out buying groceries and if she catches me on the phone with you she'll kill me and probably you, too. But I just wanted to say that I still love you, and we're going to figure something out."

This kind of talk, this saying *I love you*, it had felt so odd that first time, so desperate and dramatic. *Making too much of herself*. That's the phrase that had come to mind, a phrase Finny had heard used to describe silly women, who cried and fretted over burnt omelets or stained rugs. But now these theatrical words—*I love you, I need to see you*—it took almost no effort to say them. When she was with Earl they came to Finny's lips as naturally as *hello* and *goodbye*.

"I love you, too," Earl said. "Still."

. . .

Sometimes Sylvan visited Finny during her imprisonment. He was spending his vacation at the library, working on a paper about the Constitution and its belief in "the inherent goodness of man." That's how he described it to Finny, and she told him it sounded like something their dad would say.

"Maybe," Sylvan said, a little defensively. "But only because it's a smart idea. I thought of it completely myself."

"I'm glad you're using your powers for good."

"Someone has to," Sylvan teased her.

"And I definitely don't want to be that person," Finny told him.

Another time she had been crying. It was an embarrassing thing that happened to her every now and again over the course of that week and a half, and as usual, she tried to hide it. But since Earl had entered her life, she'd found that for some reason it was much easier for her to cry. Anything could start it. A pretty piece of music. The way the hills looked on a clear evening. She'd never understood why people cried so much—at the end of movies, or when they got a nice letter. But now she saw something about the world, about how beautiful things are always a little sad, too. She understood that, in a way, she was crying for Earl, but also for other things she had lost, or would lose. And she knew that this feeling, this endless, inconsolable longing, would forever be a part of her life, a part of what it meant to truly love. It was a vision Earl had given her without knowing it, and in the end she could never say whether it was good or bad, only that she had it now, and could never give it back.

A knock on the door.

"Go away," Finny said through tears.

Another knock. "It's me, Finny." Sylvan's voice.

She wiped her eyes on her shirt and let her brother in. He sat down on her bed.

"I'm sorry you're having such a crappy vacation," he told her. "This sucks."

She wasn't sure how to respond to this. She was concentrating too hard on not crying, and the roof of her mouth hurt. She couldn't tell why her brother was suddenly being so nice to her.

"Thanks," Finny said.

"Mom's just so pissed off. You know how she gets. Like the family's future depends on it."

She hadn't heard her brother criticize their parents before. She stayed quiet, waiting to hear what he would say.

"I think she'll get over it, though," Sylvan said. "It's just a boyfriend."

"The thing is," Finny said, "I can't figure out how she knew."

"There's lots of ways," Sylvan said. "Anyway, it's only three more days. Then once we're back at school, I think it'll be over."

"But they won't let me take lessons with Mr. Henckel again."

"Who knows? Maybe they will."

She didn't see why her brother was being so optimistic about the situation. Nothing ever worked in her favor with her parents.

"Would you do me a favor?" Finny asked her brother, since he was being nice. "I mean, if I needed it."

"Sure, Fin. Anything."

"If I want to get a message to Earl sometime, would you bring it to him? Like maybe a letter, or just something I tell you."

"I could do that."

"I don't have anything right now. I just mean, it might be hard for me to talk to him sometimes."

"He's the reason you're in trouble."

"Yeah, well," Finny said, and shrugged.

"Anyway, of course," Sylvan said.

Then Finny began to explain where Earl's house was, past the fountain, over the— but Sylvan stopped her.

"It's more of a birdbath," he said.

"How do you—" Then it hit her. She didn't even need to finish the sentence. Sylvan must have realized, too, because his mouth hung open a little.

"I'm sorry, Fin," he finally said, with an awful, sad look in his eyes. "I really am."

Finny couldn't wait for school to start again. It was probably the first time she'd ever felt that way. She had the idea that once she was back at school, once the machinery of her house was humming again, she would be a little freer to wander, to slip back into her own routines. She imagined phone calls to Earl, afternoon walks together. She looked forward to the first day of classes the way a traveler might look forward to a warm house after a long cold journey.

But the weekend before she was to go back to school, her father told her she was to pack a suitcase. "A change of plans," he said. "We've been talking to the people at Thorndon. A boarding school. A very good one, actually. It's in Massachusetts. They've agreed to take you in the middle of the year. I booked you a flight Monday. They're just finishing their winter break."

Finny's mouth dropped open. She tried to think of words to fill the space, but all that came were empty breaths.

"It's a wonderful opportunity," Stanley said. "To make some changes. To get a new outlook, if you will."

"I won't," Finny said.

"There's not much of a choice, unfortunately," Stanley said. "You've been testing the limits for a long time, Finny. And this took it too far. You just need a little time to get your priorities in order."

"My priorities are *in* order."

"A change in circumstances will be good," her mother said. "A new setting always offers a young lady opportunities for growth. And besides, there really wasn't anything else we could do, Finny. You didn't leave *us* a choice."

Finny was struck dumb by her mother's words. Once again, she'd proven less than adequate in both her parents' eyes, and she was paying for it. She didn't know how to convince them of their mistake, so she cried and hollered and pleaded.

In the end, though, she packed her bag. Like her parents had said, there really wasn't much of a choice.

She was still outraged by what her brother had done, telling on her, but she gave him a note she'd scrawled out to pass on to Earl as soon as Sylvan could. She saw now that her brother felt as horribly about what he'd done as she did, that he couldn't have known what the consequences would be. And anyway, he was the closest she had to a friend in this house.

The note to Earl said: *Sent to Thorndon School by my parents. Have to pack my bags and am leaving on Monday. I love you and I miss you and I will write to you as soon and as much as I can. Please don't forget me.*

Monday morning she left for Thorndon.

Chapter **5**

First Impressions of the Thorndon School

The Thorndon School was nestled in a beautiful pocket of forest west of Boston, and from the cab window Finny could see shreds of snow along the sides of the driveway that led to it. The main building of the school was made of a kind of smoothed stone that had a blue-gray tint in the sun. Little crystals in the stones sparkled in the light. From the front, the building looked plain and square, with large windows that were darkened like sunglasses.

The cabdriver, whose pimply neck Finny had stared at the entire ride from the airport, dropped Finny by the front door, and she paid him, remembering to tip an extra dollar. The front door of the school opened when Finny pushed on it. It was a large wooden double door, with more of the tinted glass above each side. Finny wondered why they were so careful to tint all the glass, what could be so secret. When Finny got inside, the lobby of the school was so dark she could hardly see anything once the door swung shut behind her. The walls were made of gray brick, and there were some rectangular pillars that held up the ceiling. On her right a hallway extended into a shadowy space Finny couldn't make out. A couple of exit signs provided the only light in the area where Finny stood, their green letters glowing like lamps in some medieval dungeon. Finny dropped her bags.

"Hello?" Finny said.

And then, to her surprise, a voice answered, "Hello." The voice was distant enough to be her own echo, but it offered a much deeper and more resolute-sounding greeting than her own voice had. She couldn't tell from which direction the voice came.

"Where are you?" Finny said.

"*Who* are you?" the voice said.

"I'm Finny."

"Finny who?"

"Finny Short."

"How old?"

"Fourteen."

"From what state?"

"Maryland."

There was a pause, and Finny wondered what the questioner had made of her answers. Then Finny heard a creak, and a door to her left and a little in front of her—which she hadn't seen—opened. The door was down a couple of steps from where Finny stood, and now she heard someone coming up toward her, a determined footstep on each stair. She could make out some features of the figure that approached her: it was short and squat, with short hair, and it moved steadily and confidently. By the time the figure was close to Finny, illuminated by the green light of one of the exit signs, Finny was pretty sure it was a woman.

"Poplan," the woman said in a rough voice.

Realizing this was probably the woman's name, Finny said, "Finny," once again, and held out her hand to shake, the way she'd been taught.

"Oh no," Poplan said, "certainly not."

They both looked down at Finny's extended hand, which

Finny soon dropped to her side again. It was cold in the building, and Finny crossed her arms in front of her.

"I hope you don't think I just go around shaking unwashed hands willy-nilly."

"I don't know how you shake them," Finny said.

"Really, common colds are among the most transmittable germs there are. You have to be *vigilant*," Poplan said. "I refuse to fall victim to a cold that could have been prevented by simple hygiene."

"Sorry, Miss Poplan," Finny said again.

"What?"

"I said I was sorry, Miss Poplan. I won't make the mistake again."

"No, I mean what you called me. Miss Poplan. Don't ever do that."

Finny thought she had made the mistake of calling her miss when she was really a doctor—a mistake Finny had made with her parents' friends more than once. "I'm sorry, Dr. Poplan," Finny tried.

"No, no, *no*," Poplan said. "Just Poplan. Nothing else. No miss or missus or lady. Just Poplan. That's all I'm ever called."

"Are you my teacher?" Finny said.

Here Poplan laughed. She had a wheezy laugh, like someone who'd smoked for many years. She laughed a little longer than Finny expected someone could laugh about that question.

Then Poplan said, "No."

"Then who are you?"

"I'm your dorm matron. Which means you're going to live with me."

Finny imagined this woman's home like an extension of the dungeonlike space in which they now stood. "Do I get one phone call first?" Finny said.

Poplan didn't register the joke. Instead, she walked very directly toward the wall to Finny's left and snapped on a light switch. Two overhead lights flickered, then came awake, though the rest of the building remained in shadows. Finny could now see that Poplan had an ovular head, like an egg, and a very tall and thin nose, giving her a birdish look. Her hair, which was so many shades of gray that it looked like a painter had worked on it, wasn't combed or finessed into any detectable style. It sat like a thatched roof on her head.

"We keep the lights off and the heat low during the breaks," Poplan explained. "Saves energy." Then she turned ninety degrees, with the definite direction of a soldier during a march, and said, "I'll show you to your room."

She picked up one of Finny's bags and started walking into the dark hallway. Finny followed her, holding the other bag against her hip, struggling to keep up. "You know, they had a man to pick you up at the airport," Poplan said as they walked.

"I know. I'm sorry," Finny said again. "I looked for him, but he wasn't there when my plane got in. We were very late. I took a cab."

"I think he was in the bathroom when you landed. He came back and said you weren't there. He thought you'd missed your flight." Then Poplan laughed her long, wheezy laugh. "Scared the dickens out of him."

They had to walk outside for a minute to get to the dorm, and the sudden cold gripped Finny. Poplan was only wearing a sweater, no jacket, but she didn't seem to mind. She kept on her unshakeable path.

Fewer than a third of the students were boarders, Poplan told Finny, and it was a very small school to begin with, only fifty students in a class. The school went from eighth through twelfth grade, which meant that only about eighty girls were boarders. Finny would start in the second semester of the eighth-grade class—held back a year because the headmaster believed there was no substitute for a Thorndon education. Most of the eighth-grade girls were still getting their bearings anyway, Poplan said, so it shouldn't be too difficult to slip in. The dorm Finny would sleep in, Pearlman, housed both eighth and ninth graders.

The dorm was much less striking than the school. It was a big brick house with about twenty rooms, most of them small and overheated, with gray-brown carpeting to hide stains. Poplan lived in a room on the ground floor, as did a few of the teachers. Finny's room had two beds in it. There was a small window between the beds, and a desk and closet on each side.

"Your roommate is Judith," Poplan said. "She'll be back tomorrow. With all the other girls. They took you a day early so you could settle in."

Then Poplan left Finny to herself. Finny spent the afternoon unpacking. She composed a letter to Earl about her new surroundings. *I miss you already*, she wrote. *The school is very pretty but it's lonely here without any people in it. And without you of course. But there's a funny little woman who lives in the dorm and calls herself Poplan. I don't know if it's a first or a last name. (Who would name their child Poplan?) I'll write you very soon, Earl. Love, Finny.*

She folded the note and put it in an envelope she'd brought, but didn't write Earl's address on it because she was afraid someone would find it and ask about him.

She was curious about her new roommate, so she peeked into Judith's closet. There was nothing surprising here—the usual sweaters and skirts and a couple of conservative dresses, all pastel blues and pinks. The only intriguing thing was a tube of black lipstick the girl kept on the top shelf of the dresser that was inside the closet. Finny opened the drawers of the dresser, and here she saw some interesting clothing. It was all black, even the stockings and underwear. The shirts had frills and lacy surfaces, and some of the pants were torn in ways that looked deliberate. It was as if two people shared this closet, one conservative, the other bold and exciting. Finny tried to imagine the girl who could wear both sets of clothing, and the only picture that came to mind was of Orthrus, the two-headed dog she'd learned about in Greek mythology. *Oh, everything's good, Mom, but my roommate's an Orthrus.*

She picked up the black lipstick to examine it more closely, and just as she did this, there was a knock on the door. Finny stuffed the lipstick into her pocket, not knowing what else to do, and then opened the door. Poplan was standing there, now wearing a shiny suit that looked like it was made of silk. It had some vines and flowers printed on it, and the kind of buttons you secure through loops of fabric.

"I always dress for dinner," Poplan said.

"I do, too," Finny said, and started off into the hall.

But before Finny got out the door, Poplan made a sound. *Uh.* A little catch in her throat. Finny stopped.

"Hands," Poplan said, and nodded at Finny's hands. "Don't think that just because we've hit it off I'm going to fall victim to your germs."

"I wouldn't—"

"In life, you have to be vigilant," Poplan said.

That night they ate alone in the dining hall. It was a cavernous room, with brown tile floors, stone walls, and pillars. Again, Finny had the feeling that she'd entered a medieval dungeon. Their forks clattered against their plates in the echoey space. There had been meals left for them—cold sandwiches and pasta salad and fruit salad and brownies. Poplan ate the way she walked, with focus and determination. She hardly spoke during the whole meal, except once to tell Finny it was nice having company.

Finny assumed that after dinner they would go their separate ways, but Poplan proposed a game.

"Do you know Jenga?" Poplan asked.

When Finny told her she'd heard of it but never played, Poplan challenged her to a match.

Before beginning, they each washed their hands twice,

under Poplan's orders. It turned out that Jenga was Poplan's favorite game, and she played it with a competitiveness and relish that Finny had never witnessed before in an adult. The game consisted of poking little wooden blocks out of a tower and then placing them back on top of the structure. The first to knock over the building lost. When it was Poplan's turn, she winked and lined up her index finger at a block the way a marksman might aim at a bull's-eye. She then dislodged the block with a series of deft little pokes, always keeping a finger ready on the other side, to poke the block back in the other direction should the tower begin to sway. Finally, when the block came free and Poplan had placed it on top of the tower, she let out a long, tortured breath, as if she'd just dismantled a bomb.

They played on the floor in Poplan's room, which was decorated in a surprisingly feminine way. The bed was covered in a pink duvet, and there were china animals on the shelves and the desk, the types of items young girls might buy at the mall as presents for their mothers. Finny kept getting distracted by the animals' faces, a collie's sad eyes, a parrot's rainbow beak, the arc of an elephant's trunk, and in truth, they freaked Finny out. It was like being watched by a band of loony cartoon characters. She knocked over the tower.

"Aha!" Poplan screamed, and shook her fist victoriously.

"Damn," Finny said.

"Don't be discouraged," Poplan said. "No one has ever beaten me in Jenga."

"I think I need to go to sleep."

"All right," Poplan said, and she seemed a little disappointed. "But there's one thing."

"What is it?"

"I hate to do this on your first night. I'm very sorry, but I've had orders, and one must obey one's superiors." She looked down solemnly, but with obvious determination to complete the task she'd been given.

"What are you talking about?" Finny asked.

"Oh, my life, my life," Poplan said, shaking her head, and then got up and went to her closet. She opened the door and, after digging around a moment, brought out a purple T-shirt with green lettering on it that Finny thought was the gaudiest thing she'd ever seen.

"Like I said," Poplan continued, "I'm very sorry. But they said you have a tendency to sneak around." She handed Finny the shirt.

"After talking to your father last week, Mrs. Barksdale—the principal—she thought it might be a good idea to give you something bright to wear." And then Poplan added, in a softer voice that seemed to betray the first hint of reluctance in her, "Every night after eight."

Finny looked down at the shirt. On the front, in letters the color of pea soup, it said: *Thorndon School.* And on the back, in a message that must have been botched by the printer, it read: *Shorty Finn.*

Chapter 6

Finny's Incredible New Roommate

The girls began arriving the next afternoon. Finny was in her room with the door closed, and she heard them in the halls, banging doors and suitcases, chatting, making familiar comments to each other: "Oh, it was fine, but Brian turned out to be a jerk anyway." "Do you have any more, because I'm all out?" "Kelly says she's got big boobs but her ass is fat." Finny listened to all of it, feeling tired at the prospect of making her appearance, all the smiles and handshakes. She hated the idea of drawing all those hungry eyes to her, the scrutiny she was sure to receive. And then later, when she had to wear that stupid shirt: it would be humiliating.

But just as she thought of getting off the bed and going out into the hallway, the door of her room swung open.

A girl with a big black duffel came in and threw the bag down on the floor. "Oh, hey," the girl said, shutting the door behind her. "You must be my roommate."

"Finny," Finny said.

"That's an interesting name," the girl said. "Is it Irish?"

"No," Finny said, and couldn't gather her thoughts to say anything more. The reason she was so scattered was that the girl who stood before her was beautiful. She wasn't just cute or pretty, the way some of Finny's classmates at home were. She had long blond hair that she kept back in a ponytail, tied up with a simple black band rather than the colorful, poofy ornaments other girls wore. She was tall, maybe four or five inches taller than Finny, and she had a bright, open expression, large eyes, a slightly wide jaw that somehow complimented her delicate nose and defined cheekbones, her plucky little chin. And she had breasts, full ones. She was actually more like a grown woman than a girl, and Finny could easily have imagined her on the arm of some handsome man in a suit.

"Oh," the girl said now about Finny's name. "Well, I like it anyway. I'm Judith."

The instant Judith said her name, Finny remembered the lipstick she'd stashed in her pants pocket the day before. She felt a hot gulp of fear slide down her throat.

"It's nice to meet you," Finny said. And then: "I took your lipstick." She couldn't think of anything else to say, and she figured it would be better to get it out of the way early that she was a thief.

But Judith just laughed and flopped down on her bed across from Finny. "You mean the black one? Actually, I'm glad you took it. I meant to put it in my dresser before I left, but I forgot. They would have seen it."

"Who?"

"Old Yeller. That's what we call the principal, Mrs. Barksdale."

"Why?"

"Take a guess," Judith said.

Finny didn't have a response to this, so they sat for a moment in silence. Then Judith said, "I was living alone before break. Actually, I'm in ninth grade." The way the girl began her sentences with the word *actually*, it sounded like she was correcting some unheard person. "You're in eighth, right?"

Finny nodded. "Unfortunately."

"When they said a new girl was coming, I volunteered to have you stay with me."

"Thanks a lot," Finny said. "But how did you get to choose?"

"My parents are on the board," Judith said, and then blew at a strand of hair that had come loose from her ponytail. Finny was captivated by her movements, her ease in these strange surroundings. "It just means they give a lot of money," Judith went on. "You might have seen the Turngate Auditorium? That's my last name. Turngate."

"I'm sorry you had to give up your room," Finny blurted out. She felt clumsy in the presence of big graceful Judith.

"Like I said, I wanted a roommate. My last roommate left all of a sudden, and it was lonely. Actually, I'm very glad you're here."

"Why'd she leave?"

Judith shrugged. "Family stuff. By the way, why are *you* here? I mean, why'd you come in the middle of the year?"

"I got in trouble," Finny said.

"What kind of trouble?" Judith asked. "Boys?"

"Actually, yes," Finny said. She was already beginning to talk like Judith. The girl's pull was that strong, like a huge planet on a tiny pebble.

"Did you get caught doing something?"

"Sort of." Normally Finny wouldn't have answered any of these questions. She would have shrugged, or made a smart comment about what she got caught doing. But she felt compelled to give Judith what she asked for. Finny wanted so badly to please her, to win her approval. She could see that Judith must have been used to having that effect on people. "I started taking piano lessons so I could see this boy. Then my parents found out."

"And what happened?"

"I got sent here."

"No. I mean, what happened with the boy?"

"He's at home. We're still in love."

Here Judith let out a squeal of pleasure. "How *won*derful," she said. "Have you written him?"

"I just sent him a letter this morning."

"Hm," Judith said, frowning. "Well, you have to be careful about that. Old Yeller will check mailboxes."

"Really?"

"But she won't check mine. How about you have your boyfriend send the letters to my mailbox? And then I'll hand them off to you. I promise I won't peak at anything. Unless you let me." Judith was glowing. Finny loved the way their strings were crossing, how they were winding into each other's lives.

"Thanks," Finny said.

"Nothing," Judith said, in a way that sounded faintly European to Finny, though Finny had never been to Europe. "So what did you do last night?"

"I ate dinner with Poplan. Then we played Jenga."

"Oh, so the Pussy Popper got you to play already?"

"It wasn't that bad. The only dumb thing was this shirt I have to wear so I don't run away."

"Shirt?"

Finny got up and went to her closet, pulled out the shirt. She put it on, and modeled it for Judith, striking a sassy hand-on-hip pose, the way she used to when she was modeling her rat's nest for Sylvan. Finny was beginning to feel comfortable enough with her new roommate that she could joke like this, strut around and make faces, twist up other people's behavior into these absurd shapes.

Judith laughed at Finny's display, so hard she fell back on the bed and hit her head against the wall. "Ow," she said, then laughed some more. Finny kept dancing, enjoying how silly she and Judith looked together.

"Shorty Finn," Finny said. "It's like a deformed shark."

After a while Judith stopped laughing. "Actually, that's terrible," she said. "The shirt, I mean. I'm so sorry they're making you wear that. But I think I can take care of it."

"How?" Finny said.

"You'll see."

They chatted for a few more minutes, until it was time to go down to dinner. When they had gotten their coats on and were all ready to go, Judith said, "Oh, by the way, I know you went through my dresser, and it's okay."

Finny was going to deny it, but then she wondered how Judith knew. Were there video cameras in the room? Was she psychic? Finny could have believed this girl possessed almost any powers. Maybe the CIA was working for her.

"Actually, I wasn't sure," Judith said. "But now by the look on your face, I am." She laughed. "Don't worry. Like I said, it's okay. Actually, I would do the same. No one stops at the top of the dresser."

That evening the dining hall was a completely new room, alive with the bustle of eighty girls. Finny could hear their shouts and chatter even as she came down the stairs. Judith was next to her, and by the way everyone watched them, Finny could tell that Judith held a privileged position in the school. Judith introduced Finny to some girls as they picked up their trays—one named Nora who lived on their hall, and another named Jean who was downstairs—and though Finny's head was swimming, she loved their faces, their smiles and timid, sweaty handshakes.

Judith and Finny sat down at an empty table, which soon filled up around them. They talked about so many subjects that Finny would have trouble recalling them later: hair products, favorite stores, dishes to avoid in the dining hall, what people did over vacation. Judith pointed out people to Finny. There was an upper-form girl named Cynthia Bunswaggel, whom they called Bum Wagger because of the way her ass swayed when she walked. There was a girl named Yasmin Pitzer, whom they called Pits of Death because she didn't shave under her arms and had BO. Tasha Nolan was the Jackhammer, because of her percussive laugh.

In the far corner of the room was a woman that Judith identified as Mrs. Barksdale, the Old Yeller. She wore a bright red blazer, and her stringy hair was dyed a light orange color, as if she'd been going for blond but hadn't left the dye in long enough. She was so skinny that Finny could see the muscles tensing in her face and neck when she ate, and a vein that pulsed in her forehead. There was something animal-like about her, like a starved and aggressive dog.

When they were eating dessert, the Old Yeller got up and came over to Finny's table, which became instantly silent.

"Hello, young lady," the Old Yeller said to Finny. "I'm Mrs. Barksdale."

"Hi," Finny said.

"We're happy to welcome you to our school. I hope you've settled in okay?"

"Yes. Thank you very much."

"And Poplan told you about your dress code?"

Finny nodded. She was struck by Mrs. Barksdale's voice, which seemed strained and nasal, like air pinched from the neck of a balloon. It was an almost inhuman pitch, and it cut through all the background noise in the room.

"Then I will see you at the check-in this evening. I expect you'll be there?" She made this last comment with a small laugh, as if she were on to Finny already. And then she tucked her chin to her neck and gave Finny a long look.

"That was odd," Finny said when Mrs. Barksdale had left.

"Actually, that was a typical Old Yeller moment," Judith said. "No one knows what she's thinking."

After dinner and an hour and a half of free time, which the girls used to unpack but which was normally reserved for homework, all of the girls in the dorm were called to line up in front of their rooms for check-in. Judith had been out in the halls, catching up with friends. Finny hadn't seen her since dinner, though now she took her place next to Finny. They were the first ones in the hall, and Finny wondered where everyone else was.

Then the girls came out of their rooms. Finny was shocked at the sight of them. She looked at Judith, who giggled. Finny couldn't believe what was happening.

The reason Judith was laughing was that all of the girls were wearing purple T-shirts. They looked exactly like Finny.

"What is this?" Mrs. Barksdale shouted, her voice high and grating, like nails scraped against glass. Finny had to put her hands on her ears.

When she took her hands down, Judith said, "You see what I mean about the nickname?"

Chapter 7

Finny and Judith Find Ways to Entertain Themselves

Classes began the next morning. They were all the subjects Finny was used to, but the Thorndon School called them by different names. English was "communications," history was "humanities," and math was called "SMP," for some reason related to the textbooks they were using. But once Finny got used to the titles, the courses were standard. She'd always been a decent student—not A's, but usually high B's—and here was no different. In truth, the classes were what engaged the least of Finny's energies in her first semester at Thorndon.

Finny's real life began at three o'clock, when the final class let out. She'd go first to her room, to drop off her bag and check for letters from Earl. Finny had asked Earl to start addressing his letters to Judith, and Earl didn't mind. He always included a very polite note to Judith wrapped around his note to Finny: *Thanks again, Judith, for delivering this letter to Finny. I hope I'll meet you sometime. You sound like a very nice and considerate person. Sincerely, Earl Henckel.* Judith had gotten in the habit of leaving the letters on Finny's pillow during lunch, since Judith got back to the room later in the afternoon because of basketball. (She was the center on the JV team.) Sometimes she told Finny how sweet Earl seemed, and how she couldn't wait to see them together.

"You must be the most adorable couple," Judith said, and though Finny liked the sentiment, she had the odd sensation her friend was talking about people much younger than herself.

"Cute as a button," Finny said, and Judith laughed. She could tell now when Finny was being sarcastic, and she seemed to get a lot of pleasure out of Finny's cranky comments.

Earl's letters to Finny were as sweet and careful and encouraging as Earl was in person. *Finny!* he always began, and she could picture him that day he yelled to her and waved his arms like he was signaling an aircraft. That excitement, that joy, he didn't try to contain it. He told her the news about his life, about school and his afternoons and Mr. Henckel, the words seeming to just pour out. *My dad was a little depressed after you left,* Earl confided to Finny in one letter. *He's been falling asleep a lot lately at the dinner table and during his lessons. One time he actually fell asleep onto a student, which was awkward. I think he got used to our afternoons together. He always asks me if you're going to come over for coffee sometime. I didn't really tell him everything that happened, because I didn't want him to know you got in trouble. I hope that's okay. I know he just misses seeing you, like I do. Those were fun days, weren't they?*

When she read it, Finny started to cry. "Damn," she said to herself. She meant to stay happy, skim along the surface of her days at Thorndon. But every once in a while a memory snagged her. The letter was getting speckled with tears, so she put it away.

But most of the time she was happy. Days were bright and cold and fast. Once Judith got back from basketball, panting and sweaty, they'd shower in two stalls next to each other and talk about their days, their voices reverberating off the tiled floors and walls. They'd go to the dining hall together, eat with Brooke and Mariana and Simone. Then they'd do homework together in the study room until check-in.

Now that they were into the semester, Poplan did the check-in instead of Mrs. Barksdale. At night Poplan wore a kimono. She lined the girls up, and after calling each one's name, she made them wash their hands with soap and warm water. "For your own sake," Poplan said. She fought colds with a military vigilance, and at the first sign of a sniffle or a sore throat, she would quarantine a girl in the guest room for a week. "There's no negotiating with a fever," she would inform the girls. "Your lives are in my hands."

Finny's favorite time was the night, once she and Judith were shut up in their little room together, the hallway dim, the black sky pressed against their window. There was a cozy companionship to these moments, a luxury of time, as if life spread out before them, an endless and dazzling sea. She felt such exhilaration in Judith's presence that Finny had to check herself from becoming too giggly, too overwhelmed with pleasure. So she fell back on her wry delivery, that deadpan way of making jokes. It was the sense of humor Finny would hold on to, even as an adult.

Judith seemed to know everything about everyone in the school. She stood a head taller than most of the girls, and there was a kind of authority in her walk and demeanor. At night Judith told Finny all the gossip, about who'd snuck off with which boys at the last dance. About the girls who stuffed paper in their bras. And other things. More intimate, sexier things than Finny had ever heard talked about before. Judith told her about how Cynthia Bunswaggel had once gotten her period when she was in bed with a guy, and in the morning he'd woken up in a puddle of her blood and thought she was dead. And Halley Klein, who put condoms on carrots and used them to masturbate, only one time the carrot broke off and Halley had to go to the nurse to get it extracted.

Teachers, too. They weren't safe from Judith's swath of knowledge. Finny had heard the music teacher singing opera at night in her room, and when Finny told Judith how beautiful it was, Judith said, "It's because she uses a vibrator. She sings to cover up the sound." Which Finny found hard to believe. She wasn't even quite sure how a vibrator worked, but she started listening for the sound of it beneath Mrs. Polczek's singing. Poplan dated women, Judith said. She never brought them around because she was afraid of losing her job. For some reason Judith didn't like Poplan, Finny had discovered. But when she asked why, Judith just shrugged and said, "She's not my type."

Finny never knew how much of Judith's stories were invented, or exaggerations of what had happened, tales that had been dressed up by so many tellers that it was impossible to make out their original shapes. But under the canopy of Judith's voice, a garden of images and incidents bloomed. The world of Thorndon became alive and teeming with secrets.

Then there was the game. When Finny thought back about it, she wasn't sure exactly how it had started, but it became a pattern that every couple nights one of the two girls would offer the other a dare. They alternated dares. It began simply enough. *Go outside the room after lights out.* And then the next time: *Go outside after lights out and say the word "penis" in the hallway.* Each time a step further, a little more dangerous. *Stay outside for five seconds. Do it with your pants off.*

Finny no longer had to wear the purple shirt because Mrs. Barksdale realized that she couldn't make a rule that none of the other girls could wear purple shirts. So Finny felt a little freer at night. Some nights they both put on Judith's black clothing, and her lipstick, called each other "draculady" and "phantom" and snuck into other girls' rooms to show off their looks. Judith's "dark" wardrobe was extensive, and she told Finny that when they were in the upper forms they'd go to clubs in New York where they could wear these clothes "for real."

They talked about their lives at home. Finny told Judith about her mom's social pointers, her dad's lectures and the way he popped handfuls of Pepto like an addict.

"They sound funny," Judith said. "I'd love to meet them sometime."

"Careful what you wish for," Finny said.

"No, really. I mean it. On some break. I could come visit."

"You could come during spring break if you wanted."

"It's settled, then," Judith said. "I'm going to Shorty Finn's house for spring break." Here Judith got up and pulled Finny off her bed by the arms. They did a little ballroom dancing routine they'd made up just for fun, Finny dipping and spinning Judith. When they came together in a final embrace, Finny felt the curves of Judith's womanly body pressed against her own childish frame.

"Oh great," Finny said. It sounded like the flat way she delivered punch lines.

Judith's explanations of her own family were a little harder to make out. It seemed she didn't really spend time with them the way Finny did with hers. Her parents didn't talk to each other anymore, Judith said, except when it had to do with money or plans for Judith. Her mom and dad lived in separate parts of their apartment in New York—"wings," Judith called them, "separate wings." They lived on the Upper West Side, in a building called the Beresford, which Judith said was one of the fanciest buildings in New York.

"If you tell anyone in New York that you live in the Beresford, they'll think you're a snob."

She said that most of the other people in the building were famous, or at least old and rich. She saw movie stars in the elevator, and once Peter Jennings had given her a ride in his car. The lobby of the Beresford was like a museum, with chandeliers and antique end tables and Oriental rugs. If you tripped and fell, you might break ten thousand dollars' worth of furniture in one clumsy swoop. (Finny of course imagined she'd be the one to do that, if she ever visited.)

"But it's all terribly boring," Judith said, in a way that made her sound much older. "All the smiling and bowing doormen. It's so stupid."

"It sounds very glamorous to me," Finny said.

"Well it's not."

This was the first time Judith had gotten agitated with Finny. Finny heard her friend's mattress creaking as she adjusted positions. And she wondered: Why would Judith make such a big deal of all the chandeliers and riding in Peter Jennings's car if she hated it so much?

"My dad has a girlfriend," Judith said.

"You mean a lady he takes out?" Finny was trying to get a grasp on this strange world.

"No, I mean a woman who looks like my sister. I mean, she's twenty-five or something. But she actually comes over. While I'm there. He doesn't tell us, but I've heard them together." Judith had dropped her aristocratic way of speaking. She sounded like a child now.

Finny was about to ask what she heard her dad and his girlfriend doing, but then she realized. "Oh," she said. "That's awful. What does your mom do?"

"She gets on boards."

"What do you mean?" Finny pictured the woman on tabletops, swatting at her husband with a broom.

"I mean, like at Thorndon. Or different museums. Pretty much anything she can throw a lot of money at. I don't even think she knows all the boards she's on."

"Well at least she's being generous."

"Tell me about your brother," Judith said, and Finny understood she was trying to change the subject. "Actually," Judith went on, "I don't even recall his name."

In Judith's company, Finny felt as if she moved behind a protective shield. Even Mrs. Barksdale mostly left her alone, though Finny heard her yelling at other girls numerous times. *Giving it to them*, Finny and Judith called it. *Old Yeller is giving it to someone.* Mrs. Barksdale would start at a medium volume in her rasping, discordant voice, and as she gave it to some student—who'd shown up late for morning meeting, or swiped some fruit from the dining hall—her voice gradually rose to an almost frenzied pitch, a feverish screech. She couldn't help herself, and Finny always felt sorry for the girls who were singled out. By the end the student would be holding her ears as Mrs. Barksdale shrieked and squealed. It was such a harrowing, bewildering display that students often began to cry, they were so traumatized by the effect they'd had on this woman.

Students were allowed to eat outside of the dining hall for lunch, and Finny and Judith began sitting in the hall in front of the library. Soon Brooke and Mariana and the others joined them. One time, during lunch, Chayla brought a cupcake out of her lunchbox with a candle in it, and Judith took out her lighter and lit it. She kept her hand cupped around the flame. It was Finny's birthday, and they sang to her.

"How did you know?" Finny asked when they were done singing. They'd never told each other their birthdays.

"I have my ways," Judith said. "But blow it out before Old Yeller sees."

That night a present arrived from Earl: a box of instant coffee. *Not the same,* he wrote, *but maybe it's enough to hold you over until I see you.*

In February, there was a parents' weekend, when Stanley came to visit. Laura stayed at home with Sylvan; Finny suspected it was because her mother was still angry at her over Earl. Stanley attended a few of Finny's classes on Friday, ate lunch with her in the dining hall, took Finny and Judith to dinner in Boston. (Judith's parents hadn't come.) By the end of the weekend, he seemed satisfied with the school he'd placed Finny in, though he left her with an oddly solemn quote: " 'A useless life is an early death,' " he told her as he was getting into his cab. Then yelled, "Goethe!" just before slamming the door.

At night, after Stanley's visit, Finny and Judith kept going with the dares. *Run naked all the way from our door to Clay-cie's and back. Put a love letter on Amanda's welcome mat. Shout the word "boner" so I can hear it with the door closed.* And on and on. They spurred each other with their laughter and pleased looks. Later, Finny would recognize that it was a kind of flirting, not necessarily sexual, but a testing of boundaries, of how far each would go for the other, how much they would risk. To go out in the hall, to shout something disgusting, to wait—it was all a way of saying, *See, look what I'll do.* To keep the game going, to avoid piercing this lovely dream. And what Finny hated to admit—but had to, when she thought back on those nights with Judith—was that there was a desperation in it, in her. She was clinging to what she saw as her new life. Far from being that beautiful lonely birch in her parents' yard, Finny's branches were entangled with Judith's, and she wasn't sure she would ever be set free.

One night Judith asked her to do something Finny had to think twice about. It wasn't that the act was particularly dangerous, in the sense that she was likely to get caught. It wasn't so much more daring than the dozen other stunts they'd pulled in the last couple weeks—sliding condoms that Judith had bought under the door of a sallow-looking girl named Pam, whom they called the Ice Chest; singing a full chorus of "My Girl" after Poplan had gone downstairs. But this time there was a question in Judith's dare: *Would you go this far for me?* Judith knew that Finny liked Poplan. She knew this would raise issues.

The dare was that Finny had to slip a note that Judith had written under Poplan's door. Not such a difficult thing. Finny would be the last person Poplan would suspect. They'd become friendly, to the point where Poplan had let Finny sample the cache of Asian food products she kept in her dresser: shrimp chips, salted plums, cans of fruit with names like *longan* and *rambutan*. Poplan didn't even watch Finny when Finny washed her hands at night; she trusted her that much.

What bothered Finny was the message Judith had written: *I want your pussy*. Nothing else. No signature, no instructions. Just those four words. At the time Finny couldn't say exactly what she felt was wrong with this, why this was a different sort of joke. She didn't have the words to explain what Judith was asking her to do, what loyalties she was testing.

"She'll think she has an admirer," Judith said.

"Or a stalker." Finny wondered if there was a way she could play this, if she could make just the right jokes, put it in just the right light to force Judith to see how foolish the request was.

But Judith didn't budge. "Are you worried the Pussy Popper's gonna come after yours?"

Finny laughed. "Not gonna pop mine," she said. She wasn't going to let Judith faze her.

"Then you're in?"

"Where's the note?"

Chapter **8**

A Trip to the Principal's Office

Two notes for Finny the next day.

The first was in her mailbox in the morning:

Dear Finny, the letter began:

I am writing to express what a wonderful and happy time I enjoyed with you and your new friend, Judith. I am extremely pleased that you are finding such a satisfying life in your new environment, and such a worthwhile group of friends. I would have trouble explaining all my feelings in a letter, but I want you to understand that I am proud of you, and think very highly of the young woman you are becoming.

Also, with regards to your question about Judith visiting over spring vacation: that is fine by us. We will be pleased to introduce her to the modest intellectual bastion we have maintained here at 2026 Geist.

This is the bulk of what I wished to tell you, but I feel that it may be appropriate to conclude the letter with a quotation, if you will permit the indulgence. (I will modernize spelling for your convenience.)

"Continual success in obtaining those things which a man

from time to time desires, that is to say, continual prospering, is that which men call FELICITY." (Hobbes)

With tenderest feelings,

Stanley et al.

Finny read the letter twice. In spite of the stilted language and awkward sentiments, in spite of even the fact that the quote used the word *man* to mean *people,* Finny was touched. It wasn't so much the words as the feelings she recognized behind them. She felt a rush of love for this man she'd always been wary of.

In her letter back to her father Finny wrote: *I love you, Dad. Thanks for saying those things. I had a wonderful time with you, too. Can't wait for the vacation.*

The second note of the day was stuck on Finny's door when she returned from classes. At first she thought it was a letter from Earl, and wondered why Judith would put it up where everyone could see. Then she saw the handwriting. In very neat script, the envelope read, *Delphine Short.* No address. Inside, in the same tight script, there was a brief note: *Mrs. Barksdale requests that you report to her office immediately upon returning from classes.*

Her faithful secretary,

Miss Filomena Simpkin

Finny walked into Mrs. Barksdale's outer office at three-fifteen. Her secretary, Miss Simpkin, was seated at the desk, typing out a letter. She had a dainty way of pecking at the keys, odd for such a large woman. Miss Simpkin was entirely shapeless, her body like a tower of mashed potatoes or a bowl of pudding, and she seemed to flow over and around the chair she sat in. She wore a matching sweat suit every day—today's was olive-colored—and her only attention to fashion seemed to be in the small white flower she kept tucked behind her ear.

"I got a note to see Mrs. Barksdale," Finny said.

"I wrote that note," Miss Simpkin said. Her voice was deep and husky.

"Then, does she want to see me?"

"I don't know what she wants. I only know what she tells me. She told me to write that note. I can buzz her and see, if that's what you're asking me to do." Miss Simpkin had a way of making everything you said sound like an impertinent request.

"I'm just coming because you told me to," Finny said.

"Mrs. Barksdale told you," Miss Simpkin corrected. "I am just the messenger. *She* is the voice."

"Okay. But is this the right time?"

"Would you like me to buzz?"

"Only if I'm supposed to be here."

"Nothing can be discovered until I buzz."

"All right, then, buzz," Finny said. "Please."

"Then I will buzz," Miss Simpkin said.

She made an elaborate show of buzzing, pointing her index finger upward, then steering it down onto the button like a crashing spaceship. Finny could hear the phone buzz loudly in Mrs. Barksdale's office, which was hardly five feet from where Finny was standing. The office windows were covered by blinds, but Finny could see Mrs. Barksdale's wiry shape behind them.

"Yes?" Mrs. Barksdale's voice crackled on the speakerphone. Finny could also hear her through the wall.

"Miss Short is here to see you," Miss Simpkin said. Then she looked at Finny and added, "She seems impatient."

Finny frowned.

"You can send her in," Mrs. Barksdale responded.

Finny muttered, "Thanks," and walked into Mrs. Barksdale's office.

Mrs. Barksdale's office was a small room with the same gray-brown carpeting Finny had in her dorm room. The walls were an off-white color, and if not for all the clutter, it would have been a cheerful little space. The principal had a pencil clutched in her teeth when Finny entered, and she was writing something with another pencil. Finny looked around as she waited for the principal to acknowledge her. On the wall hung Mrs. Barksdale's degree from Oberlin, and two pictures. The first was of the principal with her husband, a diminutive man who looked a decade older than Mrs. Barksdale and who was completely bald. In the picture Mrs. Barksdale had seized her husband in what she obviously considered an affectionate embrace, only her husband's expression appeared more one of terror than fondness. The expression seemed to betray the belief that his wife was trying to kill him.

The second photo on the wall was a family portrait, featuring the husband again, and also a young girl whom Finny took to be the principal's daughter. The girl sat between her two parents, in a neat white dress, a look of distress on her face, as if she still couldn't accept the fact that, of all the couples in the world, God had chosen to place her with this one.

Finny wondered why the principal had chosen to hang these particular photos on the wall. She noticed that Mrs. Barksdale's desk—a large wooden desk that took up most of the room—was strewn with pencils. The pencils had teeth marks on them from eraser to point, as if a dog had chewed on them, and some were broken in half. Behind Mrs. Barksdale the window let in shafts of dusty sunlight. It was hot in the room, and there was a sour smell, like spoiled milk.

Suddenly, Mrs. Barksdale ejected the pencil from her mouth. She stopped writing and looked at Finny. "What's this I hear about you writing notes?" she said.

"What?" Finny said. For a moment she was stunned. She wondered how Mrs. Barksdale could have found the notes to Earl, whether the principal had in fact gone through Judith's mailbox.

"You've got a lot of boldness, young lady."

"Boldness?"

"But you've crossed lines here."

"Lines?"

"Yes, I would certainly say so," Mrs. Barksdale said. "But then again, you deserve a fair hearing. Let me buzz Miss Simpkin for her response."

Mrs. Barksdale made the same show of pressing the button that Miss Simpkin had made a moment before.

"Yes?" Miss Simpkin responded. Finny could hear her voice through the door as well as the telephone line.

"Miss Simpkin," Mrs. Barksdale said, "you know the details of Miss Short's case. Now, would you go as far as to say that she 'crossed a line'?"

"Certainly," Miss Simpkin said.

"I thank you," Mrs. Barksdale said, and hung up. "It's settled, then. Miss Simpkin has made everything clear, as usual. She believes you've crossed a line. And Miss Simpkin has impeccable moral judgment."

"Oh," said Finny.

"I'll give you one chance to speak for yourself," Mrs. Barksdale said, "because I know that is the fair thing to do."

While Mrs. Barksdale's words remained calm, Finny could hear that this was a struggle for her. The woman's nervousness seemed to be suppressed by the greatest effort, the way you might throw all your weight on an overstuffed suitcase to contain the clothing inside. Finny could tell that Mrs. Barksdale was heading toward a screech. This was how it always began before she lost it, before she *gave it to someone.* Finny shuddered at the thought of the Old Yeller letting loose in this tiny room.

"I—I didn't know that I couldn't write my friends," Finny sputtered.

"*Friends?*" Mrs. Barksdale said. "Do you treat all your friends in such a—*perverted* way?"

"Perverted?"

Here Mrs. Barksdale buzzed again. "Miss Simpkin, I have called to ask your advice on another matter of principle."

"Shoot," Miss Simpkin said.

"Would you go as far as to call Miss Short's actions *perverted*?"

"Undoubtedly," the gravelly voice answered.

"I thank you," Mrs. Barksdale said, and hung up. "From the mouth of a woman who could have been a Supreme Court justice," she informed Finny. "An unerring sense of fairness."

"I'm sorry—" Finny said.

"I'm not the one you should be apologizing to," Mrs. Barksdale cut in. "Do you know that Poplan was humiliated by your little note?"

Finny's mouth dropped open. Her mind scurried for words. She never imagined it could have been the note to Poplan that Mrs. Barksdale was talking about. That silly prank. And it had happened only last night. She was sure she'd been alone in the hall. Who could have told on her? A horrible flash of an idea appeared in Finny's mind.

"Let me cut the mystery short," the principal said, and her voice was edging toward panic, like the needle on a record beginning to lose its grip, to skip and scratch. Finny glanced at the picture of the little man cowering in the Old Yeller's grasp, the gnarled pencils on the table. "I can see that you're astonished at my ingenuity. So let me just say that you were observed, that a student saw you sneak downstairs with that dirty note, and heard you giggling when you came back up. She told us you were up to something, and when Poplan showed us the note, we put two and two together. Or I should say, Miss Simpkin put two and two together. I owe everything to the unconventional genius of Miss Simpkin."

"Thank you," Miss Simpkin called from the outer room.

Mrs. Barksdale buzzed her.

"Yes?" Miss Simpkin said.

"You're welcome. But may I kindly ask you to use the buzzer next time," Mrs. Barksdale said.

"I'm sorry," Miss Simpkin said.

"Quite all right," Mrs. Barksdale said, and hung up.

Who was it? Finny thought. Who would have followed her all the way downstairs to the teachers' rooms, then stood and watched in the dark? Again, the horrible idea flashed in Finny's mind, and she shook her head, like she had water in her ears.

"It was a stupid prank," Finny said now. "We didn't mean anything—"

But here Mrs. Barksdale cut in, unable to contain herself any longer. "And to think Judith Turngate offered to room with you! One of our brightest stars! And you go performing your filthy pranks!"

Finny couldn't take it. It was like a radio with bad reception turned to the highest volume. Mrs. Barksdale's voice slashed and stabbed. It bounced off the walls like a misfired bullet. Finny put her hands on her ears.

"Don't you cover your ears in front of me!" Mrs. Barksdale screeched. When she screamed, the tendons in her neck tensed like the strings in a marionette. She reached across the desk and tore Finny's hands from her ears. "You're going to listen to me!"

"But—" Finny started.

"But nothing!" Here Mrs. Barksdale stopped to take a breath. She must have realized the scene she was making, because when she began again, it was in a slightly calmer voice. "Let me just make this clear. We considered calling your parents, Finny. What you did was that wrong. This is a much more serious offense than you think."

Finny nodded. "Please—" she began again.

But Mrs. Barksdale made a sound—*chuf*—like a little bark. "I have no time for this. I'm going to explain our decision, and then send you off to deal with it. We've decided you'll have one chance to get this right, Finny Short. You're going to be housebound the next three weekends before break—no parties, no walks except to and from the dining hall."

"Okay," Finny said, having feared the punishment would be much worse.

"And of course you'll have to apologize to Poplan. She's very hurt. I'll leave it to her discretion how to handle you. She'll see you tonight after dinner. Now you can go." Mrs. Barksdale made a shooing motion with her hand.

Finny was getting up to leave when the phone buzzed. "Very fair," Miss Simpkin said on the other end of the line.

"I thank you, Miss Simpkin," Mrs. Barksdale returned. "I'm honored that you should think so. You have true moral fortitude, Miss Simpkin. . . ."

Chapter 9

Finny Tries
to Make Amends

"Come in," Poplan said after Finny knocked on the door. Finny went inside and closed the door behind her. Poplan's room had a pleasant smell, like something sweet was baking in it. Her bed was neatly made, the porcelain animals arranged and dusted on her shelves.

"Hi," Finny said.

"Hello," Poplan said. She was wearing a very simple kimono that evening, a jade color with no pattern on it. Her hair was wet from the shower. She was tidying up the room, smoothing out the duvet on her bed.

"I came because I had some things I wanted to tell you." Finny had an anxious feeling in her chest, like it was puffed up with helium. Her fingers were trembly and cold, and she was sweating a little under her arms.

"What things?" Poplan said. She kept smoothing her hand over the duvet, even though it looked perfectly smooth to Finny. Finny could see she wasn't going to make it easy for her. She wouldn't even look Finny in the eyes.

"About the note you got under your door last night. It was my fault. I mean, I did it. I put it under there. I'm sorry,

Poplan." The words just rushed out of her, like she was coughing some sour-tasting thing out of her mouth.

"Why did you do it?" Poplan asked, still smoothing the cover, not looking at Finny.

"I just—" Finny started. "I didn't think—" She couldn't seem to get the right angle to charge at it. "It was supposed to be funny," she finally got out. "But it wasn't."

"You actually scared me."

"It was a dumb thing to do. It was supposed to be a joke, but we didn't stop to think what would happen."

"We?" Poplan looked at Finny. She'd stopped smoothing the cover, and her hands hung by her sides. "Was it your idea?" she asked.

"It was just a joke," Finny repeated. "I regret it. I'm sorry."

Poplan shook her head. "I'm surprised you did it, Finny. I thought we were friends."

Finny looked about her, as if for someone who might come to her defense. But all she saw were Poplan's animals, watching her, waiting to see what she'd say.

Then something happened to Finny, all at once, so fast it was like a wave washing over her. She began to cry. It was a bitter kind of crying, and she had to take long breaths to slow it. She stood there in the room, the tears falling off her face, saying, "I'm sorry, Poplan. I'm sorry." She felt ridiculous for making a scene, but she couldn't stop it.

And then Poplan's arms were around her. "Okay," Poplan said. "Okay." Her voice was steady and calming. Poplan held Finny and stroked her hair, and Finny wept. It was partly that Finny was sorry, but also that Poplan had loosed something in her. Finny knew she didn't deserve this woman's affection.

"All right," Poplan kept telling her. "It's okay."

And finally, when she stopped crying, Poplan asked her again, "I just want to know if it was your idea, Finny. Did you come up with it?"

Finny shook her head.

"I had a feeling," Poplan said. They were still standing close, and now Poplan pulled out her desk chair and gestured toward it with an open palm. Finny sat down. Poplan sat on the bed, facing Finny.

"Now I'm going to say something," Poplan began, without any of her usual brusqueness. She seemed softer, as if Finny's tears had awakened some motherly instinct in her. "I know this might sound strange. Maybe it'll even be uncomfortable. And I know you probably won't believe me. But I think I'm saying it for your own good."

"What?" Finny managed to ask.

"Judith is a bad influence," Poplan said. "I know that everyone loves her, and that you and she hit it off. I know it seems like she's your best friend in the world right now. And it's not to say that she doesn't like you or want to be. It's just that she has a need to act out. I've seen it. And she doesn't always think about the people around her when she does it."

"Why are you saying this?" Finny asked. She was shaking her head. She didn't want to hear it, didn't want to see mud splattered on her beautiful canvas.

"I know it's not going to sound right to you. I know you're probably going to hate me for it. But I like you, Finny, and I feel for you. I just don't want to see you getting hurt."

"Are you mad at Judith for something?"

"I'm not mad at her, and I'm not jealous," Poplan said. "It probably seems that way, but I'm not."

"Then why? What did she do to you? Besides this stupid prank?"

"She didn't do anything to me." Poplan looked at the ceiling and muttered something that sounded like "Oh, my life." Then asked Finny, "Did Judith tell you anything about her last roommate?"

Finny didn't understand why Poplan would ask that, why it had anything to do with what was happening now. She knew she should stop the conversation here: she wasn't ready for any shattering truths.

And yet, her curiosity nudged her on, like when she'd stood in front of Judith's dresser, wondering what was inside.

"She said she had some family stuff," Finny offered at last.

"Her name is Jesse," Poplan said. "Judith and Jesse. That was the team. I caught them on the roof with a bottle of hooch."

"Of what?"

"Porch climber. Tiger milk." Poplan's forehead was creased, as if Finny were the one speaking a strange language.

"I don't know what you're talking about," Finny said.

Poplan leaned toward Finny and whispered, "Alcohol." Then, in a louder voice: "Which is why Judith doesn't like me." She paused, seeming to consider her next words. "They were daring each other to lean over the edge. It was dangerous. I had to turn them in, Finny."

"All right," Finny said.

"The next thing I know, Jesse's expelled," Poplan continued. "Judith was the victim. She'd been dragged out of sleep, hardly knew where she was going. Her parents had a long talk with the school. The administration was afraid to mention alcohol to the other students, so none of them ever found out what happened." Poplan looked Finny over the way she sometimes scrutinized girls while they washed their hands at night, then added, "I'm telling you this in confidence, of course. I trust this conversation will remain off the record."

Finny nodded. Her thoughts were too stirred for her to speak. It wasn't that she felt betrayed; she knew Judith's parents held power at the school, and Judith had probably been told not to mention what happened to anyone. Finny was just surprised at herself, at how easily she'd been taken in.

"Look," Poplan said, and made a chopping motion with both hands, like a politician coming to a point, "it's not that

I'm telling you not to be friends with Judith or go on about your life here and have fun. I'm happy to see that you're enjoying yourself and making friends. I'm only saying you need to be your own person. Judith seems like she knows everything, but she doesn't. If you follow your own judgment, Finny, I think it'll turn out all right."

Finny wanted to stop Poplan, to protest, but didn't know how to do it. And it was true, there was a sense in which Finny had been less of herself since she'd come to Thorndon. Part of it was Judith, her overwhelming influence. But part of it was also Finny, a new desire in her to please and be rewarded, so different from her old life, her old way.

And now that other question appeared in Finny's mind. *Who told?* She was certain Judith wouldn't have snitched, or even tipped someone off about what Finny was doing, but still, the idea was there. It was a mark of Judith's power, Finny realized, that you could imagine her doing inexplicable things, for her own reasons. But also a sign of Finny's own insecurities, that she could believe her closest friend had betrayed her.

"Anyway, that's all I wanted to say about that," Poplan concluded, and stood up. She'd regained some of her military bearing. "Now, there is one thing you can do to make this up to me, and I hope you won't refuse."

"What is it?" Finny asked.

"It's an important task."

"What?"

Poplan smiled.

They set up the blocks on the floor.

"Don't think I'm going to let you win either," Poplan said, "just because you had a bad night."

"I don't," Finny said.

"And if I catch a cold from this, you know who I'm coming to."

"I do."

When Finny knocked down the tower, Poplan jumped up and performed a little boxing routine in the middle of the floor. "Yahoo!" she screamed, giving the air a final jab with her fist.

Chapter 10

The Vacation Begins, a Bit Early

They crept toward spring break, more slowly than Finny had hoped. Her punishment made the days drag. But Judith was a model friend, spending nights in the dorm with Finny while the other girls went out. Finny didn't mention the story Poplan had told her about Jesse, since she'd promised Poplan she wouldn't. Finny could see both sides of it—why Poplan was annoyed that Jesse had gotten the brunt of the punishment, but also why Judith was upset over her friend's moving away. It made sense why Judith didn't talk about it.

One afternoon, a couple of weeks after the note incident, Finny returned to her dorm room and there was another letter on the door. *Delphine Short*, it said on the envelope, and inside was Miss Simpkin's familiar handwriting: *Mrs. Barksdale requests that you report immediately to her office. If we do not see you by the end of your lunch period, she will seek you in your next class.*

Her faithful secretary,
Miss Filomena Simpkin

. . .

Today Mrs. Barksdale's office had an even stronger odor of spoiled milk. It was hot in the room, and when Finny walked in, the principal looked agitated, some sweaty curls of hair adhering to her temples. Mrs. Barksdale had a gnawed pencil in her mouth, and when Finny shut the door behind her, she heard the utensil snap in Mrs. Barksdale's teeth.

"Tuh," the principal said, and spit the splintered pencil onto her desk, among the remains of other decimated utensils. "Please have a seat."

Finny sat down across from Mrs. Barksdale. She glanced at the photo of the principal's husband. The tiny man's frightened expression seemed to warn Finny of some impending danger.

"His birthday," Mrs. Barksdale said about the picture of her husband, noticing Finny was looking at it. "I got him good."

"I guess you did," Finny said.

"Surprise party. It took him a few days to recover."

"I'm sorry."

"Psh." She gave a dismissive wave of her hand. "He's so excitable."

"Anyway, what is it?" Finny said, impatient to hear what she'd been dragged here for. Did they figure out she'd snuck a cigarette with Judith during gym class? Or that she'd been the one screaming "boner" in the hall after lights-out?

"Did I do something?" Finny asked.

Mrs. Barksdale shook her head vigorously at Finny's suggestion, like a dog drying itself after a swim. "No," the principal said. "No."

"Did you want to ask me something?" Finny tried.

But Mrs. Barksdale shook her head again, this time more slowly, her lips pressed together.

"I have some bad news, Finny," Mrs. Barksdale said. "Tragic news, I would say."

"What is it?" Finny said. "What are you trying to tell me?"

"Let me just say," Mrs. Barksdale continued, as if Finny hadn't spoken, "that your mother would have been the one to tell you this, but when she called during your lunch hour and we couldn't find you—do you not eat in the cafeteria?—she asked us to relay the message to you, since this is going to be a very busy and unpleasant afternoon for her."

"Please," Finny said. "Could you please just tell me what you want to say?"

"Your father is dead," Mrs. Barksdale blurted out. And then seemed to recover herself. She must have realized how abrupt this sounded, because she clapped a hand over her mouth. Finny noticed the tendons tensing in the principal's neck.

The phone buzzed. "Passed away," Miss Simpkin's voice said in the speaker. "*Passed away* would have been more sensitive."

"I thank you," Mrs. Barksdale said, and hung up. She then went on to tell Finny, "The message remains the same. You are to pack a suitcase and return home on a flight at seven forty-five this evening. The funeral will be in a couple days. All of your teachers will be apprised of the unfortunate news, and they will arrange it so you can finish your courses in a comfortable amount of time, without having to repeat any next year."

Once Mrs. Barksdale had finished this speech, she let out a long breath, like she'd finished climbing a steep set of stairs, or had reached a bus she was running to catch. Her shoulders sagged, and she looked at Finny to see if she had anything to say.

"Do you have any questions?" the principal asked, the way teachers do when they've finished a lecture.

But all Finny could think to say was, "What happened?"

Here Mrs. Barksdale seemed confused, and began glancing into corners of the room, as if the answer would appear there. She looked like a trapped mouse. When at last she relinquished the search, she turned her eyes back to Finny. For a moment Finny had the distinct impression that the principal would have liked to reach across the desk and touch her, offer some reassurance in the face of this terrifying news. It was as if Finny had been walking along on a fine, clear day, and all of a sudden came upon a huge dark hole, something mysterious and out of place, and which she'd never be able to cross. She felt more startled than sad.

Mrs. Barksdale pressed her lips together, her eyebrows knitted like she was about to cry. Then she said, "I don't know."

Poplan was waiting outside Finny's door when Finny got back to her room. Finny had begun crying on her way back from the principal's office, and the sight of Poplan in a bright orange jumpsuit did nothing to calm her. Poplan held out her arms, and Finny collapsed into them. The dorm was empty, since the girls were in class, so Finny just cried and cried, holding on to Poplan, pushing her face into the warm folds of Poplan's jumpsuit. After a few minutes, Poplan suggested that Finny open the door so that maybe they could go inside and sit down. Like when Finny had come to her room to apologize about the note, Poplan was gentle and kind. She seemed to be able to shed her official manner as easily as her kimonos and wraps.

In the room Finny lay down on the bed. "I don't understand," she said, turning on her back, her hands over her eyes, shaking her head like she just couldn't believe what was happening. "He seemed completely fine when he visited."

"I'm sorry," Poplan said. She sat down next to Finny and stroked her arm as Finny cried.

In a little while Poplan suggested, "Maybe you should try calling your mother."

"That's another thing I don't get. Why wouldn't she tell me herself?"

"Maybe it was too hard right now. Maybe she tried to call you and couldn't reach you and was just too tired and stressed out to keep trying."

"Maybe she was being a thoughtless bitch," Finny offered.

"You don't know that," Poplan said.

"You don't know my mother."

Poplan stayed in the room while Finny packed, sitting on Finny's bed. Every once in a while Finny would say, "It's okay, Poplan. You don't have to sit here all day."

"I don't mind," Poplan said. "It's good to have company."

Soon Finny could hear the girls coming back from their classes, chatting about their scores on quizzes, how much homework they had.

"Karina farted in humanities," Finny heard Nora say.

"She's a humanitarian," Brooke answered. And then some laughing and snorting.

On other days Simone or Jean or Nora might knock and come visit Finny for a little while, but today nobody knocked. The voices seemed to get quieter as they approached Finny's door, as if the girls were observing some sort of decree. Finny had the sense that word had gotten around about her dad, or at least that the others knew something was wrong with her, since she hadn't been to any of her afternoon classes. She had an odd feeling of being isolated by her grief, the way Poplan quarantined girls who had caught a cold or the flu. Finny felt sick herself, like no one would want to touch her or be near her. Loss always did this to you, pushed you in a corner where no one wanted to go.

Later Judith came in, after her lacrosse practice. She was sweating, and had a purple bandana tied around her hair. She looked lovely, and for the first time Finny resented her for it.

"I heard," Judith said. "My God, Finny, I'm so sorry." Then she noticed Poplan on the bed. "Hi," Judith said to her.

"Hi, Judith," Poplan said, and Finny heard the effort Poplan was making to be friendly. "You know, I think Finny might want some time to herself, to get ready now."

Judith looked at Finny. There was a moment of silent struggle between Poplan and Judith, over who would get to stay with Finny.

Finally Finny said, "If you don't mind, Judith, I'm just not up for talking now."

Judith took the hint. "Oh," she said, and Finny could see she was surprised, and a little offended. Judith hated losing, no matter the circumstances. "Actually, I was planning to head to dinner early anyway. I just needed to grab some clothes."

Judith gathered an outfit from her closet. Before she left the room, she walked over to Finny, who was standing in front of her own closet.

"I am so sorry," Judith said, and gave Finny a long hug. "Look, I know you're not up to discussing anything now, but give me a call when you feel up to it. I hope you can come back soon. I'll miss you, Shorty Finn."

Finny felt her eyes fill up again. "I'll miss you, too," she said.

Then Judith took her hand like she was going to shake it. But instead Finny felt a cold metal object placed in her palm. She looked at Judith, and Judith smiled sadly. Finny knew it was the black lipstick.

"Thanks," Finny said.

She didn't call her mother that afternoon. She knew Laura was too overwhelmed to deal with anything, and she figured she'd get all the information from her brother when she got home. Poplan said she would drive Finny to the airport. When Poplan turned on the car, some lively Irish fiddle music blared through the speakers, and Poplan had to hurry to turn it off. "Sorry," she said. They fell silent for the rest of the ride. The last thing Poplan mentioned was that she had some cousins in Virginia she visited a lot, and that she'd love to stop by and see Finny in Maryland during a vacation sometime if Finny wouldn't mind a visitor.

At seven-twenty Finny boarded the plane that would hurtle her back into a very different world from the one she had left only ten weeks before.

Chapter 11

A Sad Time

The Haberdasher Funeral Home was just off Reisterstown Road, one of those four-lane commercial havens lined by strip malls and representatives of every chain store under the sun. The funeral home was an olive-green A-frame house with black shutters, nestled between a Target and a John Deere outlet. Inside, the floors were varnished pine, the walls wine-colored. The doors between rooms opened by a latch rather than a knob. The windows were small and square, and the strangled light that pushed through them left the house dim and shadowy, even in the middle of the day.

Which was the time now. Laura had brought Sylvan and Finny along to help her make decisions about the funeral. She'd read an article the night after Stanley died that said a grieving widow must bring people with her to the funeral home with whom she can discuss options, because she won't be in a condition to make appropriate decisions herself. This proved to be true in Laura's case, as evidenced by the fact that she'd brought her children here.

The house was lit only by some electric lights that looked like candles, encased in glass jars that were mounted on the walls. The floors creaked as the Shorts toured the facilities. Finny could hardly believe they were getting ready to put

Stanley's body in the ground. She kept thinking of her father's face completely still, like he was sleeping, and that seemed the closest she could get to accepting he was dead. She remembered him telling his stories, reciting his quotations, and she couldn't find a way to fit that liveliness into the picture of him lying motionless in a coffin. She remembered the letter he'd written her only a few weeks before, all those feelings he'd never been able to share.

But she stopped herself. He was gone now, drained from the world like bathwater from a tub.

Mrs. Haberdasher was a short and very stout woman in her sixties who walked with a cane and whose nose always seemed to be twitching as though she had an itch there. She wore a green velvet cap like a loose-fitting beret. She walked slowly, and knocked her cane against the floor with every step. Mr. Haberdasher allowed her to lead when they were walking. He was a demure man, tall and with the approximate body type of a string bean. His voice was soft as a whisper, his yellow-gray hair silky as a baby's.

"Now," Mrs. Haberdasher said, "there are two basic options for coffins." She was indicating the two options displayed on tables in front of the Shorts.

But before she was able to explain the options, Mr. Haberdasher let loose a gigantic sneeze that echoed in the small room.

"Holy Christ!" Mrs. Haberdasher yelled, and jumped away from her husband, much more dexterously than you would expect a woman with a cane to jump.

Mr. Haberdasher shrugged and wiped his nose on his shirt cuff.

"Now," Mrs. Haberdasher said, coming around to the coffins again, "as I was saying, there are two options to consider. The first, to your left, is the standard coffin. Made out of wood, with the tapered shape. And we can offer you a variety of interiors and exteriors for that. The second is a cas-

"Now, do you want to take care of this today?" Mrs. Haberdasher said.

"Certainly," Laura blurted out. Then stood there, waiting.

"Mom, your credit card," Sylvan said.

"Oh," Laura said, "of course," and handed the Haberdashers her card.

"I am very sorry for your loss," Mrs. Haberdasher said to the Shorts as she swiped Laura's card.

"Thanks," Sylvan said.

"It's a tough road, young man," Mr. Haberdasher said.

"Are *you* the expert?" Mrs. Haberdasher asked him.

He shrugged and wiped his nose on his shirt cuff.

And then, as if in response, Mrs. Haberdasher released an echoing shriek of a sneeze, which caused Mr. Haberdasher to actually run around the counter, and then half a dozen strides away from his wife.

"My ghost just departed," he said, when he'd finally come to rest.

The burial was the next morning. Mr. Haberdasher drove the hearse, and he seemed to take great pride in the duty, wearing a black chauffeur's cap he reserved for the occasion. Mrs. Haberdasher navigated. Finny saw the little woman hop into the cab of the hearse, like a jockey mounting a horse, already informing her husband that he was the last person *she* would choose to drive for *her* last ride. She sat on the armrest between the driver's seat and passenger seat, and as they all pulled out of the funeral home, Finny saw her directing Mr. Haberdasher with her cane, pointing to road signs and passing traffic.

The graveyard was not far from the funeral home, and the Shorts followed the hearse in their car. They stood around the grave. Finny recognized a number of the mourners—faces from her father's office Christmas parties, her parents' dinner parties, family reunions. She saw Aunt Louise, rubbing her ball of tissue across her nose. Mr. Hedgwick was there, the farmer who cleared the Shorts' driveway in the winter with his tractor and who'd let Finny play with his golden retriever puppies. There was Arnold Arnold—a cruel joke by his parents—who used to give Finny rides to soccer games when she played on the Cockeysville rec team. And Kitty Plinket, who always wore red and had shown Laura how to dance the tango.

Earl, of course, was not there. Finny knew he would have wanted to come and that Laura would have objected, so Finny decided she wouldn't tell him until it was over.

When the priest said the line about "As for man, his days are like grass . . . ," Finny burst into tears. Sylvan put his hand on her back, and she watched the rest of the service through bleary eyes.

Then they were lowering the casket into the ground. A few symbolic shovelfuls of dirt were tossed into the hole. There was an awful tapping sound when the dirt hit the metal casket, which made Finny erupt into tears again.

And then it was over. The mourners were saying how sorry they were, telling Finny and Laura and Sylvan how much they'd miss Stanley. Aunt Louise offered her condolences, a hand clasped to her breast as she spoke to Finny. There were the sounds of doors clicking, motors starting, a man telling his wife they needed to stop for gas on the way. And finally, Mrs. Haberdasher could be heard informing her husband, as they got back into the hearse, that his feet were very much in the way.

After dinner that night, Finny excused herself and went upstairs. She sat on her bed, staring at the dark window. She knew her brother would come, and in ten minutes he did. She heard a knock on the door, and opened it.

"Hey," Sylvan said.

"Hey."

"I want to tell you what happened with Dad, since it doesn't seem you'll ever get the full story from Mom."

Finny nodded. Motioned for him to come in. He shut the door and they sat down together on the bed.

"She's acting crazy," Finny said.

"She just can't handle it. It's like she's overloaded."

"She hauled all Dad's stuff out. I mean, like, all of it."

"I had a feeling. I heard her last night banging around. Then she took a bunch of trash bags to the dumpster this morning."

"Aren't you pissed off?"

"I'm more sad than pissed, Finny."

Finny hated when people said her name like that, like a rebuke. She was about to strike back at Sylvan, but instead she said, "Okay. What?"

"Dad died on the toilet."

"What?" Finny said again, and started to laugh. She felt guilty for it, but she couldn't help it. "Are you kidding?"

Sylvan shook his head. He explained that he'd gotten the whole story while the paramedics were on their way. It seemed that Stanley had woken up before five and told Laura he was going to the bathroom. "Probably to 'brush his teeth,'" Sylvan said. When he didn't return after fifteen minutes, Laura assumed his indigestion was worse than usual and fell back asleep. Stanley must have thought the same thing, because when Laura woke two hours later and went to the bathroom, she found him sitting on the toilet, his chin resting on his chest. The indigestion had been chest pains. He'd had a heart attack.

"I don't believe it," Finny said, still laughing. "I'm sorry. I don't think it's funny. It's just so—*perfect* for Dad."

"I know," Sylvan said, and he began to laugh, too.

Then they started to laugh harder. Finny couldn't have explained it, but soon they were falling back on the bed, gasping for breath. She laughed until her sides hurt, until hot tears sprang to her eyes. She pressed her face against Sylvan's shoulder, and laughed until she could have puked.

And then at some point the laughter became crying. It was a funny thing. Finny wasn't sure exactly where the transition was, the two acts felt so similar. But soon she and her brother were hugging each other in the bed, sobbing onto each other's shoulders because they didn't want to show their faces. She felt her brother's breath on her neck, his chest rising and falling, tears on her shirt. She'd never seen him cry before. They stayed like that, holding each other, until at last they fell asleep.

Chapter 12

Things Begin to Brighten

It was easier now, during Finny's spring break, to sneak over and see Earl, since Laura was on another planet. Laura spent most of her day in the bedroom, or else running small, unnecessary errands for the house, such as getting rugs cleaned, or buying new cords for the phones. When Finny said she was going out, Laura said, "Okay, sweetie," and rarely asked where. Still, it was sad for Finny to see her mother this way. It was as if after Stanley died Laura's foundations cracked. The façade was the same, but Finny knew the inside was crumbling.

Besides Sylvan, Earl was the only person Finny felt comfortable talking to about her father. When they went for walks, Finny explained to Earl how she felt as if Stanley had been snatched away from her, just as they were beginning to have some understanding of each other, just as they were beginning to get close. She told Earl about the letter Stanley had written her, how he'd said he was proud of her, and when she started to tear up, Earl hugged her and let her cry. Another boy her age would've gotten shy around all those feelings.

One day she took Earl to the old vineyard. Their feet scuffed the dirt path. Finny noticed their heads almost reached the top of the green walls on both sides of them. Yet there was a feeling of being sheltered. They stopped, faced each other, half-covered in shadows from the vines. Earl held her hands.

She let Earl lower her onto the dirt. He sat beside her, and they kissed for the second time. She put her arms around his neck. "Oh, Earl," she said, and kissed him on the cheek, "I missed you so much when I was at school." His cheek was scratchy. He smelled like oatmeal, and a little like pears.

They fell back on the dusty ground together. She snuggled close to him in the deep shade of the vines, her head burrowing in his neck, in the heat from his skin. He kept his arms around her, holding her like they were sleeping. At first Finny thought they would have to tussle around like she'd seen people do in movies, but neither of them tried to do that. They just lay there. It was what they wanted to do together, to curl up and sleep in each other's arms. It was the most intimate thing Finny could imagine. Years later, holding Earl like this in a tiny apartment in Paris, Finny would feel just as warm, just as protected as she did now. More than kissing, even more than sex, this holding would always be Finny's favorite part of love with Earl. It was when she could imagine them growing old together.

Most afternoons they would lie in the vineyard for hours and talk. Finny felt a remarkable freedom during these afternoons. She told Earl things she'd never thought of telling anyone, not because they were particularly private but because they seemed like thoughts you would keep to yourself, thoughts no one would be interested in. She told him about how she used to look at the fuzzy green ribbon of horizon from her bedroom window and imagine walking there one day, finding some magical landscape of mountains and waterfalls. She told him about the day after they'd met, when she'd gone to the pasture and seen that no one was there, and her heart sank because she thought Earl had already forgotten about her. Finny had never spoken so easily about her feelings, but something in her grief had liberated her. She spoke more directly now, and without fear of what people would think.

"Show me your house," Earl said to her one afternoon, and they walked along the fence to Finny's backyard. She pointed at her window.

"That's it," she said.

"I can imagine you there," Earl said, "looking out."

"Sometimes I thought I could see your house. I liked to think that."

"Maybe I can come over one day. When your mom is feeling better."

"Maybe," Finny said.

There was another change in Finny that spring when she was fifteen. It had to do with her outlook on love—or rather, an aspect of love. She'd always thought of sex as silly, a little crude, all that poking and moaning and rolling around. It was hard to take seriously. And though she still saw the comedy in it, there was a part of her now that yearned for it, to be abused in that particular way. Sometimes when she lay with Earl in the vineyard, she felt herself getting warm, a kind of tingly excitement spreading over her body. She had to wrap her legs around Earl and squeeze him in order to push the feeling down in herself. At night, when she was dressing for bed, she noticed her breasts were plumper, the development she'd waited so long for. She felt a heaviness in her nipples, and sometimes she pinched them just for the electric thrill of it.

She was the one who started the touching. Reaching down to rub him, feeling him grow hard beneath her hand. She loved that—his almost instant response. He followed her lead, touching her the way she touched him. At first they felt each other above the clothes, and then just the underwear, then beneath it. Hidden between the green walls of the vineyard, Finny's desire swelled. She was bolder than she'd ever been.

Once, she reached down to her own underwear and felt they were soaked, she'd become so aroused.

"Oops," she said to Earl.

"Well, you can always wear mine," Earl said.

And they laughed together. She didn't need to hide or explain with him. She wasn't worried about him judging her. With Earl sex could be funny, and Finny saw how important that was, too. When she got home that day, she looked at her underwear and saw a few dots of blood, he'd reached so far into her.

One day, when they were lying in the vineyard, Finny said to Earl that she thought he'd make a good dad.

"What makes you say that?" he asked.

"Just a way you have. Of making people feel good for the things that make them who they are. The important things. I don't think you'd make a fuss over test scores and being the best on the soccer team."

"Well, since my test scores aren't so good and I can't kick a ball straight, I don't think that would make sense."

"That's what I mean," Finny said. "You're not stuck-up."

"I'm very proud of my ability to prevent car accidents when my dad falls asleep at the wheel."

Finny laughed. "That's important."

"Especially for me," Earl said.

"Do you think you'd want to be a dad sometime?" Finny asked.

Earl was silent a moment. Then he said, "Yeah, I think so. It's just hard to know how your life will turn out."

Finny wasn't sure what he was trying to tell her, so she asked him, "How do you want it to turn out, Earl?"

He thought for another moment. "I think I'd like to be a writer."

And though Finny wasn't sure what this had to do with the issue of children, she asked him why.

"Because there's so much stuff you never get to say. Or

never take the time to figure out how to say. There's so much in the world, and I want to get it down somewhere. I just don't know if I'd be any good at it."

"I think you'd be a great writer, Earl. You're more sensitive than anyone I've ever met. I'd read anything you wrote."

"Thanks," Earl said. "Then I know I can sell at least one copy."

"And it better be signed."

"I'll write you a personal letter."

"Deal," Finny said.

"Oh, I forgot to mention it," Laura said to Finny one morning at breakfast, "but we can't afford Thorndon anymore."

"Why?" Finny said. Though she'd had a feeling this news was coming. She'd be sad to leave Judith and Poplan, but she'd be closer to Earl and Mr. Henckel. It had to be one group or the other. Sometimes she wished she could just round up all the people she loved and move to a commune.

"You'll be going back to the Slope School in the fall, with Sylvan. They offered you some assistance."

"Assistance?"

"We need it," Laura said.

Judith came to visit Finny the last weekend of Thorndon's spring break, even though Judith knew Finny wasn't coming back to school with her. She'd already gotten her tickets, and figured Finny could use the company anyway. Finny, Laura, and Sylvan drove to BWI to pick her up.

Judith stepped off the plane with her hair back in her usual ponytail. She was wearing a black sweater that hugged her well-formed curves, revealing the tiniest sliver of belly when she lifted her arms. She had a brush of makeup on her cheeks. She looked gorgeous, Finny thought, like some starlet, and Finny was struck once again by the thought that she didn't deserve this beautiful girl's attention. Finny was about to introduce her friend to her mother and brother, when Judith said, "Hi. I'm Judith Turngate. I'm very pleased to meet you. I was so sorry to hear about your family's loss. Mr. Short was so wonderful to me when he came to visit Thorndon. I have the nicest memories of him." She spoke with the poise of a woman twice her age. She held out her hand and shook Laura's and Sylvan's hands in turn. Then she stood there with her shoulders back, smiling sympathetically at Finny's family.

For a moment they were speechless. There was a beat of silent appreciation, until Laura finally said, "We're pleased to meet you, too, Judith."

Finny understood they were both a little awed by Judith. She knew what that was like. It was the usual response, and she forgave them for it.

In the car they asked Judith where she was from, and about her family. She spoke about her life in New York in a completely different way from how she had to Finny. She explained that her father traded bonds, how he loved to play bridge and go for jogs in Central Park in the afternoons. "A pretty easygoing guy," she said. Her mother was "a philanthropist." Judith said she was working to try to make arts more affordable and accessible in the city, and she'd butted heads with a few politicians as a result. Her mother was tough, "but I know she's a good person and has everyone's interests in mind. Everyone but herself, I guess." Judith laughed.

At dinner that night everyone seemed more animated than they'd been in the last couple weeks, like the colors and sound had been turned up on a television. They ate and talked in the bright dining room, in front of the wide windows that looked across the valley, the constellations of lights from the neighbors' houses, the stretches of dark fields and trees. Finny laughed at how attentive Sylvan was to Judith, asking her if she needed more salad or bread. She'd never seen her brother so cowed by someone his age. But now he mumbled and blushed, smiled too much, asked awkward questions about the weather in Boston and what Finny and Judith had done on the weekends. Finny knew he was trying to figure out if Judith had a boyfriend. But it felt good to Finny, like her family was coming back to life.

Saturday was a lazy day. Laura made toaster waffles and eggs for brunch. Finny and Judith watched videos and read magazines and ate microwave popcorn. By dinner they were all feeling antsy. They went out for Chinese food, and then ice cream, and the whole family was in bed by ten o'clock.

After Finny and Judith had settled into Finny's bed, Finny said to Judith, "I heard you were pretty close with your roommate before me. Jesse, right?"

Finny felt the covers rustle. "We had fun," Judith said. "Actually, I can tell you this now: the reason she left is we got caught drinking together, and my parents bailed me out. But I'm really glad you came, Shorty Finn. You're the closest friend I've ever had."

On Sunday, Finny woke up before Judith. She knew she had a couple hours before her friend would want to get up. Her brother was already downstairs in the family room, seated on the couch, hunched over a large book, his hair flopping in front of his face. He was working on an English paper about Walt Whitman that was due in two weeks.

"Dork," she said, pointing to him.

"Argument for birth control," he said, pointing to her. It was pretty funny, Finny had to admit. Now that Judith wasn't in the room, Sylvan was free to take up their usual arguments.

"You going to be working the whole day?" Finny asked him.

"Mom went out," he said.

"Um," Finny said, not knowing how to make the request she had in mind.

But Sylvan cut her off. "It's okay," he said. "Go see your boyfriend."

"I'll make a pie for you later," Finny said, and hugged her brother around the neck.

"How about you just give me the money you'd use to get the ingredients?" Sylvan said. "I'll tell Judith you're out."

"I'll bet you will."

"What's that mean?"

"Just don't go making kissy faces while she's asleep."

"You want me to tell Mom where you went?"

"Okay, okay," Finny said. "Thanks!" And she ran out of the room.

At Earl's house, Finny and Earl had a cup of coffee with Mr. Henckel. He told Finny a story about how, after his concert career had collapsed, he'd joined a traveling act.

"A kind of cabaret, shall we say," he confided to Finny with a half dozen smile-frowns. "But the costumes were very expensive, especially for the ladies. So they came upon this formula. Which is to say they realized the gentlemen patrons would pay more for less costume. A win-win, if you will. So the ladies' costumes were gradually, shall we say, removed from the budget." Mr. Henckel was practically drenched by the time he finished this confession. He mopped his face with the yellow handkerchief, but it was like trying to stop a waterfall with a dish sponge.

Finny couldn't believe that Mr. Henckel was telling her he'd worked in a strip show. "What kind of music did you play?" she asked.

"The classics, mostly," he said. "It was a rather arty production. There was a grand finale involving the William Tell Overture."

"How did they dance to *that*?"

"You see, young lady, the music is of very little consequence in this sort of performance."

"I guess so."

"We'd been on the road for nearly three months when I realized that possibly this wasn't the greatest use of my talents."

"Of course not, Mr. Henckel. But what did you do?"

"Thus began the long and cold decline into the life of a teacher, my dear."

"Dad," Earl said, "I think Finny and I are going for a walk."

"Okay," Mr. Henckel said, offering a single smile-frown, like he'd just told them about his first time on a Ferris wheel.

Back at home, Finny went upstairs to meet Judith in their room. She pushed open her door without even thinking to knock. Finny was three steps into the room when she looked up and saw something that made her stop: it was Judith, lying on Finny's bed, next to Sylvan. They were kissing, and Sylvan had his hand on Judith's breast.

"I'm sorry," Finny said. "Oh my God." And she started out of the room.

"Finny," Judith said, sitting up.

But Finny wouldn't stop now. She heard Judith call her again, but she just kept walking, out the door, down the hall, down the stairs, into the kitchen, where Laura was scrubbing some dishes.

"You look like you just saw a ghost, sweetheart," Laura said.

"No, I didn't," Finny said, but couldn't think of anything else to say.

They spent the rest of the day with Finny's family—whom Finny used as a kind of shield—and Judith left in the evening. She called the next week to try to explain about Sylvan, but

Finny said, "Look, I don't want to get between you and my brother. I just think I'd prefer not to hear about it, if that's okay with you."

And when Sylvan broached the subject, Finny said, "You two can do whatever you want. But if you ever ask me for condoms, I'll kill you."

Chapter **13**

Another Visitor

April to June was a busy time for Finny. Since her mother couldn't afford the room and board at Thorndon, Finny completed her classes by mail, with a few phone calls to teachers and one conversation with Mrs. Barksdale, during which Finny had to hold the phone several inches from her ear. Mrs. Barksdale told Finny again how sorry she was for Finny's loss, and assured her that everyone had missed her during the final months of classes.

Poplan called. "I just wanted to see how you're doing," she told Finny.

"Where are you?" Finny asked.

"At my cousins'. In Virginia. Remember?"

"What's that in the background?"

Finny heard some brassy, syncopated music playing, and a squeaky voice saying, "Cha-cha-*cha*, cha-cha-*cha*," to the beat of the song. She couldn't tell if it was the voice of a woman or a young girl.

Then Poplan said to someone in the room, "Alana! Put down that maraca *right now*."

After a brief pause, Poplan said, "Sorry," to Finny. "They get so wound up when they hear a good mambo."

"Understandable," Finny said. She was just so pleased to hear Poplan's voice on the other end of the line.

"It might be my vacation," Poplan continued, "but I remain vigilant."

"Of course."

Poplan then told Finny she was going to be passing through Maryland on her way back to Thorndon, where she'd be spending the summer. "I thought maybe I would stop by to say hi."

"That would be great."

"Of course, it would be impossible to do that without proper directions and an ETA."

"ETA?"

"What time do you want me to get there?"

"Oh. Sorry," Finny said. "Noon? But it's still a little weird here. Maybe we could meet at my friend's house . . ."

Finny was at Earl's house at eleven, and she heard Poplan's decisive knock at 11:42. Finny started up out of her chair. Mr. Henckel snorted awake.

"No," Earl said to Finny. "Sit. Let me get it. I'm so excited to meet your friend."

Finny sat back down, and Earl went to the door.

When he opened it, Poplan was standing there, wearing a bright shawl made from a red and gold fabric that looked Indian. She had on lipstick, and some dangly gold earrings. Earl invited Poplan in, and when she strode into the small living room, Finny heard Mr. Henckel let out a gasp. Finny looked at him, and noted that his face was nearly white, his lips parted and trembly, like he had something important to say. Finally, after several seconds, he gathered himself enough to whisper to Finny, "She . . . she's *radiant*."

"Who?" Finny said. "Poplan?"

"Poplan," Mr. Henckel repeated, as if Finny had taught him

the name of some rare and delicious fruit. And in truth, Poplan did look striking in her red-gold suit. Her hair was pushed off her forehead from the breeze outside. Her cheeks glowed. Finny could see how with a little imagination someone could even call her "radiant."

Finny walked over to Poplan, and just as she was about to speak, Poplan said, "Now tell me you've washed your hands."

"Of course!" Finny said.

"Then give me a hug."

Finny put her arms around Poplan, and the two women held each other for what felt like a full minute. Finny had to check herself from getting teary. She hadn't realized how much she'd missed Poplan, how much this older woman meant to her.

After their hug, they all got down to the business of the visit. What Finny had known about Mr. Henckel but hadn't quite had the opportunity to observe in full effect was how intensely and painfully shy he was around new people. Earl and Poplan had introduced themselves at the door, and now Poplan looked to Mr. Henckel, who was standing by Finny's side. Any other adult would have taken the opportunity to introduce himself at this juncture, but Mr. Henckel, who was not like any other adult, was silent.

"I'm Poplan," Poplan said.

Mr. Henckel nodded and thrust an elbow into Finny's side. Taking the hint, Finny said, "This is my friend, Mr. Henckel."

"Pleased to meet you," Poplan said.

Mr. Henckel nodded again, and offered a quick smile-frown as his only response. They all sat down at the kitchen table.

Then began a long series of proddings and gesturings by Mr. Henckel, for the purpose of getting Finny—who had the bad luck of being seated next to him—to perform various tasks for Poplan. First she was offered a better seat at the kitchen table. Then, when it was observed that she might not be comfortable enough, Finny received an elbow to her side to inform her that a cushion should be brought from one of the living room chairs. Once this was done, the coffeepot was nodded at, and then the cream pitcher and sugar bowl successively. Finny poured the coffee, then added the cream and sugar in turn. After one spoonful was added, Finny received another painful jab from Mr. Henckel to suggest that Finny should ask whether Poplan preferred one spoonful or two.

"Two," Poplan responded, after Finny asked, and a completely unnecessary jab informed Finny that she would have the honor of adding the spoonful to Poplan's cup.

Because of Mr. Henckel's reluctance to speak, conversation was somewhat strained. But Earl and Finny made do, talking about some of the walks they'd taken recently. Then Finny explained how Poplan loved to play Jenga, and was the best player at the school. Mr. Henckel looked impressed, and nodded appreciatively, signaling his admiration with an extended series of smile-frowns.

After several minutes of conversation, Poplan stood up and stated that she had brought a gift for her hosts but had waited for the proper moment to present it. Now was that moment.

Poplan returned to the house carrying a beige tote bag with the words *Buloxi Regional Square Dancing Championships* in green letters on it. Inside the bag was some round, heavy object, about the size of a human head. Poplan set the bag down on the living room floor. Immediately, a smell of rotting meat filled the room.

"What *is* that?" Finny said.

"What is what?" Poplan said.

"That smell."

"It's our snack."

"Is it alive?" Finny asked.

"Not anymore," Poplan said. "I suggest we repair to the kitchen. By the way, Mr. Henckel, do you own an extremely sharp knife?"

Finny and Earl looked at each other. Earl's forehead was creased, like he was trying to figure out a difficult math problem.

But Mr. Henckel nodded eagerly, and took Poplan by the hand into the kitchen—a very bold move for him—to show her where the knife was.

"Mr. Henckel, have you washed that sweaty hand you're holding me by?" Poplan asked.

Mr. Henckel nodded, still unable to speak. Finny had warned him to wash his hands before Poplan arrived.

Finny and Earl followed them to the kitchen. By now the scent had filled the entire house. To Finny it was like the smell of a garbage bag that should have been taken out the day before. They saw Poplan examining the knife blade. Approving it, she fetched the tote bag from the living room floor and placed it on the kitchen counter.

"Is this going to be bloody?" Finny asked. She and Earl were standing behind Poplan, a few feet away from her in case anything sprang out of the bag.

"Not if it's done right," Poplan said.

Then she opened the bag. The first thing that struck Finny was the smell. It was overpowering, like someone's old gym socks. She coughed, hardly able to breathe, and covered her nose and mouth with her shirt. She could see that Earl had the same reaction. He didn't want to seem rude, Finny knew, but he was taking small breaths from his mouth like he was sipping from a straw.

Poplan and Mr. Henckel seemed unaffected by the odor. Or rather, they seemed to enjoy it. Both inhaled deeply through their noses, and Mr. Henckel's pleasure was intense enough to prompt him at last to speak. "That's astonishing," he said. "What is it?"

"It's a durian," Poplan said. "A kind of fruit. A delicacy in Southeast Asia."

Poplan explained that she had procured the fruit from

friends who shopped at the markets in Chinatown in New York. It was a spiny fruit, actually a bit larger than a human head though with the same oblong shape. When Poplan hacked into it, a cloud of the offensive odor wafted over Finny, and even Earl had to cover his nose to prevent himself from choking.

"Is it rotten?" Finny asked.

"It's perfect," Poplan said.

The flesh, Finny saw when she could bring herself to examine it, was yellow-white, like a used undershirt. The texture looked mushy, and a little grainy.

"I can't eat that," Finny said.

"You have to try it," Poplan said, with an assurance Finny was afraid to question.

"It smells rich," Mr. Henckel said. "Like almonds. Or butter. Or custard, almost." He seemed to have forgotten his shyness in his enthusiasm about the durian.

"Exactly," Poplan said. "Some people can't stand the smell, and they think it looks terrible. But the people who love it would choose it over any fruit in the world. It's all in your tastes. And how you see it."

Mr. Henckel looked overjoyed by this explanation, and he offered up several enthusiastic smile-frowns to demonstrate his approval.

Poplan handed pieces of the fruit to Earl, Finny, and Mr. Henckel. Then she took a piece for herself. "Bottoms up," she said.

They each placed the fruit on their tongues. Mr. Henckel and Poplan had contemplative looks, like they were sampling a fine bottle of wine. Finny squished the weird fruit through her teeth. It had the texture of an apple that had gone completely soft. She and Earl ran to the sink at almost exactly the same moment and spit their helpings into it.

"I'm sorry," Earl said, looking at Poplan with an expression close to terror. His cheeks were ashen and glistening with perspiration, like he was about to puke. "I just can't." He bolted out of the house, forgetting even to shut the door behind him.

Poplan and Mr. Henckel laughed. Finny watched them for a second, unsure what to do. Then she dashed out after Earl, shutting the door behind her.

After she caught up to Earl, they walked around the valley for an hour, until they were sure the fruit had been either eaten or disposed of.

"That was the most disgusting thing I've ever tasted," Finny said.

"It was nice of her to bring it," Earl said. "I felt so bad running out like that."

"Poplan doesn't mind. She seems tough, but she's really nice."

As they approached the house, Finny could already hear the piano music. It was the same piece she'd heard Mr. Henckel playing that day when Earl had first invited her over, that swirling melody, sweet but somehow sad. When they were in front of the door, she grabbed Earl's arm and held a finger to her lips. They stood and listened. The music was arrestingly beautiful. Almost painful. It brought tears to Finny's eyes.

Then it was done. Earl opened the door and they walked back into the house. Mr. Henckel was at the piano, and Poplan was standing beside him. The smell of the durian filled the house, but more faintly now. The silver coffee set was on the kitchen table, and Finny saw two drained coffee cups there.

"Welcome back, my young friends," Mr. Henckel said. He looked in remarkably good spirits. It was only a little after one o'clock, though it seemed the earth had shifted in Finny and Earl's absence.

"By the way," Poplan said, "the durian has been finished."

"It is the perfect accompaniment to coffee," Mr. Henckel said, and he and Poplan laughed over this for a long time.

Chapter 14

The Deal

A tapping on Finny's window. She was drifting in and out of sleep, and the sound became fingernails on a table in her dream, then crows' feet on gravel. She heard it again, and this time realized it was something in the real world. She pulled herself up from the depths of sleep, through layers of dreams, into her bedroom, where she was lying with her face against the wall. This was several weeks after Poplan's visit. It was a little after midnight, she saw by the blue numbers of the alarm clock on her shelf. She got up.

The sound again. *Tic. Tic. Tic.* She walked to the window and drew the blinds. The yard was dark. She couldn't see much. The floodlights had been turned off, and everyone in the house was asleep. Maybe she had imagined the sound?

Just to make sure, she opened the window, by a little crank on the windowsill. She stuck her head into the warm night, and as she did it, she felt a sharp poke on her cheek.

"Ow," she said.

"Sorry," a voice called from below. It was Earl's. She looked down and saw he was directly below her window. There were some white pebbles where he was standing that the landscaper had put in. Earl must have been tossing them up at the window.

"You hit me," Finny said.

"I feel terrible," Earl said.

"Hold on. I'll be right down."

She closed the window. She walked to her closet and opened the door. Put on the fastest outfit she could make: the green reaper and a pair of gray sweatpants. Then she went downstairs to the sliding glass door. Raskal was asleep in the mudroom, his chin resting on the tile floor. Finny tiptoed around him, yet he heard her and raised his head, his collar clinking. She shook her head, held up her hand to tell him to lie still. He stared at her. She opened the sliding door, and backed out slowly. She thought Raskal might bark, but instead he put his head down and went back to sleep. She closed the door.

Earl was standing with his hands in his pockets, even though the temperature must have been in the sixties. It was humid, and Finny could already feel sweat budding on her lip. There was a three-quarter moon, and under its light Finny had a good view of Earl. He looked tense and distracted.

"Hey," she said.

He turned toward her. "Hey. I remembered which one it was from when you showed me."

"Hopefully you won't start tossing knives next time," Finny said. She walked right up next to him and wrapped her arm in his, kissed him on the cheek. "What is it?" she said.

"I've had a crazy night," Earl said. He was taking deep breaths, and he kept staring at things—the sky, the ground, anything his eyes fell upon—the way Laura did just after Stanley died.

"Bad?" Finny asked.

Earl nodded. "Strange. I found out a lot of things."

Finny pulled him closer. She nuzzled into the gap between his neck and shoulder. She was several inches taller than him now, and she had to lean down to do it.

"What?" she finally said. "What is it? You look like someone hit you on the head."

"I feel like that."

"Is it something with your dad?"

"Sort of." He moved his lips like he was about to speak, but no sound came out. At last he got around to saying, "He told me some things tonight."

"What?"

"Can we find somewhere to talk?"

They went to the vineyard. At this time of night, there were no lights from the houses, but they sat beneath a dome of stars, nestled between the walls of their hideout like children in a fort made of sofa cushions. Earl had brought a flashlight, and he led Finny into one of the dirt rows between the vines. They sat. Finny asked him to keep the light on, in case any animals came, so he wedged it into the dirt.

Earl began by explaining that Mr. Henckel had taken a phone call that night, during which he'd asked Earl to go to his bedroom. After an hour Mr. Henckel was still talking, and Earl peeked out and saw that his father's face was wet, like he'd been sweating or crying. Soon Mr. Henckel called Earl back into the room, and his father said that he had some things to discuss with Earl. Mr. Henckel then promptly fell asleep.

"So I shook my dad until he woke up."

"What did he say?"

"Let me just explain first that I always thought my mom was dead."

"Your mom?" Finny said.

"Or maybe not dead. But not available to me. Like she had another life and I would never be part of it. Some of my dad's relatives had even told me she was dead, and that I shouldn't think about her. So I guess I listened. I just assumed I was never going to see her. I knew my dad met her through his performing, but I never asked him a lot about her. I could tell he didn't want to talk about it."

"Were they married?"

"They were never married. I found that out tonight. You remember when my dad told you that story about how he was part of a traveling act?"

"Yeah, the strip show, right?"

Earl nodded, the shadows lengthening and shortening on his face. "Well, it turns out my mom was a . . . performer."

"A stripper?"

"He never said that. He just said he'd met her there. He told me he was popular because of his piano playing, and that they were all artists and a little crazy. He said that he and my mother had carried on for a while—that's how he put it—and then stopped. The only thing was, she was pregnant."

Finny could imagine Mr. Henckel trying to get this story out, the sweat pouring from his brow, the way he dabbed his face with the handkerchief, the nervous smile-frowns.

"So what happened?"

"It was a big mess. It tore the whole group apart. My dad wanted to live with her at first, to raise me, but they weren't happy together, and she knew it would be the end of her career if she had to take care of a child. So they struck a deal."

"About you?"

"About me. My dad would quit the act to raise me. He had money at the time, because his family is rich. He didn't think I would get in the way of his performing career, since he could hire babysitters and maids, and he told me that the bottom line was he didn't want to part with me, even though I wasn't born yet. He didn't know that his parents were going to disown him and he was going to stop getting money, once they found out all the stuff that happened. He said they called him a disgrace and an embarrassment, and that was when he lost his confidence for good.

"Right after I was born, my dad took me away. He even said that my mom asked the nurses not to show her the baby, so she wouldn't get attached."

"That's so sad," Finny said.

"But the deal was that whenever my mom was ready, they would have to share me. I mean, I'd have to live part of the time with her. It was the only way she would agree to let me go, if there was a chance she could see me later. So my dad agreed to it, thinking it would never happen."

"But how would he know when she was ready?"

"He promised he would trust her. The trouble started last year, when my mom said she wanted me back. He never told me till now. The problem is, she lives in France."

"What does she do?" Finny asked.

"She's a hairdresser now. But the point is, it would be impossible to have me flying back and forth all year."

Now Finny's breath came harder. She knew what Earl was going to tell her, and the thought of it was like a weight in her chest. The stars seemed to spin above her. It was like a dream, sitting here surrounded by miles of darkness, hearing this strange and almost unbelievable story. It took all her energy just to keep herself propped up on the ground in the vineyard. She felt dirt and rocks pressing the palm of her hand, leaving marks.

"Are you moving to France?" Finny asked. Her voice was high, breathy, barely audible.

Earl nodded, the shadows moving again on his face. She heard the sound of leaves shaking, an animal scurrying in the bushes. Suddenly she was afraid. They could be eaten, or attacked. There was nothing to protect them.

"I'm sorry, Finny," Earl said. "I begged my father tonight. We stayed up till after midnight talking. He said he'd done everything he could to keep me with him, that he'd made every possible argument—about how I was comfortable here, about how it wouldn't be fair to take me away from what I knew. But in the end there was still the deal. He couldn't get around that. I can come back and visit, but I'm going to be with my mom through high school. She wouldn't accept anything less."

"It was a stupid deal," Finny said, angry now. "How could anyone make a deal like that?"

"My dad knows that. But he said it was the only way. She even made him sign a contract. He didn't want to give me up. He finally fell asleep tonight, while we were still talking, and that's when I decided to come over and tell you. I wanted you to know right away."

Questions twirled like snowflakes in Finny's mind. She grabbed for one, and then another, and finally settled on: "When are you leaving?"

"That's the other thing," Earl said. "My plane's in a week."

A lot could be said about how they talked and cried, the plans they made to escape, which they later abandoned. But in the end the sun rose, and they walked back to their houses.

At a little after six the following Friday evening, Earl's plane took off, headed for France.

Chapter **15**

An Interlude

Sunlight. A fence shadow printed on the lawn. Grass leaning in the breeze like thousands of tiny arms. A gauze of clouds draped across the sky. Trees waving their leafy limbs. A row of gorgeous days ahead, strung like jewels on a necklace. This was the world after Earl left, as calm and bright as ever, like one of those persistently cheerful party guests who refuse to talk about anything but favorite restaurants and places to vacation.

So the summer bloomed and faded. Fall arrived, bringing school and the old routines. Finny returned to kids she had left nine months before, though some of them seemed changed as well. They'd had braces taken off of or put on their teeth, had grown taller or fatter or skinnier, had longer hair or new outfits or breasts. She was welcomed back to the Slope School with smiles and hugs, though she knew they wouldn't have thought of her ever again if she hadn't returned. Since she'd been held back at Thorndon, she had to reenter Slope as a ninth grader, which meant she was in different classes from the students she knew anyway.

High school is not the place to linger in Finny's story. It wasn't a place Finny gave much thought to, even though she spent four years there. When she remembered it, she had the feeling she'd glided over that time in her life. It was as if she had done enough living for a while, and so she set the controls to autopilot, put her hat over her eyes, and slept.

But of course there were events. Rarely do four years pass without events. In her memory they appear like a slide show, a parade of snapshots projected on the screen of her mind.

First the move. Laura saying, "It's time to downsize." They left the Geist Road house that fall. Boxes, a giant truck, sheets with boot prints on them tossed over the furniture. Laura throwing away and throwing away, until there was hardly anything left. The new house—smaller, on Old Court Road, up the street from the Slope School so that Finny and Sylvan could walk. A sunny kitchen with a skylight. A little backyard in which there was a sculpture of a lion made out of crisscrossing wires. It caught the leaves when they fell that season.

Some lines from Earl's letters:

Our apartment is one big room. It's in an apartment building on the border between the 9th and 10th arrondissements in Paris. That means the 9th and 10th districts, which are where a lot of artists live. Our street is called Rue du Faubourg Poissonnière. (Try to say that!) My mom rents the apartment from a rich American lady who lives part of the year in New York. The apartment used to be her maid's room. We have to walk up five flights of stairs to get there, and the apartment always feels stuffy because there's only one window and it doesn't open very far and the steam from the shower comes into the room. The toilet is in the hall, and we share it with the lady next door (who I've never seen), but the sink and shower are in a closet in our room. I guess all the bathrooms are like that here. I hate going to the bathroom in the middle of the night because it's freezing in the hall and really dark, and you have to keep hitting the switch to get the light to stay on. . . .

My mom works just down the street. She's an assistant to a "master" hairstylist, and one day hopefully she will take over his business. As of now, she washes people's hair and sometimes does the haircuts when it's a customer the master doesn't like. It's been strange getting to know my mom. It's like we're not even related. We're both shy with each other and don't always have a lot to say. But she's very nice to me. She buys me loaves of French bread to eat while she's at work, and once in a while little cans of this stuff called "foie gras," which is made out of liver and is supposedly a delicacy. It looks and smells disgusting, but actually tastes good when you get used to it. I have to be very thankful when she buys it, because I guess it's expensive and a treat. . . .

I go to school in an English school, which is good for me because my French is horrible. It sounds like I'm choking when I talk. . . .

Some things I like to do: walk to Montmartre and watch the artists sketch. Go to the Tuileries. Eat crêpes stuffed with Nutella and bananas. (I know how to say that in French: Nutella banane!) Go to the English movies with my mom. . . .

I don't think I'm coming home for winter. My mom says it's a very expensive time. Spring is better. Damn. . . .

And in the spring, an announcement from another friend, arriving in the mail: *We kindly ask you to reserve the date of July 12th for the observance of matrimonial vows by Menalcus Henckel and Joan Poplan.* Finny had some questions about how often Poplan and Mr. Henckel had seen each other, but all she could think was, *Joan?* when she read the invitation. How could someone as weird as Poplan have a name like Joan? When she called Poplan to ask about it, though, Poplan's reply was succinct. "We shall never speak of it again," she said.

The ceremony: held outdoors at Mr. Henckel's house, under a tent pitched in the yard. Earl was there, as the best man. It turned out this was the first time he could make it home. A few teachers from Thorndon were there, too. Finny was the maid of honor. It was a small party, but lively, helped along by the Irish fiddler Poplan had hired, and the somewhat raucous dancing of her cousins. By the end they were all step dancing together. Earl was Finny's partner. The night ended when the remaining guests gathered in Mr. Henckel's living room to listen to him play a song for Poplan.

Earl stayed for a month. He and Finny spent as much time together as they could, but their houses were farther apart now, and their dates depended on Sylvan or Mr. Henckel acting as chauffeur, since neither Finny nor Earl could drive. Earl wanted to spend time with his dad, too. Mr. Henckel had delayed his honeymoon so that he could be with Earl as much as possible during Earl's time in the States. Finny tried to get over to see them both, but it wasn't always easy.

Then Earl left. More promises of visits and letters. Tears. A kiss goodbye.

Phone calls from Judith. Sylvan handing the phone to Finny every time. Sometimes it didn't even ring, and Finny knew that Sylvan had been the one to call. Judith seemed even brasher than when they'd been at school together. Every other sentence was about someone *fucking* someone else. *Oh, they fucked a long time ago. She used to fuck him. Fucking is overrated.* Like a role she was trying to play, some jaded New York socialite.

A weekend when Judith came to visit, and Finny was pretty sure she and Sylvan had sex after Finny went to sleep, because they were acting so strange in the morning. Another time: Sylvan coming into the den in the new house, telling Finny he was going to New York for the weekend. Finny saying okay, okay, not letting him tell her why.

A line from one of Earl's letters: *It was so great to see you this summer, Finny. It feels so long ago now! I haven't talked to you in forever.*

A winter night. Finny waking up and hearing Raskal whimpering in the kitchen. The wind whistling around the house. Waking Laura and Sylvan. Raskal lying down, squealing, shivering, vomiting. A seizure, the vet said in the morning.

They buried him next to the lion. He was so big they needed to ask their neighbor the UPS man to help dig.

Afternoons with Poplan and Mr. Henckel. Coffee. The silver pot, the little silver spoons. Piano music when Finny was lucky. Every Asian snack food imaginable: sheets of beef jerky sprinkled with chili flakes, cakes made out of sweetened rice with salty peanuts on top, little doughy balls covered in sesame seeds with a paste inside made from mung beans. Married, and having left her job at Thorndon, Poplan seemed to have become a new person. She still required hand washings and Jenga games, but she was less rigid, less severe than she used to be. She wiped crumbs from Mr. Henckel's sleeve, which seemed to Finny the tenderest act in the world. Poplan was the one who drove with Mr. Henckel to his lessons on Mondays now, in case he fell asleep at the wheel. It was one of the great joys of Finny's early life to see them together. She felt an intense, disproportionate sadness whenever she left the little brown house, as if she'd never visit again.

Phone calls from Judith tapered off. A last one, telling Finny that Judith was pretty sure she would be going to college in New York, at Columbia. Her parents had influence there, too. Asking Finny where she thought she would go, and Finny saying, "To tell you the truth, I don't really care."

Not so many letters from Earl. Most of them full of the kind of news you'd tell a stranger: taking tests, a trip to Italy, a cold he just got over.

A boy in Finny's math class named Gregory Bundt sitting next to her almost every day. They scribbled notes to each other, drew pictures of the teacher and laughed behind their notebooks. He was thin, pale. His hands left sweaty marks on her desk. He asked her to a dance. He leaned forward, kissed her in a clumsy hard way. The next time, they sat apart in math class. A mutual decision.

A picture of Sylvan on the front steps of Widener Library. He'd been accepted to Harvard. He wrote Finny, *Cambridge is nice, except for the Harvard students. It's kind of a know-it-all group.* Meaning, Finny knew, that he was afraid they were smarter than him. Finny wrote back, *You should fit right in.* And when she visited him, it seemed he did.

"And what do you hear lately from my globe-trotting son?" Mr. Henckel asked one Sunday afternoon.

"Nothing," Finny said.

"He's had quite a semester."

"Why?"

"Take a guess."

She couldn't help thinking: a girlfriend, an engagement. Her stomach churned. "I really have no idea," Finny said.

"A straight-A student," Mr. Henckel announced, to Finny's great relief. "Finally, the Henckel genes are kicking in. He showed me the report card when he visited last month."

"He visited last month?"

Mr. Henckel must have realized his mistake, because he had to pass through many smile-frowns before he was able to say, "It was a brief trip, Finny. I'm sorry." And in a short time he fell asleep.

After that the landscape of Finny's school days flattens out. She graduates. She's leaving for college, arriving at college, saying goodbye to her mother. She stands there, waving, waving, perched on the edge of a whole new set of adventures.

Book Two

Reunions and New Friends

Chapter 16

Judith Has a Party

It was a cold and rainy November evening, two months into Finny's freshman year at Stradler College in Pennsylvania, and Finny was in a taxi, racing toward the Upper West Side of Manhattan. She was on her way to visit her old friend Judith Turngate, at Judith's parents' apartment on West Eighty-First Street, near the park. Finny was nineteen. This was her first time in New York alone—she'd been several times with her parents, when her father was alive—and so she'd decided to spring for a cab, uncertain of her ability to navigate the unfamiliar letters and numbers of the subway.

Though, on another occasion Finny would have been the first down the subway steps in a new city. She wasn't the type to get intimidated by foreign places. It was just that she wasn't quite herself tonight. Hearing Judith's instructions on the phone, she'd felt suddenly small, like she was fourteen again, marveling at the mysterious life of more mature, more beautiful Judith. Finny knew she wasn't bad-looking herself. In her long wool coat, she cut a slim, attractive figure. She still had the apple cheeks, the freckles and red hair of her childhood, though the freckles were fainter, the hair not so stridently red. Only, next to Judith, Finny knew she'd appear awkward and bumbling, a plain and flat-chested girl.

Judith, now a sophomore at Columbia, was the one who'd initiated the contact. She'd written Finny a long letter just after Finny had left for Stradler. She addressed the letter in care of Laura, and asked Finny's mother to forward the letter to Finny, since Judith didn't know where Finny was going to school. In the letter Judith said many kind things about the memories she had of Finny, and their time together at Thorndon. She brought up some of the old nicknames Finny hadn't thought of in years: Old Yeller, Pits of Death, the Jackhammer. They still made Finny laugh. She had such a good time reading the letter, reliving those old memories, that she'd almost forgotten it had been nearly two years since she'd talked to Judith. At the end of the letter Judith wrote, *I've just been thinking about all the fun we had, and how sad it is that we don't even talk anymore. I was hoping that maybe we could reestablish the contact a little bit. What do you say, Shorty Finn? I miss you.*

Finny was touched. She wrote Judith back the next day, and in the letter she said, *I'm so glad you took the time to write, Judith. You've always had the balls in this relationship. (Excuse the expression.) I love you for it. I'm looking forward to getting back in touch.*

Soon phone calls started. Long, giggly conversations that went on late into the night. Talking to Judith, Finny felt like they were back in their dorm room together, after lights-out, nestled in their private space between the hall and the black windows. She could still make Judith laugh, sometimes so hard her friend dropped the phone. Like when they were in school, Finny waited for that decisive clunk. She told Judith about the sweet Midwestern girl who danced like a stripper at parties, whom Finny called the Moving Violation, and about the drunk boy whom Finny made out with at a rugby party who then pretended he didn't know her when they were introduced the next day in the dining hall. Finny's conversations with Judith got her through the first awkward months of college, made her feel solid enough to raise her hand in class, eat in the dining hall alone. Her phone bill was astronomical in October. She bought a phone card.

Then, a few days ago, Judith had called and told Finny, "I'm having a party this weekend. My parents are out of town. You should come."

For a moment Finny couldn't speak. She was suddenly, desperately nervous. Somehow, she hadn't imagined taking this relationship beyond the phone. "I have a midterm on Monday," she got out at last.

Judith laughed. Then she said, "Oh, you're serious. Well, you could just come up for the night. Actually, New York is only an hour and a half from Philly."

"Okay," Finny said.

"When you get off at Penn Station, just grab a cab. It'll save you time."

"Okay," Finny said again. She didn't really have the extra money to *grab* a cab, but she felt Judith's old confident grip on her, like she was leading her through a crowded room.

"Well then I'll see you Saturday."

"See you Saturday," Finny repeated.

Now, in the cab, the taxi driver said to Finny, "North side. South side."

"What?" Finny said.

"You want north side of *street*? South side of *street*?"

"Oh, I don't know which side," Finny said. "The Beresford."

"Oh," the taxi driver said. "Very snobby."

The cab pulled over. Finny paid and got out. She gripped the package she'd brought for Judith under her left arm. Inside was a purple T-shirt with the name Shorty Finn stenciled on the back, in the same pea-soup-green letters that had been printed on Finny's shirt when she was fourteen. She thought the present would make Judith laugh.

When Finny got to the door of the Beresford, it swung open. The lobby was everything Judith had said it would be: a chandelier the size of a dining table, ornate rugs so plush you could hide in them, an elegant-looking wooden chair parked next to an end table with spindly legs, huge mirrors with gold-plated frames, old-fashioned molding around the ceiling. Finny froze for a minute in the doorway, afraid to go farther. What was she doing here? How could she even think of fitting in in a place like this? The door was still open, and cold air streamed into the lobby. Then a timid voice said "Miss?" and Finny realized that a small man in a red coat and hat was holding the door.

"Oh, sorry. *Sorry*," Finny said.

The man nodded, and made a little bowing gesture with his head.

Finny bowed back.

"You're here for 15J, miss?" the man in the red hat said, once the door had swung shut. He had a thin mustache, black hair and dark eyes, and he spoke in what seemed a studied English.

"Turngate," Finny said.

"Yes, miss," the man said. "Could I have your name, please?"

"Finny," Finny said.

He gave her a puzzled look, as if waiting for more, then picked up a small phone from the wall and pressed a few buttons. In a moment he said, "Yes. We have a Finny here for you." There must have been some noise in the background, because the man was forced to repeat, "A *Finny* for you, Miss Turngate. A *Finny*!"

The man cleared his throat. Finny felt a little embarrassed having her name shouted in the lobby of the Beresford. But Judith must have caught it the third time the man said it, because even Finny could hear the scream on the other end of the line. The man held the phone an inch away from his ear, blinked twice, then said, "I'll send her right up, Miss Turngate."

"Finny!" Judith screamed again when she opened the door to the apartment. Her face was flushed, and she leaned across the doorway at an odd angle, as if she'd had to lunge to open it. Somewhere in the apartment some bassy dance music was playing, making the walls of the old building vibrate, and there were loud voices in the background. Judith looked almost the way she had at Thorndon except, somehow, completely different. Her features were more defined now, her cheeks sculpted in the way beautiful women's often are. Even her somewhat wide jaw was alluring, like a canvas for the glossed lips and white teeth she loved to display. Her hair seemed darker, styled in a more fashionable way, with bangs and a deliberately tousled look. She wore a fitted black button-down shirt, with the cuffs flared, and some gray wool pants that hugged her form. The outfit would have been conservative on someone else, but on Judith's body it had a calculated sexiness. She was exactly the woman Finny had imagined she would turn out to be.

"It's so good to see you," Finny said, trying to keep up the excited tone of their meeting. She felt the way she had when she'd just met Judith, as if this gorgeous young woman had handed her a heavy tray of glasses and Finny had to make sure not a single one dropped.

"Come in, come in," Judith said, waving Finny in from the hall.

Finny came through the door, and Judith shut it, then gave Finny a long tight hug.

"I brought you a present," Finny said, and handed Judith the package she'd been gripping in her sweaty hand.

"A present? You didn't have to bring anything," Judith said, smacking Finny with an open hand on the shoulder. Then she began untying the bag.

"Oh my *God*!" Judith screamed. "I don't believe you. Shorty Finn!" She was hugging Finny again. "This shirt is hi*lar*ious. I'm going to change into it right now." Then she padded off to a room directly in front of Finny and closed the door.

Finny took the opportunity to look around the apartment. The floors were parquet, and beside the door in front of Finny, there was another door to her right. The door to her right was also closed, and Finny heard voices and music behind it. To her left was an enormous living room, with a wraparound couch that could have seated twenty people. Though at the moment it held only eight. Everyone was holding drinks in real glasses with some silver cross-hatching and gold rims—not the plastic cups Finny was used to from college parties. Behind the couch was a large wooden dining table, and a grand piano that must have been as big as Mr. Henckel's. There was a window that took up the whole far wall of the apartment, and since Judith had the shutters open, Finny got a sparkling view of the city at nighttime, like the stars outside her window when she was a kid. To the right of the city lights was a dark swatch that must have been Central Park.

"Hey there," one of the boys on the big couch said to Finny, and held his glass up to her like a toast.

"Hey," Finny said, and because she was still frazzled from the whole scene in the lobby, she gave a small bow.

The boy began to laugh hysterically, so hard that he spilled some of his brown drink onto the sofa. "Oh shit," he said, and then got down on his hands and knees and put his mouth on the sofa cushion, trying to suck the stain off. The curly-haired girl next to him started to laugh. "You're good at that," she said.

Then Judith emerged from the room. "How do I look?" she said, hands on hips, modeling the shirt for Finny the way Finny had modeled hers at Thorndon.

"Beautiful," Finny said, and it was true. The shirt was supposed to be a nightshirt, but it fit Judith as snugly as the black shirt she'd been wearing a minute before.

"Your coat," Judith said, and began helping Finny out of her coat. When it was off, Judith placed it on the coat rack by the door. Finny tried to straighten herself—*Shoulders back, boobies up*, she'd once heard a model advise on television—but she found herself retreating into a comfortable slouch. The shirt she'd picked out—a blue sleeveless with brown polka dots, which a girl at Stradler had told her looked "hot"—felt clownish now.

"Let's *meet* people," Judith said, and took Finny by the arm into the living room. The music was softer here, a faint throbbing. Judith picked up a glass off an end table and pressed it into Finny's hand, saying she was drinking it before but decided she didn't want it.

"This is Carter," Judith said now, holding a palm out to the boy who had a moment ago been sucking on her couch. He stood at attention, not even saying *Excuse me* to the curly-haired girl he'd been talking to, though she didn't seem to mind. His dark hair was long for a guy's, and tousled like Judith's. He was frighteningly skinny, his eyes dark around the lids like he was wearing eyeliner, the veins in his arms plump as electrical cords. His clothes fit tightly—faded blue jeans and a bright yellow shirt that said *Ship Shape* across the front and showed a stick figure lifting a dumbbell on the deck of a boat.

"This is my very old and dear friend Finny," Judith said to Carter.

"Pleasure, darling," Carter said.

Finny held out her hand, but Carter leaned forward and smacked a kiss right on Finny's lips. For a moment she could hardly believe he'd done it. She stood there, stunned, lips tingling. The curly-haired girl watched them impassively. *The nerve*, Finny thought.

But before she could say anything, Judith told Carter,

"Finny got me this shirt. Tell me what you think of it." Judith did a quick spin in front of Carter.

"Look at you," Carter said. "Gorgeous." He put a hand on one of Judith's breasts and squeezed. "I could eat you alive."

Finny was speechless, scandalized by Carter's boldness. She took a long sip of the brown liquid in Judith's glass, which burnt her throat and made her cough. Judith must have noticed Finny's discomfort, because she quickly told her, "Don't worry. Carter's gay."

"As your shirt is purple," Carter said. He sat back down on the couch, falling almost immediately into conversation with the girl next to him, as if she'd been waiting for him to finish a point.

"He's an actor," Judith went on. "Very dramatic. He actually had a small part in *Cats*."

"The second-greatest play in the world," Carter piped up from the couch.

"And what's the first?" Judith asked.

"*Phantom*, of course!" Carter said. He told something to the curly-haired girl that Finny didn't catch, but the girl laughed and nodded vigorously.

"Then Carter was, um, replaced in the play," Judith explained, "which was very sad."

"Tragic!" Carter said, and then immediately began talking to the girl again.

"That's too bad," Finny was starting to say, but before the words were even out of her mouth, a very muscular set of arms wrapped themselves around Judith's waist. The boy they belonged to must have been several inches over six feet. He was wearing a long-sleeve T-shirt, and the sleeves looked stuffed like potato sacks. It took Finny a few seconds to get around to his face, but when she did, she noticed he had a particularly wide jaw, as if to complement Judith's. His face was all straight lines and hard angles, like some masculine appliance, a drill or a big-screen TV. His wide eyes didn't just glance at, but took hold of, everything they saw. Finny knew these were qualities a lot of women would have found attractive—the intensity, the assurance, the muscles and chiseled jaw—though Finny couldn't help feeling a little threatened by them.

"Oh, hey," Judith said, warmed by the boy's touch. She looked up at him, like a young girl at a favorite uncle. "This is my friend Finny. Remember I told you about Finny? We went to boarding school together. Only for a few months, but she was my best friend."

The boy released Judith, and Judith took a step to the side—a routine they'd obviously practiced: they were as proficient as ice dancers.

"Finny, this is Prince," Judith said.

"Huh?" Finny said, thinking she hadn't caught the second half of his name.

"Prince," Judith said.

"Oh," Finny said. "I'm Prime Minister." When the boy just stood there, staring, Finny went on, "Sorry. Bad joke. It's nice to meet you."

She shook Prince's hand, which enveloped hers. He shook amiably, though he squeezed a bit harder than Finny thought a guy should squeeze a girl's hand, as if to prove the strength he held in reserve. He was wearing cologne. A musky-sweet cloud drifted from his body. At college she'd realized she was allergic to cologne. She let go of Prince's hand.

"Great to meet you," Prince said, and Finny could almost feel the vibration of his deep voice.

Finny sniffed again, then sipped the brown liquid in her glass. When she was done, she rubbed her nose with her knuckle, trying to get it to stop itching.

"Are you all right?" Prince asked.

"Yeah," Finny said, "I'm just—" And then she sneezed on him. It came so quickly she couldn't even put her hand up to muffle it. She felt the spray of it, and she knew he must have, too. Her sneeze was accompanied by a sound—*yak*—like a cat throwing up a hair ball.

"Oh God. I'm sorry," Finny said.

But Prince offered a friendly smile and said, " 'Renunciation is not getting rid of the things of this world but accepting that they pass away.' " He wiped his hand on his pants.

"Huh?" Finny said again.

"Prince is into Eastern philosophy," Judith explained.

"Buddhism in particular," Prince said. "I used to be a very angry person. But I've figured out how to renounce. I've found equilibrium."

"He was recruited for football," Judith continued, "but now he's honors in English!"

" 'But, soft,' " Prince began to quote, " 'what light through yonder window breaks?' " He spoke the words competently, though there was something chantlike about them. " 'It is the east, and Judith is the sun.' " He concluded the quotation, smiling in a way that could have been either self-deprecating or prideful, Finny wasn't sure. She felt a pang of sadness, thinking of her father, who quoted much more convincingly than Prince.

Then Carter began to sing his own quote, "'Mid-niiight, not a sound from the paaaave-ment. Has the moon lost her memmm-ryyyy?"

The curly-haired girl seemed transfixed.

"Webber," Carter said to Prince, as if he'd asked.

"Okay, Carter," Prince said. He smiled again in that practiced, good-humored way—it seemed to be his response to a fork in the road of any conversation—though Finny noticed a vein pulsing in his temple, almost to the beat of the bassy music in the background.

"Don't get upset," Judith said to Prince.

"I'm not," Prince said. He leaned over and kissed Judith on the temple. As he did it, Finny saw one of his large hands gather into a fist, then relax, like he was trying to pump the last dregs out of a tube of toothpaste. Finny sipped her drink.

Then Prince said to Carter, " 'Your worst enemy cannot harm you as much as your own unguarded thoughts.' "

"Am I really your worst enemy?" Carter asked.

"Jesus, Carter," Prince said. "Let's give it a rest. Have you ever heard the saying 'Do not speak unless it improves on silence'?"

"Oh, it always improves," Carter said, and turned back to the curly-haired girl.

"Listen, though," Prince said now to Judith, wrapping one of his substantial arms around her waist, "I have to head out."

"Okay," Judith said, leaning into him.

"Bye, babe," Prince said, sliding his hand onto Judith's hip, giving her a peck on the lips.

"Bye," Judith said.

Prince walked out of the apartment, forgetting to say anything to Finny.

"By the way, your boyfriend is a douche," Carter said to Judith now. "And that anger management program is *not* working."

"He's just kidding around with you," Judith said.

"He seems nice," Finny said to Judith, balancing that heavy tray.

"Just so you know, his real name is Milton," Carter told Finny. "But now he's Prince, the football player formerly known as Milton. He got into Columbia because he's a Hollibrand, which is basically as good as a Kennedy around here. And incidentally, Mr. and Mrs. Hollibrand are very good friends with the Turngates. Did I miss anything, Judith?"

"I think that's about it, Carter."

"Oh, and one more thing," Carter went on. "If you ask me, he's a closet homo."

Finny was laughing. She was starting to like Carter.

"Well, no one asked you," Judith said, and took Finny by

the arm, leading her back toward the entryway where Finny had come in.

"So, you ever talk to Sylvan anymore?" Finny asked. The question had just popped out. It was the first time she'd ever asked Judith about Sylvan.

"Um. A little," Judith said. "I saw him one weekend. He came down. We hung out."

"Oh," Finny said. She tried to catch Judith's eye, but Judith looked away.

"Let's go see what they're doing in there," Judith said, and took Finny toward the closed door on the other side of the entryway. As they walked, Finny placed her glass on the end table from which Judith had plucked it earlier. The music was loud behind the door—some kind of electronic music, echoing chords and a persistent, rhythmic static. The voices were nearly shouting. Finny wasn't sure if some kind of argument was going on.

Judith opened the door. It was a moment Finny would think about for many years to come, a moment when her life seemed to change course, like a car pulling off a highway.

At first there was nothing terribly surprising about the room. Four disheveled-looking boys in different variations of black-on-black wardrobes were seated in a circle next to a large canopy bed with a pink comforter, which Finny guessed was Judith's. The boys were all drinking from coffee mugs, and talking heatedly about something intellectual. "It's not an issue of *pragmatism*," one of them said. The room smelled faintly of smoke.

Behind the bed there was a couple making out on a hard-backed chair. The girl had an ample backside, which was pretty much all Finny could see of her, because she was straddling the boy, who looked skinny and had a large tattoo of something like an anteater on his neck. The boy had his hands pushed up under the girl's shirt, and she kept making exaggerated sounds of surprise. They didn't even pause when Judith and Finny came in.

Then Finny looked into the back corner of the room. What she saw there made her stop in the doorway. She opened her mouth to speak, but her voice caught in her throat. Sitting by himself, his chin propped on his hand, nodding off in a cushioned chair, was Earl Henckel.

Chapter **17**

The Party, After Finny's Discovery

"I didn't know it was *the* Earl," Judith was saying a minute later when the three of them had congregated in the study next to Judith's bedroom. It was a small room, with a desk that wrapped around three of the four walls, and a rolling desk chair behind Finny. There were some built-in bookshelves above the desk. A message in bubbly letters floated across a computer's black screen: *Judith's Computer, Don't Touch*. The windows of the study were shuttered, the door closed, and in this quiet space Finny felt almost completely removed from the world, suspended above the music and conversation of the party, the horns blaring and trucks rumbling on the streets.

"I guess we were introduced when you came in," Judith went on. "But how would I know it was you?"

"You guys never met, did you?" Finny said. Earl was just staring at her, speechless.

"No," Judith said. "Remember, it was that time I came to visit you in Maryland, and I stayed in with your brother when you went to see Earl."

"Oh my God," Finny said to Earl now, staring at him again in disbelief. "I just can't believe it's you." And she hugged him, put her arm around his shoulder, brushed his stubbly face with her fingers—anything just to touch him, to make sure he was real.

"It's me, Fin," Earl said, shaking his head. "This is unbelievable."

When she stood back and looked at him, she was amazed at the transformation. It was still Earl—the manly face and torso, the slight blush in his cheeks, the pudgy fingers, the adorably stubby legs—but he looked like he'd aged so much. His skin seemed darker, weathered, and his sandy hair longer, flopping on his forehead, so that sometimes he had to brush it away with his hand. He had the faint shadow of a beard, and he seemed to stand a little straighter, his chest puffed out like he was being challenged to a fight.

"Who'd you come with?" Judith asked. "Not that I'm not thrilled you're here. I'm *ecstatic*. I'm just wondering how this all happened."

"It's weird," Earl said. "I didn't even realize where I was going. I was just having a drink with a friend, and he said he wanted to stop by this party. He told me your name was Judith, but I guess I didn't catch your last name. His name is Paul Lilly."

"Sure. Paul," Judith said. "He's an English major at NYU," she explained to Finny.

"I actually don't know where he is," Earl said. "He was talking to some people, and I just got in from France so I'm ridiculously jet-lagged. I decided to go off and close my eyes for a minute."

"I saw you sleeping," Finny said, smiling at him.

Earl laughed. "Did I snort when I woke up?"

"It was hard to hear over the music," Finny said, "but I think so."

Judith seemed thrilled by everything Finny and Earl said to each other. She watched them like they were the most entertaining movie in the world, a budding smile on her lips.

"You know what?" Judith said. "This is silly. Why am I standing here getting in the way? I'm going to leave you two alone to catch up."

"It's okay," Finny and Earl both said at the same time.

But Judith shook her head. She pulled Finny and Earl into a three-way hug. When they let go, Judith said goodbye and blew a kiss to them both. She walked out of the study, and Finny heard the music and voices swell for a moment. Then Judith shut the door behind her, and they were alone again in their quiet space.

Finny turned to Earl. "This is strange," she said.

Earl nodded.

"I feel like when you're a teenager and your friends lock you in a closet with a boy you like. Not that that ever happened to me. But I've heard about it happening."

Earl smiled. Even though he was exhausted, Finny could see the effort he was making with her, how much he wanted to please her. They stood there for a minute, looking each other over, marveling at what they saw. It wasn't an uncomfortable silence, more like the hush in a museum when people are looking at beautiful paintings. She didn't feel shy; she knew he understood. There was so much to say, and she couldn't think of where to start.

At last, though, and without speaking, they fell into each other's arms. This time they held each other tightly, with more conviction than they had in front of Judith. Finny started to cry. Earl smoothed his hand over her back. He kissed her neck, her cheek, her forehead, her lips. His mouth against hers was like some longed-for taste, a food she remembered from childhood, a feeling that had been part of her so long she couldn't remember a time before it.

"My God," Finny said again, pulling her lips away from his, her hands still holding his face. She felt quivery and strangely light. "Why are you here?"

"I'm trying to be a writer," Earl said. "I'm still figuring out the best way to do it. But I thought New York would be the place to start. I took some time off work. I wanted to come here for a few weeks and see if I could make it."

He explained that he'd met some Americans last winter in Paris, after he'd finished school and was deciding whether to come back to the States, whether to go to college. Earl had a job in a restaurant, cleaning chickens and stocking the bar and washing dishes. He wasn't sure if he really needed college to do what he wanted to do. The friends said he could come to New York anytime, crash at their apartment in the Village. They were NYU students, and had cheap student housing. They loved to argue about books and French movies. They'd all grown up in the city, attended Fieldston or Horace Mann or Bronx Science. Earl decided to take them up on the offer this year. He needed to get away from home for a bit, to look around and see what was out there for him. He'd flown into New York the night before.

"So here I am," Earl said.

"And for how long?"

"Maybe a few weeks. A month. Longer. It depends."

"On what?"

"On what I see, I guess."

"Well, what do you think so far?" Finny said, standing back from him, striking one of her silly hand-on-hip poses.

But Earl simply said, "What I see is great, Finny."

She kissed him then, put her arms around him and squeezed like she used to. "Oh, Earl," she said, feeling those familiar gears begin to turn.

After a little while, Earl said, "Do you think we should go back to the party?"

"I don't want to," Finny said, "but maybe we should."

"I'd love to just go get coffee with you somewhere and talk."

Finny hesitated. "Me, too," she said. "I'd just feel bad, since I came all the way up here to spend time with Judith. I wouldn't want her to think I was ditching her."

"That was really nice of her, leaving us alone to catch up. She seems like a thoughtful person. A good friend."

"She is," Finny said. And she realized Earl had done it again, built someone up from the scraps of her personality, into a beautiful shape.

"You have a good sense for people," he said. "I think my dad is as happy as he's ever been."

She laughed. "They're adorable together, Earl. When I go over, he pours the coffee, and she tells him to wash his hands before he touches hers. Then when he falls asleep, Poplan brushes the crumbs off his sleeves and shakes her head in this severe way, but you really know she loves him. And then he plays the piano for her, or tells stories and she never interrupts him. It's exactly the way a marriage should be."

Finny was going to say more, but a prickly thought snagged her.

"Earl," she said, steadying herself, "there's something I need to ask you."

"Yeah?"

"I want to know what happened. Why'd you stop writing and calling? I found out from your dad you'd been in town and didn't even tell me. It really hurt me when I heard that. And then tonight again. You're sitting there in my friend's bedroom, and I didn't even know you were in the country. Couldn't you have written? Your dad knows my address."

"Finny," Earl said, but for a moment he couldn't say more. He stood there, with a look of such pain that Finny began to feel sorry for him. Yet the splinter of his betrayal was still lodged in her.

"When I heard that from your dad, I almost died," Finny said. It was dramatic, she knew. And yet the words conveyed something of the horrible, sick feeling she'd had, like she'd

Chapter 18

A True First Date

The midterm, which was in philosophy, went well. Finny handed in the test, sweating and red-faced, as she always was after exams, and went back to sleep in her dorm room.

Her roommate wasn't there. She hardly ever was. Her name was Dorrie Kibler, and she was on the swim team. She was tall and broad-shouldered for a girl, though with a gentle voice, a thin nose like some invisible fingers were pinching it. She was exceedingly polite, always asking Finny if she needed anything when Dorrie went to the co-op in town, or if Finny minded if Dorrie kept her light on at night to study. Dorrie was in the campus Christian fellowship, and her social life revolved around that group. Friday nights were spent in prayer group, Saturdays baking cookies and breads for charity, Sundays at church, and then the church brunch. Dorrie had a boyfriend in the group, a nice and very dull junior named Steven Bench whose only mark of rebellion was a small silver hoop earring in his left ear. Dorrie spent a lot of nights in Steven's room—Finny hadn't realized what a time commitment not having sex was—and often the only trace of her in their room was a faint odor of chlorine.

So Finny had the room to herself that week, to her thoughts and worries and hopes about Earl. Her night with him in New York already felt like a dream, something you wish for so much your mind makes it true. And then that awful feeling of waking up, knowing it was all in your head. It was especially tough because she hadn't gotten any word from Earl since the night of the party. She'd told him she would be busy studying, so it was perfectly reasonable that he wouldn't call. But still, she wanted him to. Just to say *Hi, I'm here*. What a mess I am, Finny thought.

It was during this time that Finny went to the music library to look for the piece Earl's father had played that first day she met him, when Earl took Finny to the little brown house. It was an odd thing: now that Earl was so close, the distance and the time apart were almost unbearable. She needed some part of him to be close to her.

Finny sat there, going through album after album of piano music. Earl had mentioned Brahms once, so she tried Brahms. Then Chopin. But she couldn't get the piece. She asked the music librarian, a man with a goatee who stroked his facial hair in a creepy way as you talked, but her descriptions didn't help. She could hear it, but when the music librarian asked her to sing a little portion, she faltered. She'd always been a terrible singer. So the music stayed inside of Finny. She gave up on her search. She could have called Mr. Henckel, but she didn't want to have to talk about Earl.

Then, on Wednesday, the phone rang.

"Hello?"

"So, what do you feel like doing this weekend?" It was Earl's voice. Relief washed over her.

"Whatever. I just want to spend time with you."

"But we have to *do* something, don't we? It would be boring just sitting around the apartment."

"What do you like to do?"

"Um," Earl said, "just walk around mostly."

"Walking around sounds good."

"Anywhere in particular?"

"Anywhere you want," Finny said. "I'll let you choose."

"Then how about Central Park?"

It was the week before Thanksgiving, though it felt like September in the city. The afternoon was warm, the light on the buildings golden, the sky a gemstone blue. Finny walked out of Penn Station, into the tide of shoppers and commuters, feeling as if she were being swept up in the energy of the place, a powerful wave guiding her to shore. She smelled smoke from the man cooking kebabs on the corner, heard a woman speaking into a megaphone, "Jesus Christ is your savior, honey. Let me ask you a question: If ya don't trust Jesus, who *can* ya trust?" And a man, in torn canvas pants and an overcoat, with a scraggly beard and a mane of frazzled hair, yelling back at the woman, "Ma toes is itchin'! Ma *toes* is itchin'!"

She decided to walk uptown; she'd only brought a backpack with her. She was meeting Earl at three at the southeast corner of Central Park, and she had time.

She passed Times Square, walked under the hot lights of the theaters, past the windows with displays of women in lingerie, the video shops with dirty movies, the pizza parlors, the jewelry stores, the clothing racks, the blankets spread on the sidewalk paved with scarves and hats and purses. She crossed Sixth Avenue at Fiftieth Street, peeked in at the ice skaters doing laps at Rockefeller Center, some of them wearing only T-shirts. She walked up Fifth Avenue, past the doormen in caps and jackets, the Bergdorf Goodman window displaying an elaborate crime scene enacted by mannequins, the Paris Theatre. She stood at the corner of the park, waiting, smelling the barnyard smell of the horse carriages, watching tourists have their portraits sketched, the cabs swinging around the bend onto Fifty-ninth Street.

Then Earl was coming out of the park, a thick book in his

hand, saying, "It was so beautiful, I spent the day reading. How long have you been waiting?" It was 3:45. His face was clean-shaven now, his eyes wide and excited.

"I just got here," Finny said. "What are you reading?"

"Dickens. *David Copperfield*. It's the funniest book I've ever read."

They slipped into each other's arms, like they'd been meeting here every week. He kissed her. He took her backpack and strapped it on his shoulders. They held hands, walked into the park.

"I saw the skaters at Rockefeller Center," Finny said. "Isn't it early for that? It's so strange in this weather. But it looked fun."

"Do you like to skate?"

"I like it, but I'm terrible at it. I've only done it a few times."

"Let's go skating," Earl said. "I know another place. It's less crowded."

She was happy to be led by Earl, to give herself up to the flow of his intentions. She didn't want to make decisions today. She was content to watch the world, the shafts of sunlight through the tree branches, the startlingly green lawns, the fat golden leaves dropping from the trees.

They went to Wollman rink, which was less crowded than Rockefeller Center, as Earl had predicted. They rented skates and a locker for Finny's bag, then set out on the ice. Big band music was playing on the speakers, and Earl did a little dance step to the rhythm, crossing his right skate over his left. He was a good skater, Finny noticed with surprise. For some reason she'd expected him to be clumsy, timid, but instead he turned effortlessly, backward and forward, his feet swishing along the ice.

Meanwhile, she was the one with ankles turned, feet shuffling and slipping. Earl took her by the hands, and he skated backward while she went forward, like they were dancing. She warned him when there was someone in the way—a slow skater like herself, or a fallen child. Finny flinched every time she heard someone fall—*whup! whoa!*—as if the unfortunate skater were going to pull her down with him. But Earl didn't let her fall. He always had a hand on her, an arm around her, keeping her balanced.

"Where did you learn to skate?" she asked him.

"In Paris," Earl said. "My mom and I would go a lot of weekends every winter, outside the Hôtel de Ville. It's free, and my mom is actually a great skater. Since she'd been a dancer, she's very graceful. She can even do some figure skating, pulling her body in and spinning on one skate. That kind of thing."

"So you did a lot together?"

"That was the most fun thing we did. Or the most natural, I mean. The other times it was forced. There was always this barrier. I guess it's like that when you don't meet your parent until you're a teenager. There are always these questions. Why did you do that? Why didn't you want me? Even though I tried not to think those things, I couldn't help it. When we were ice skating, we could just enjoy each other's company, and we only had to think about getting around the rink."

"But you think she loves you, right?"

"I do. And I care about her a lot. She has such a lonely life in Paris. She only half-speaks the language, after all this time. But she's also really hard to get to know. You'll see one day, when you meet her."

"You think I'll meet her?" Finny said.

"I hope so," Earl said.

"You know," Finny said, "I used to imagine the way your life was in Paris, what you were doing at that exact moment, that kind of thing."

"Really?"

"I wondered things. Like, did you have other girlfriends?"

"Well," Earl said, and Finny noticed he had a brush of color on his cheeks, "not really girlfriends."

She realized then that she didn't want to hear about it, no

matter how many or few girls he'd dated. She'd had her own dark little tussles with boys on her campus, understood the fuzzy embarrassment surrounding them. So she was glad when Earl started on a new topic. "By the way, how's your mom?" he asked.

"We hardly talk," Finny said. "In a way, I think it was a relief for both of us when I went to school. But I think she's good. Same as always."

"It's so funny that I've never met her."

"It is."

"And your brother."

"And my brother. I know. But you should still be mad at him for turning us in that time. He's the reason I got sent to Thorndon."

"But you wouldn't have met Judith if you didn't go to Thorndon. Then we wouldn't have met in Judith's bedroom. Everything has different sides."

"That's true," Finny said. "It's crazy. All of this."

"Are you going home for Thanksgiving?" Earl asked.

"I am. Are you?"

"At least for a couple days. I have to see my dad and Poplan. I promised them. So we'll spend some time when we're both at home?"

"Sure," Finny said.

After they'd taken a couple more laps, Finny had to stop because her feet hurt—though she would have liked to go round and round the rink all night. They returned their skates. It was evening now—darkness at five o'clock, a reminder that the warm weather wouldn't last. The temperature was dropping, and Finny got an extra sweatshirt out of her bag.

"Hey," Earl said when she put it on.

"What?"

"That sweatshirt. What do you call it?"

"Oh. The green reaper. It's pretty torn up now. But I just can't seem to part with it."

"I love it," Earl said. "Don't ever part with it."

They decided to take the subway back to the Village, near where Earl was staying. They walked to an Italian restaurant Earl knew, several blocks south of Washington Square Park. He seemed to know a lot of the restaurants in the neighborhood, and he pointed some out to Finny, saying that they'd have to try this one or that one together sometime. It was as if he were building up a future for them—dinners in the city, trips to France—the way he built people up, out of moments, glances, words. The world was gleaming with possibilities.

At dinner—in their private nook next to the waiters' station, where Finny could hear one waiter complaining about a customer "dicking" him—she said to Earl, "I want to read something you've written." The idea had just occurred to her. They were sitting over nearly finished bowls of pasta, both of them having been hungry from the skating.

"Sometime," he said. "When I have something good enough to show you."

"It doesn't have to be good," Finny said. "I'm just interested."

She realized she'd said the wrong thing when she saw Earl's expression, the way his lips tightened.

"What I mean is, I just want to know you. To know that part of you." And it was true. She felt as if Earl were some great expanse of land, like that green ribbon of horizon she'd watched as a child, and she wanted to walk every inch of his terrain.

"But I know it will be good," she told him.

"Thanks," he said, and they didn't talk any more about it.

The apartment where Earl was staying was on Tenth Street, near University Place—an odd-shaped building, one of its four corners jutting out so that two of the walls were longer than the others. There were four rooms in the apartment: a common room and three bedrooms. The rooms were small and stuffy, cluttered with textbooks and soda bottles and ragged furniture. There were dishes in the sink, a little puddle of something that looked like ketchup on the counter, turning brown, which no one had thought to wipe up. Earl was sharing a room with one of his friends, a guy named Eric, but he mentioned that his roommate wouldn't be coming back tonight. In fact, at this hour—a little after eight—none of his friends were home.

So Finny and Earl decided to watch a movie in Earl's bedroom, on the small TV Eric kept on the window ledge, in front of the window fan. Finny could see flashes and glimmers of the busy street below, through the fan's plastic case. Earl rifled through Eric's movies, saying to Finny, "I'm sorry. The selection's not great. They're a little snobby about movies."

"Well, I'm a little snobby about clean kitchens," Finny said. "So we're even."

Earl laughed and put in a cassette: *Jules and Jim*. He said he remembered watching it with his mom once and liking it. He and Finny sat on the bed, backs to the wall, knees at their chests, their legs and arms pressed against each other but not linked.

It turned out not to matter what they were watching, because soon Finny and Earl were kissing. Actually, Finny had liked the movie—the doomed energy of the characters—but she liked kissing Earl more. She found herself closing her eyes, her mind floating off as he pressed against her. They lay down. He touched her stomach, her back, her breasts. It startled her, the sudden closeness.

"Are you okay?" he said.

"Yes," she said. "I'm just—this all feels so strange. But in a good way."

"I'm really happy I found you, Finny."

She smiled at that, and let him go on, touching, stroking, kissing. He took her shirt off, then his own. He still had a strong chest, square shoulders, but a lip of skin hung over his belt. She thought it was adorable: a place to rest her hands. His skin was pale, etched with dark hairs like pencil marks. He took off her bra, with surprising competence, like when he'd dashed onto the ice in his skates earlier. He put his mouth on Finny's nipple, and she felt a shock of excitement. She sighed.

He was gentle with her. Each time he'd start something new, he would ask her, "Is this okay? Do you like this?" And she would nod, too feverish to speak. He guided her hand down his stomach, beneath his belt, and she felt his erection.

"Do you want to have sex?" she finally got out, through heavy breaths. She remembered the time she'd returned from one of their sessions in the old vineyard, and her underwear had been dotted with blood from their investigations. She felt as if he'd made a promise to her then, begun something he needed to finish.

"If you do," he said.

"I do."

"I have a condom."

"I do, too," she told him, just so he'd know.

They ended up using his. She watched him roll it on. Thinking of what he'd said before while they were skating: *Not really girlfriends.*

But she loved this. Every part of this. Not just the rushes of tingly warmth but these funny unsexy moments, like when they had to stop to get their pants off, or put the condom on. You never saw those parts in movies. Though to Finny they were just as much a piece of the experience as the panting and the moaning.

When he pushed into her, she felt a pinch, like from a thumbtack. Then a surge of quivery heat passed through her body. Her leg trembled. Tears filled her eyes. "Oh God," she said, realizing she'd come. She tilted her head back, let her mouth fall open, and moaned. She felt him plunging, plunging. It wasn't painful, as she'd feared it might be. When he came, his mouth dropped open, too. She pulled him to her, wanting to protect him, and also to feel him thrust inside her one more time.

Afterward, he wrapped the condom—which was only slightly bloody, a not unpleasant pink—in tissues, and dabbed himself off. She laughed at his fastidiousness.

"What?" he said.

"Nothing. Just you. I love you."

"You can have it as a present," he said, holding the ball of tissues up for her, then kissing her on the ear. "And by the way, I love you, too."

Chapter **19**

A Potential Conflict Arises over Eggs and French Toast

The next morning they had brunch with Judith and Carter at a restaurant Judith picked in the East Village. They stood in line for an hour, waiting to have their names called. Everyone outside seemed to be in their twenties, attractive and dressed in a consciously haphazard way, with carefully mussed hair, spotless tennis shoes. Finally they were seated at what seemed to Finny a perfectly good table, in the quiet back of the restaurant. Though for some reason Judith didn't seem pleased.

"She's just sore because she heard they seat all the good-looking people in front," Carter said when they sat down.

"That's not true," Judith said, turning red.

"I knew I should have taken more time with my hair," Earl joked.

"And I should have worn my good dentures," Finny added. "These chompers are not what they used to be."

Carter was laughing. Judith scowled at him.

Actually, it was a pretty place inside, a row of windows in the front with little square panes letting in a wash of sunlight.

A large oak bar in the center of the room. Some very green plants next to the windows along the side walls. A lot of funky artwork featuring animals depicted in colorful blocky forms.

The menu was simple, and inexpensive: eggs, bagels, pancakes. They ordered a lot, all of them starved from the long wait outside.

"So, what did you guys do last night?" Carter asked, after the food arrived.

"We just stayed in," Finny said. "Watched a movie."

"A little alone time?" Carter prodded.

"You need to learn when to zip it," Judith told him. Finny could see her friend was still smarting over Carter's comment about the table.

"You're wrong on two counts, darling," Carter countered, stuffing a hash brown into his mouth. "First, you will never find out anything interesting without asking. Second, your friend Finny is perfectly capable of deciding whether or not she wants to tell me which sexual positions she has mastered in the past twenty-four hours."

Finny felt herself blushing now. She didn't dare look at Earl, who must have been the color of the ketchup bottle.

"Listen," Carter said to Finny, "I'm just teasing. I'm bitter because I spent my Friday night catering on Park Avenue at some retirement home they call an apartment building."

"I didn't know you catered," Finny said.

"If someone in New York tells you he's an actor," Carter said, "you better believe he knows how to pass a tray of salmon croquettes."

Earl laughed at that. "Yeah, you know that *writer* and *waiter* are only one letter apart."

"I've never heard that," Carter said. "That's *golden*."

Finny wasn't sure if she liked this kind of joking. It was true, they were both struggling. But they were doing what they loved. She had no idea what that would be for herself.

So she said, "Well, you two are only one *seat* apart, so if you want to make out at any time, just let us know and we'll turn our heads."

"To vomit," Judith added, though Finny could see she was having a good time now that her food had arrived. She'd ordered French toast, and was stacking it on her fork, dousing it with maple syrup the way she used to in the Thorndon dining hall. That was the thing about Judith: she had these little pretensions, like about the table, but after a minute she would drop them and just have fun.

"So how about you?" Finny asked Judith. "What did you do last night?"

"Prince and I went out for dinner."

"Oh," Finny said. She wasn't quite sure what to say about Prince, since she knew Carter didn't like him. She took a bite of her omelet.

"And you should tell her who's coming to visit after the holiday," Carter said to Judith. "Because that's an important piece, too."

Judith rolled her eyes. "He's talking about your brother." Then to Carter, "The reason I didn't tell her was that she told me a million years ago not to talk about what I did with her brother. Isn't that right, Fin?"

"Yeah," Finny said. "But I guess it's different now. I guess it's okay if you tell me."

"Well, then," Judith said. "Actually, Sylvan is coming the Saturday after Thanksgiving, on his way back up to Boston."

"Does he know about Prince?" Finny asked. She couldn't help it.

"That's the *other* other piece," Carter said, then stuffed another hash brown in his mouth.

Chapter 20

A Difficult Thanksgiving

Finny spent the rest of the weekend with Earl, meeting Judith once more for a quick cup of coffee on Sunday before she went back to Stradler. She told Judith she would be coming up to the city a lot, so there would be no tearful goodbyes.

Then three days of classes at Stradler, and Finny was on the train to Baltimore Wednesday evening.

In Baltimore, Laura was waiting for Finny outside the train station. She still drove the green Oldsmobile Stanley used to drive. She got out when she saw Finny, and they hugged each other.

"So *good* to see you, sweetie," Laura said.

"You too, Mom," Finny said. Though she'd only been away three months, for the first time Finny noticed how much her mother had aged. Her neck looked thin, and her skin was loose around her jaw. Her hair looked drier, and was a white-blond color in front, where it used to be a honey-brown. She still had it cut short like she had just after Stanley died.

They got in the car and started driving. Coming home had such an odd feeling for Finny, since she didn't really think of Laura's house as her home anymore. And her mother—she was more like a distant aunt or an old teacher than a parent.

Hard as she tried, Laura was not what you'd call a superb

driver. Some other words you might not use to describe her driving included: smooth, safe, or within any reasonable range of accepted driving codes. She'd gotten by without having to drive much while Stanley was alive, but now she was full captain of the Oldsmobile, and Finny and Sylvan suffered the consequences whenever they came home to visit. Finny especially, because she'd never learned how to drive; she just hadn't wanted the responsibility.

So now, when Laura merged onto the Jones Falls Expressway by cutting across two lanes of traffic without using her blinker, Finny was not surprised to hear the horns of angry drivers sounding behind them. In fact, a chorus of horns followed Laura wherever she drove. Though rather than taking the honking as a sign of people's aggravation with her, Laura seemed to believe they were offering some kind of greeting or helpful encouragement. Her universal response, whenever anyone honked at her, was to wave. Sometimes the wave was accompanied by a small, pleased grin, or even a playful tap on her own horn. Any automotive difficulty—from a near-collision to a tailpipe spewing smoke like a chimney—could be solved with a wave. Watching Laura drive, you might have believed that world peace and a cure for cancer were only a wave and a smile away.

"So tell me about *you*," Laura said now to Finny, applying a curious combination of brake and accelerator, as if in rhythm to a song. The car behind her honked and flashed its headlights. Laura waved and kept up her rhythm.

"I was in New York last weekend," Finny said.

"Really? Why?"

"To visit my friend Judith Turngate. You remember Judith, Mom?"

"Oh," Laura said. "Oh sure. She's lovely." Laura was speaking in the distant way she sometimes did when Finny approached a topic that might reference Stanley.

"Well, anyway, I saw her. And also another old friend who's

in the city." She was still debating whether to tell her mother about Earl. It had been so long since Laura had gotten angry about him. Another era. What harm could it do?

"Actually," Finny went on, channeling Judith's confidence, "it was Earl Henckel. The boy from next door. You remember him? The one Sylvan caught me kissing a long time ago?" Finny laughed, trying to strike a pose where she could joke around over old battles and grudges.

The funny thing was that Laura seemed just as unsure about their relationship as Finny. She smiled hesitantly. "Well," she said to Finny, "that's *int*eresting. What's he up to?"

"He's trying to be a writer. He's living with some friends in New York."

"How is he making money?" Laura asked, and it was at that moment that Finny decided not to introduce Earl to her on this trip.

"I think he has some saved up," Finny said.

"By the way," Laura said, "we'll have an extra guest at Thanksgiving this year."

"Who's that?" Finny asked.

"A man named Gerald. A friend of mine."

They were coming up on Greenspring Station, where the expressway funneled into Falls Road, the country road they used to take all the way out to the Geist Road house. The three-lane road narrowed to a single lane here, and now Laura put on the brakes, with the ostensibly helpful purpose of letting others go ahead of her. It's not often that someone comes to a full stop in the middle of a forty-mile-per-hour road, and it must have thrown some of the other drivers for a loop, because one man sped past and yelled through an open window, "Take a *fucking* driving class!"

For a moment Laura appeared shocked. She put her hand to her mouth and widened her eyes, as if she'd seen something extraterrestrial. But soon her politeness got the best of her, and she waved.

. . .

On Thanksgiving day, while Laura and Sylvan were cooking, Finny decided to give Earl's house a call.

"Hello," said Poplan's voice on the other end of the line.

"Hey," Finny said. "What's that in the background?"

There was some loud synthesizer music playing, and Finny heard the squeaky voice of Poplan's cousin saying: "All the ladies in the house, can ya *hear* me?" And then some other voices—presumably the other cousins—answering, "Yeah!"

"Oh, the cousins. They're into this dancehall music now," Poplan said. "Hold on one second." Then Finny heard Poplan calling, "Alana! Take that salad bowl off your head and do *not* use the tongs as percussion instruments!"

"Sorry," Poplan said to Finny when she got back on the line. "How are you?"

Finny said she was good, enjoying the break from school. They wished each other a happy Thanksgiving. Then Finny asked about coming over on Friday.

"I'd love it," Poplan said. "The only thing is, Menalcus has a show."

"A show?"

"I'm his manager now," Poplan said.

"Manager for what?"

"Why don't you come and see? I know Earl is planning to come. And I need to get away from the cousins for a night. If I hear the word *breakdown* one more time, I might take it literally."

"All right. Where am I going?"

"It's called the Tender Crab."

"Sounds lovely," Finny said.

Gerald Kramp was a darkly suntanned man in his sixties, with silver hair that looked wind-blown, as if he'd just come in from a walk on the beach. His teeth were impressively white, small, and sharp, and against his tanned skin, they looked a bit like the teeth of a jack-o'-lantern. From what Finny gathered, her mother had been "seeing" him since September, just after Finny left for college. They had met at a movie at the Baltimore Museum of Art, talked all through the reception, then gone out for a drink afterward and talked some more.

Gerald seemed perfectly nice. When he came in, he gave Laura a restrained peck on the cheek, then shook Finny's and Sylvan's hands with his own very clean and manicured hand. Sylvan—who now wore his hair parted, pushed back off his face with his fingertips—asked Gerald if he'd like a glass of wine, and when Gerald said sure, Sylvan asked if he'd prefer red or white.

"Whatever you want," Gerald said.

"How about red?" Sylvan offered.

"That would be great," Gerald said, then seemed to hesitate. "Except," he went on, "there are some advantages to starting with white. Your teeth won't get stained, for one. Not that I care. I only mention it because I thought you'd want to know."

Laura smiled.

"Then how about white?" Sylvan suggested.

"That's fine with me," Gerald said. "If you'd prefer. Really, I'm very flexible."

Sylvan poured the white wine for everyone, and they sat around the dining room table, which was separated from the kitchen by only a small island where Laura kept pots and pans. The meal was nearly ready. The turkey was resting on the stove top, and the side dishes were warming in the oven. They were eating early. It was only four-thirty. Since it was windy outside, leaves kept falling onto the skylight above them. The lion sculpture looked like it was dressed in a colorful cloak.

"Should we eat now?" Laura asked everyone. "Or should we enjoy our wine for a few minutes?"

"Whatever," Gerald said, a wide grin displaying his white teeth.

"I'm not that hungry yet," Finny said. "So maybe let's wait."

"That's absolutely fine with me," Gerald said. "I actually haven't eaten anything all day. So it doesn't hurt me one bit to wait another hour. It doesn't get me riled up the way it does some people."

"Well, if you haven't eaten all day," Finny offered, "maybe we should start soon."

"If that's what you'd honestly prefer," Gerald said. "This is not my house, so I don't aim to alter your routines in the slightest. I want you to do just as you would if I weren't here."

So they ate. They set up the turkey and side dishes on the island and everyone helped themselves to a plate, then sat back down again. Sylvan asked Gerald what he did for a living, and Gerald said that he was a businessman.

"What kind of business?" Sylvan asked.

"Spices," Gerald said. "It's the future of cooking."

"What do you mean?"

"Smoked paprika. Wild oregano. You name it. Actually, I provided the spices your mother used in this dinner. We wanted to keep it a surprise."

"So you sell the spices?"

"Not yet," Gerald said, "but I'm working on it. I'd say it's my current project." He grinned, and his bronze skin seemed to redden slightly, as if he were being warmed under the broiler.

Laura nodded supportively.

"I don't need to bore you with the details," Gerald said, "but it's going to be very interesting, isn't it?" He looked to Laura.

She nodded again.

As at every Thanksgiving, Laura went through the process of naming every dish on the table and saying how delicious it was. Sylvan and Finny offered their agreement where they could.

"How about the spices?" Gerald added. "Very important. Spices."

Finny said yes, she agreed that spices were important.

"Aha," Gerald said. "You see?"

"Would you like to open another bottle of wine?" Laura asked Gerald.

"Doesn't matter," Gerald said.

"I'm fine," Finny said.

"Me, too," Sylvan said.

"Only," Gerald said, "I've heard that at least two glasses of wine every evening is very beneficial for your heart. A weak heart runs in my family. So, for example, at my house, I would move toward opening a second bottle—only because I don't want to die tragically of a major heart attack. But that's my house. In your house, you should do whatever you want."

They opened a second bottle.

"To heart health," Gerald said, raising his glass.

And if two glasses of wine were beneficial for the heart, Gerald must have believed that each successive glass increased the benefits. He drank the majority of the second bottle, replenishing his glass almost as soon as he'd drained it, and by the time they got around to proposing a third bottle, Gerald accepted on behalf of all their hearts, and then sought to spare their livers by inflicting the brunt of the bottle on his own.

Laura wore her impenetrable smile the whole evening. For Finny, who had felt the gap between herself and her mother widening ever since her father's death, it was as if a canyon had opened up between them. Laura seemed so small and far away that Finny hardly saw the point in reaching toward her. She made faces across the table at Sylvan, who laughed and shook his head.

When they had finally finished and the plates were cleared,

leftovers sealed in Ziploc bags, Laura said to Gerald, "You can't drive home."

"I'm fine," Gerald said, though he was leaning like a tree in a heavy wind. "But if it'll make you feel better, I'll stay." It was only seven o'clock, though already Gerald's eyelids looked heavy.

"Yes, honey," Laura said. "It would."

They were all in bed by nine. Finny's room was next to Laura's, and that night Finny heard a thumping against her bedroom wall. The sound lasted for only a couple minutes, but it was enough to gross Finny out.

Chapter **21**

The Tender Crab

The Tender Crab was, as one might guess, a seafood restaurant, and it was located in the ring of waterfront shops at Harborplace in Baltimore. Finny had convinced Sylvan to drive her, and to attend the performance—which was not difficult, since Gerald Kramp had spent the day at the house, and both Finny and Sylvan were happy to leave him and Laura alone for a while.

When they got to the restaurant, Earl was waiting in front. Finny heard the water sloshing beside them, some boats knocking into one another in the marina.

"Hey," Earl said, and gave Finny a kiss on the cheek.

"This is Sylvan, my brother," Finny said. "Sylvan, this is Earl."

She could see that they were both looking each other over as they shook hands.

"It's great to finally meet you," Earl said.

"Likewise," Sylvan said. "I'm glad Finny decided I was presentable."

"Only now that you've gotten a haircut," Finny said.

Sylvan blushed. "I was hoping the rat's nest would come back in style," he said.

Earl explained that Poplan was inside, saving tables for

them. They walked under the neon sign, into the restaurant. It was dark inside. The room was cavernous, with wooden rafters in the ceiling, and fishnets hanging from the rafters, to give it the look of a ship's hull. To the left was the family section, booths with hanging lights over them, tables covered with paper and the carcasses of crabs. The pungent smell of Old Bay drifted through the restaurant.

Earl pointed to the right, which was the bar section. Here the round tables were much smaller—they fit only two people—and the main attraction was a stage area toward the back of the room. Even though the music hadn't started yet, there were a few dedicated drinkers already seated at the tables. One man was nodding to an unheard beat, and a woman with teased hair and a considerable amount of tattooed cleavage kept licking her lips like she had food on them.

"In front," Earl said.

Then Finny saw Poplan, who was wearing a visor. She had two tables reserved, right in front of the stage. She waved to them, and they walked toward her. The floor in this section of the room was made of cement, painted a rust color, what must have been a last-minute budgetary decision by the owners. The wooden stage was elevated about two feet, and on it sat an upright piano and a straight-backed chair.

"Hey," Finny said to Poplan, and gave her a hug. Poplan hadn't gotten up—she must have been worried about keeping her seat. Now that Finny was close, she could appreciate the full effect of Poplan's wardrobe. In addition to the visor, Poplan was wearing a white button-down shirt, tuxedo pants, and a black vest—like two pieces of a man's three-piece suit. She also had a black armband around her left arm.

"Is it poker night?" Finny asked Poplan.

"What are you talking about?" Poplan said.

"Your outfit."

"*This*," Poplan said, giving her shirt collar a tug, "is what I wear to all of his performances. It is my manager outfit. I be-

lieve it imparts a sense of respect to anyone who might observe me." She nodded significantly when she finished saying
this, as if it were clear that many people were observing her.

"This is my brother, Sylvan," Finny said.

Sylvan held out his hand.

"Have you washed that?" Poplan asked.

Out of Poplan's line of sight, Finny nodded vigorously.

Taking the hint, Sylvan responded, "Yes, of course."

"Then it's a pleasure," Poplan said, shaking Sylvan's hand.

"And I'm Earl," Earl said to Poplan.

"What a beautiful name," Poplan said, shaking Earl's hand,
which she must have been sure was washed. Finny was happy
to see that Earl and Poplan had developed a rapport with
each other.

"Since there's not enough room at this table for all of us,"
Poplan said, "you boys are going to have to make due with
that one." She nodded at the table next to them. "And by the
way, you may order what you like to drink, but just make sure
it looks enough like a soft drink that I won't have to answer to
anyone."

Finny was a little nervous when she realized that Earl and
Sylvan would be sitting alone, without her there to guide
them through conversation. Finny was still afraid that Sylvan
would dislike her friends, this other family; but when they sat
down, Finny noticed that Sylvan and Earl fell almost immediately into conversation.

In a minute they all ordered drinks from a waitress who
was chewing gum and called everyone "hon."

"So tell me about this act," Finny said to Poplan when their
drinks arrived.

"Well, he's backstage now," Poplan said. "The act really isn't
anything special. I don't want to tell you too much. You'll just
have to see."

It was then that the stage lights went up, and Mr. Henckel
walked onstage. Some of the chairs behind Finny had been

filled—it was a solid little audience—and everyone clapped enthusiastically. Mr. Henckel took a gracious bow, as if he were onstage at the Meyerhoff, rather than the Tender Crab. He was wearing a full tuxedo, with cummerbund, and he had his comb-over slicked across his scalp.

"Doesn't he look handsome?" Poplan said.

Mr. Henckel's first piece was a Chopin mazurka (Poplan had the set list), a jaunty piece that set the audience hooting and applauding. He gave a little nod of acknowledgment, then launched into the final movement of the Moonlight Sonata, playing it in an agitated fury. The audience was silent, captivated. Mr. Henckel knew how to pause just long enough in the rests to make you yearn for that next note. He knew how to set off across the keys, his fingers running like the legs of centipedes. And he knew how to strike down on chords, making them ring in the large room. It was funny, Finny thought, but the music, which might have seemed plain in an auditorium, felt special here. In a way, it was more beautiful than it ever could have been in Carnegie Hall or Lincoln Center; it lifted you above the noise and clutter of your everyday life.

Then the piece ended. The audience clapped and whistled. And Mr. Henckel nodded, once, twice, three times. Only now the nod was different from before. Finny recognized it from her lessons, all those years ago. She saw him drifting, drifting. And then he was asleep, his chin resting on his chest. His comb-over stayed where it was, fixed by whatever hair product Poplan had used to slick it down.

"Oh no," Finny said, looking at Poplan in alarm. The audience was completely silent. Poplan sat there, lips tight, waiting. When Finny tried to speak again, Poplan held her finger to her lips. Finny looked back at Earl. Earl shrugged. They waited some more. Finny felt awful for Mr. Henckel, embarrassing himself like this in front of all these people. She knew that soon someone would get up, lift him off the stage. She wondered why it hadn't happened yet. Were they calling an ambulance? Was there a doctor on the way? It would be humiliating, whatever it was, and probably the end of Mr. Henckel's new performing career.

Finally, after an excruciating five minutes, Mr. Henckel snorted awake. He looked around the room dazedly, cleared his throat, then said to his audience, "You'll have to excuse me. It just comes upon me."

What happened next was a miracle to Finny: the audience burst into applause. They cheered and cheered, stomped, smacked their hands on the tables, gave him a standing ovation. What's going on? Finny thought.

Then Poplan leaned over and said in Finny's ear, "You see, this is the business part of what I do. I knew he'd be falling asleep once in a while during performances. He can't help it. So we set up this arrangement. There is a man backstage who times how long Menalcus sleeps. If it's more than five minutes, everyone who's attending the show gets a free drink. The regulars all know. It keeps them coming back. That's how you turn a liability into an asset. Like I said before, it's all in how you see it." Poplan winked at Finny after she said this, and it might have been then that Finny first appreciated what a woman of vision Poplan truly was.

After the show, they chatted a bit. Mr. Henckel came out from backstage and enjoyed a cup of coffee with everyone. They told him what a wonderful job he'd done, and he said, "Oh, no, no." Though a string of smile-frowns betrayed how proud he was of his newfound success.

Soon it was time to go, and everyone said goodbye. When Finny was giving Earl a hug, he said to her, "Oh, I forgot to tell you. I'm going back to France in a week."

"What?" Finny said, pulling back from him. How could he say it so casually, like he was running out to grab some milk at the supermarket? She felt as if a trapdoor had opened beneath her, and she was falling, falling. "That's terrible."

"I know," Earl said, "but I really should spend the holidays with my mom. She doesn't have anyone else. And New York is getting expensive."

"When am I going to see you again?"

"Soon," Earl said. "The thing I wanted to ask you is whether you might consider coming to Paris over the holidays to stay with me."

Finny thought of the holidays at her own house—listening to her mother and Gerald thumping to the rhythm of "God Rest Ye Merry, Gentlemen"—and Finny said to Earl, "Of course I'll spend the holidays with you. I'd love to!"

"So, what did you think?" Finny asked Sylvan while they were driving home from the performance. Sylvan had his eyes on the road, and didn't turn toward Finny when she spoke.

"The performance was great," Sylvan said. "I had no idea your friend was so talented."

"And what about Earl?" She almost pinched herself after saying this. What if Sylvan didn't like Earl? Would she never mention him to her brother again? She wasn't sure she was ready for Sylvan's judgment.

But he offered it before she could stop him. "Earl's great. I have a lot of respect for what he's doing. The writing, I mean. I could never put myself on the line like that. I've always played it safe with my choices. He's really got courage."

She could hardly believe what her brother was saying. As a child, she'd never known him to be a particularly modest person, but here he was, showing admiration for Earl. People had an endless ability to surprise Finny.

"What did you guys talk about?"

"Mostly about you," Sylvan said, and raised his eyebrows in a way that let Finny know he was kidding. "Actually," he went on, "we just talked a lot about what we're doing. And a little about Judith, since I gather you guys have seen her. I was just curious what she was up to."

"What did Earl say?" Finny asked quickly.

"Not much. Just that you met at a party, then had brunch together."

"Yeah," Finny said, grappling with herself over whether to go further. She decided to ask her brother some questions. "So I hear you're going to be stopping by."

"Tomorrow," Sylvan said. "I think Maryland has done what it can for me. I'm going to stop for a night in New York, then head back up to school."

"What are you guys planning on doing?"

"Just hanging out. Maybe catch some movies, or a museum or something."

"Where are you staying?"

"I actually hadn't really thought about that. I figured I'd, uh, see how it goes."

"Do you guys see each other a lot?"

"You have a lot of interest all of a sudden," Sylvan said, glancing at Finny as he settled into the middle lane of the Jones Falls. They were heading out of the city, past the broken factories and warehouses, the teeth of the shattered windows glittering in the expressway lights.

"I was just curious—"

"Then let me tell you everything," Sylvan interrupted. "If you want to know. I need to say it anyway. The story is that I've been going down to New York every couple months since Judith started at Columbia. Usually we just hang out for the day, and sometimes I spend the night in her apartment. Or else I head back up really late and sleep on the Chinatown bus. I don't think either of us was really sure what we wanted, but we liked spending the time together. And you might not want to hear this, Finny, but Judith was the first girl I ever slept with. Actually, the only one, if I'm being completely honest."

"It was that time she came down to visit in the new house, right? When you two were acting so strange at breakfast."

Sylvan nodded. "That was the, uh, first time, yeah. And it

wasn't that I felt awkward with her afterward. It was more that I really liked her—more than I expected."

"I know what you mean," Finny said. "I know exactly what you mean."

"But anyway, the reason I'm telling you all this is that, in a funny way, your boyfriend was an inspiration for me. He's dead set on becoming a writer, and he hasn't given himself a way out. He's going for it, damn the consequences. And I realized that I don't have anything like that in my life, anything I'm that passionate about. Except Judith. I can't be a writer or an artist or anything like that. But I can learn to put myself on the line a little, Finny, if it's for something I care about."

Now they were winding into the suburbs, past the Cold Spring Lane exit, the Exxon sign twirling on its pole like a lollipop in the big dark mouth of the sky. Finny felt, with every breath she took, like a balloon was expanding in her chest. She couldn't stand to watch her brother set himself up this way. She'd always joked that he was a pretentious jerk, but in truth she knew him to be as delicate as that cracked candy plate Laura used to keep on the marble buffet in the old house.

"Do you know what else is going on in Judith's life now?" Finny asked.

"Nothing in particular. She always says she's busy with classes. She talks about her friend Carter a lot. Other than that, I don't think she hangs out with a lot of people."

"Listen," Finny said, unable to bear the weight of her knowledge any longer, "there are some things I want you to know about Judith. It's just that—" And she thought how to go on. She felt as if she were plunging into some dark, cold water—like the water outside the Tender Crab. "You have to understand that Judith is a little reckless sometimes. She's a very close, dear friend of mine. I owe her everything for helping me fit in and get along the first time I left home. She's full of energy, and good intentions. But sometimes she doesn't see all the consequences of what she's doing."

"What are you trying to tell me, Fin?" Sylvan said.

And suddenly a memory struck Finny. It was that time Poplan sat Finny down in her room at Thorndon, after Finny had delivered that awful note, and Poplan said, *Judith is a bad influence*. Finny hadn't wanted to believe it could be true at the time, and she didn't want to believe it now. She couldn't betray her friend, as much as she couldn't betray her brother.

So she said to Sylvan, "I'm not trying to tell you anything, except what I said. Which is that Judith is a good person, but I don't want you to expect too much of her. I'm glad you guys have fun together. She's great for that. But in the long run, I'm not sure what kind of wife she would be. Once she loses her figure, she's liable to get cranky."

"That's good to know," Sylvan said. "I'll keep it in mind."

And Finny left it there, hoping what she'd said was enough.

Chapter 22

Finny Goes to Paris

Two hurdles before winter break: Laura and finals.

Finny had already gotten her passport the week after she'd left home, just in case the opportunity for a trip arose. So she didn't have that to worry about. It turned out Laura wasn't anything to worry about either. When Finny told her mother she was thinking about going to France with a friend for the holidays, Laura said, "Sounds great, honey. I'm jealous. I guess Gerald and I might be opening presents alone, if Sylvan doesn't come." And Laura must have been excited enough about that prospect that she didn't even ask Finny who the friend was.

Finny called Earl, told him everything was clear at home, wished him a safe trip back, told him she'd see him soon.

The next day she called a travel agent and spent half her life savings on a round-trip ticket to Paris.

Then she was caught in a haze of studying and paper-writing, a fog of days and nights in the library, short naps that she optimistically called "sleep." She saw a lot of her room-mate; Dorrie studied in the room, so as not to be distracted by Steven Bench.

During this time Finny got a quick note from Sylvan. She had written to tell him she wasn't coming home for winter vacation, in case it affected his plans. He thanked her, saying that he probably wouldn't go home for too long in that case. *I'm not sure where I'll go. Maybe I'll spend part of the time here, and part in New York. Then maybe Baltimore for a week or two. And by the way, things went well with Judith the other weekend. Just thought you'd want to know.*

Finny wondered what "well" meant. She had to fight the urge to call Sylvan and talk the whole situation over again. But she saw Dorrie, hunched over a chemistry textbook, and it was enough to yank Finny's mind back to where it needed to be. She'd give Sylvan a call as soon as she got back from France.

Then finals were over. No time to organize, she just threw some clothes in a bag. She boarded the plane a little after seven, and promptly fell asleep. She didn't wake up until she was in France.

Earl was there to meet Finny's plane. In the airport they kissed, held on to each other like they'd been apart for years, rather than a few weeks. He took her through Charles de Gaulle, through what seemed an endless series of buses and escalators and walkways, until they finally got to the B3 metro, which would shuttle them into Paris.

"My mom wanted to be at home to meet you," Earl said when he and Finny were on the train, "but she had to work."

"I completely understand," Finny said. "I don't want to put her out at all."

"She's just excited to meet you."

"That's cute."

"And anyway," Earl said, "this is better because now you can go back and nap, and you don't have to feel like you need to stay up and talk. You must be exhausted."

"Actually, I'm wide awake."

It was true. Whether because it was Finny's first full night of sleep in a week, or whether it was just the excitement of being here, on this new continent with Earl, Finny couldn't even imagine sleeping. Every little thing thrilled her: the language, the beautiful women, the sour odor of the man holding the pole next to her, the little crank on the metro door you had to turn to get the door to pop open when the train stopped.

After one transfer, they walked upstairs, onto the street. Earl rolled Finny's suitcase for her, and she kept her backpack strapped on her shoulders. She was surprised to see that the streets looked pretty much like the streets in a big American city. Except there were bakeries on the corners instead of delis. And the magazines on view in the magazine booths showed pictures of actual topless women, their breasts displayed like meat hanging in a butcher's window. She and Earl walked up a small hill, until they reached the address Earl had written on the envelopes of his letters to her when they were in high school. There was a double wooden door that must have been ten feet tall, with brass handles that looked like they were made for giants' hands. Earl punched in a code on the call box next to the door, there was a small click, and then they pushed through the doors into the building.

The space they walked into was dark, and very cold, and soon Finny realized that they weren't inside at all. They were in some kind of tunnel, their feet on a stone walkway, and Finny could see light ahead of them. Earl pressed a switch on the wall, and the tunnel lit up. There was a small apartment to their right, which Earl explained was a superintendent's room. As they walked forward, Finny could see that the bright space ahead of them was a courtyard. They walked into it, a gorgeous green square of lawn. Around it were garages for the cars of the presumably wealthy people who lived here. A stone path bordered the grass, where the cars could drive. It was quiet here, walled off from the city. Finny looked up at the majestic building, its beige walls nearly golden in the bright winter sun.

"In France, it's a big deal to live on the third floor, which they call the second," Earl whispered to Finny. "There are a few ground-floor apartments here that are smaller and a little less expensive. A photographer lives in that one." He pointed to a window through which Finny could see a television set. "And a lady who works as an, uh, escort, lives there." He pointed to another window, which was shielded by a curtain at the moment. "For a while I didn't understand what she did. I kept asking my mom, and she would always laugh. The lady advertises as a massage therapist. She sometimes has different guys waiting in the courtyard at lunchtime. It's pretty funny. No one really cares. One time, just for fun, my mom went in to ask for a massage, and the lady said she was all booked up. Even though there was no one inside."

It seemed like here there was a frankness, an everydayness to sex, which Finny liked. She said to Earl, "Have you ever gone in for a 'massage'?"

"Um," Earl said, turning red.

"Really?"

"My mom bought me one for my eighteenth birthday. It was kind of awkward, but I told her I'd go through with it."

Finny laughed, clapping a hand over the ugly jealous voice in her head. She didn't want to acknowledge all that pettiness. What was the big deal about a "massage"? And it wasn't like she hadn't thought of other boys during the last four years either.

So she said, "Your mom sounds funny. I'm looking forward to meeting her."

"Well, if you're not tired, we can go over soon and visit her at work. She said she wanted you to come by when you woke up anyway. Let's just go stick your stuff upstairs."

Earl led Finny to a door on the far side of the courtyard, which he opened with a key. It was still cool inside, and he had to hit another switch to get the light to go on.

"We gotta move fast," he said. "Or else the light goes off and I have to grope for the switch."

They hustled up a very narrow, tightly wound staircase. Earl said that it was only five flights, but it felt like it would never stop because they were turning so much.

"The regular staircase is nicer," Earl said. "But this one is the only way to get to the maids' rooms."

He pointed at the door on the third floor and said, "That's the American lady my mom rents from. I don't even think she's around."

When they reached the top landing, there were doors on either side of them, and a door behind Finny, which Earl said was where the toilet was. He opened the door to their right with another key, and they walked into the room.

It was stuffy, as Earl had said—and unbelievably small. There was a kitchen counter, with a sink and two burners in it, a small refrigerator beneath it. A table was pushed into the corner between the counter and the wall, and there was only enough room for two chairs beneath it. There were some red cushions stacked against one wall, which Earl explained could be spread out to make a bed for them later. And on the far wall, a little window through which Finny could get a view of the rooftop next door.

"Where does your mom sleep?" Finny asked.

"She's renting the other room, across the hall, too. The lady who was living there moved out, and my mom had saved a little money. She decided she needed the extra space. So we have this room to ourselves."

"Wow," Finny said. "An apartment in Paris to ourselves."

"Not bad," Earl said, "right?"

"I can hardly believe it."

Earl's mom worked in a hair salon on Rue La Fayette. It was only a five-minute walk from Earl's apartment. The salon occupied a very small storefront, sandwiched between a jewelry store and a chocolate shop. The sign on the door said *Salon de*

Coiffure, and then beneath that: *Ramon de la Peña.* Earl led Finny inside, a bell on the door ringing as they entered. The shop was tiny, only two barber's chairs and two chairs with the heated domes that came down over your hair for drying, one sink for washing hair. There was a small desk in front, which was empty at present. In fact, there was no one in the shop. Finny and Earl placed their coats on a coat rack by the door.

Then Finny heard a woman's voice from the back of the store, which was shielded by some black silk screens with pictures of purple cranes on them. *"Bonjour!"* the voice said.

"Hey, Mom," Earl said.

The woman who emerged from behind the screens was taller than Finny had expected her to be. Probably because Earl and Mr. Henckel were so short, Finny had expected Earl's mom to be, too. But this woman had the opposite of their squashed frame: she was almost unnaturally elongated, with arms and legs that seemed stretched like taffy—so thin and white. Her pallor was accentuated by the simple black dress she wore, and by her dark hair, which was pulled back in a tight bun, moistened by some kind of hair product. She had a strong nose, and thick, somewhat square eyebrows. Her whole body seemed pliable as dough when she walked, and Finny had the feeling she could pop into a handstand at a moment's notice.

"Hello, hello," Earl's mom said to Finny and Earl, waving dramatically, like they were much farther away.

"Hi," Finny said, and held out her hand to shake.

But the woman took Finny in her slender, surprisingly strong arms and gave her a long hug. "Finny," Earl's mom said while they were still hugging, "I'm so, so happy to meet you. I've been waiting so long for this day."

"Me, too," Finny said, a little taken aback by the intensity of the greeting. She wasn't sure what to call Earl's mom, since she knew she wasn't a Henckel.

Finally, Earl's mom let go. Finny had to take a deep breath, since all the air had been squeezed out of her lungs.

"I'm Mona Trebble," Earl's mom told Finny. "But you should call me Mona."

"You should call me Finny," Finny said.

"You're stunning," Mona blurted out. "One of the most beautiful young women I've ever seen."

"Uh, thanks," Finny said, though she wanted to say more, as if there'd been some obvious error she needed to explain.

But Earl saved her. "Finny slept her whole flight," he told his mom, "so she didn't need a nap. We decided we'd come right down and see you."

Mona's reaction to this statement was a bit more pronounced than Finny would have expected: her eyes flooded with tears. "This is the most wonderful day of my life," she said, sniffling and trying to collect herself.

Finny supposed that she hadn't realized the importance of this visit to Earl's mom, how honored Mona must have been that Earl would bring his girlfriend all the way to France to meet her. Only later did Finny see how extreme Mona's emotional reactions were to everything; you could have held the door for her and she would have burst into tears.

"I'm really happy to be here," Finny said.

"To have my son and his love together in my home. Who could imagine a greater joy?" She was beaming, her eyes reflecting the overhead lights.

"Not me," Finny said.

"My son is such a wonderful, thoughtful child," Mona went on.

"Mom," Earl said.

"I'm just so excited," Mona said. "To think that under a roof I have provided, you and your lover will be snuggling up together, kissing, petting, whatever else you do—it's the greatest accomplishment I could hope for."

"So inappropriate, Mom," Earl said, his cheeks glowing.

"Anyway, I have a surprise for you," Mona said to Finny. "It's something very, very special, to welcome you to France." She looked at Earl. "Is now a good time, honey?"

"Sure," Earl said. Finny could see he was already tired from this visit with his mom. "Why don't you see if Finny wants to do it, though?"

"Oh, of course, of course," Mona said, clasping her hands over her heart like she was trying to catch a scurrying mouse on her chest. "Of course we wouldn't do it if Finny wasn't interested. But it's such an honor." She looked at Finny. "I couldn't imagine you not being interested."

"I promised I wouldn't tell," Earl said to Finny. "But definitely don't feel like you have to if you don't want to."

"What is it?" Finny asked.

"Ramon has agreed to cut your hair. *For free.*" Mona whispered these last two words, as if they were too unbelievable to say at full volume.

"Actually, I just got a haircut not that long ago. I don't want to inconvenience you."

"Ramon comes all the way from Madrid," Mona said. "People normally pay two hundred dollars for a trim. This is not a haircut. This is"—she seemed to hesitate, struggling for words—"a blessing."

"I really just wash and go," Finny said. She felt uncomfortable being fussed over. But she looked at Earl, who shrugged and raised his eyebrows, like he couldn't help the situation. Mona was practically panting with excitement.

"But yeah," Finny went on, "why not? It's worth treating yourself once in a while, I guess."

Mona sighed. She smiled, then called out, "Rrramon!" rolling her *R*'s in the Spanish style.

Almost instantly he appeared from behind the silk screen, in a sort of flourish, like a flamenco dancer at the first strum of a guitar: a handsome man hardly five feet tall, with earrings in both ears, his black hair slicked back from his face the same way Mona's hair was slicked into her bun. He wore all black, too, which was evidently the dress code in the salon; his wardrobe was made up of a black T-shirt and some extremely tight-fitting slacks that produced a considerable bulge at his crotch. He walked toward Finny, around the drying chairs and the sink, and Finny noticed he had an odd way of navigating a room, walking in very straight paths, with short quick steps, and making sudden turns, only at ninety-degree angles.

"*El Maestro,*" Mona said to Finny as he approached. It took him a bit of time to get to Finny, considering all the objects in his way, and the fact that the room was not conducive to perpendicular walking. When he finally arrived in front of Finny, he offered a quick nod to Earl, who nodded back.

"*Bonjour. Buenos días.* Hello," Ramon said to Finny, who held out her hand to shake. Again she was disappointed in her attempt, though, because instead of reaching for Finny's hand, the maestro grabbed a tuft of Finny's hair and said, "Esplendid." He then let go of her hair, made a quick ninety-degree turn, and held out his hand toward the chair in front of the sink.

After Mona had washed Finny's hair, Finny sat in the empty barber's chair, the other being occupied by Ramon. She expected him to get up and start cutting her hair, but instead he stayed seated, watching her with his eyes barely squinted.

"Oh," Finny said. "Just a little trim. Kind of like it is now, but maybe with some more layers and—"

Ramon shook his head. Mona waved Finny off frantically, as if she were stepping in front of a speeding truck.

Ramon kept watching Finny. She wondered what was happening.

Just when the staring contest was becoming painful, Ramon got up from his chair and walked over to stand in front of Finny. He stepped on a bar, and her chair went down, nearly to the ground. He leaned over her, looked straight down at her scalp. Then he stepped on the bar and her head came back up to nearly the same level as his. He bit his lower lip and looked hard at her temples, her hairline.

Then, for no reason Finny could discern, he began to nod. He held out his hand, palm up. Mona placed a comb in the hand. He took several swipes at Finny's hair with the comb, parting it strangely in the center of Finny's scalp.

"Ah," Mona said.

"Ouch," Finny said.

After several more swipes with the comb, Ramon transferred it to his left hand, then held out his right again. This time Mona placed a pair of scissors in the open hand. Ramon shook his head, grimaced, looked tortured. He sighed. He put his hand on his chin.

And then, out of nowhere, inspiration struck. He nodded and grinned, raised the scissors to Finny's bangs, and took four decisive snips. He then walked around behind Finny and took a series of eight or ten snips in what seemed to be random places around Finny's head.

Then he stopped, rubbed his forehead and breathed loudly, put his fists against his waist and stomped.

But here inspiration seemed to find him again, because his eyes widened and he made a final snip just above Finny's left ear. He then gave Finny a quick nod, like he'd given to Earl when he'd walked out from behind the silk screen.

"Ah," Mona said.

The maestro looked pleased with his work. "Esplendid," he said again, handing the scissors and comb to Mona. He then zigzagged his way to the rear of the shop, his shoulders back, hands on his hips, his substantial pelvis thrust forward like a bullfighter exiting the ring.

"It looks fantastic," Mona said, with a kind of childlike awe.

To Finny it looked exactly the same as it had before it was

cut, but since she didn't want to hurt Mona's feelings, she said, "It's the best haircut I've ever gotten."

"He's a minimalist," Mona explained. "It's as much about the cuts he doesn't make as the ones he does."

"Interesting," Finny said. "What do you think, Earl?"

Earl looked up from his magazine. "Nice. I really like it," he said. She could have been sporting a mullet and he would have said the same thing.

"Well, you two should go enjoy the afternoon now. I'll meet you back at the apartment before dinner, Earl?"

"Yeah," Earl said. And they walked into the Paris streets.

Chapter **23**

La Maison des Fantaisies

"So that's my mom," Earl said as they headed down a street called Rue Montorgueil toward the Seine. They'd walked into a market area and were now passing shops displaying cheeses of every shape and color, some looking like they were dusty, even covered with mold; or meats of vibrant reds and pinks, little roasted hens or rabbits tied to spits, spinning round and round; or pastries, lacquered with butter or sugar and bursting with fillings. Even on this winter day, some of the shops were open to the cold air. Finny saw one store that sold only foie gras, the stuff Earl had told her about in one of his first letters from Paris. Colorful tins lined the walls.

"She's great," Finny said about Earl's mom. "I want to get her something to thank her for setting up the haircut for me."

"Come on, tell me the truth. Do you even notice a difference?"

Finny smiled. "It was still nice."

"Ramon said he's going to take her in as a partner in the business soon. They're going to call it Ramona."

"That's great."

"It gives her something to look forward to," Earl said.

"Is she not happy?"

Here Earl took a breath, then let it out slowly. "It goes up and down with her. She can be excited and bubbly, like today. Then there are times when I catch her crying for no reason. There's a lot I didn't understand about her for a while. She's not the most stable person in the world."

"What do you mean?"

"I mean, she has a history. When she was with my dad, it was right around the time she had a breakdown. She was barely eighteen. She cut all her ties with her family and joined that traveling act my dad told you about. Part of the reason she couldn't see me after I was born was that she was in a psych ward. I think my dad didn't tell me that stuff because he wanted to spare me—or at least to respect Mom's privacy. But gradually the story came out. She told me some weird stuff, Finny. She started hallucinating when she was in the hospital and she said that all day she could smell the color purple, and when she ate, it tasted like the sound of birds chirping."

"Jeez," Finny said. "I had no idea."

"I didn't want to make a big deal of it, but that's one of the reasons I came back. To check up on her."

"That's why she thinks you're a wonderful son."

"She thinks everything is wonderful, when she's happy. Then when she's sad, it goes the other way."

"So is she all right? I mean, you said she's not so stable."

"She takes a lot of drugs now. Medicine, I mean. It keeps her within range."

"What about Ramon?" Finny asked. "Is there anything going on there?"

Earl smiled. "You mean, like sex? I don't think Ramon sleeps with women. I actually don't think he sleeps with men either. He's pretty content with himself."

"Does your mom date at all?"

"Once in a while. But her French isn't good, so she doesn't have many options. And I'm not sure she's really built for relationships. She has some weird hang-ups about sex. She can be very frank about it—like before when she embarrassed me—but then sometimes she also seems afraid of it."

And Earl? Finny thought. What mark had it left on him?

Now the street they were walking on ended, and they came upon a plaza with some pretty gazebos in it where Finny could imagine people eating lunch in warmer weather. There were some benches, and small trees, even a fountain.

"We can walk right through this," Earl said. "It's a shortcut. The Pont Neuf is on the other side."

They walked down another short street, and came out by the river. Holding hands, they walked onto the bridge, over the wide water. Because of their long walk, Finny didn't feel cold anymore. She squeezed Earl and made him pose with her for a picture along the railing of the bridge, which another American tourist ended up taking for them. Earl pointed out some of the sights: the Louvre, the Tuileries, the Orsay, Ile de la Cité and the buttresses of Notre Dame at its far end. They planned some places to visit. Earl told her about the *bateaux-mouches* you could take a ride on at night, and how the rich people who lived on the Seine complained about the lights from the tour boats shining in their windows.

They spent the first part of the afternoon walking around some Left Bank neighborhoods, which Earl said he liked better than the Right Bank. He took Finny to a café where Gertrude Stein used to come for parlor sessions with her writer friends. They stopped at a fancy ice cream shop on Ile Saint-Louis, with brass tables and counters. Finny tried a flavor with chocolate and orange and hazelnuts, and when Earl asked if she was ready to go, she considered getting another scoop, but decided not to spoil her dinner. He took her to a little Picasso museum in the Marais, which he said was one of his favorite museums in Paris. He taught her some useful expressions, like *"Où est le métro?"* and *"C'est combien?"* which Finny then proceeded to butcher with her abominable French accent. Earl laughed, then tried to correct her and ended up bungling it himself, which made Finny laugh. They were practically falling over by the time Finny learned to say "I would like to order the steak."

They got back to Earl's apartment building around seven. Finny was exhausted, so Mona suggested they stay in for dinner. They made a meal of baguette and cheese, salami, some rabbit pâté Mona had picked up at the farmers' market held every week on her street. Mona walked them to the door of Earl's room, then said to Finny and Earl, "You two must have some catching up to do. You can relax, give each other massages, talk dirty if you like. I'll plug my ears."

"Mom," Earl said. "Please."

"Sorry," Mona said.

Then they all said good night.

After Finny had washed for bed, they made up the red cushions for themselves, and Finny lay down on them while Earl was getting ready. She must have closed her eyes at some point, because the next thing she knew she was blinking awake in a shower of sunlight from the high window. Earl was asleep, and Finny got up on a chair to look out the window. She heard voices below, and when she looked into the street, she saw children congregating in front of an iron gate. Since it was the holidays, Finny imagined they must have been friends meeting up for some outing. One very big child pushed a small one into the road and laughed. Cars honked at them. Finny got down off the chair, and she saw that Earl was now awake.

"Sorry I fell asleep," Finny said. She wasn't sure if he was disappointed they hadn't had sex. "I guess I was more tired than I thought."

But if Earl was disappointed, he didn't show it. "Come here," he said to Finny, holding out his arms, and she got back in bed with him. They hugged each other under the warm covers, and for some reason it put Finny in mind of chickens in an oven.

"We're roasting," she said.

It would be what they'd always call this morning time together, when they held each other under the covers. It was Finny's favorite part of the day. On this particular morning, though, as Mona had predicted, it led to more than just holding. Soon they were kissing, undressing, and Finny was scrambling into the cold air to find a condom in her bag. Earl laughed at the sight of her running naked through his room. Then she was back under the covers, and they were moving through all the familiar, warm routines they'd established that weekend in New York. They moved slowly, and it took a long time, but by the end they were both breathless. What a wonderful way to begin their vacation together! What a perfect morning in Paris!

It became the way they started every morning. Too tired for love—and usually a little drunk—when they returned at night, they went straight to sleep. But in the mornings they lingered, roasted, made love, sometimes fell back asleep for a while longer. Then they'd eat cereal, or else go to the corner for an espresso and a croissant. (Finny always got chocolate.) They didn't make a lot of plans, but they always had enough to fill a day. There were exhibits they wanted to see, restaurants they wanted to try, walks they wanted to take. They went to Angelina on the Rue de Rivoli to drink *chocolat africain*. Finny bought postcards, chocolates, key chains for her friends and family. In the evenings they told Mona about their days, and she relished every detail. She licked her lips when Finny described the hot chocolate. Earl showed Finny a little square in Montmartre with a bust of a French actress in it, surrounded by some lovely old houses that had been converted into apartments. There were a few park benches, a circle of lawn, some walls draped with ivy, a fat oak tree. He said this was where he'd choose to live in Paris, if he ever had the money.

That evening—it was the first week of January, a scoured

winter smell in the air—Earl and Finny ate crêpes in a piano bar and listened to a man play Billy Joel songs for tips. Afterward, walking down the slope of the Rue de Maubeuge, they saw a prostitute who was clearly a man—though he was wearing heavy makeup and a fur boa—pick up a client in a business suit. The couple walked into an alley, whispering and laughing. The man behind Finny and Earl—who walked with a noticeable limp, and kept wriggling inside his overcoat, as if his clothes didn't fit properly—shrugged at the couple who walked off together. Finny laughed.

"You know, I like the way people are about sex here," Finny said. "They treat it like it's slightly funny. Which it is, if you think about it. I mean, in a certain way. I could get used to that."

"Used to what?" Earl said.

"Being here, I guess."

"Really? You could live here?"

"I think so. Why?"

Earl shrugged. "It's just good to know. Since I'm not sure where I'm going to be."

Finny felt a bubble of anxiety expand in her chest. What was he telling her? She looked at Earl, and caught a glimpse of the limping man behind them, who seemed unable to control his pace on the steep hill. He kept wriggling in his coat, as if he were trying to shrug it off. His feet made a quickening rhythm on the pavement—*du-duk, du-duk, du-duk*—and Finny thought of asking if he needed a hand.

But first she said to Earl, "You mean you think you might want to live here for good?"

"I'm not sure about for good," Earl said. "It's just, right now, I feel like I should be with my mom. She needs me more than my dad. He's got Poplan."

"But what am *I* going to do?" Finny burst out. "I can't drop out of school. I just started. *We* just started. Now you're telling me we're going to have to put it all on hold again?"

"I'm just saying everything's up in the air. We haven't even talked about being a couple. We don't even know if this is going to work out."

"What?" Just this morning she'd been planning their life together. Though now, and suddenly, like a thunderclap on a clear afternoon, another thought struck her. "You're not seeing other people, are you?"

"What do you mean?" Earl asked. Which told her everything she needed to know. She saw it in his face, in the scurrying confusion in his eyes, the familiar glow in his cheeks. She didn't need to push on, and yet, against every good instinct, she did.

"I mean," Finny said, summoning her old bluntness, "have you had sex with anyone besides me since we met at Judith's party? Is that clear enough?"

But Earl didn't want to fight anymore. "Yes," he said. "I have."

"Who?"

"A girl I knew from high school. Camille. It wasn't serious. I didn't realize I couldn't—"

"It's not about *couldn't*."

"You're on a different continent, Finny. I don't see how we can—"

But she stopped him. She felt the bubble of her emotion bursting, a hot flood in her lungs, and she said to Earl, "You can't do this to me. You *can't*, Earl. I can't live that way." She was practically screaming. They'd become one of those unhappy pairs who fought in the street—something she'd told herself they'd never be.

Before Earl had a chance to answer, though, they were interrupted. The limping man, whose pace had quickened even more, bumped into Earl with his shoulder. All Finny saw of him was his bristly jaw, like some overused hairbrush. At first, she thought the man was falling, but when she reached out to grab him, he tore her purse off her arm and started to run down the street, no longer limping at all. Earl was on the ground.

"Oh my God," Finny said, and leaned down to help Earl up. But Earl got up on his own. He started down the street, chasing the purse-snatcher.

"Hey!" Earl screamed. "Stop! *Connard!*"

"No!" Finny screamed at Earl. "Come back!"

But he wouldn't stop. The two men rounded the corner at full speed, and Finny had to run to keep up. Earl was still screaming at the man, and Finny wanted to tell him she didn't care about her purse. But Earl was too far away, and yelling too loudly to hear. She'd seen the look in Earl's eyes when he'd gotten up from the pavement, a kind of blind outrage, and she knew that nothing she could say would stop him. For the first time she'd glimpsed something reckless and impulsive in Earl, a piece of him she hadn't known existed, and she found she was running as much away from that vision, those raging eyes, as toward Earl and the thief.

"Please!" Finny shouted. "Please come back!"

She followed them down the street, Earl chasing the thief, yelling, *"Mais quel connard!* Thief!" and Finny calling after Earl to come back. All of a sudden the man darted into an alleyway off the Rue de Maubeuge. "Don't!" Finny yelled to Earl. But Earl kept going, into the dark side street. Finny had no choice but to follow.

When she made the turn, it was at first difficult to see anything. She could hear Earl's footsteps ahead of her, and more distantly, the thief's. She kept running toward Earl, her own feet smacking the pavement. None of them were screaming any longer; there were no other people around to hear them. The alleyway must have been made of cobblestone, because Finny's feet kept getting turned between stones, her ankles strained. But she was a good runner; she wasn't going to give up. She passed a dumpster. She could make out the shadows of the men ahead of her.

Farther down the alley was a small light, encased in what looked like the head of an old-fashioned streetlamp. It illuminated an orb of alleyway, and Finny could see that the street dead-ended just beyond the light, at a cement wall with some graffiti on it. She knew now that they were headed for a face-off with the criminal. Earl was gaining on him. The man was slowing his pace. There was nowhere else to run.

The man was nearly to the lit-up spot at the end of the alleyway. Finny heard the *tok-tok* of his shoes on the pavement, echoing in the tight space between the buildings. Then, suddenly, the man opened a door that Finny hadn't seen, next to the light, and ran inside.

"Okay!" Finny screamed to Earl. "Okay!" It was all she could think of, and she was too out of breath to get out more than a couple of syllables. She figured that here Earl would have to give up.

But instead Earl yanked open the door that the man had disappeared behind. He ran into the building, still chasing the man.

Finny was coming up on the lighted patch herself. She considered giving up, going back. Why risk herself? But she couldn't leave Earl that way. It would be too much to bear if something happened.

The door was painted red, and it squealed when Finny opened it. Above the lintel there was a tiny sign, which you couldn't have seen if you hadn't known exactly where the door was. In bright red letters the sign said: *La Maison des Fantaisies*. A brothel, Finny thought as she went inside.

The first room she entered was square, about the size of the dining room and kitchen in her mother's house. The room was painted the same red color as the sign outside the door. It was very warm, and there was an odor of burnt almonds. There were chairs and couches of various shades of red, and six or eight people were sitting reading magazines like in a doctor's office. The people—both men and women, which made Finny question her idea that it was a brothel—looked normal enough. They wore dresses and suits, leggings for the women, scarves or earmuffs piled in the seats next to them. One man had on a hooded sweatshirt with the hood up. Finny saw Earl darting past a door on the far side of the room. He was yelling *"Au voleur!* Stop!" but no one seemed to be paying attention.

Finny ran through the room, then down the hallway Earl had run down. The hallway was painted white, and had a tile floor like in a hospital. Here there was an astringent smell, as of bleach or some cleaning product. Earl ducked into one of the rooms, where he must have seen the thief running, and in a moment Finny followed.

But when she got there, Earl had already moved on. It was a cream-colored room that seemed to be set up like a classroom. There was a portable blackboard in one corner, stocked with chalk and erasers. A woman in a too-large tweed coat stood at the board asking questions of a very small man—he could have been a midget—who was seated at a child's desk in front of the board. The man was wearing a schoolboy outfit, short pants and a starched shirt. He had a satchel tucked under his chair.

"Quelle est la capitale du Nicaragua?" the woman questioned, tapping a piece of chalk against the board so that the tip crumbled.

"Bogotá?" the man answered.

"Non!" the woman screeched. Then she slapped the man across the face.

"Huit moins cinq," the woman said.

"Quatre?" the man answered.

"Non!" the woman screamed, and knocked him out of his chair with a blow to his shoulder. The woman looked pleased by the result. *"Vous êtes un mauvais élève!"* she said. She kicked him in the ribs, and he moaned with satisfaction. Neither glanced in Finny's direction. A pickpocket would never get caught here, in the confusion of these rooms.

Finny ran back into the white hallway. She heard scuffling in a room ahead of her, to the right. "Earl?" she said. "Earl!" She was afraid he'd caught up with the thief, that they were fighting, or maybe the criminal's friends were attacking Earl. She just wanted to get him out of this crazy place. She ran to the room where the sounds seemed to be coming from and she opened the door.

Inside the room, a very pale young woman was lying naked on the floor, her arms and legs splayed like she was making a snow angel. She lay on a rug the color of a fresh wound. She was almost sickly thin, her stomach sucked under a pronounced rib cage, her arms as brittle-looking as twigs. She had something like bread crumbs dusting her chest. And next to her—the part that Finny could hardly believe—was a live swan. The bird was enormous, probably four feet tall with its neck extended, and brilliantly white. Its eyes were encircled with black, giving it an angry, determined look. The swan craned its neck and nibbled a few bread crumbs off the woman's chest. It didn't walk toward her, and Finny saw that there was a small collar on the bird's neck, fixing it in place. When the swan's beak touched the woman, she giggled like a small child.

"Oh my God," Finny said, hardly believing what was happening. She felt as if she were in some kind of demented dream.

She stumbled into the hall. For a moment she did nothing but breathe, look at the floor, and try to collect her thoughts. And then she looked up. Ahead of her, unbelievably, she saw the man who had taken her purse. He was running toward her. She realized now that he was only a boy—fifteen or sixteen, maybe—with some early stubble on his chin. The limping must have been an act he'd perfected to catch people off guard. He had wide, excited brown eyes, and he was breathing heavily, as if he couldn't get enough air.

"It's okay!" Finny called to him. It was the first thing that

popped into her mind. She didn't even realize that he probably didn't understand her, probably spoke only French. She
just had the urge to comfort, assuage.

In a second Earl was coming around the corner, chasing
the boy. They were both headed right toward Finny. She
didn't know what to do. Should she put her arms out and stop
the boy? Or scream, which didn't seem to have much effect in
this place. Or should she just let him go and grab hold of Earl,
make him stop? But before she had a chance to make a decision, the boy kicked open a door in the hallway marked *Sortie*
in green letters, and ran into the street. Earl chased him.
Finny followed Earl.

Outside it was cold again. She was in another alley. This
was a different door from the one they'd come in. Finny saw
her breath in the cold air. Ahead of them was a major street,
Finny wasn't sure which. There was some kind of street fair
or celebration going on. A swarm of people moved along the
road, which was too crowded for cars to pass. Music was
playing, drums and horns. The people were eating sweets out
of paper bags. Finny knew that if the boy made it to the
crowd, they'd never find him.

But here something else unexpected happened. The boy
simply tossed the bag onto the pavement, waved to Earl with
both hands as if to say, *Okay, you got me*, then jogged off into
the crowd. Finny let out a long breath, relieved that their
chase had ended. She almost hoped the boy had taken some
money for his trouble.

Earl was picking the bag up off the pavement when Finny
reached him.

"What just happened?" Finny asked. She was out of breath.
Sweat ran down her sides. Her throat was dry and felt
scratched, like she'd swallowed a mouthful of steel wool.

"That was the craziest place I've ever seen," Earl said as
they stood there in the alleyway, panting. Then Earl said,
"Check to make sure everything's there."

Finny opened the bag. Money, keys, credit card, passport. It was all there.

"Nothing's missing," Finny said.

Earl had a small grin on his face.

"Jesus," Finny said.

"What?"

And then she punched him in the chest.

"Ow," Earl said.

She punched him again.

"*Ow*. What?"

"Don't do stupid things," Finny said. She was nearly frantic, with worry and rage and panic and relief. "You hear me? I don't care about my goddamn purse."

"I thought you'd want—"

"*Don't*," Finny said.

"Okay," Earl said. "I'm sorry."

And then, in spite of herself, she was hugging him, crying into his chest, her tears soaking the spot where she'd punched him a moment ago. "Oh my God, Earl," she sobbed. "I can't even tell you. I thought he'd kill you."

Earl was stroking her hair. "I did it for you, Fin. I thought it's what you'd want."

"I know," Finny said.

They didn't talk any more about their living arrangements during the trip, or about how exclusive their relationship was. It was as if their conversation before the purse-snatching hadn't happened. Finny was just so relieved that everything was okay, that they were alive and safe and enjoying each other's company. They were affectionate with each other, stopping to kiss in the street, touching the other's arm or hand when they were sitting in restaurants. In the mornings their love was, if anything, more vigorous, more urgent.

Then, out of nowhere, the trip was over. Finny was packing

for her plane ride back to the States. She was flying into New York, because it turned out to be cheaper on the return trip. She was going to stay with Judith for the night. Earl cried while Finny was zipping up her bag, and then Finny started to cry. They had dinner with Mona in a restaurant she liked near the Gare du Nord. Ate foie gras, since it was a special occasion. Finny liked it spread on toast, with the little fruits and nuts they gave her. They drank too much wine, and Mona began to cry, too, more heavily than anyone, saying how much she'd miss Finny and how she hoped she would come back soon. Earl had to comfort her. Finny understood that he must not have shared all the details of his social life with her. He hugged his mother and looked at Finny over her shoulder, signaled that it was time to be heading back. Like a father with a young daughter.

In the morning Finny and Earl woke up early so they could roast in bed together for a while before she left. They didn't even have sex. They buried their faces in the warmth from the other, and already Finny was feeling lonely and a little depressed. Would life always be this way? she wondered. Would there ever be a place she could rest?

They took the train to Charles de Gaulle. They had breakfast in an airport café—some cold coffee and an American bagel that tasted like rubber. Then it was time. Finny strapped on her backpack, kissed Earl goodbye. Told him she had a great trip. Nothing about the future.

Just before she walked away, Earl said, "Wait." He took an envelope out of the bag he was carrying. "Here," he said, handing it to Finny. She could see his hand was trembling. "Promise you won't open it till you get on the plane."

Chapter **24**

My Father the Collector

The summer before I went to college and left my dad behind in the little brown house with all our animals, I only wanted to read. I had a job in a restaurant, yanking the cold guts out of chickens and rubbing the fat birds down with oil till they shined like prizefighters, hauling crates of dusty soda bottles up a shadowy staircase that squealed with the anguish of a dozen thwarted safety inspectors; but my real life began when I switched on my bedside lamp and read things like: "All happy families are alike; each unhappy family is unhappy in its own way." Every minute I spent listening to my manager holding forth on the latest addition to his entertainment center and the virtues of layaway financing ("Nothing this month, Chris. Not a *single penny*!"), I was counting in my mind the pages I had left to read that night to stay on pace in *The Grapes of Wrath* or *Candide* or *The Republic*. Every evening I would come home exhausted and smelling like an herb garden, pluck some leftovers from the refrigerator, and lock myself in my room with Shakespeare and Dostoyevsky and Marx. It was late when I'd emerge to find my father at the kitchen table, reading selections from his favorite book, the Guinness book of world records, to our parrot, Romulus. He would ask

me if I could guess how long the longest toenails in the world
were. . . .

Finny looked out the plane window for a minute while she
tried to absorb this opening paragraph of Earl's short story,
"My Father the Collector." At first, she couldn't help hearing
the words in Earl's voice, like he was reading them to her. She
knew she was looking for the little trail of footprints that
would lead her to some hidden enclave, some stashed-away
part of him. But she couldn't enjoy the story that way. So she
stopped doing that; she just read.

It turned out the story was about a lonely teenager in his
final year of high school, preparing to leave his even lonelier
father behind in the house they'd shared for Chris's entire life.
There was no mother in the picture. Chris's father wants to
have some fun with Chris, the way they used to, so he takes
him out to an abandoned field they'd sometimes visited, to
toss an old easy chair down a big hill, just for the fun of it, to
watch it break. But when they throw it, the chair ends up hitting a stray dog they hadn't seen, and Chris sees his father
break down, devastated over what he's done:

> And I stood there, not knowing what to do or say, because
> what could you do or say in a moment like this? I watched my
> father in the dirt just crying and crying. It was like he'd been
> broken; he couldn't stop.

And then the scene shifts. Chris is leaving home, saying
goodbye to his dad. There's a brief epilogue that takes place
some time later, after Chris's father has died, where Chris
comes back to the house to sort through his father's things:

> I made a last pass through the rooms, checking under beds
> and in drawers for anything left behind. I knew my father was

a great collector, and he could have hidden his findings anywhere.

For some reason, this line touched Finny. She finished the
story in tears.

More than anything, her first reaction was relief—relief
that it was good. After the time in the Italian restaurant when
Earl had gotten upset because Finny had said she'd enjoy
reading his work even if it wasn't good—after that, she'd been
worried that when she did finally read one of his stories, it
would be silly, or too intellectual, or like a million other stories twenty-year-olds write. Finny knew that Earl wouldn't
settle for that. She could tell, by their conversation in the
restaurant, that this was more than a hobby or a dream for
him. And she was excited to see he had real talent to back it
up. Confused as their relationship was, he was someone special.

Finny was amazed that the story didn't "sound" like Earl at
all. She caught pieces of Earl in Chris—the way Earl had used
his experience working at the restaurant in France in Chris's
summer job at the restaurant, the complicated relationship
with a quirky father, the little brown house—but Chris was
not Earl. Earl had transformed himself, used the scraps of his
own experiences to build an entirely new character, to show
something about the world. In a way, it was like how Earl
built up the people around him, making them livelier, more
interesting, better than they ever could have been on their
own.

And it was funny. She'd been afraid that because Earl took
writing seriously, his *writing* would be overly serious. But
there were several parts where she laughed out loud. She
thought the father's character was marvelously strange. The
story was about something sad, though Earl hadn't been
afraid to make it funny. This made sense to Finny, because
her view of life was very much that way—that it was both hi-

lariously funny and devastatingly sad. And only if you saw both things could you ever have a realistic idea of the subject.

Of course there was a part of her that wondered where Finny was in all this. She'd had a small hope that the story would be about a love affair, about a couple being apart for many years and then coming back together, that the beautiful heroine would be based on Finny Short, that Earl would reveal all his hidden hopes about their future—but Finny quickly jogged herself back to reality. She knew that life was more complicated than that, and that a story wasn't some kind of secret message. She was touched by how sensitively Earl had captured certain aspects of his own life. In the end, Finny was happier that it was a good story *not* about her than if it had been a bad story about her. She concluded that Earl was a talented writer, and that, as in other areas, he just needed time to grow, to see more of the world, to practice.

"What's that you're reading?" the woman next to Finny asked when Finny put down the story. She was a small woman, though she wore a large hat with flowers sewn into the brim. She had a squawking voice. As she looked at Finny, the woman had an expression of intense concentration on her face, and Finny knew she was gearing up for a long chat.

So Finny did something she'd never done before. She put a hand to her own throat and mimed like she was being choked.

The woman looked confused. Finny tore off a square of paper from the bottom of Earl's story, took a pen out of her purse, and wrote, *I just had an operation on my throat. Can't talk. Very sorry.*

When she showed it to the woman, the woman made a *hmph* sound and turned back to the movie she'd been watching, as if it were Finny's fault for getting the operation right before this opportunity to have a lovely discussion. Finny felt bad, but she just didn't want to talk about Earl's story with the woman. When the stewardess came down the aisle for drink orders, Finny had to point at what she wanted.

Finny was going to be staying at Judith's apartment in Morningside Heights for the night, then heading back to Stradler on Sunday morning. Her classes began on Monday. It was fine with Finny that she'd be staying in Morningside Heights, since she figured she'd be more comfortable there than at the stuffy Beresford. Finny was looking forward to having a night away from the intensity of her time with Earl, her swirling thoughts about him, and Judith always provided a good distraction.

At a little after eight, Finny arrived at 110th and Broadway, where Judith lived. The street was quiet: only a D'Agostino grocery store and a Chinese takeout were open. Judith had mailed Finny the extra set of keys, in case she wasn't home when Finny got in, so Finny opened the lobby door, then took the elevator up to the ninth floor.

The hallway here was much less adorned than the one at the Beresford. There was a gray carpet that was coming up at the sides. The walls had at some point been white but were now scuff-marked from top to bottom because of all the people moving in and out with bulky furniture. One ceiling light was out, and another blinked on and off, giving a disco effect to the hallway. At the door of 9G, Finny knocked, just in case Judith was in the middle of something. No one answered. Again Finny knocked.

This time the door swung open, revealing Judith with tears streaming down her face, saying, "Oh God, Finny, I'm so glad you're here. Please help me."

Chapter **25**

In Which the Potential Becomes Actual

Judith's apartment had an odd design. The entrance faced one wall of a small hallway that led to the right of the front door. To the left of the door was a bedroom that Finny guessed was Judith's because of the Thorndon bumper sticker tacked to a corkboard. The room was tidy: a bed, a desk, a dresser—not unlike Judith's half of the dorm room at Thorndon. There was a frilly blue and white quilt on the bed, and a framed poster of the Edward Hopper painting "Nighthawks" on the wall, which Finny had seen in about a dozen dorm rooms at her school already. Finny wondered if Judith still had the black clothes. She guessed not.

"I didn't mean for it to happen," Judith was saying to Finny. Judith was still crying as she led Finny down the hallway. Finny dropped her bags here, not knowing what else to do with them. The wooden floorboards creaked under their footsteps. "It just got out of hand," Judith said.

They passed the kitchen, a pretty room with large yellow tiles on the floor, a little window with long white curtains.

"What's going on?" Finny asked. "Is someone hurt?"

"No," Judith said. "At least, not yet. By the way, your brother's here."

The hallway turned to the left. There was a *Bonnie and Clyde* poster on the wall, Warren Beatty holding Faye Dunaway by her hips like he was about to kiss her. There was a bathroom on the left. The hallway ended at a glass-paned door that was now shut, a curtain pulled over the glass panes so that you couldn't see into the room. Finny heard voices behind the door. She couldn't make out what they were saying over her own creaking footsteps. But then someone yelled, "And I'm not fucking around anymore!"

Finny recognized Prince Hollibrand's voice.

Judith turned the door handle, and the door squealed open. The scent of Prince's cologne filled the room, like a thick sweet mist. Finny sneezed.

The first Finny saw of the room was a large television parked in front of a window that looked onto the apartment building across the street. There was a gray sofa facing the television, and beside the sofa's arm was Prince, standing with hands on hips, that vein bulging in his temple. He looked every bit as chiseled and exaggeratedly handsome as he had when Finny met him. Only now his forehead was damp, as if he'd been under some strain. His skin reflected the overhead lights.

At first Finny couldn't find Sylvan in the room at all. Prince took over the space, the way a large, colorful painting can dominate a gallery. Finny wondered if Sylvan had found a way out while Judith was getting the door.

"Hey," Finny said to Prince, hoping that the presence of a near-stranger might calm him down.

"Hey," a voice said. But it wasn't Prince's. It came from behind the gray couch. "Sylvan?" Finny said.

Sylvan stood up from behind the couch and looked at Finny. His eyes were unfocused, and he had a strange, excited smile on his face. Finny noticed a trickle of blood running from his mouth.

"Hey, Fin," Sylvan said. "How was your trip?"

"What are you doing?" Finny asked.

"I just came to visit." He was speaking casually, as if they were all sitting around over drinks, discussing their evenings. "It was supposed to be a surprise." He laughed. "I guess it was." Here Sylvan's head dipped forward, and he had to brace himself on the back of the couch to keep from falling. He looked dizzy, and a little sick. He was paler than normal, and his hair flopped in a funny way over his ears.

"It was a big misunderstanding," Judith said now. "I didn't invite anyone, but they both showed up a little while ago. I was planning on spending the night with you, Finny."

Finny nodded. She didn't like the way Judith was appealing to her sympathies now, as if this were all just some funny scheduling mistake. But it wasn't the time to tell Judith what she thought of the situation, of Judith's part in it.

"I don't like this," Prince was saying to Judith. "This is the *old* me. This conflict is bringing out the worst in me, Judith. Could you please *take care of this*?" He spoke these last words through clenched teeth, and to Finny it sounded like a threat.

"I'm not leaving," Sylvan said, and shrugged.

"It might be better if you did," Finny said. She figured Sylvan was the best person to reason with. "It'll give you all a chance to cool down. I'm sure you can talk it over once you settle down."

"Oh, I'm settled," Sylvan said. "I'm down."

She wasn't even sure he knew what he was saying. His head was drooping again. His eyelids began to close, like he was falling asleep. Then he started awake, and his eyes came wide open.

"Are you okay?" Finny asked him.

"This guy pushes pretty hard," Sylvan said, nodding at Prince. "I might have knocked into something. And I have to admit I had a few drinks before."

"You're drunk," Judith said.

"I don't like to do this," Prince said to Finny about the pushing. " 'An outside enemy exists only if there is anger inside.' "

"I think there's some anger," Sylvan said.

Prince stepped around the sofa arm and pushed Sylvan to the ground. He landed behind the sofa with a loud thump, and Finny worried that he'd hit his head again. She sneezed twice in the cloud of Prince's cologne.

"Judith," Prince said now, "could you *please* tell this ball boy to leave?"

"Stop it, Prince," Judith said. "Stop hurting him, okay?"

"What am I supposed to do?" Prince said, turning to Judith. "I come over to my girlfriend's apartment and I find some scrawny little penis-pulling matchstick trying to get into her bed."

"You're mixing metaphors," Sylvan pointed out. "How can a matchstick pull a penis?"

"I never invited you over, Prince," Judith said. "And I never said we were exclusive."

"I'm hurt by this," Prince said.

"So am I," Judith said.

"Me, too," Sylvan added from the floor.

"I would just leave, Sylvan," Finny told him. "I really think it'll end up better for you in the long run if you're the one to walk away."

"I thought of that," Sylvan said, using the back of the couch to help him onto his feet again. He'd wiped most of the blood off his chin, and now there was just a faint red smear around his lips, like he'd been drinking tomato juice. "But it's like I told you over Thanksgiving—I need to stand up for myself. I love Judith." He turned to Judith. "I love you," he said again, for her benefit.

"You don't have to do this," Judith told Sylvan. "It's silly."

"It's worth having this brute beat on me a little if it helps you see how much you mean to me."

"I'm not a *brute*," Prince said, and then shoved Sylvan again. It was enough to set Sylvan off balance, but soon he regained his wobbly stance behind the couch.

"That's it, Prince," Judith said. "If you touch him one more time, I'm not talking to you. Ever. I mean it."

"You hear that, you giant penis?" Sylvan said to Prince.

"*Stop* it," Finny told her brother. "Stop taunting him." She walked over to Sylvan and put an arm around him, intending to help him out of the room. She wanted to get him away from the apartment, away from Judith and Prince and this absurd scene.

But as they walked toward the door, Sylvan hesitated in front of Prince. For a moment he looked like he was going to toss out another insult. But instead he spat on Prince. Finny couldn't believe it. The spit splashed Prince's face, and a small gob of it landed in the crook between Prince's neck and his shoulder.

"What the *fuck*?" Prince said. His hand flew to where the spit had landed, as if he were swatting a mosquito. When he felt the wet spot on his shoulder, Prince's eyes widened. And then, without warning, he swung at Sylvan.

Finny saw the blow coming. Her perceptions were startlingly precise. It was as if she were watching the world at some slower speed than normal. She saw Sylvan duck out of the way. She heard Judith gasp. She saw Prince's enormous fist coming toward her temple.

A shock of lights, a roaring noise, a moment of explosive pain.

Then everything went black.

Chapter 26

Finny's Convalescence

She woke with the cloying scent of Prince's cologne in her nostrils. Her head felt like it was locked in a vise. Where was she? She heard some banging, someone in another room calling, "Medics! Open up!"

Then she recognized the gray sofa she was lying on, the television across from it. She saw a woman folding laundry in the apartment across the street. Sylvan was standing above her, saying, "Fin? Are you okay, Fin?"

"Bags," she said.

"What?" Sylvan said.

Finny was trying to say that she'd left her luggage in front of the door, and that was why whoever was banging couldn't get in, but she couldn't seem to form the words. She was too tired. And it felt like someone was tightening the vise on her head.

"Where's Judith?" Finny asked.

"She took the gorilla into the other room. He kept saying he was sorry, and wanted to stay and make sure you were okay. But Judith wouldn't let him. You scared us, Fin. You were out cold for a second."

"You're an idiot," Finny said to her brother.

"I'm sorry, Fin," Sylvan said. "I really didn't mean for any of this to happen. I just didn't want to back down. I'm sure that's what he expected."

Finny sneezed. "Ow," she said.

Then the paramedics burst into the room. There were two of them, wearing orange vests. One of the men had a large belly and, in his tightly cinched belt and vest, had something of the look of a trussed turkey. The other man was extremely thin, his face pocked like an orange peel, and his vest was so large on him that it billowed when he walked. They were rolling a metal gurney that clanked in the small room. Judith was behind them, trying to peer around at Finny.

"Okay," the fat medic said in an unnecessarily loud and deliberate voice, like he was speaking into a megaphone. "Please tell us where the body is."

"You're okay," Judith said, seeing that Finny was awake. Finny could hear the relief in Judith's voice. Then Judith told the medics, "It's not a body; it's my friend."

"I'm fine," Finny said to the paramedics. "Really." But when she tried to sit up, the screws tightened on her head and she had to lie back. "I just need a minute."

But the fat paramedic shook his head. He was bald, and had a triangle of orange hair on his chin, a silver hoop earring in his left ear. "You are coming in to get checked out," he informed Finny in his megaphone voice.

Then the thin one piped up, "Why don't you just give her a minute, like she said?" His voice was actually deeper than the heavy man's, and there was a sandpapery roughness to it. He had a couple days' worth of stubble on his face, and his black hair looked unwashed, oily.

"You better go in and get checked out," Sylvan said to Finny. "You look like you might be getting a black eye."

"Then the toughs won't mess with me at Stradler," Finny joked.

"Seriously, Fin," Judith said from behind the paramedics, "you should go."

"All right," Finny said. "Sure. Why not?" Her head really did hurt.

"Okay," the fat paramedic said, "we will *now* load you on."

"Do you have to announce everything?" the thin one said.

They helped her onto the gurney, and started to push her out of the room.

"It's not going to make it around the bend with her on it," the thin man said. "I can see from here. There's no point."

"The procedure is to try once before we make adjustments," the heavy one said.

"You and your procedures," the thin one said.

As predicted, the gurney couldn't make the turn with Finny on it, and the men had to pick it up and tilt it.

"We will first tilt to the left," the heavy paramedic said.

"You need to tilt right," the thin one said. "The hallway turns right."

"The procedure is left first, then right."

The thin man rolled his eyes. The gurney swayed. Finny felt seasick from being tilted left then right. But she didn't complain. She didn't want to make the tension between the two medics worse.

"You need to go *with* the turn," the thin one said. "It's obvious."

"Obvious is not necessarily right," the fat one said.

"Are you crazy?" the thin one said. Then he looked at Finny. "Will you verify this guy is crazy?"

"Sticks and stones may break my bones," the fat man said.

But the thin one went on, "Everything is rules, rules, rules. We had an old lady say sayonara the other day because fat Joe over here insisted Broadway was the shortest route to the hospital. Who takes Broadway through midtown in an ambulance? What are we, a fucking tour bus?"

"Sticks and stones," the fat man repeated.

Finally they got Finny around the turn and out of the apartment. Prince must have left, because Finny didn't see him during her trip to the elevator. Downstairs, as they were loading her in the ambulance, Sylvan said, "I feel so awful, Fin. That punch was meant for me."

"Don't worry," Finny said. "I think I can take a punch better anyway."

"I'm sorry!" Judith called to Finny as they were closing the ambulance doors.

"Don't take Broadway," Finny told the paramedics.

Finny spent a woozy night in the emergency room, getting poked, prodded, x-rayed, and blood-tested, shuttled from room to room. She was exhausted because of her long flight, the time change, and probably also the punch she'd taken. She fell asleep a couple times, and they had to wake her, telling her it was bad to sleep if she had a concussion. During the night she found her mind playing tricks on her because of the fatigue. At around two in the morning she realized you could rearrange the letters in *concussion* to spell *unconscious,* if you added a *u*. This seemed an urgent discovery, and she wanted to alert one of the nurses to it, but no one seemed to care. She attempted to notify a doctor, but this only caused him to believe she was *suffering* from a concussion, which prompted more tests, more hours of sleeplessness.

Then the doctor told her everything was okay. He let her sleep a couple hours in a hospital bed. In the morning, when they discharged her, Sylvan and Judith were in the waiting room, their eyes bloodshot from lack of sleep. Judith's hair was coming out of her ponytail, and her face looked puffy, as if from crying. Or maybe because she'd taken a nap.

"You're *not* going back today," Judith said.

"I have to," Finny said. "I have class tomorrow."

"It's one day," Sylvan said. "I'm sure you can make it up."

"People are adding and dropping classes anyway," Judith said. "Just come back and rest. I called my parents and told them you had a fall last night. They said we could stay at their place. It'll be more comfortable for you. Come on."

"Do it," Sylvan said. "For your health, Fin. I'd feel awful letting you go back the way you are."

"Are *you* coming?" she asked her brother. She wasn't sure what his status with Judith was.

"I have to go back to Boston," Sylvan said. "But call me tomorrow, okay?"

Finny agreed—more for her brother's sake than hers, since she could see how guilty he felt.

Sylvan got on the subway. Judith paid for a cab to the Beresford for Finny and herself.

Inside the apartment at the Beresford, Judith told Finny, "You're going to stay in my room. Don't even *think* of protesting. You can go rest now. My dad is at his bridge game, and my mom is at a meeting. I'm going to get your bags from my apartment this afternoon, and I'll be back by the time my parents get home for dinner."

Finny lay down in Judith's bed, and the next thing she knew it was five-thirty in the afternoon. She got up and looked outside at the darkened streets. Then she picked up a copy of *The New Yorker* magazine Judith had in the magazine rack by her bed. Finny started to read a long article about spices, thinking of Laura's boyfriend, Gerald, but almost immediately her head began to feel like it was getting screwed into the vise again. She put down the magazine and lay back on the bed. In a minute she picked it up again, and read the first line. *Gregory P. Mark is not the sort of man you'd expect to find in a police lineup.* But then Finny's vision went blurry, and she felt like her brain was about to pop out of her skull. Several more times she tried to read, and each time the headache came back worse than before. Finally she dropped the magazine back into the rack.

There was a light knock, and the bedroom door opened. "Hey," Judith said. "How are you feeling?"

"Weird," Finny said. "I can't read anything."

Judith looked concerned. "Well, maybe you should eat something. You haven't eaten all day. My parents said we could have dinner early."

"Sounds good," Finny said. "How's my eye look?"

"Not bad, actually," Judith said. "I'll give you some cover-up."

Judith's parents turned out to be not at all as Finny had imagined them. Because of Judith's stories of her father's trysts, Finny imagined a well-dressed, confident man. But the man who appeared in the dining room was neither of the above. He had a hunched posture, pinched features, and spindly legs that emerged like stalks from the running shorts he wore to the dinner table. He was soft-spoken, with a funny nervous way of talking. He asked Finny how she was feeling, and before she could even answer, he began to mutter a train of almost unintelligible courtesies: "Yes, yes, very good, thank you, nice to meet you, great, great, how lovely . . ."

Mrs. Turngate, on the other hand, was an authoritative woman. She had short dirty-blond hair, which she kept in a spiky style Finny was used to seeing on high schoolers. Judith had clearly inherited her wide jaw from her mother, whose flat cheeks and sharp little nose appeared the way a ship's hull might look if it were approaching you while you were swimming. Mrs. Turngate's features were like a clumsier version of Judith's, and they put Finny in mind of how thin the line is between beauty and strangeness. Mrs. Turngate wasn't a particularly large woman, but next to the stuttering Mr. Turngate, she was impressive with her straight posture and jutting bosom. She wore only gray clothes. Even her shoes and earrings were gray.

"Charcoal is my shade" she said when Finny commented on how well-coordinated her host's clothes were. "Once I learned that, I have never worn anything else."

Finny thought it was an odd look, but of course didn't

question this distinguished woman's tastes. Mrs. Turngate asked Finny again how she was feeling after her fall, and Finny said she was doing much better. The cover-up that Judith had applied completely masked the bruise.

They sat down to dinner, which Judith's mother had prepared. She said that it was meat loaf and vegetables, though to Finny it appeared as several indistinguishable gray mounds. They ate with heavy silverware, off the kind of china that feels light and breakable but that Finny knew to be very expensive. Their dining table—made of a glossy chocolate-cherry-colored wood—must have been twelve feet long, but they sat gathered in the middle, like animals huddled in the cold. Behind Mrs. Turngate there was a foggy modern-looking painting that heavily featured the color charcoal-gray. Instead of wine, everyone was served a glass of cranberry juice in the gold-rimmed glasses Finny had seen at the party where she'd run into Earl.

"My dad thinks cranberry juice is the cure for everything," Judith said.

"Panacea," Mrs. Turngate said.

"Delicious," Finny said.

Mr. Turngate followed this up with a string of polite comments: "Good, good, a lot of benefits, glad you like it, please come any time, help yourself, thank you, thank you, enjoy—"

"Linus," Mrs. Turngate said to Judith's father. "Let the girl eat."

"Yes, very sorry, beg your pardon, please enjoy, so nice to have you . . ."

For a while they ate in silence. Judith hardly looked up from her plate. It was not the glamorous butlered meal Finny had envisioned when Judith had described her parents to her in their dorm room at Thorndon. Though none of them seemed uncomfortable with the silence. Finny guessed this must have been the way they spent all their meals.

Once they were finished with their food, and they had all

drunk their cranberry juice, a stage of the meal Mr. Turngate observed with particular interest, Mrs. Turngate said to Finny, "I hear you are acquainted with our future son-in-law."

"I believe so," Finny said, wondering what Mrs. Turngate meant.

"Mom," Judith said. "I'm not seeing Milton anymore."

"What are you talking about?" Mrs. Turngate said. "Linus, did you hear that?"

"Yes, yes, well, takes time, all for the best, whatever makes you happy, your mother knows best. . . ."

"What?" Judith said to her father. "I don't understand what your point is."

But her father looked positively terrified at being caught between Judith and her mother. He shrugged and turned the color of his cranberry juice.

"He's been behaving badly," Judith said to her mother about Prince. "You wouldn't approve of it, Mom."

Mrs. Turngate raised her eyebrows. "The Hollibrands are a good family," she said. "I don't know what you mean by 'behaving badly,' but you know I've always thought highly of Milton."

"I know you have, Mom. But you hardly know him."

"I know his family."

And she left it at that. They asked Finny a few polite questions about her trip, and then everyone scattered to different rooms of the apartment.

Later that night, as Finny was brushing her teeth, Judith came into the bathroom and said to her, "I hope you know I'm never talking to that asshole again, after what he did to you. He can't control himself. I didn't want to get into it with my mom, since she's best friends with Prince's mom and they have this idea we're going to end up together and live in the Hollibrands' house in Westhampton. But it's bullshit. I just want you to know that, Fin. I think Prince is an animal, and as far as I'm concerned, we're done. I told Sylvan that last night, while we were waiting for you."

Finny rinsed her mouth and spat into the sink. "Then what's going on with you and Sylvan?"

"We're going to see how it goes," Judith said.

"That's great," Finny said. She looked at the skin around her eye, which was purple and a little puffy.

"Thanks," Judith said. "I thought you'd approve."

"Sylvan is an ass," Finny said, "but he comes from a good family."

Judith laughed at that for a long time, and Finny was glad to see Judith had a sense of humor about her mother.

"What's the status with you and Earl?" Judith asked.

"I think 'seeing how it goes' about captures it."

Finny tried to read the spice article again before she went to sleep, but the headache came back and she had to put the magazine down.

"What is it?" Judith said. They were sharing the bed, the way they had when Judith came to visit Finny in Maryland all those years ago.

"It's my head. Every time I read."

"I think you should take a few days here, Fin. Till you feel better. It won't make a difference. Actually, they never discuss anything the first week anyway."

"Maybe you're right," Finny said, because her head really did hurt, and she worried about traveling if she couldn't read any signs. Plus, what use would she be at Stradler if she couldn't read?

"I'll give it another day," Finny said.

"Perfect," Judith said, and they went to sleep.

Chapter **27**

Several Significant
Developments

"*Mas*ter of the *house*, *kee*per of the *wine* . . ."

Finny was blinking out of sleep as she heard the words to this familiar song. The digital alarm clock by the bed read 10:48. "Holy shit," Finny said.

"And good morning to you, too," said the voice that had been singing a moment before. Carter stood by the bed where Finny lay, his skinny body clothed in a brightly patterned child-size argyle sweater, fitted jeans, and red sneakers. His hair was mussed in the careful way Finny had seen it at Judith's party, swooping over his right ear and sticking up like a cowlick in back.

"I hope you're ready to make something of this afternoon," Carter went on. "I've been assigned to entertain you while Judith is in class, and my call time isn't till four-thirty, so you better be ready to enjoy this goddamn beautiful day."

"How's it going, Carter?"

"Lovely, darling," he said, bending over to smack a kiss on Finny's cheek. "By the way, that's a nasty bruise you've got."

"It's from a nasty bruiser, as you might have heard."

"Bits and pieces."

"Can you give me a few minutes to make some calls and brush my teeth?" Finny asked.

"Well," Carter said, with an exaggerated air of frustration, "if you must. Then I suppose I could be persuaded to investigate the contents of the Turngates' well-stocked liquor cabinet. But just know that you are responsible for driving me to such extremes of behavior."

"You're going to drink at eleven in the morning?"

"New York is a tough, tough city," Carter said, and then left in search of the liquor cabinet.

Finny found her phone card in her backpack. She was delighted to see that her headache wasn't as bad when she read the instructions on the back. The first call she made was to Sylvan. The machine picked up, so she left a message. "Hey, Syl, it's your sister. I decided to stay at Judith's an extra night because my head was bothering me yesterday, but I'm feeling better today and will probably head back tonight or tomorrow. Judith told me that you and she are talking, and you have my, uh, blessing, I guess. Take care. Bye."

The next call was to Dorrie. She told her roommate that her flights had been delayed but that she'd be back soon and not to worry.

The third call was a bit longer distance. She knew she shouldn't be making a bunch of overseas phone calls to a man who wasn't even her boyfriend; but still, Earl would appreciate knowing she'd gotten in safely. And she needed some kind of closure to her trip. She figured a phone call might put the proper seal on it. She decided not to mention anything about Prince and the black eye, because what would be the point? Angry as she was, it would be impossible to explain to Earl that she also felt bad for Prince. Luckily, Earl picked up.

"Earl, it's Finny."

"Hey!" Earl said, in the excited way he always greeted Finny's voice. "How was your trip?"

"Good," Finny said. "Listen, I'm on a phone card and can't

talk long. But everything's fine. I ended up staying at Judith's an extra night and couldn't get away to call you. The main thing is, I want to tell you I read your story and I loved it. It's so good, Earl."

"I can't tell you how great that is to hear, Finny."

There was a pause, as if neither of them knew where to go from here. Then Earl said, "I guess I have one other piece of news, which is that I sent the story to a literary magazine in the States and they accepted it. They're going to publish it in their next issue."

"Oh my God!" Finny screamed. "That's amazing! Congratulations!" She was astonished. A publication! Earl was only twenty years old.

"I'm glad you're excited, too," Earl said.

"Earl, you're really talented. I always had a feeling. But it's great to see it. What's the magazine called?"

"You've probably never heard of it. It's called *Aftershock*. But it's a pretty good one. They sell it at Barnes & Noble. I'm even getting a check."

"The first of many, I'm sure," Finny said.

"Well, thanks. I hope so."

Another pause. Like a little wall, an obstacle they had to hop over every time they spoke to each other. Why had Earl placed this barrier there?

She was about to tell Earl how sad it made her, when he said, "I know you have to head off, but I wanted to tell you that this stuff with the publication made me think about some things. And there's something else I want to talk to you about, when you have—"

But here the line clicked off. The phone card was out of minutes.

"*Damn*," Finny said. She picked up the phone and began to dial Earl's number again, breathless for his news. But then she hesitated. She wasn't sure what Judith's parents would think of getting a call to France on their phone bill—even if they could have afforded several thousand calls to France. She decided she'd get a phone card while she was out with Carter, and call Earl back as soon as she returned to the apartment. She'd have to wait to call her mother, too, but Finny wasn't so worried about that, since Laura hadn't even asked the exact day when Finny was coming home.

"Okay!" Finny called to Carter after she'd washed up and gotten dressed. "Let's go!" She'd found the cover-up and applied it again over her bruise.

"Yoorall better," Carter said when he saw her. She smelled what she thought was gin on his breath.

"You on the other hand."

But Carter didn't pay attention. "I'm ship shop," he said. "Shape soap." He shook his head. "Shipshape. There we go."

And they went.

"You're probably starving," Carter said when they were on the street. "If you were subjected to Bonnie Turngate's cooking last night."

"So you've tried her food?"

"Murder. Absolute murder. She could sap the flavor out of a bottle of hot sauce."

It was a bright, cold afternoon, the branches of the trees along Central Park clacking in a gusty wind. The fresh air seemed to have diminished the effect of the alcohol on Carter. A man in a spandex running suit trotted past them, his breath clouding. Sunlight glittered on the cars. Finny could smell nuts roasting in a cart sitting at the entrance to the park.

"I guess I am kind of hungry," Finny admitted.

"Then there's only one solution," Carter said. "Chinatown."

They took the train to Canal Street, then walked down the Bowery. Finny had never been to this part of the city before, with the roasted ducks hanging in the windows, the bags of Asian sweets lined up in the grocery stores, the smell of fish and frying oil in the alleyways. She recognized a number of products from the cache of Asian food Poplan had kept in her room at Thorndon. Though now Finny could see what the fresh fruits looked like: pods of jackfruit in their bumpy cases, lychees, soursops, and kumquats. A man ran out from one of the restaurants and dumped a bucket of fish heads into a drainage grate by Finny's feet.

"Brunch, anyone?" Finny said.

Carter took Finny to a Vietnamese restaurant he knew in a little horseshoe street off the Bowery. The restaurant was in the windowless basement of a somewhat run-down building, a festive shade of red paint flaking off the walls, and when they walked in, they were the only customers. A bored-looking staff eyed them as they made their way to a table. When the waiter came, he nodded to Carter, as if he knew him, and Carter told him the dishes they wanted in Vietnamese.

"No *banh xeo*," the waiter said, shaking his head.

"Come on," Carter said. "Just one."

"Let me check," the waiter said.

"We go through this every time," Carter said when the waiter had left. "I ordered this Vietnamese crêpe, which is the best thing on the menu, but they hate to make the batter, so they only serve it to Vietnamese people and tell everyone else they're out of it."

The waiter came back. "One order," he said to Carter. "All we have."

"That's great," Carter said, and the waiter left again.

The crêpe turned out to be delicious. It was a thin, crisp pancake made from coconut milk and eggs, folded like an omelet around pork, shrimp, and bean sprouts. You wrapped lettuce leaves and fresh herbs around it and dipped the pieces in a salty translucent sauce.

Over the crêpe Finny said to Carter, "I feel bad intruding on Judith's parents."

"Why?" Carter said. "I'd do it if I could. In fact, since your little run-in, I've been considering getting punched by Prince just so I could live it up in the Turngate apartment for a week."

"Yeah, but I feel like I'm in the way. Judith used to tell me, when we were at school together, that her father lived a certain kind of lifestyle."

"You mean like cranberry juice and bridge games?"

"No, I mean like extramarital affairs. She said he liked to bring his girlfriend home in the middle of the day."

For a second Carter stared blankly at Finny, his mouth open, displaying a half-chewed bite of *banh xeo*. Then he erupted in laughter. He laughed so hard he nearly slid out of his chair, and the waiter who had served them shook his head, as if he'd wasted the crêpe on someone who obviously wasn't fit to eat it. Finny wasn't sure what was so funny about this— she actually found the situation with Judith's parents a little sad—but by the time Carter had seated himself again, he was gripping his stomach as if in pain.

"I'm sorry," Carter said. "It's just—I've never heard anything so ridiculous. Could you imagine Linus Turngate conducting an affair?" Then Carter launched into a brief imitation of one of Mr. Turngate's polite litanies: "Yes, thank you, please only lick my left testicle, yes, very nice, do you want it harder? Good, good, very nice to see you, do I make you horny? Very good, bye."

Finny laughed, but she couldn't help feeling a little hurt, too, as if Carter were making fun of Finny's credulity as much as Mr. Turngate's trains of courtesies. "Where did she get that idea, then?" Finny asked Carter. "Why would she say all those things?"

Here Carter stopped laughing. He watched Finny for a moment, the way a doctor might before delivering a poor prognosis to a patient. "There's something you have to understand, Finny," Carter said. "About Judith."

Finny recalled the talk she'd had with Poplan about Judith, way back at Thorndon, a talk that had begun similarly. And the discussion with her brother, only a few weeks ago, where Finny had seemed to be the expert on Judith.

"Sometimes she says things she doesn't really mean," Carter went on. "It's not that she's lying, exactly. It's that she likes a certain kind of attention. So she'll tell you things to get that attention. I can imagine that when she was fifteen, and just learning how a penis fits into a vagina—excuse the language—she would be coming up with all kinds of theories about whose was fitting into whose. But I can tell you for a fact that your brother was the first guy she slept with, and that Prince Hollibrand was the second. There was one other, once, as a payback to Prince. But that's the whole sexual history of Madame Turngate, whatever else she might lead you to believe."

Just as Carter was finishing his speech, the waiter arrived with their entrées, a steamy beef noodle soup and a plate of panfried beef cubes with lettuce and tomato and a sauce that had flecks of pepper floating in it. The waiter removed the plate that had held the crêpe, still shaking his head, as if over the loss of a close friend. Both Carter and Finny stared at the new food without moving.

"This is delicious," Carter said, pointing at the beef cubes. "You dip them in that sauce, which has lemon juice, salt, and pepper. You're going to go crazy over how it tastes."

Finny looked at the food for a few seconds. She knew that Carter was bringing attention to it to save Finny from the embarrassment of her mistaken assumptions about Judith. How many people could Finny get wrong? Suddenly she wasn't hungry anymore.

"Do you think we could take some of this home?" she said.

"Look," Carter said, "I love Judith, Finny. The same way you do. She's magnetic. She's big and beautiful and smart. And even though I'm as gay as a poodle in a peacoat, I'd still probably bone her once, the same way I would Judy Garland or Andrew Lloyd Webber—just to say I did it.

"But I don't trust a word that comes out of her mouth. That's why I'm always on her case. Especially around you. Because I know she's playing it up for you. She thinks you see her as some gorgeous, vivacious, cosmopolitan woman, and she likes to think of herself that way."

"I suppose I am taken in by some of that," Finny admitted.

"As you damn well should be," Carter said. "Just know it for what it is."

"Okay," Finny said. "Thanks."

"Now eat some of this *bo luc lac* before I smack you." Carter smiled. "As a friend."

Finny called Earl when she got back to the Beresford, but there was no answer. What had he wanted to say? What could be so important that he hadn't told her while she was in France? She decided to hang up before the machine came on, so she wouldn't waste her phone card minutes. She was considering calling her mom but instead decided to pack. It was only four. She could still get back to Stradler at a reasonable hour.

Carter had left for his catering job, which he'd described as "seven hours of getting fucked in the ass in a way even *I* can't enjoy." Finny liked Carter more and more the better she got to know him. He was dramatic, she was aware, but he really was very good at knowing people for what they were, as he'd put it. It was like he couldn't help saying what he thought, no matter how discordant. Which reminded Finny of the way *she* used to be.

When she was done packing, Finny tried Earl again. It was almost eleven o'clock Paris time, and she couldn't imagine where he would be at that hour. The phone rang once, twice, three times.

Then someone picked up. *"Allo?"* It was Earl.

"Hey," Finny said. "I'm sorry I lost you before. My phone card ran out of minutes."

"It's okay. I figured."

"I tried you before, but you weren't around. You said you wanted to talk to me about something?"

"Yeah. It's actually why I wasn't in my room. I've been discussing it with my mom all evening."

"What is it?"

There was a pause. "I think I'm ready to leave Paris," Earl said.

"What do you mean?" Finny asked.

"I mean, I think it's time for me to move away. When I was in New York, I realized I could do it. Live there. And getting this story published was a huge thing for me. It gave me confidence that I'm on the right track. I've been thinking about what we talked about the other night. About how things would be with us. And you're right. I don't want to be apart either. I want to be with you, Finny. Completely with you. I want to move to the States for you.

"I told my mom tonight, and actually she took it surprisingly well. She's really happy for me. She loves you. She said she would come visit us. I think she'd be okay. I know this is the right thing. I mean, if you're still up for it."

It was all coming so quickly, Finny thought. She didn't know what to say. *Happiness* wasn't the word to describe what she was feeling. More like *shock*.

"Finny?" Earl said.

"Yeah."

"Well? What do you think? I thought you might have a response."

"I think it's the best news I've ever gotten."

She could hear Earl exhale on the other end of the line. She wanted, as she had many times before, to reach across the phone wire and touch his face. "I'm so happy to hear you say that," he said. "I just have this whole idea of how our life can be. I'll rent an apartment near your school. I can get a job somewhere close by, at a restaurant or something. I'll write in the mornings. We'll have every night together. I'm really ready for this."

"It sounds like a dream," Finny said. "I couldn't imagine anything better."

"You don't have to imagine," Earl said. "This is real."

The rest of the afternoon, though, passed somewhat like a dream in that Finny had the sense she was floating through it, or maybe above it, not totally there. When Judith returned, Finny told her she was going to head back to Stradler that evening. She said she'd love to spend the night with Judith but that she wanted to get to school and see her grades before her mom got them. And Finny was still deciding between two English classes, so she wanted a chance to sit in on both. She told Judith to thank her parents again for letting her stay, and she hoped she hadn't been too much of a disturbance.

To Finny's surprise, Judith didn't protest. She said she understood. She said it was probably time for her to get down to work, too, but that she'd call Finny over the weekend. She said that Finny's face looked much better, not puffy at all, almost completely healed.

At Penn Station, Finny decided she'd take the Amtrak back to Philadelphia. She didn't think she could stay focused enough to make all the transfers on the New Jersey Transit. She was reeling. Visions of her new life kept flashing in her mind: roasting in bed with Earl; the two of them reading together at night; meals at their little kitchen table; Earl coming back from work, exhausted but happy, falling into her arms. She was giddy with the possibility of it.

On the train she opened her bag to find some reading material, something to slow her spinning thoughts. She pulled out a magazine, and realized it was *The New Yorker* she'd been reading at Judith's parents' apartment. She must have packed it with her things by mistake, she'd been so absentminded.

She opened the magazine back to the article she'd been reading about spices, deciding she'd give it one more go. She was still having trouble focusing on anything, but she got the gist of the first page, about how spice importers grind up all kinds of things and try to pass them off as rare spices. How they set up phony identities and business records. How they pull in gullible investors.

Finny flipped the page and began to read about a man named Gregory P. Mark, who went by various pseudonyms and who owned a company called Futurecook. The company sold extremely rare spices that you could buy only in very small quantities. As she read, she felt a twitchy uneasiness in her chest. She knew she was going to have to ask her mother some questions.

Dorrie wasn't in the room when Finny got back. Finny dialed Laura's number the minute she put down her bags. She'd read the article from start to finish on the train. She knew what she had to say.

"Hello?" Laura said when she picked up.

"Mom," Finny said.

"Hi, sweetie. How was your trip?"

"It was fine. Great, I mean. But, Mom, I need to ask you a question."

"Finny, it's unfortunate, but I must tell you that people will take offense if you don't begin a phone conversation by asking how they are."

Finny sighed. She knew her mother must have been in particularly good spirits, since she was back to offering her opinions as objective truths. She'd hardly done that since Stanley had died. Finny assumed things must have been going well with Gerald, which was a good sign. It meant that maybe Finny was wrong about him, or possibly that Laura hadn't been pulled in yet.

"I'm sorry, Mom," Finny said. "It's just that, what I have to ask you is pretty important. Really important, actually."

"Oh," Laura said, and Finny could imagine the blank look on Laura's face. It was an expression she'd begun to have after Finny's father died, and it seemed to reappear whenever bad news was about to be dropped.

"I wanted to ask you what's going on with Gerald," Finny said.

"Oh," Laura said again, her voice much lighter. "Is that it? Well, it's going fine. Thanks for asking, sweetheart."

"No, Mom. I mean— I guess I'm not being clear. I was just reading this article. I think there might have been a part about Gerald in it."

"He's a very well-regarded businessman. People like that have articles written about them all the time."

"But this article, Mom—it wasn't about business, exactly. It was about stealing. It was about a scam that a guy named Gregory P. Mark is pulling. He has a bunch of fake names, and I realized that Gerald's name, Kramp, is P. Mark backward."

"Such a funny coincidence," Laura said.

Finny knew the way Laura had of pushing uncomfortable details to the side, smiling that undefeatable smile of hers, waving at drivers who wanted to kill her.

"It's not a coincidence," Finny went on. "I'm pretty sure it's Gerald. Your boyfriend, Mom. Everything in the article sounds like him. I think he's a criminal."

Finny went on to explain how Gregory P. Mark's fraud operated. He would attend events that were often populated by single women with money—widows or divorcées. Lectures in the middle of the day, museum tours, wine tastings and cooking classes—these were the places he'd locate his targets. He would start casually, simply striking up a conversation, and then usually the conversation would continue in some more private setting—a bar or a restaurant. It would be like a date, except Gregory would spend most of the time talking about his business ventures, how successful they were, how much money he'd made from certain deals. If the woman was impressed, he would keep seeing her over time, and talk more and more about his new project: spices. He offered samples, even began to interest some local specialty businesses in his products. The spices were really just combinations of other store-bought spices you could buy for almost nothing. But Mr. Mark hired a food scientist to blend them, and then they gave the spices exotic names. He could sell a small jar for a hundred dollars. He'd even fooled some very knowledgeable tasters. All of which gave the women he dated more confidence in him. They practically insisted on backing his company.

The problem came when the products were tested. The business would fall flat at that point. But Gregory P. Mark was always able to wriggle free of legal ramifications, claiming he'd been duped by his suppliers. He'd shake his head and manage to walk away with a significant amount of the money the investors had given him, which he'd remove to various offshore accounts. He'd pulled the scam in a dozen states. And he was yet to be indicted.

Finny read to her mother a short passage in the *New Yorker* article she thought would be particularly persuasive. " 'The key to Gregory Mark's success as a con artist is not his business savvy or the initial results he supplies; it's his manner. He seems on the surface to be easygoing, almost inhumanly flexible. He's known for using the catchphrase that has become his business motto: 'Whatever you want.' Yet one of his former business associates remarked, 'The funny thing is, it always turns out that Greg gets whatever *he* wants. It's just that you'd never suspect that such a fool could be swindling you. And once you do, he's out the door with your money.' "

Finny stopped there. She waited for her mother to comment. She hadn't wanted to present her case quite so forcefully, at least not yet.

"Mom?" Finny said.

No response.

"Mom, are you there?"

In a moment Finny heard a choked sobbing on the other end of the line, and she realized her mother must have been muffling her crying with a towel or a pillow.

"I gave him everything," Laura said. "Everything I had."

"Oh God. Listen, Mom," Finny said. "You have to listen to me. Mom?"

"Mm-hm."

"I think the worst thing you can do now is tell Gerald you suspect anything. The second you do that, he'll be in another state and you won't even be able to find his phone number."

"So what do I do?" Laura sounded so much like a child that Finny had to remind herself she was speaking to a fifty-six-year-old woman.

"We'll think about it," Finny said. "I know someone who might be able to help."

Chapter **28**

The Spice Trade

There was one nice surprise for Finny when she started classes the next day: she'd received A's in all her classes the first semester. Well, almost all. An A– in her philosophy class, which was a nagging disappointment. But she realized she was being a perfectionist. She hadn't studied quite as hard for the philosophy final, since she'd found the contemporary philosophers such a chore to read. She'd done pretty well for her first semester, especially considering all the disruptions. She let herself be proud.

Her roommate was hardly around at all anymore. Finny had to practically hunt Dorrie down to give her the Eiffel Tower key chain she'd bought for her, and the package of chocolates from Angelina. Dorrie thanked Finny profusely but seemed distracted. She was spending every night in Steven Bench's room. *Please screw him already*, Finny wanted to tell her roommate. *You'll probably go to hell for thinking about it so much anyway, so why not at least enjoy it?*

Finny's eye had healed well enough by Friday that she hardly needed any cover-up. She called Sylvan, told him she was going to visit Laura, that their mother was having some "relationship issues." Sylvan asked if she needed help, but Finny said she'd be fine. On Friday afternoon she took the Greyhound to Baltimore. Her mother offered to pick her up at the station, but Finny insisted she'd get a cab. She wanted to keep her head clear for what she knew would be a difficult evening with Gerald Kramp, and a car ride with her mother was not the best way to stay focused. Plus, Laura had her own part to prepare.

Finny arrived at Laura's house a little after six. She had just enough time to shower and get dressed for dinner. The dinner guests were due at seven o'clock.

The first to arrive were Poplan and Mr. Henckel, whom Finny greeted with enthusiastic hugs, thanking them for coming. Poplan kept her gloves on when she shook hands with Laura, who was in no state to deal with hand washing requests. Finny had hashed out the plan with Poplan; she knew Poplan would be meticulous about the details.

Mr. Henckel, who hadn't been informed that there was a plan at all, was delighted with the invitation to such a "distinguished party," as he put it. He was dressed in what Finny took to be his finery, which consisted of a black suit in the boxy zoot suit style, complete with a gold watch chain and a jaunty wide-brimmed hat, with pictures of playing cards, dice, and poker chips on the band. The outfit gave him something of the air of a retired pimp. Fortunately, he removed the hat at the door, revealing his usual comb-over style, except that Poplan seemed to have slicked down the unruly flap of hair that sometimes flopped over his ear when he fell asleep.

Poplan, who was of course well apprised of the plan, had sought to match Mr. Henckel's exuberant choice of attire with one of the many fashions available in her extensive wardrobe. She'd chosen a 1920s-style blue and gray flapper dress, with black stockings and a feathered hat that suggested less the era of gangsters and prohibition than some sort of wildlife conservation project.

When she saw Finny's response to the hat, she said, "What? You asked us to dress up."

"And you did," Finny said.

"Well," Poplan said, removing the hat to display her cropped gray hair, "I wouldn't expect everyone to have such an acute sense of fashion as *I*."

They all said how glad they were to meet one another, and Laura thanked them for coming to help her. Finny had simply explained that Poplan and Mr. Henckel were her former teachers. Finny's mother seemed shaky and a bit nervous, so as they made their way to the kitchen, Finny touched Laura's arm and told her to relax, that it would all go fine.

Mr. Henckel, on the other hand, seemed remarkably at ease in these new surroundings. Whereas he had been so shy before when meeting people, it seemed that having Poplan around emboldened him. He strutted through the house, one hand jammed in the pocket with the watch chain, the other swinging by his side, snapping lightly to the beat of his footsteps. In the dining room, he looked through the doors at the lion sculpture and said, "Nice lion."

"Thank you," Laura said.

Mr. Henckel greeted this response with a nod, and several rather suave smile-frowns.

"So," Poplan said to Finny and Laura, "I take it our friend isn't here yet. Are we all ready?"

"The stew is done," Laura said. "And Gerald knows he's bringing the spices. He said they would be some very special ones, since I told him we're having guests."

"That's great, Mom," Finny said, patting Laura again on the arm. "And I put some white wine in the refrigerator."

"Wonderful," Poplan said.

Gerald arrived at seven-fifteen, completing their party. He greeted everyone with hardy handshakes, flashing his brilliantly white canine smile. He was dressed in what looked to Finny like an expensive gray suit, with wide lapels and polished shoes. He'd brought with him several small pouches of spices, and Laura directed him to the stew she'd made, inviting him to "go to work."

"I'd love to know what you're putting in there," Poplan said.

"This first one is called *baharat*," Gerald said. "It's a blend of some of the finest spices from around the world: Sri Lankan cloves, Saigon cinnamon, Spanish paprika, Chinese tien tsin peppers. Only the best of each, of course."

Then he sprinkled another pouch of spices over the tray of vegetables Laura had roasted in the oven.

"This one is a very rare wild oregano found only in the mountains of Greece. They call it *rigani*, but that name refers to all the wild Greek oregano. This one is particularly hard to procure." He flashed another blinding display of teeth.

"They must be very expensive," Poplan said.

"You wouldn't believe it," Gerald said.

"Is it hard to make sure they're pure?"

"It is," Gerald said, pleased that Poplan was so interested in his business. "But of course I do all the work to make sure these are one hundred percent. That's why people are willing to pay the big bucks for them." He nodded at Laura, and they exchanged smiles.

"Let's have some wine," Finny said. "What do you think, Gerald?"

"Whatever you want," he said. Then, in a moment, he added, "Though I do happen to know that a nice bottle of medium-bodied dry white wine is the best thing to bring out the subtle flavors in these exquisite spices. But that's neither here nor there. You should enjoy them any way you like."

"Then I guess we should have white wine," Laura said. She seemed to have relaxed once Gerald had come in the door. She delivered the line convincingly.

"That's fine with me," Gerald said. "I just want you to be happy. All of you."

In the *New Yorker* article, Finny had read how Gregory P. Mark liked to have everyone drinking when they tried his spices, especially if the tasters were experienced. They were more easily impressed that way.

Finny popped open a bottle of wine and poured everyone a glass. She was especially careful to pour Mr. Henckel a full glass.

Mr. Henckel drank swiftly, which prompted an extended confession about a time when he had been touring with the "dance" troupe and the dancers had persuaded him to join them onstage for a "disrobing routine."

"I was actually quite successful at it," Mr. Henckel added, his free hand still swinging and snapping by his side. "Though I must admit that certain aspects of the male anatomy undergo changes when subjected to sudden cold." Here he began to sweat, and had to momentarily cease his snapping in order to mop his forehead with the handkerchief he always carried with him.

Poplan was shaking her head at him, but everyone else seemed to be amused, to Finny's relief. Even Laura smiled, though she probably hadn't absorbed a word of the story. Gerald was laughing especially hard. He must have thought Mr. Henckel was joking.

Finny opened another bottle of wine and poured glasses all around. Gerald was drinking much more slowly than he had at Thanksgiving, probably because he wasn't sure how distinguished Poplan's and Mr. Henckel's palates were, and he wanted to make sure their perceptions were adequately dulled.

In another few minutes they sat down to dinner. Laura and Finny served the stew, which was made from braised lamb and potatoes. Laura had roasted all kinds of vegetables to go alongside: carrots and beans and broccoli and tomatoes. Mr. Henckel was helping himself to a third glass of wine by the time everyone was ready to eat.

They all took a bite.

"Delicious," Finny said.

"Astounding," Poplan said.

"You see?" Gerald said. "Spices."

Laura nodded supportively.

After a few more bites they looked to Mr. Henckel for his opinion. He had also been nodding at people's comments, but Finny could see that his eyelids were drooping. In a moment he slumped forward, his nose only inches from his stew. Poplan had told Finny the wine would have this effect. Plus, he would sleep for longer, which would give them the time they needed.

"Oh my God," Poplan said now, looking alarmed.

"What?" Gerald said. "What is it?"

"He's— Oh, Jesus," Poplan said.

"Is he okay?" Gerald asked.

"What's happening?" Finny said.

"Should I call an ambulance?" Laura asked.

"Do you know what's in the stew?" Poplan asked.

Laura listed the ingredients: lamb, tomatoes, olive oil, salt, pepper, flour, onions, wine, brown sugar, balsamic vinegar, potatoes.

"Yes!" Poplan shouted. "Go! Go! Call an ambulance! Tell them he could die."

Laura dashed out of the room.

"Why?" Gerald said. "What's wrong with him?"

"He's got very serious food allergies," Poplan said. Her military bearing suited this situation well. She appeared like the sort of person who could be calm but firm under extreme pressure.

"To what?" Gerald said.

"The two things he absolutely can't eat," Poplan said, "are nuts and marjoram. Marjoram makes him pass out. Nuts make his throat close up. If he eats them together, it's a lethal combination."

Gerald's face went white. He gulped several times, and looked around the room, like a trapped rabbit. Finny had read in *The New Yorker* that the most common counterfeit oregano used marjoram instead of the wild plant, and that ground nuts were often substituted for the more expensive ingredients in Middle Eastern spices.

"I never thought to mention it," Poplan went on, "since Laura told me what she was making, and of course your spices are so pure. That's why I asked you what was in them."

"I—" Gerald started, but he couldn't seem to get the words out. This was exactly what Poplan had guessed would happen. Gerald was a con artist, not a killer; he didn't want to be responsible for anyone dying.

"What?" Finny said. "What is it?"

"There might be some marjoram in there. And some nuts, too," Gerald said. His lips looked dry, and he kept moving them after he'd finished speaking, though no sounds came out.

"I don't believe this," Poplan said. "What are you telling me?"

"The spices," Gerald said. "They might not be a hundred percent pure."

"Do you know that for a fact? Because I need to tell the paramedics what shots to give him. Tell me exactly what was in what."

"There is marjoram in the oregano, and nuts in the *baharat*."

"But I thought you said it was pure," Finny said.

"I have a guy," Gerald blurted out. "Sometimes he mixes in some extra ingredients."

"Why does he do that?" Finny asked.

"He . . . Well— People can't tell the difference. It saves a lot of money."

"So you're lying to people?"

"Not lying," Gerald said. "Marketing."

Mr. Henckel's breathing was becoming heavier and more agitated. He was beginning to snore.

"Oh God," Poplan said. "His throat is closing up."

"What can we do?" Gerald said. "Please save him."

And then Mr. Henckel snorted awake. Gerald leapt out of his chair and put his hands over his face. Laura must have heard the snort from the other room, because she walked back in at that moment.

Gerald slowly took his hands away from his eyes and said to Mr. Henckel, "What's this? You're okay."

"I'm very sorry," Mr. Henckel said, shaking his head. Finny could see that he was embarrassed for falling asleep at the dinner table. "It just comes upon me."

"You have nothing to be sorry for," Poplan told Mr. Henckel.

"You did great," Finny said.

Mr. Henckel seemed satisfied with these compliments. He produced a winning smile-frown and resumed some light snapping under the table. Gerald, on the other hand, didn't seem to know what to make of these developments. He stood there, next to the dining room table, his mouth moving but no words coming out.

Then Poplan brought the tape recorder out of her pocket. It was a Dictaphone—the type lawyers use to dictate memos. Poplan held the recorder up toward Gerald and very carefully pressed the stop button. The click sounded loud as a gunshot in the silent room.

Gerald looked at the tape recorder for what felt like a full minute without saying anything. His lips just kept moving around words no one could hear. He glanced at Laura, then back at the Dictaphone.

"I read an article about you in a magazine," Finny said to Gerald.

Then Poplan continued. "We know you're in a lot of trou-

ble, so we're willing to offer you a deal. This tape has everything on it. You say exactly which spices you used, and admit
that they're phony. In addition," Poplan couldn't help adding,
"you sound like an ass."

Gerald must have been too wounded to even acknowledge
this final swipe, let alone fight back. "Deal?" he said.

"All we want is my mom's money back," Finny said. "You
give her the money, we give you the tape. If you don't give us
the money, we're making copies of the tape and sending them
to the police and *The New Yorker*. We know you've already got
a lot of money to run away with, so this is a pretty good deal
for you."

"Okay," Gerald said, nodding vigorously. "That's fine. I can
give you a check and we can go to the bank tomorrow and
cash it together. Or else I can try to get you large bills. What
do you prefer?"

Finny smiled, and said, "Whatever you want."

Chapter **29**

Back at Stradler

It was a funny thing. The plan had worked perfectly: Gerald had written a check for the exact amount Laura had invested in his business, and they'd deposited the money and handed over the tape; and yet Laura seemed less than thrilled with the results. She was of course very polite. Who would have expected anything less of Laura Short? She continued to thank Poplan and Mr. Henckel for everything they'd done. She said she'd be forever indebted to them. She told Finny she would never forget what a wonderful daughter she was, or how she'd come to Laura's aid in her time of need. And yet, Finny could tell there was something missing. There was a hollowness in Laura's voice when she talked about Gerald. As much as she spoke of her relief and the exhilaration of fooling the man who'd taken her money, Finny knew her mother was depressed.

Still, they parted amiably. Laura took Finny to the train station on Sunday, and Finny gripped the seat and smiled as her mother risked their lives numerous times in speeding traffic. Finny could see that her mother was hardly looking at the cars in front of her. It was like the way she'd stared at things after Stanley died, and Finny understood for the first time how afraid her mother was of the world that had betrayed her again and again. That startled, nervous look she'd always had when Finny misbehaved as a child—it was fear, Finny saw, fear that all the smiling and cleaning and organizing in the world couldn't stop life from making a mess.

Nonetheless, Finny and her mother hugged tightly in front of the doors of the train station, until a traffic cop asked Laura to move her car. "Thank you, sweetheart," Laura said, waving to Finny as she pulled away. The driver she'd cut off honked at her, and Laura waved at him.

Back at Stradler, Finny decided to walk to her dorm by the main path through the center of campus rather than by the side route she normally took. It was a gorgeous, bright, cold afternoon, and Finny liked walking along the tree-lined road, the bare limbs of trees twitching in the wind like bony fingers. There was something Finny enjoyed about these days before Earl arrived, about the anticipation, but also the loneliness itself, like she was standing outside a house where a loud party was taking place. She liked long walks on cold afternoons, dinners by herself, the comfortable solitude of her life at Stradler. She saw that it would be different when Earl was there, that she'd lose some of this private space.

And another very strange thought struck her now, as she was walking up the path that ended at the columned façade of Griffen Hall. She realized she'd be okay if she were by herself. Not that she wanted to be. But that she could be. She hoped and intended to spend her life with Earl now that he'd come around, but if for some reason it didn't work out, she knew she wouldn't risk all this again. She'd be content with her walks and her studies and the small joys a lonely person experiences: the scent of laundry, sunlight filtered through leaves, dinners with friends, rain tapping on a window. It was enough to get you through.

Behind Finny on the path was a tour group. The guide was telling a crowd of prospective students and their parents that the grounds of Stradler were a national arboretum. Then she began to talk about faculty-to-student ratios, graduate school statistics, majors and minors.

But someone must have raised a hand, because the guide stopped talking and the questioner asked, "Do you think that *rules* are well enforced on campus?" Finny felt as if someone had placed a cold hand on the back of her neck. She would have recognized that voice anywhere. Its screeching, broken sound had marked so many important transitions in her young life. She turned around, and was of course confronted by the familiar figure of her former principal, the Old Yeller, Mrs. Barksdale.

The woman's stringy orange hair was blowing every which way, over her face and ears, and the veins in her neck strained every bit as ferociously as they always had. Next to Mrs. Barksdale was the small, cowering, entirely bald man that Finny had only glimpsed in the photo on Mrs. Barksdale's wall; and a fifteen- or sixteen-year-old girl who looked like a younger version of the Old Yeller. Finny took her to be the daughter. Mrs. Barksdale held the small man by the cuff of his jacket, pulling him along, and the daughter had her arms crossed in front of her chest, as if to prevent her mother from taking any similar action against her.

Finny turned away as the tour guide was beginning her stammering answer to the Old Yeller's question. Finny wanted to talk to Mrs. Barksdale about as much as she would have liked to purchase a selection of spices from Gerald Kramp. Finny started off the path, across the lawn, hoping to avoid any contact with her former principal. But it turned out to be too late. "Hey!" a squealing voice called. "Delphine Short!"

Damn, Finny thought, and turned around.

Mrs. Barksdale had broken off from the tour group, which she claimed was fairly useless anyway. The bewildered guide was left to pull her diminished group on to the next sight. The Old Yeller was very happy to see one of her former students in such a good liberal arts school. She introduced her husband and daughter, who both nodded uneasily at Finny.

"Now, let me see," Mrs. Barksdale said. "You were very good friends with Judith Turngate, one of our shining stars, right?"

"The brightest," Finny said.

"And have you kept in touch?"

"I saw her last weekend."

"So she must have told you she was coming to Thorndon this weekend," Mrs. Barksdale said.

"Actually, she didn't mention it."

"There was an alumni basketball game last night. It was a big fund-raiser for the school. Judith came back because she had been so dedicated to the team while she was at Thorndon. I would have sent you an invitation, but I suppose you're not on the alumni mailing list since you didn't graduate with us."

"I guess not," Finny said. She did find it a little weird that Judith hadn't mentioned anything.

"In any case," Mrs. Barksdale went on, "I actually had the good fortune of spending a large portion of the evening with Judith, who seems to be doing fabulously as an English major at *Columbia*."

"That's wonderful," Finny said. She was running out of supportive comments to make about Mrs. Barksdale's run-in with Judith.

"But the greatest pleasure for me," Mrs. Barksdale said to Finny, and here her voice seemed particularly strained by the emotion she felt, "was to see what a fine young gentleman she has chosen as a life partner. That is the most important decision a young woman can make for herself—to find the right man to embark on the journey of life with." Here Mrs. Barksdale leaned over and planted a forceful kiss on the top of Mr. Barksdale's bald head. He seemed to cringe, just slightly, at her touch.

Finny was puzzled. "Was it the first time Judith's boyfriend visited Thorndon?"

Mrs. Barksdale was nodding. *"Fiancé,"* she corrected. "But yes, I had never met Milton Hollibrand before. Though he is just the sort of boy who can make a very ambitious, beautiful, and intelligent young woman like Judith Turngate happy. Because aside from cutting a very handsome and dignified shape, it seems he is also an intellectual. He is very knowledgeable about Eastern philosophy."

"Oh," Finny said. She felt as if all the words had been knocked out of her by the assault of Mrs. Barksdale's news. She wanted to leave, and excuses dangled in her mind.

But Sarah Barksdale beat Finny to it. "Mom," she said to the Old Yeller, "if we don't go to Griffen Hall now, we're never going to have time to see the athletic center."

"Very true," Mrs. Barksdale said. "You know that my good friend Miss Simpkin has always said that physical activity is as important as mental. And Miss Simpkin is never wrong."

Alone in her room, Finny's first impulse was to call Sylvan. She dialed the numbers for his room at Harvard. The phone rang once.

Then Finny hung up. She had to think this through. If she called Sylvan first, and for whatever reason Mrs. Barksdale's story was untrue or incomplete, Finny would have set a suspicion rolling in Sylvan's mind that she knew he'd never be able to stop. He'd always be looking out the corners of his eyes, checking phone messages and receipts. He'd never be able to completely trust Judith.

So Finny decided she had to call Judith first. She owed it to her friend to give her one chance to explain what happened.

Finny tried Judith's apartment in Morningside Heights, and Judith picked up on the second ring.

"Hey," Finny said, "it's me."

"Finny! I meant to call you this weekend. I wanted to see how you're doing. The time just got away from me. I guess the first week of classes isn't as tranquil as I thought."

"It's okay," Finny said. "I was actually out of town. Visiting my mom."

"Is everything okay?"

"It is now. She was having some trouble with her boyfriend. But I think she's gotten everything resolved."

"Good," Judith said.

"How are things with you and your boyfriend?" Finny asked.

"Actually," Judith said, "things are good. Though I'm not sure I'd call him my boyfriend yet. We're still working that out."

"Are you going to see each other anytime soon?"

Judith paused here. She must have been puzzled at Finny's sudden fascination with their relationship. Outside her door Finny heard some of the boys on her hall whooping and applauding. She knew what they were cheering for. There was a boy named Hector who pedaled his bike at full speed down the hall, then jammed on the breaks at just the right moment so that his front tire stopped only inches from the wall.

"Maybe next weekend," Judith said. "We're taking it slow, Fin. Anyway, what's the news with you? How are you feeling?"

"I'm feeling okay. My headaches are completely gone, and my eye looks almost normal."

"I'm so relieved."

I'll bet you are, Finny thought but didn't say. She remembered the rushed way Judith had said goodbye to her earlier that week, claiming she had to "get down to work." Finny now understood what Judith must have been working on, and the fact that she'd been doing it while Finny was still in her apartment, bruised and dizzy, made Finny practically shake with rage at Judith. She had probably gone to meet Prince while Finny had been out with Carter—or else she'd been planning to meet him that night. It came back to Finny how Judith had downplayed Finny's bruise that afternoon, saying it looked almost completely healed when Finny still had to apply about five pounds of makeup to hide it. Of course Judith would want to say that the bruise wasn't that bad, if she was planning on getting together with the animal who had caused it.

But Finny calmed herself enough to say to Judith now, "You're not going to believe who I ran into when I got back to school today—"

"Actually," Judith cut her off, "I can probably guess. Was it the Old Yeller?"

"How'd you know?"

"I was at the alumni basketball game last night. Actually, I just got back into town myself. I was going to tell you. Actually, that's why I was so busy this weekend. The Old Yeller told me she was going to visit your school with her daughter when I saw her."

Outside her door Finny could hear Hector pedaling back into place for another run. Finny saw that Judith must have been hoping Finny wouldn't bump into Mrs. Barksdale, that the Old Yeller wouldn't get a chance to mention whom Judith had been with.

All of this deception made Finny even angrier. She wanted to scream at Judith. But she knew she had to stay calm for another minute, so she simply said, "I heard you were with—"

But Judith stopped her. "Prince had been planning to come for months, Finny. He'd already bought his ticket. It would have been too awkward to change things."

"You know what else is awkward?" Finny said. "When you get punched in the face."

"It was a mistake," Judith blurted out. "Sylvan spat on him. It caught him by surprise. He feels awful."

"But that's not the point," Finny said. She wanted to ask Judith why she was defending Prince anyway, if she was supposed to be "seeing how it goes" with Sylvan. But instead

Finny focused her argument on the most important parts. "Why didn't you tell me you were going to Thorndon?"

"I knew you wouldn't understand," Judith said. "I couldn't expect you to, after what Prince did to you."

"That's bullshit," Finny said flatly. "You're lying to cover your ass, Judith." She felt like a shaken bottle of soda, ready to burst.

"Relationships are complicated, Finny," Judith said.

Somehow, this feigned wisdom, this apparent assertion that Finny was somehow naïve about the complexities of adult relationships—it was enough to blow the cap off Finny's rage. "What's complicated is being a *whore*," she told Judith. "Carter warned me you were a liar, but I was stupid enough not to believe him. You'd do anything to get what you want. You don't think about anyone but yourself, Judith."

Finny expected Judith to come right back at her with some biting line. But instead there was silence. And then, something about Judith's breathing made Finny realize she was crying.

"You're not going to tell him?" Judith whined into the phone. "Sylvan, I mean."

"Of course I'm going to tell him," Finny said. "I'm sorry I didn't tell him before. I had too much faith in you."

Here Judith seemed to break down. Finny heard her sobbing into the phone, her breath pounding the receiver. Then Judith said something Finny would remember for a long time: "Not everyone's as lucky as you are, Finny. Not everyone finds the perfect person. You don't know what it's like not to be sure."

Which was partially true. She was lucky to have found Earl, to be expecting him in a matter of weeks. Though *perfect* hardly captured their relationship up till now. Finny didn't want to quibble with Judith's word choice. Whatever Judith's difficulties, it wasn't an excuse for what she'd done.

Outside there was a squeal of brakes, a tense moment of silence, and then a small thud when Hector must have hit the wall. "I'm okay," she heard him telling the other boys. "I'm fine."

As they applauded, Finny hung up the phone, wondering if it would be the last time she'd ever hang up from a call with Judith.

Late that night she dialed Sylvan's number again, and he picked up.

"Sylvan, it's Finny."

But he cut her off. "I talked to Judith," he said. "I can't talk about this any more tonight, but I wanted to thank you for looking out for me, Fin. I'll call you sometime. When I'm up to it. I'm glad to hear you're doing better. Judith told me your headaches are gone."

"Did she tell you about Prince?"

"She told me she'd seen him. I was pretty disappointed."

"Okay," Finny said. She remembered the night she and her brother had held each other, crying over their father. She wanted to provide the same comfort for Sylvan now. She wanted to hold him and tell him it would be all right.

But she couldn't. She knew there was nothing she could say. So she said goodbye.

Chapter 30

Earl Is Coming!

Earl was due to arrive in the beginning of March, which gave Finny only five weeks. She was familiar with these kinds of weeks, though, which were so different from the kinds of weeks she'd spent in Paris. These kinds of weeks stretched on and on, like enormous glaciers, or perfectly calm seas, endless and unvaried. She knew it was simply a matter of waiting, of a certain number of breakfasts, lunches, and dinners, walks to the library, nights alone in her dorm room. She knew that everything was settled, tickets were purchased, goodbyes were being said; and yet, the distance between herself and Earl's arrival seemed monumental, nearly untraversable. Especially now that she wasn't talking to Judith, and Sylvan appeared to have dropped off the face of the earth.

Dorrie had moved in with Steven Bench. He had a single in one of the more desirable dorms on campus. Dorrie left some clothes and textbooks in the room, but she came back only a couple times a week, and she always knocked like she was a guest. When Finny saw her in the halls, it was like running into an old classmate, someone she'd known a long time ago. Dorrie was nothing if not polite. She always treated Finny like they'd been better friends than they were.

One afternoon in the middle of February, Finny and Dorrie

happened to both walk into the dining hall just as it was closing its lunch service. They hurried through the buffets,
pulling out random fried items and making quick mis-
matches of food on their plates. They sat down together at
one of the window tables. It was a gray day. They picked at
their unattractive food, talked in a scattershot way about
their lives, then moved to their relationships. Finny told Dorrie that Earl was coming in a couple weeks.

"That's fantastic!" Dorrie said. She had her hair pulled
back, which gave her nose a pointy look.

"I know. I can hardly wait," Finny said.

"Does he know where he's going to live?"

"I think in an apartment near here. Maybe in a building
with some Stradler students."

"Wow," Dorrie said, practically glowing over Finny's news.

"It feels like he's never going to get here," Finny said.

Dorrie breathed quickly from her nose—like a laugh, but
without smiling. "I know how that is," she said. "But you
should try to enjoy it."

"Enjoy what?"

"The waiting, I mean. You still have all these ideas about
how it's going to be and what you'll do together and the way
your place will look. But the thing is, it's never quite like that,
exactly. I mean, it's never the way it is in your mind. Not that
it's bad. I love living with Steven. But there's something different about being *in* it. It doesn't have the same sparkle."

"Do you love Steven?" Finny asked.

"Of course I love him," Dorrie said, with what seemed like
the first hint of annoyance Finny had ever glimpsed in her. "It
has nothing to do with whether I love him. There's other
things. I'm just telling you, there's something nice about having stuff to look forward to. Once you're there, you realize it's
just the same from here on out."

"Have you guys talked about what you'll do after Steven
graduates?"

Then Dorrie came out with it. "I'm pregnant, Finny." She must have been working around to it the whole time, but when she couldn't find a space for her news, she just said it, dropped it like a piece of unwanted mail. Finny understood Dorrie had no one else to tell.

"Does Steven know?" Finny asked.

Dorrie nodded. And then she burst into tears. "And we haven't even really had sex yet," she sobbed. "We thought we should wait." Dorrie lost herself to crying for a moment, though in between bouts of tears she described to Finny—in surprising detail—the medieval methods of birth control she and Steven had employed while technically not having sex. Finny felt terrible for her roommate. She wanted to ask her why she hadn't just gotten some condoms from the health center. But of course that advice would have been useless now.

"So, what are you going to do?" Finny asked.

"What do you mean?" Dorrie seemed puzzled by the question.

"I mean, about the baby."

"We're going to get married over spring break," Dorrie said, as if the answer were obvious. "I'm not going to get really fat until summer. Then I have to decide if I want to come back in the fall or take a semester off."

She started to cry again, and Finny found herself reaching across the table to touch Dorrie on the shoulder. This produced a fit of tears, and then a surprising statement from Dorrie. "I'm so happy about all this, Finny. It's just—this isn't the way I expected it to happen. I just have to accept that God's plans aren't always clear to us."

Finny took her hand back and put it in her lap. She wasn't convinced God had anything to do with it. Finny picked up a piece of fried zucchini and took a bite. The zucchini was soggy now, floppy as a cooked noodle, and it left a puddle of oil on the plate. Finny put it down and wiped her hand on a napkin. She wasn't sure how to respond to Dorrie.

"How does Steven feel about all this?" Finny asked.

"He seems to be taking it in stride," Dorrie said. "He said we could get an off-campus apartment next year, if it'll make things easier for me."

Or him, Finny thought. But she said, "That's nice."

Dorrie nodded. She looked out the window, at the gray day. Something seemed to have caught her eye, but Finny couldn't see it.

"For a second," Dorrie said, still looking out the window, "right when I found out, I wondered if I wasn't making a huge mistake."

"About what?" Finny said, hoping Dorrie would say, *Steven* or *Having a baby when I'm nineteen*.

But Dorrie shrugged. "I don't know," she said, and turned back to her meal. She plucked a piece of lettuce out of her salad bowl with her fingers and ate it. "That's the thing," she said. "I don't know what my problem is. I think it's just the hormones making me like this."

"Time to go!" one of the dining hall staff yelled at Finny and Dorrie. Finny knew the man. He'd come around and bang on the tables if you didn't get up.

"Well," Finny said. They bused their uneaten food to the conveyor belt that would carry it back to the clattering kitchen.

"I'm sorry," Finny said to Dorrie when they were walking to the door. It was the best she could do.

"It's okay," Dorrie said. "I'm just being stupid. It's all a gift."

"No, you're not," Finny said.

But Dorrie didn't seem to hear. They walked out under the heavy sky, going separate ways.

Then March came. The day of Earl's arrival was warm, and something about the sudden change in weather made Finny feel as if spring were decidedly here. The air smelled of grass.

Cross-country runners trotted across campus in shorts and T-shirts, and girls in tank tops laid down blankets on the stretch of lawn Stradler students called "the beach," in front of Griffen Hall. Finny knew it was too early for this weather, that it had to be a false spring, but still, it brought hope.

And then, just as Finny was heading out to meet Earl, taking her keys off the desk so she could lock the door behind her, the phone rang.

She picked up.

"Hello?" Finny said.

"Finny, it's Earl."

The moment she heard his voice she deflated. He was supposed to be on the plane. How could he be calling her?

"I have some sad news," he went on.

"What?" she said. "What is it?" She could already feel the wave crashing down on her.

"My mom. She's in the hospital."

There was a pause, in which Finny knew Earl must have been trying to collect himself.

"What happened?"

"She tried to kill herself," Earl said.

It turned out that Mona had been more upset about Earl's leaving than he'd let on. He'd wanted to convince himself that she could make it on her own, yet she'd cried most days, once she knew he'd bought his ticket. Often the fits would strike her out of nowhere. They'd be sitting at a meal, or watching a movie, and all of a sudden she'd just crumble. It was like watching her collapse, Earl said, the way she started to tremble, tears spilling from her eyes. She had become so dependent on him; she didn't have anyone else in Paris. Her doctor was a psychiatrist in a state hospital, and he called her prescriptions in from his vacation home in Nice.

Plus, Mona would never leave France. She'd moved there

in desperation, fleeing her personal and familial problems. And now she was too scared to go anywhere else. She'd never held such a stable job as the one in the hair salon.

Some days she told Earl she'd be okay, that he should live his life, and yet she could hardly get the words out before she was practically shivering with grief. As he told Finny about it, she heard Earl begin to cry himself.

"I always thought she might do something," he said. "Ever since I came to France in high school, I've felt like she was my responsibility. I felt like she was given to me in a way, to take care of. Like a baby on the doorstep or something. It's a terrible way to think about your mother."

But Finny saw that Earl felt this way about both his parents. It had been something she'd admired about him, his instinct for caregiving. She remembered the way he used to help his dad out, offer encouragement, take over the wheel of their car when Mr. Henckel fell asleep. It was what Finny had seen in Earl's story, in the way Chris fretted about leaving home. He felt a responsibility, as Earl did, to make sure everyone was all right.

"Who found her?" Finny said, stupidly, since she already knew the answer.

Earl was sobbing. "She was so out of it," he said. "She took pills and tried to cut herself. Oh God." Finny heard his breathing. "This is just so sad," he finally got out. He sounded like a frightened child.

"But she's okay now?" Finny asked. It was the best way she could think of to be encouraging.

Earl didn't answer. All he said was, "I can't come, Finny."

She didn't know what to say. How could this gift be torn from her again?

Finally she asked, "How long are you staying for?"

"I can't leave," Earl said. "I can't do that to her."

Finny looked at her keys, which she'd now placed back on the desk. "What are you saying?" she asked.

"This is where I'm needed. I don't have a choice."

"What are we going to do?"

Then it happened. She didn't know how, but she felt it, that slightest shift, like a cloud passing over the sun. "How can you ask me that?" he said. "Honestly. How can you worry about *yourself*?"

She felt a hot wave ripple down her body. She realized it was hatred she felt—hatred toward Mona. For being so helpless. Demanding so much. The feeling was so intense as to be physical, like hunger or cold. And then, with the same swift certainty, she felt her anger turn toward Earl. It was a wretched, jarring move, but she couldn't quiet her own clamoring needs. She'd never felt anything so strongly in her life. She hated him. She hated Earl. He'd done this to her. Made her into this. Only now could she see how her old self—that gutsy, bold, rebellious girl—had been squelched by her love for him. Maybe that was why Mona's neediness made Finny so angry—it was so much like her own.

"Don't do this," she said to Earl. Her voice was rough, like her throat had been scraped. It didn't even sound like her. "It's an excuse. You're nervous about coming. Take a minute to think—"

"Don't analyze me."

"Your mom could easily fly over here when she's better. There are plenty of places she could work."

"That's not the point, Finny." Something about hearing her name made her feel small, like when her parents used to lecture her about doing her homework or cleaning her room. "Don't you see I need to be with her? That's what I have to think about now. She's asking how much I care about her."

So am I, Finny thought. And she didn't want to ask anymore. All he had to say was that he'd do it, he'd leave for her. Then she'd relent. It would be proof enough. She saw that the argument had become a kind of test—of what he felt for her, how much he'd sacrifice.

"I can't do it anymore," Finny said. "Live this way. I can't sit around waiting."

"Then don't."

A week later he called again. They talked a little about their fight, about how angry each had gotten, both trying to make light of it, to salvage what hadn't been swept up in the torrent of it. Actually, it made Finny feel a little better, like they might be able to hoist themselves out of what had seemed an impossibly deep and dark hole. But when she asked him what he was up to, he said, "Not much. Just catching up with friends."

She didn't know why, but some instinct told her to ask, "Who?"

"I don't know," Earl said. "Just some high school friends."

"You slept with her, didn't you? Camille."

"I guess."

It was like a door clicking shut in her mind. To think she'd waited so long, expected so much. The idea of how gullible she'd been made her almost physically ill. Like Earl in his fiction, she'd invented a character, built someone up out of the air, because she'd wanted so much for him to be real, to be what she needed.

"Okay, Earl," Finny said at last. She wasn't even angry anymore. Just tired. "All right. That's enough."

Chapter 31

Another Interlude

After Earl's call, Finny felt as if the train that had carried her through her days had ground to a halt. There was a squeal of metal on metal, a hiss of breaks, the slow sigh of an engine coming to rest. The world seemed fixed in place. Eventually, though, it began again. The engine whirred, the train jolted forward. Life went on.

And so did Finny's story. Once again, this is not the place to linger. Here is another album of memories, a few handfuls of time.

Schoolwork. She found that if she just sat there, her mind would wander. She'd stare at the wall, thinking of Earl, of what they'd said, of how they'd ended things. But if she fastened her mind to a task—to reading a certain number of pages in a physics text, or completing an English paper—she could keep herself from drifting back. Her grades were still strong. She hadn't let herself slip.

A call from Sylvan. Finally. Her brother saying he was sorry he hadn't called sooner. It was a tough time. He'd had to accept that Judith wasn't the right person for him. But he'd been feeling better lately. He said he'd been thinking of changing his major. He'd always been interested in psychology. He'd planned to be a history professor, but couldn't see himself as a stuffy academic anymore. Something new in Sylvan's voice. Not pain exactly. But he sounded older.

A letter from Earl. His mom was doing better. *I'm sorry I've been disappointing*, he wrote. *I just couldn't think about anything clearly. I know you're very angry at me. And you have a right to be. Just know that I still love you and think the world of you. . . .*

Dorrie coming back to school with her belly round and taut as an overinflated beach ball. Her feet turned out when she walked. Finny putting her hand on Dorrie's stomach, feeling the miniature Steven Bench give a couple of mild kicks. Then, a few weeks later, Dorrie showing up at Finny's dorm room with a little red-faced howling infant. Not particularly cute, so Finny ended up telling Dorrie he was "quite a baby."

Another surprise in the mail: a videotape in a plain brown envelope, no return address. Playing it on the VCR in the lounge in her dorm. A picture of a female newscaster came on the screen, saying, "Now, here's a story about a Baltimore couple who are making a difference in *their* community. . . ." Then the screen flashed to a film of Mr. Henckel conducting a group of six- and seven-year-olds through the Bach minuet Finny used to play. Mr. Henckel's comb-over flapping to the rhythm of the music. The story was about an after-school arts program that Poplan and Mr. Henckel had set up, funded through a charity Poplan had established. There was a clip of Poplan explaining how she wanted the program to be a fun, safe place for these kids to go. Then the tape cut to a picture of Poplan lining the children up to wash their hands before a game of Jenga. The story concluded with a quote by Mr. Henckel. "I just want these children to know that here the coffeepot is always warm for them."

A form arriving, asking Finny to check off a box for which major she'd like to pursue. She had no idea. She hadn't even thought about it. Deciding to check off English, since she had the most credits in that one. Then she checked off a box for a minor in education, for no reason other than that it looked better than just a plain English major. And with that one stroke, a decade of her professional life was decided.

A hot morning in September. The first day of classes Finny's junior year. Walking into Griffen Hall and seeing Sarah Barksdale holding a notebook, checking her mail. Finny was about to run. Any reminder of Finny's former principal made Finny grit her teeth. But she decided she had to say hi. She walked over and tapped Sarah on the shoulder, reintroduced herself. Though Sarah was cursed with her mother's grating voice, it turned out she had a sense of humor. She told Finny that Mrs. Barksdale had tried to get Miss Simpkin to spend a night "under cover" in the dorm with Sarah, in order to "evaluate the social dynamics." But Sarah had convincingly argued that no one would act normally around Miss Simpkin, and furthermore, the idea of Miss Simpkin under cover of anything but a sweatsuit was ludicrous. Finny laughed, and she and Sarah ended up having lunch a couple times a month.

Evenings in the library, sitting by herself at a synthetic wooden table in the periodicals section, surrounded by the garish orange carpeting the school had laid down in a misguided attempt to keep students awake. Finny liked to sneak off here some Friday nights, when she was feeling gray, and thumb through old women's magazines, laughing at the sex tips and social pointers, the pictures of smooth-skinned women lounging with their boyfriends on white comforters. It was a way to escape, to think that five blow job tips could save your relationship, or that you could find your career through a multiple-choice survey. She even took some of the surveys. Found out she'd be best suited for woodworking or pet clothing design.

A party in one of the Stradler frat houses. Dim lighting, throbbing music, the sour smell of beer. Finny didn't normally go to parties, but she'd promised Sarah Barksdale she'd stop by this one. They danced together for a while, until a tall, muscular boy with hair as red as Finny's asked Finny to dance with him. The dancing turned out to be a lot of calculated rubbing, which, in combination with the three cups of astringent fruit punch she'd drunk, did the trick of putting Finny in the mood to stop by the boy's dorm room. Finny said bye to Sarah and stumbled with the boy across the cold, dark lawn to his dorm. Inside his room, which was decorated with posters of jazz musicians, they kissed clumsily to a Bill Evans record, then began to take off their clothes. They ended up sleeping together a couple times before he graduated, after which they never talked again.

A vacation with Sarah Barksdale in Mexico over spring break Finny's senior year. Getting conned into paying rental insurance on the already overpriced rental car by a sweaty man who kept shrugging and saying, "This is Mexico. Anything can happen." On their way back, at the Cancún airport, Finny and Sarah stopped in a duty-free to buy souvenirs for their families. There was a counter where an old white guy with silver hair was pouring samples of jarred salsa into plastic cups, and when Finny looked closely, she recognized the man. It was Gerald Kramp. When he saw Finny, he turned as red as the salsa. Finny bought two jars of mild from him, telling him she could do without the spices.

Graduation. A muggy morning. Finny lifting her robe to get some air on her legs. Afterward, Laura and Sylvan taking Finny to lunch at a Chinese restaurant. They got seated at a table for two, since it was all that was available and no one had thought to make a reservation. Laura looked much older than she had when Finny started college; when she smiled, lines appeared on her face like cracks in ice. For the first time, Finny could imagine the way her mother would look as an old woman. Laura grinned a lot, but Finny and Sylvan did most of the talking. They both knew this was the routine now when they visited their mother, who hadn't been the same after the trouble with Gerald. The lunch made Finny think about her father for the first time in a while, and they all laughed when the waiter brought out a plate of General Tso's chicken and Finny insisted on calling it Chicken à la Picasso.

Another publication for Earl. He wrote Finny with the news. They'd communicated a little by mail—no calls—keeping each other up to date. Finny didn't see the harm in it, since they weren't getting back together. This time his story was coming out in a magazine called *Trophy*, which Earl said could be found *in the most dimly lit and out of the way corner of Barnes & Noble.* . . . Finny wrote him congratulations. When the story came out that summer, she read it, sitting in a Barnes & Noble café. The story was beautiful—about a woman who goes to a doctor to get a skin cancer treated, and it ends up bringing up all these memories about her father dying and her losing the man she loved. It was a long, wandering, lyrical story, and it went back and forth in time. By the end, Finny had a sense of such great loss and sorrow that she actually began to weep in the middle of the bookstore. She'd been transported by the story, and she didn't know how Earl could write so convincingly about a middle-aged woman. He seemed able to tap into some sadness in his stories, some truth and wisdom he didn't always have in real life. She wrote him again that night to say it was one of the best stories she'd ever read.

The move to Cambridge. Finny had loved the area when she'd visited Sylvan at college, and so, on a whim, she decided to move there. More boxes, more dirty bedsheets flung over furniture. She and Sylvan had actually traded places, since Sylvan was now pursuing a Ph.D. in psychology at Bryn Mawr, outside Philadelphia. Finny got a job hostessing at a restaurant near Harvard Square. She liked the work, though she knew she could hardly make a career of it. So she started interning for a literary magazine at Harvard, reading their fiction submissions, hoping to put her English degree to work.

It didn't even occur to her that both her jobs were in exactly the areas Earl worked in. She didn't analyze herself that way. She simply wrote Earl the news, and they even chatted on the phone once in a while. Earl told Finny he had an agent now, but it was hard to sell a collection of stories. He was still living across the hall from his mother, because it was cheap and it allowed him the mornings to write. She didn't ask if he was living with anyone. Mona had become a partner at the salon, as promised. Finny asked Earl if he was writing a novel, and he said, "No. Stories are my thing." He was almost finished with an undergraduate degree in France.

An invitation forwarded from Laura, to attend "the union of Judith Marie Turngate and Milton Gaylord Hollibrand." Finny had been in Cambridge a couple years already, but had never given Judith the address. The wedding notice was written in a simple blue script, on a white background, with a plain blue trim. Finny knew they must have spent thousands on the invitations alone. She looked at the two boxes: *Yes, I will attend* and *With regrets, I am unable to attend*. There was no room on Finny's card to add a guest. She thought of simply not returning the card. Then she thought of checking the regrets box and adding a little note. But in the end, she decided to attend. Anything else would have been too dramatic. And she had to admit—she was curious.

The ceremony, which the Turngates and Hollibrands had set up through their many connections, was held at the Metropolitan Museum of Art. They rented out the Egyptian tomb area for the reception, which turned out to be a five-course formal catered dinner. The only whimsical element was that when the glasses for the toast were handed out, Finny realized they contained cranberry juice—which must have been a point of great importance to Mr. Turngate. Hal Hollibrand offered a toast to the married couple, in which he called their union "the greatest merger I've ever seen," and afterward he shook hands with the Turngates like they were sealing a business deal.

Luckily, Finny was seated nex\
of entertaining commentary on a rter, who provided lots
guests. He told Finny that Prince's distinguished-looking
rather small—had adopted the muta ts—who were both
Turngate had made noise about adopti ince when Bonnie
They were always trying to show each o baby from China.
that the only thing tackier than having a up. He also said
on top of a national treasure was if they ha lding reception
the bar *inside* the Egyptian tomb, giving th ctually set up
mummies to stir their drinks with. uests little

Halfway through dinner, he came out with his news. "I
have a boyfriend, Finny. A steady one. First time in my life.
His name is Garreth, which is the gayest thing I've ever heard.
And my name's Carter." It was then that Judith and Prince
started making their rounds. Judith appeared at Finny's table
looking almost too beautiful, her cheeks slightly blushed, her
skin golden against the white dress. Prince was grinning, his
enormous chest nearly bursting the seams of his tuxedo.
Finny did have to admit they looked pleased together. "I'm so
happy you came," Judith said to Finny. And Prince added, "It
means so much to us." Judith and Finny said they'd have to
get together, though Finny knew her former friend would
never call. Only when the newlyweds walked away did Carter
say, "I'll bet his dick is the size of a Mike and Ike."

Finny chatting with one of her managers at the restaurant
during a slow afternoon. Mentioning she had a minor in education. "Are you serious?" the manager said. Her name was
Brandy, but everyone called her Bee. She told Finny that a
friend of hers was responsible for hiring at a kindergarten in
Boston and they were looking for a teacher's assistant. Asked
Finny if she might be interested. Finny said sure, and got the
job at the interview. In a month, when one of the head teachers left to have a baby, Finny took over her position. It was a
fluke, but she loved her new job. The kids called her Miss
Finn.

Some dates: a der at the restaurant where she'd worked; a divorced r of one of the kids she taught; a man she'd been set up who worked in film and kept talking about all the peo e knew at HBO and how close they were to buying his cts. Sometimes Finny slept with them; sometimes she dn't. It was based more on how lonely she felt at the time an how attracted she was to the man. Nothing lasted fo more than a couple months, which was fine with her.

Finny apartment in Cambridge: the bottom floor of a two-story hone owned by a Brazilian couple. The house's address was on a little one-way street called Berkshire Street, but the place was tucked behind another row of houses, so you could access it only by an alleyway. Quiet in the apartment all day. Plus it was enormous—a bedroom and a study off the large kitchen, and then a separate living room down the hall. It was one of the reasons she found it so hard to contemplate leaving Cambridge. She was paying less than a thousand a month. The Almeidas liked her, and they saw no reason to change tenants.

Sundays she met Bee from her old restaurant job, or other teachers at her school, and they stood in line at the S & S deli to get a table for brunch. Latkes and blintzes, mimosas in soda glasses. Dinner plans once or twice a week, or stopping by to see her aunt Louise, who happened to live just outside Boston with her new crop of cats. Concerts—at Symphony Hall or the Middle East or the Orpheum—which Finny was happy to attend by herself if no one else wanted to go. Last-minute theater tickets, or catching the Alvin Ailey or Paul Taylor troupes when they came to town. Coffee shops she loved, and bars and restaurants and bookstores. Laughing at the women's magazines like she used to in college, even once sending in a letter to the editor (*I mastered all twenty "blow his head off" orgasm techniques*, she wrote, *but my kitchen still doesn't look as clean as the one in the photo*), which came back to her with a polite rejection slip saying they valued her subscription and would she like to renew it with a special "career woman" rate? Dim sum at China Pearl. The Museum of Fine Arts, which was free for Finny since she was a teacher. Time rolling by. Another summer and another.

Sarah Barksdale calling Finny from her place in Philadelphia, saying, "Finny, I'm engaged!" Finny congratulating her, having to hold the phone a couple inches from her ear, the way she had with Sarah's mother. Then, a month later, another call. "We had a fight. It was the dumbest thing. About who was paying the security deposit. It just blew up. We broke it off." Sarah crying into the phone, Finny telling her it was okay, better they found out now. Thinking of Earl, the time they'd fought in Paris before her purse was stolen. She told Sarah to give it a few weeks. She would know if it was the right thing. There was nothing they couldn't take back. And Sarah thanking Finny, saying she knew Finny was right.

Teaching. Finny loved the children, all the adorable comments they made, the seriousness over cutting out paper circles, gluing glitter to a square of cardboard. Finny laughed at their little arguments. A boy telling a girl that Christmas was about family, and the girl disagreeing, saying she was pretty sure it was about Jesus. They went back and forth for several minutes until Finny said it was about something different in everyone's house, and in her house it was about presents. Which both seemed to like. Nice to dispatch of problems so neatly, like putting silverware in a drawer. And the health benefits were good. And she had her summers free. She couldn't see any reason to change, so she just kept renewing the contract, accepting the little salary hikes she got each year.

Until one summer, when she was achingly bored with the job, and on a whim she applied for an internship at a small women's magazine called *Doll's Apartment* in New York. She found an artist who was willing to do an apartment swap with her, so she ended up with a disheveled studio in Chelsea that reeked of insecticide. Finny was in her thirties, hardly the type to take an unpaid pencil-sharpening position, but still, it was an adventure. She wrote little captions beneath the photos they gave her, read the slush pile, even contributed a couple of small opinion pieces. (One she particularly liked about the locker-room way men always refer to male writers by their last names and female writers by their whole names.) The editor she worked under, Julie Fried, an almost frighteningly tall and broad-shouldered woman who wore no makeup and kept her red hair in a loose ponytail, liked Finny a lot. Told her she was "fresh." Offered her a permanent job at a bracingly low salary. The work was fun, but not something Finny could make a career of, so she said thanks, but she'd bow out at the end of the summer.

The call from Sylvan: "Did you hear?" he said. Finny on a plane to Baltimore the next morning. She and Sylvan sitting by their mother's hospital bed, watching her nap. An enlarged heart, the doctor had said. Funny, it was so much like what had killed their father. A warm, cloudless afternoon, the sun golden as an apricot, slipping behind the buildings outside, casting the room in a honey-colored light. The hospital seemed unnaturally quiet. Shadows stretched across the floor. Laura's mouth twitched as she slept, and once in a while she whispered things Finny couldn't make out. A nurse placed a tray of food in front of Laura while she was still asleep. Sylvan mouthed *Thank you* to her.

Laura waking in the middle of the night and saying, "You have to understand." She stared at Finny and Sylvan with her eyes wide, burning.

"It's okay, Mom," Sylvan said, stroking her hand.

"No!" Laura said, looking at Finny. "I just wasn't strong."

"It's okay," Finny said.

"I just wanted everything to be nice," Laura said. "I thought everyone would hate me if it wasn't nice."

Finny thought of her mother's pointers, the childlike way

Book Three

From Here On Out

Chapter **32**

Finny Gets a Glimpse into
the Lives of Her Friends

It was Judith Turngate, again, who brought them all back together. This time she'd sent an email, inviting everyone to a
Memorial Day weekend at her summer house on Dune Road
in Westhampton Beach. (She and Prince also had an apartment in the city.) The email went to three people: Finny,
Sylvan, and Carter. But they were told to bring friends or
significant others, anyone they wanted. Finny's invitation was
followed by a personal note from Judith. *Hey, Shorty Finn! I
just thought of having this "reunion" at the last minute. The
weather's been beautiful on the island. Prince and I have the
barbecue set up. I've just been thinking how it would be nice if
we could all be friends again. Please come if you can.*

"Did you see that email from Judith?" Sylvan asked Finny
on the phone the same day she'd received the invitation.

"It was pretty unexpected," Finny said.

She and her brother talked on the phone a couple times a
week, now that their mom had passed away. Sylvan was working as a counselor at Stradler College, Finny's alma mater. They
talked about the news in their lives, about old memories, anything that came up. Finny felt closer to Sylvan than to anyone

else in the world. Maybe it was just that she and her brother had been through so much together. But she also had a lot of respect for Sylvan, for how he'd dealt with his pain, for who he'd become. She was certain he'd be an excellent therapist.

"Are you gonna go?" Sylvan asked.

"I don't know. Are you? If you do, you should bring Mari."

"The thing is, she's going to her mother's that weekend. I actually have nothing to do."

"Well then," Finny said.

"Well then, what?"

"I think we should go. Maybe it'll give some kind of closure. Prove that we're over it and we can just have a nice time together. You shrinks are into closure, aren't you?"

Sylvan laughed. "We're into charging for it."

"Who knows? You might get a chance to do that, too."

"At least it'll be a chance for us to catch up. I have a surprise for you. I'll save it till when I see you."

"Is it a bill?" Finny asked.

"That's coming in the mail," Sylvan said.

Finny took the Chinatown bus to New York on Saturday afternoon, then the subway to West Fourth. She was planning to meet Carter at the restaurant his boyfriend managed, just off Washington Square Park. Then they were going to ride out to Long Island in Carter's car. Their plan was to get to Judith's for dinner.

Carter was waiting in front of the restaurant when Finny arrived. She was wearing her backpack the way she did when she used to visit New York in college. It was a gray afternoon, the clouds above them thick as batter, threatening rain. Carter was talking to a shortish man with a beard who looked to be about forty. Finny assumed it was Garreth, the boyfriend. He was soft-looking but attractive, and he wore a somewhat shiny tan shirt and dark slacks. Both he and Carter were smoking cigarettes.

"Now," Carter said, smacking a kiss on Finny's lips, "look what the D train dragged in. It's beautiful to see you, Finny Short."

"You, too," Finny said. She noticed Carter was looking a little soft himself, not his usual shipshape skin-and-bones self. His belly pushed at his black Jimi Hendrix T-shirt like a pumpkin beneath a sheet. His hair was parted neatly, not bedraggled like it used to be.

"I'm clean and I'm not smoking anymore," Carter said, taking a long drag from his cigarette, then tossing it into the street. "That's why I look like a damn oven stuffer roaster. All I have are bonbons to keep me warm. By the way, this is Garreth."

Garreth shook Finny's hand, told her it was nice to meet her, that he'd heard so much about her. He seemed a little shy, Finny thought, but pleasant. He looked her in the eyes when they shook hands.

"I have to move the car," Carter said to Garreth. "Just remember Yvonne gets the dry food, and Curly the mix." Carter looked at Finny. "Dogs," he said.

"Which one gets the dry?" Garreth said. "Kidding. You really are becoming my mother." Then he kissed Carter goodbye, told Finny again how nice it was to meet her.

"You have dogs?" Finny said to Carter when they rounded the corner.

Carter took a set of keys out of his pocket and pressed a button, causing the blue minivan in front of them to chirp and flash its lights. "And if you say anything about the minivan," Carter said, "I'm going to lock you in the doggy cage and you're not coming out till we get to Westhampton."

Once they'd settled into their lane on the Long Island Expressway, Finny said to Carter, "It seems like there've been some changes on your end."

"You mean the hair?" Carter said.

"Among other things," Finny said. "Have you joined a mahjong club?"

"It's the damn married life. Turns a decent couple into the gay version of the Partridge Family. Maybe that's redundant."

On their right some strip malls flashed by. Finny saw a fried chicken restaurant, an adult movie store with blackened windows, a defunct Shell station with boarded-up gas pumps. The sky was still gray, but not as ominous, more like a thin milk shake than batter. It seemed the storm might pass without rain.

"What about you?" Carter said. "What ever happened to that cute boyfriend of yours I met in New York? I thought you were on the slow boat to marriage, too."

"You mean Earl? I think that boat stopped off on some Caribbean island and never got going again. We're not in touch anymore."

"Anything happen?"

Finny shrugged. She didn't know exactly what to call it.

Carter sighed. "So what are your projects nowadays?"

"Work, mostly." She was going to say something about the magazine job she'd been offered, just float it, but she couldn't think of how to do it without inviting questions.

Carter wrinkled his eyebrows. "Are you kidding me? I'm as sober as Nancy Reagan at a MADD meeting, driving a fucking minivan to a Memorial Day barbecue, and you're not going to tell me about getting your buzz on and titty-fucking a stranger in the bathroom of a club called Nerve? What the hell am I driving you around for anyway? Don't you know that when a married person asks a single friend what's going on, it's the equivalent of buying porn?"

"Are you and Garreth really married?"

"In spirit," Carter said. "We call it 'committed.' I think of it as a life sentence, with only the very dim possibility of parole. And not for good behavior."

"Can I ask you, though, seriously," Finny said, "what made the change? I mean, I didn't really expect you to settle down so soon."

"Yeah, well," Carter said, and then twisted his hands on the steering wheel, like he was wringing out a soaked towel. He seemed to be considering what to say next. It might have been the first time Finny had ever seen him hesitate.

Then he said, "I found out I have the bug, Finny." She must have looked confused, because Carter went on. "HIV. Not the grand prize. But a solid runner-up."

"Oh God, Carter," Finny said. "I'm so sorry." Her vision went blurry for a second, then came back, like she'd been shaken. "What happened?"

"I'd just been swinging for too long. It catches up with you. I can't even tell you the life we were leading, Finny. I know Garreth looks tame. But trust me when I tell you that our first night together I was snorting a line of coke off his dick and he was fucking me senseless while I vomited in the toilet. I don't mean to say this to gross you out. Well, maybe a little. But what I'm trying to tell you is that we were out of our minds. Possessed. I don't know if it was love or what, but it went crazy.

"Anyway," Carter went on, "we had this party. Drugs, booze. Both of us getting fucked left, right, and sideways. It's the way we lived. Our only agreement was that we'd use condoms. So this one time I didn't. I don't remember if we were out, or I was too lazy. But of course I got it. One mistake, and I had doctors telling me my life expectancy."

"It's hard to imagine—" Finny said.

"And that's not the worst of it," Carter interrupted. He was as serious as she'd ever seen him. He wouldn't look at her while he spoke, but kept staring ahead through the windshield, almost like he was summoning the story from the gray sky. "Garreth kicked me out. It was the one thing we'd agreed upon—the one thing we both did for the other person, for us—and I'd broken his trust. He said he couldn't forgive me.

"I found this little rat hole, deep in Hell's Kitchen, and just started going really hard at the drugs and the booze. I had these days I called 'missed days,' which were times when I woke up and started drinking, and the next thing I knew it was tomorrow. It went on for a couple months like that. I think I was trying to kill myself. I lived next to a strip club, and I made some money selling drugs to the dancers and running little errands for them. Buying them tampons and whatnot."

Carter took a long breath, like a drag from a cigarette, and then exhaled it slowly. "Then one day Garreth showed up at my door. At first I didn't even recognize him. I didn't believe it could be him. I thought my life was over." Carter sniffed, and Finny saw that he was blinking away tears. "He came in and sat me down at my kitchen table. I only had one chair. But he made me sit while he cooked me an egg. It was the only thing in my refrigerator. He sat there on the counter and watched me eat it. Then he asked if I was eating okay, if I was getting out. He was concerned. He said that since I left, things just didn't feel right."

Carter sniffed again, then sighed. He rolled his shoulders like he'd been sitting in the same position for too long.

"He loves you," Finny said. "I can tell by how he looks at you."

"Eh," Carter said, waving Finny off. "I feed his dogs."

"Everyone needs a dog feeder."

"Anyway, now we have our place near Ditmas Park with our little backyard. I'm taking all the drugs my measly Healthy New York policy can afford, and doing pretty well. I have a flower business. I actually do the flowers at Garreth's restaurant. I would have shown you if I hadn't been feeling sick from all the doggy planning."

"I admire you," Finny said.

"But my point," Carter said, as if Finny hadn't spoken, "is that it is up to you to provide the drama, Finny Short. I cannot deal with a boring weekend. And I think you and I have both seen enough of Judith's drama. She's probably as bored and horny as I am, anyway. So you better think quickly of some interesting stories, or else make some Memorial Day resolutions to find some."

"I'll do my best," Finny said.

"And one more thing," Carter said as they were rolling into the pine barrens. There had been a fire here a couple summers ago, Finny knew, and beside the highway the new trees, bright as grass in the early spring, were beginning to peek through the dull forest floor. "I haven't told Judith about the whole being-sick thing. I don't exactly see her as a shoulder to cry on, if you know what I mean. So maybe keep that quiet?"

"You can trust me."

"I know I can, Finny Short. It's one of the many reasons I like you."

Carter took the turn into Judith's U-shaped pebble driveway, and Finny listened to the stones crunch beneath the tires. The clouds had parted, like curtains unveiling the late-afternoon sun. Dune Road was simply a strip of land—wide enough for only a two-lane road with a house on each side—shielding a portion of the south shore of Long Island from the ocean. The houses on one side of the road backed onto the ocean, and on the other side the bay. Judith's property was on the bay side, sandwiched between a large white modern-looking house that was shaped like a bullet, and a gray house that looked like something a child might make out of blocks. The Hollibrands' house itself was all on one floor, beach-bungalow style. Finny could see through the front windows that there was a large living room in the center, and then a wing on each side, where she assumed the bedrooms were. Behind the house was the bay.

Judith must have heard the minivan in the driveway, because she came out of the front door waving both hands, saying something Finny couldn't hear. Carter pressed a button to lower the passenger-side window, and Finny caught the words " . . . my best friends."

They got out of the van. The air was warm and salty. Judith was wearing a purple dress with a swath cut out of the neckline, revealing an extensive view of her suntanned breasts, which seemed impossibly larger to Finny, round and brown as two cantaloupes. Judith had put on makeup—some eye shadow, blush on her cheeks—though she seemed to have applied it with a heavier hand than she used to, like she was about to walk onstage. Finny could see a crinkly border of cover-up around her eyes. Judith hugged Carter and Finny in the driveway, and again Finny felt that old creeping discomfort, like she'd been asked to give a speech she hadn't prepared for. She felt herself hunching, and she tugged at the little black sweater she was wearing. Carter pressed the button to make the minivan chirp.

"What is *that*?" Judith asked, laughing.

"*That*," Carter said, "is your future. You laugh now, but no one can escape the minivan. It's like wrinkles and nursing homes."

"It even has a doggy cage," Finny offered, "which you get locked in if you make fun of it."

"By the way," Judith said to Finny, "your brother's already here. We're having drinks on the patio. Why don't you stick your stuff inside. I'll show you your rooms. Then you can meet us out there. Prince is driving out with his sister. Unfortunately, she'll be spending the weekend with us, too." Judith seemed out of breath when she finished these announcements. Finny could tell she was excited to have her friends back.

"Just show me the hookers and the hot tub," Carter said.

"You have an entirely mistaken idea about the Hamptons," Judith said.

"Sorry," Carter said. "Do the hookers prefer saunas?"

Outside on the patio, Sylvan was lying on a chaise longue, with a red fruity-looking drink in his hand. Unlike Carter, Sylvan had kept his thin shape into his thirties, though he'd been less successful at keeping his hair. For a while he'd tried to hide the coin of scalp at the back of his head, combing and growing his hair in different ways—including a brief, ill-advised bout with a ponytail—but as his hairline eroded, Finny convinced him that the only sensible route was to face the music and shave his head. Actually, it didn't look bad on Sylvan. It made him seem older than he was. But that was how Finny thought of him anyway. And the brushstrokes of gray in the stubble at the sides of his head only contributed to a look of distinction.

Judith told Carter and Finny to have a seat while she brought out some more strawberry daiquiris.

"Make mine a virgin," Carter said. "I never thought I'd say that."

"Are you kidding?" Judith said.

"Does that goddamn minivan look like I'm kidding?" Carter responded.

Judith slipped into the kitchen through the sliding glass door. Everyone said hi. Hugs and kisses all around. Sylvan and Carter knew each other from when Sylvan used to date Judith. The chairs on Judith's patio, which extended the length of the house, were faced toward the inlet behind the house. The chairs were all made from the same unfinished wood, which Finny knew was calculated to give a rustic effect, and the furniture would have been a chore to move. Around the patio were some reeds and dune plants, and farther down, a strip of beach and the lapping water. It was late afternoon, and the sun spilled its colors across the water. There was a boat doing laps around the inlet, dragging a water-skier. Every once in a while Finny could hear the boat's driver give an excited shout. She smelled smoke in the air from someone's barbecue.

Judith came back out with the drinks for Finny and Carter, and then sat down next to Sylvan. Finny sipped her drink, and winced at the amount of rum in it.

"Is it okay?" Judith asked Finny. "I make them a little sweeter than Prince does. He likes to really taste the alcohol."

"Oh," Finny said. "It's good, then."

"So," Judith said, "Sylvan was telling me you're teaching in Boston." When she said this, Judith brushed Sylvan on the arm with her fingertips. Finny saw her brother start, like he'd gotten a static shock.

"I am," Finny said.

"So how's that?"

"It's pretty good," Finny said. "I only hit the kids when they don't shine my shoes properly."

Judith laughed. Finny could see she was having a good time, and Finny found it endearing that her friend could be so thrilled just to sit around and talk with her. It's what Finny had always liked about Judith—how much fun they could have together, how genuinely Judith enjoyed the company of her friends.

"What about you?" Finny asked Judith. "What are you doing?"

"I'm boring the heck out of myself," Judith said. "It seems like Prince and I are out to dinner or at someone's party every night. I'm getting my real estate license. The course is a joke. I think I'm ready to have kids. I'm horny as hell, and I keep telling Prince we should take advantage of it."

Finny looked at her brother when Judith made this comment, and she saw his eyes dip to Judith's cleavage for a moment. Judith must have noticed, and been pleased by it, because Finny saw her smile, as if in response to a compliment. It all happened in an instant, but suddenly Finny was worried. She saw that it might have been a mistake to get everyone back together, as if they could just go on as friends. And there was something else Finny saw in that moment. It was something teasing in Judith, something Finny had only glimpsed that summer after she'd left Thorndon, when Judith had talked all the time about "fucking" and how good or bad it was, and who was fucking whom. That summer, Judith had seemed to grow up and become more bitter both at once, and somehow, the woman who sat before Finny now, with her blushed cheeks and swollen breasts, seemed the fruition of a seed that had been planted all those years ago.

But maybe Finny was wrong. Maybe she was taking it too far. She looked at Carter, and saw that he was practically asleep, probably cursing himself for having driven all this way to listen to other people talk about how boring their lives were.

Then Prince arrived. He opened the sliding door and walked onto the patio, trailed by a petite woman with frizzy blond hair who was wearing an oversize T-shirt and patched-up jeans. She looked a decade older than Prince, and if Judith hadn't mentioned before that the woman was his sister, Finny would never have known. Prince's sister had a large brown and black dog on a leash, who sniffed at the boards of the deck.

"How's everyone?" Prince said, waving, smiling his famous smile. Everyone greeted him, and he leaned down to give Judith a kiss, which Finny noticed her brother observing with special interest. For Prince's part, he looked more clean-cut and professional than he had when he was in college. His dark hair was slicked with gel. He wore a polo shirt and khaki shorts, and appeared just as muscular as he always had, only with maybe a bit more of a belly from all the daiquiris. He seemed comfortable in his role as host, happy to share his good fortune with his wife's friends. Finny was pleased to note that he no longer doused himself in cologne.

"This is my sister, Korinne," Prince said.

"And this is Homer," Korinne said, presenting the dog as if he were a guest. "He's part Doberman, but don't worry. He is the best and sweetest dog in the world."

"I hope no one's allergic," Prince said. "I asked her to leave him in the city."

"He doesn't shed," Korinne said sharply. "And besides, there's no way I could leave him. He gets depressed when I'm not around."

"How do you know he's depressed?" Finny said.

"He just mopes and droops. Mopes and droops."

"So would you like a drink?" Prince said to his sister. He already seemed a little exasperated by her. "Or are you all hungry?"

"Well," Korinne said, "it's not that I'm hungry or thirsty. *I* don't matter. But when I look at this poor sweet dog. When I look into his dear little eyes"—and here she got on her knees and performed this very task—"he's telling me he not only wants to eat, but he *needs* to eat. I can't deny such a darling creature." She scratched Homer on the head, lifted his left ear then his right. The dog raised one eyebrow at her.

"Do you want me to pick up some dog food?" Prince asked.

"Ha!" Korinne said. "You must be joking. Are you joking? Because it seemed like you were joking, knowing what you do. You said we were going to grill tonight. Homer likes his burger medium-rare, a little pink in the middle."

"I can just make it for him now," Prince offered. "Then we could all enjoy a drink." He smiled at everyone, which appeared to take some effort.

"You'd have to be crazy if you think he's going to eat alone," Korinne said to her brother. "That would just be sad."

"Then he might mope and droop," Carter offered. Finny could see that he found Prince's sister funny, and he was going to take full advantage of the tension. Carter seemed to have come back to life, roused by the first hint of entertainment in this crowd. "We don't want to keep the puppy waiting," he went on. "Maybe he enjoys a little drink before dinner? A glass of wine?"

But Korinne didn't seem to see the humor in this. "He only drinks tequila," she said. "Don Eduardo. One shot on special occasions. He's not a lush." She flattened her mouth and shook her head at Carter.

"Of course not," Carter said. "In fact, maybe he'd enjoy some of this strawberry milk shake Judith made me. I can't finish it without the booze."

"The only fruits he likes are mangoes and pomegranates," Korinne said, and then went inside with Prince to change for dinner.

"Prince," Carter called, "I think you might have to go to the market!"

Finny and Judith were left to make the salad in the kitchen while Prince and the other men worked the grill and Prince's sister took Homer for his walk. Judith's kitchen would have been plain—white cabinets and a white tiled floor—except for the view of the water through the glass doors that were one wall of the room. Through the glass, Finny could also see the corner of the deck where the boys were working on the barbecue, though she couldn't hear them. Prince was getting the coals ready, Sylvan was nodding approvingly, and Carter was squirting little streams of lighter fluid onto the coals from a large plastic bottle.

"This is so nice," Judith said. "Having you here. I feel like we're back at Thorndon."

"Then I'd have to think of a dare," Finny said. "I think yours was the last one. When I stuck that note under Poplan's door." She glanced at Judith after she said this, to see the effect of her words.

Judith laughed. "I felt so bad about that. Telling on you. I had a guilt complex for years."

The news struck Finny like a blow from behind. "And here

I thought you were my friend," she said. Then she laughed at her own joke just to make sure Judith knew she was kidding. Finny could see how much effort Judith was putting into this weekend, how much she wanted to be friends again, and Finny didn't want to spoil that. So she tried to ask Judith her next question as casually as she could. "But why'd you do it? We were getting along so well."

Judith shrugged. "I saw how close you were to Poplan. I guess it bothered me."

Finny remembered the story Poplan had told about catching Judith and Jesse with the alcohol. How angry Judith had been at Poplan. And Judith could see how close Finny and Poplan were getting. She must have realized that for Poplan, not knowing who had written the note wouldn't be half as bad as knowing Finny had betrayed her.

"Anyway, it was a long time ago, Finny," Judith said, and opened the refrigerator. It was like Judith to diminish any topic that didn't cast her in a flattering light. Finny wanted to say more, but she held back. They had the whole weekend in front of them.

A minute later, while Judith was washing the lettuce, she asked Finny, "How's your sex life?"

Finny was slicing some pears into long strips. "It's more of an afterlife," Finny said. "I don't have that much time since I'm heading the after-school program, too."

"I take it you don't see Earl anymore, then?"

"No," Finny said. For some reason she didn't feel comfortable getting into it with Judith. She hoped her friend wouldn't ask any more questions.

Judith seemed to take a moment to absorb the information. Then she said, "Prince and I tried anal sex for the first time recently."

Finny wasn't sure how they'd arrived at this topic, or whether she really needed the inevitable mental pictures it would inspire. "That's funny," she said, "I just had calamari for the first time."

Judith looked puzzled. "I'd always been afraid of it," she went on. "I just thought of it as somehow dirty. Like something they'd do in a porno. We'd tried it once, about five years ago, but Prince couldn't even get in me. This is going to be gross, but I have to tell you: it felt like I was taking a shit backward. I know, I know, it's disgusting."

"I felt the same way with calamari," Finny said. She finished with her pears. "What else?" she said to Judith.

"There's a nice aged Gouda in the fridge," Judith said. "You can take that out and chop it up."

Finny opened the heavy door of the refrigerator, hoping that the previous topic had passed, but as soon as Finny had the cheese on the counter, Judith started up again. "I realized the trick," Judith said as Finny saw the grill light up outside in a whoosh of flames, the guys all leaping back for cover. "The trick is to get really lubed up. And then you bring your knees way up, like, almost to your chest. He needed to work his finger around in there for a while to get me to relax. But then he slipped right in. I can't even tell you how amazing it was. I came three times."

Now Judith was spinning the salad dry, and she looked at Finny. "I'm sorry," she said. "I can see I'm making you uncomfortable."

Finny waved her off. "I love Gouda."

"It's just that I don't have girlfriends to tell this stuff to. I'm not even really sure what other women's sex lives are like. I mean, we do it all the time. Prince says he needs it every day to go out there and sell his funds or whatever. So I give it to him."

"It's okay. I'd tell you my stories if I had any."

"By the way," Judith said, "your brother looks really cute with his head shaved."

"I've been telling him to do it for years," Finny said.

"I think Prince is cheating on me," Judith said. "In fact, I know it."

They were joined at dinner by a friend of Prince's named Bradley Miller. Brad had gone to Columbia with Judith and Prince, and he now worked with Prince in finance. He was probably a couple of classes ahead of Judith and Prince, because he looked older, maybe his late thirties. Not unattractive, though. He was nicely built, with strong shoulders, his shirt opened a couple buttons at the neck so Finny could see his bristly chest hair. He was paler than Prince and Judith, with dark hair that was just beginning to make a widow's peak, and he had silvery half-moons under his eyes. Finny guessed he spent a lot of time at the office. He seemed to know about wine and food. He'd brought the bottles of Brunello they were drinking with dinner, and he explained about his travels to the town in Italy where the wine was made, how the long hot summers and mild winters made it the perfect climate for the Sangiovese grapes.

"Is this real silver?" Brad said, touching his knife.

"Yeah," Prince said. "We got it for our wedding."

Brad nodded. "It's nice," he said.

They were eating at the large round table in the living/dining room, in front of the glass doors that led to the deck. It was dark now, and constellations of lights speckled the inlet. You could hear crickets, waves pawing the shore, boats knocking the dock. There was a lazy Susan in the middle of the table, where Judith had laid out all the platters of grilled meats and buns and salad and potatoes, and people spun the wheel back and forth to get what they wanted. Homer ate his burger off the same china the other guests did, lying on the floor next to Korinne, and Prince's sister frequently stopped the conversation to point out something about Homer's tastes—such as that he liked onions but abhorred pickles—and everyone had to agree how interesting it was before the conversation moved on. Brad had traveled a lot in Europe, and he and Finny had a long exchange about their favorite things to do in Paris. When Brad mentioned a restaurant Finny hadn't tried—it sounded very expensive—he said, "Well, I'll have to take you sometime." Judith grinned at Finny when he said that, and Finny said she'd have to check her calendar.

"What the hell do you people do here on the weekends?" Carter said, amidst the clacking of knives and forks. Finny could tell he'd been fighting the urge to sip from the glass of wine set before him. His abstinence must have been making him cranky.

"Mostly quiet stuff," Judith said. "We can go to the beach tomorrow. Take a walk in town."

"Or maybe do some knitting," Carter suggested.

Sylvan laughed, but Prince didn't seem to find it funny. "When you have a long hard week of *work*," he told Carter, emphasizing this last word as if it were a foreign term, "it's nice to have a little peace and quiet at the end of it. Judith and I take a long bike ride most mornings, then go for a swim in the bay and have a big breakfast."

"I'd actually love to check out the town," Sylvan said, and Finny recognized the therapist's instinct in her brother to defuse the tension. "I'm curious to see some of the shops."

"I'll show you around," Judith said quickly, and flashed a smile at Sylvan. Judith pushed a strand of hair behind one of her ears—a gesture Prince couldn't have noticed because he was seated next to her—and Finny once again got the distinct impression that Judith was flirting. She was wearing another low-cut shirt, made of a loose gold netted fabric, and a diamond necklace that dropped into the shadows between her breasts.

"That would be great," Sylvan said, and smiled back at Judith.

"I've been meaning to ask you, is this real?" Brad Miller said, brushing his hand along the marble top of a cabinet behind him. But before anyone answered, he said, "It's beautiful."

Finny excused herself to use the bathroom.

"You can use ours," Judith said. "It's right behind you."

Finny went into the master bedroom and closed the door. The room was more disheveled than Finny had expected, clothes on the bed and floor, and only a small window, now shielded with blinds, above the large mahogany bed frame. The carpet was a faded pastel blue, and felt damp under Finny's toes from the sea air. The bathroom was to Finny's right, and she was just about to step in when she remembered something. What she remembered was the day she'd arrived at Thorndon and looked into Judith's dresser before Judith had gotten there, seeing all of Judith's black clothes. Now Finny looked at the large armoire next to the bed, made of the same mahogany as the bed frame, with a matching ornamented trim. Of course Judith and Prince would have a bedroom set in their vacation home. But what interested Finny more was what Judith had *inside* her closet now. She felt an almost unbearable urge to open the mahogany armoire.

So she did. She wasn't normally a snoop. But Judith seemed to bring it out in her. Finny needed to get to the bottom of her friend's mystery. She wanted to know who Judith Turngate actually was, behind the smiling and the makeup and the sex talk. What was the reason for all of it?

Most of the clothes on the hangers were standard beach stuff—sundresses, and cute little tops, shorts, and some skirts and dresses for the evenings. Tucked in between were some racier samples of lingerie: lots of lace and silk. Finny went on to the drawers. Here were G-strings and push-up bras. They weren't things that Finny would have ever worn herself, but still, somehow she'd expected more.

She was careful to keep everything in the exact place and

folded in the exact way she'd found them. Finny was about to close the armoire, resigned to the impenetrableness of Judith, when she saw on the top shelf of the dresser, in precisely the spot where she'd found Judith's black lipstick twenty years before, a small stack of photographs. Finny lifted the stack, making sure not to smudge the photographs, and began to thumb through them.

The first few were standard couple photos of Judith and Prince, arms around each other, smiling at the camera. But as she went through the stack, the photos changed. There was one of Judith naked, taken from below. She was straddling a man who must have been Prince, cupping her breasts in her manicured fingers. Another photo showed Judith in one of her lingerie outfits—a black and pink one—bending over to display the pink rim of her anus to the camera, smiling shyly, almost timidly, over her shoulder, like she'd been cajoled into taking the picture. There was a photo that must have been taken in the mirror, of Prince mounting Judith from behind, flexing his biceps. What the hell *is* this? Finny thought. And yet she couldn't stop. Not until she got to the final photo—of Judith wearing dark lipstick, her mouth shaped like an *O*, ready to accept Prince's penis (which Carter had correctly identified as tiny).

Just as Finny was stacking the photos back up, a small slip of paper fluttered out of the top of the pile, which Finny had only skimmed through. The paper sailed to the floor like a feather in a breeze. Finny picked it up. A note was written on it: *You shouldn't be looking at these.* It was in Judith's handwriting—the same writing that had been slipped under Poplan's door at Thorndon. Finny turned around. She had the uncanny sensation that Judith was in the room with her. Yet no one was there. Finny remembered Judith's comment at Thorndon that "no one stops at the top of the dresser," and now Finny saw the wisdom of it, of what Judith had known at such a young age: once you've opened the door, you've already crossed over. Finny wondered if the note was intended for her.

Finny gathered everything as well as it could be gathered. She knew that eventually Judith would probably figure out what Finny had done. The certainty was in the note. A beautiful woman like Judith knows people will want to go through her stuff. It's probably why Judith had told Finny to use the master bathroom in the first place.

Finny put the photos back on the shelf and went to the bathroom.

Back at the table, Judith asked Finny, "Are you okay?"

"Yeah," Finny said. "Just more to drink than I'm used to."

Brad looked concerned. "Drink a lot of water," he said. "In London, since the bars close so early, we used to pound a dozen beers, then drink a gallon jug of water so we could walk home."

"If Homer's stomach is upset," Korinne offered, "I crush up Pepto-Bismol tablets in his food. It's funny: he's very picky. He'll only eat Pepto, not Tums or Mylanta."

"He would have gotten along with Dad," Sylvan joked to Finny.

She smiled at everyone. She had the feeling the room was spinning, or rocking, as in a large boat. "Really, I'm fine," she said.

And Judith grinned in the knowing way she had earlier, when Sylvan had looked at her breasts.

After dinner they turned on a movie. They sat on the enormous wraparound couch—enough room for fifteen people, like the couch Judith's parents had at the Beresford—which was behind the dining table. The movie was some silly action story that Finny couldn't put the effort in to follow, and besides, she was distracted by the fact that every time there was a sex scene, Korinne let out a little shriek and placed her hand over

Homer's eyes, claiming, "He's very sensitive. He's offended by gratuitous nudity." Carter was asleep. Prince and Brad were talking about investments. Judith was in the kitchen, washing dishes. She'd insisted that no one could help her.

"You want to go for a walk?" Sylvan asked Finny.

"I can't tell you how badly," Finny said.

They walked down to the belt of beach around the inlet. It was quiet here, with just the sounds of the water and the boats. Finny could see into the houses of some of the other people who lived on the water—warmly lit kitchens and living rooms, the flicker of television sets.

"So, what's your surprise?" she said to her brother. They were walking barefoot, and the sand and seaweed were cold on Finny's feet.

Sylvan laughed. "I was just going to tell you," he said.

"So?"

"I'm engaged," he told Finny.

She stopped and punched him on the arm. "Hey," she said. "Congratulations!" She hugged him. She was thrilled for her brother. With only one reservation: for some reason she couldn't get the image of him looking down Judith's dress out of her head.

"Thanks," he said, in his awkward way. "I know, it's weird."

"Are you happy?"

"I think so," Sylvan said. "She's great." And then he added, "Mari, I mean."

Back inside, Carter had gone to bed. He was going to be sharing a room with Finny that had two twin beds in it. Sylvan had the room across the hall, which had a double bed, since Judith hadn't been sure if he was going to bring Mari. Korinne was sleeping on the couch, since she said that Homer liked to get up at four-thirty for his walk, and Prince said that no one else would want to hear that.

Brad was ready to go. He kissed Judith goodbye and shook hands with Sylvan and Prince. Then he said to Finny, "Walk me to the door?"

They walked outside and stood on the front porch together. A few cars sped past on Dune Road, their headlights briefly lighting the pine trees in front of the house.

"I waited for you to get back before I left," Brad said to Finny. Finny could see now that he was swaying a little from the Brunello. His eyes moved up and down Finny's body in the appraising way he looked at Prince's expensive things, and Finny half-expected him to ask if she was real.

She was about to make a joke, when Brad leaned over and kissed her on the mouth. He then put his hands around her waist and drew her to him. Normally Finny would have pulled back, or kicked him, or screamed, but something about the suddenness of it, the confident—even forceful—way he drew her in, it surprised her. She felt a hot spark of lust, a familiar spreading warmth, and she found she liked kissing him.

In a few minutes, after some hasty examinations of each other's bodies, Brad said, "You know, I'm in Boston all the time for business. I'd love to take you out for dinner." He pulled a card from his pocket with his number on it. "I really enjoyed, uh, talking to you."

He squeezed her hand, then got in his car—a purple Audi—and drove off.

Inside the house, Judith said, "I guess you guys hit it off."

"I think so," Finny said, still a little dizzy from the wine and the sexual charge of Brad's embrace.

"I had a feeling," Judith said.

Carter was snoring when Finny came into their room. He was passed out, an episode of *The Golden Girls* playing on the little TV in front of the bed. "I should always meet men lying down," the Southern character said. Then the sassy old woman said, "I thought you did." Canned laughter spilled into the room. Finny flipped channels on the TV for a few minutes; she didn't feel like sleeping. She washed up in the bathroom and came back out in her pajamas. It was after midnight. She assumed everyone was asleep.

Then she heard a door click open in the hall. It was Sylvan's door, and Finny rushed to the door of her own room to catch him. She didn't know what she'd say, but she wanted to talk to him.

She opened her door, and was on the point of speaking, when she saw that it wasn't Sylvan coming out of his room. It was Judith, wearing a silky Asian-printed nightgown that barely covered her backside. The nightgown was only loosely knotted around Judith's waist, as if she'd put it on in a hurry.

Finny and Judith looked at each other across the dark hallway, silently acknowledging the other's presence. But they didn't say anything. Judith walked back to her bedroom.

In the morning Sylvan was seated on a stool at the island in the sunny kitchen, hunched over a bowl of Cheerios. He was reading the *Times*, which they'd gotten early, and sipping intermittently from a mug of coffee.

"Hey," Finny said when she walked into the kitchen.

"They're fighting," Sylvan said.

At first Finny thought he meant Prince and his sister, since they'd seemed testy with each other the night before. But then Finny heard Judith shouting behind the bedroom door, "Nothing. It didn't mean *anything*."

"What happened?" Finny said.

"I don't know," Sylvan said. "I woke up and things seemed okay. I said hi to Judith. Then I went to wash up, and when I came back, they had the door closed and were yelling at each other. I don't know if I had something to do with it."

Finny kept looking at her brother, to see if he would say more, mention Judith's trip to his bedroom last night. But he just shook his head and stuffed a large spoonful of Cheerios in his mouth.

"Not again!" Prince screamed. "I'm sick of this, Judith. Your behavior is disgusting."

Finny heard Judith crying, then Finny said to her brother, "Where's Korinne?"

"Walking the dog. How about Carter?"

"I think he's planning to sleep through the whole weekend. He's had a hard time, Sylvan. He's just getting his life together."

"Tell him to let me know how it feels," Sylvan said, and Finny wasn't sure if it was an invitation to ask about what wasn't together in Sylvan's life.

"You feel like you're ready to get married?" Finny tried.

"I'm ready for a change," Sylvan said. "Yeah, I'm ready. I feel like I'm going in circles now, and I need to head down a path. I love Mari. I really think she's a good person. We have fun together."

Finny nodded. It was another bright, calm day outside. The water in the inlet was so still it reflected a perfect view of the sky. Seagulls sat on the dock pilings, their eyes ticking over the scenery. Then Judith shouted, "You *bastard*! Give me those!"

"Beautiful morning," Sylvan said.

But Finny felt she had to say something. "Sylvan," she started, "really, do you think you have anything to do with it? With why they're fighting?"

Sylvan shrugged and looked back at the newspaper. He read for a couple of seconds. Then, without lifting his eyes, he said, "If Judith can't let go, it's certainly not my fault."

"But don't you think it's better for you both to let go?" Finny prompted him.

Before Sylvan could respond, though, Korinne burst

through the front door with Homer on a leash. "I've been up since four-fifteen!" she shouted into the house.

The door to Finny's room opened, and Carter came out in his boxers and an undershirt, scratching his stomach. "Woo-hoo," he said. "Hope you all didn't wait for me."

"Wait for you?" Korinne said. "We've already walked five miles. Homer prefers walking on the beach, which is a better workout anyway. And we had to stop at the bakery in town for a linzer torte, since that's his favorite breakfast in the world. He gets the sugar all over his face and it looks like—"

But Korinne was interrupted by a crash from the bedroom. Then the door swung open, and Judith stepped through, shutting it behind her. She strode into the living room, wearing shorts and a sleeveless athletic top. "Leave me alone!" she called back to Prince. Her eyes were red and her face was splotchy. For the first time this weekend she wasn't wearing makeup, and her skin had a puffiness that made her look tired.

The door opened again and Prince was standing there, in a loose-fitting T-shirt and spandex biking shorts. "And take your fucking whore photographs!" he said, tossing a handful of photos into the living room after Judith. Prince slammed the door so forcefully the house shook, and as they recovered from the sound, the photos twirled like snowflakes through the room.

"Oh God," Judith said, running to snatch all the pictures before anyone saw them. Of course Finny knew which photos they were. Prince must have tossed them into the room just to humiliate his wife.

Judith couldn't grab them quickly enough, though, because in a moment Korinne let out a long howl, as if she'd been struck down in battle. She clapped her hand over Homer's eyes, keeping her own shut, and screamed, "It's too awful for words! He's going to be traumatized!"

"Oh, let me see," Carter said, bending over to pick up one

of the photos. He examined it, and said, "Judith, this is a good angle for you."

Judith fell on her knees, buried her face in her hands, and wept, her chest heaving, her shoulders shaking. Finny expected Sylvan to run to comfort her—it was what he always did—but this time he just sat there, watching her from his stool in the kitchen. So Finny went over and kneeled down. Put her arm around Judith's shoulders. Helped her up off the floor. The others watched, quiet as a theater audience. Only Korinne repeated the word *traumatized,* as if to make sure everyone had heard. She still had her hand over Homer's eyes.

Then the phone began to ring. Once, twice, three times, the jangling covering up Judith's crying.

"You want me to get it?" Sylvan said.

Judith didn't respond, so Sylvan picked up the phone. "Hello?" he said. Everyone's attention turned to him, as if the caller might provide the comfort they were waiting for. Finny could tell it was a woman's voice on the other end, because of the tinny sound.

Sylvan said, "Uh-huh. Yeah. Sure. I'll get her."

He held the phone up, and Finny was about to tell him he should probably take a message, when Sylvan said, "Finny, it's for you."

Chapter 33

Another Trip

The next half hour—which involved Finny racing around the house to gather her things, get dressed, and purchase airplane tickets—provided a much-needed distraction from that morning's episode. Everyone seemed to rally around Finny, and all the energy that had previously been directed toward the conflict between Prince and Judith was now rerouted toward getting Finny to her plane. Sylvan agreed to get on the computer to check prices and schedules, and then call various airlines if it was too last-minute to purchase tickets on the Web. Carter helped Finny comb the bedroom and bathroom for dropped clothes and personal items. Judith made Finny sandwiches from the leftover meat and packed them in a Zabar's bag. Korinne performed the double duty of keeping Homer out of Finny's way and making sure Homer wasn't frightened by the commotion of Finny's departure. Even Prince finally came out of the bedroom and offered to give Finny a ride to the airport, or pay for a cab, though Sylvan said he was planning to take Finny.

The flight was from MacArthur airport, in Islip, a good fifty-minute drive from Judith's house. When Finny had her bag packed, she said a hurried goodbye to everyone, not even taking the time to give hugs since she was in that much of a hurry. She told Judith she would call her, and thanked Prince for letting her stay at his house. Then she thanked everyone else. She couldn't even think straight; she just wanted to get on the road. Finally, she was strapped into her seat in Sylvan's car. She said to her brother, "I know you're normally not a speed demon, but you're going to have to zoom a little for me. I can't miss this plane."

"I know," Sylvan said.

And so his Ford Taurus was driven as it had never been driven before. Tires screeched, the engine groaned, turn signals were neglected, traffic lights ignored.

"Who's going to pick you up when you get there?" Sylvan asked.

"I'll call the airport shuttle," Finny said.

"That's going to waste your time. Why don't I call from my cellphone once I drop you off?"

"I don't know the number."

"I'll get it," Sylvan said. "Don't worry." He patted her on the leg. "I'll give them your flight info."

She was glad Sylvan was the one driving her to the airport. He was good at reassuring her in times of crisis. And there was some continuity in sharing these moments with her brother. They'd been through so many together. She wouldn't have felt as comfortable with anyone else.

"How did she sound?" Sylvan asked Finny now.

"Not like herself," Finny said. "It's the first time I've heard her really panic."

"What else did she say?"

"She gave me a long explanation about how she'd gotten my number. I guess I'd mentioned to her that I was going to Judith's for the weekend. So she called Thorndon and got the number of the beach house from the alumni directory. I wasn't sure why she was telling me all that stuff. I think it was just the first thing that came into her head. It was almost like she couldn't hear herself talk. Her mind was somewhere else."

"It's scary when that happens."

"Especially with someone like Poplan," Finny said. "I always expect her to be in control."

"You can't control this," Sylvan said. "Did she say anything about how he was doing?"

"She said he'd been having stomach pains. And then he just passed out at the dinner table. At first Poplan thought he'd fallen asleep, but when she saw the way he was breathing she realized it was worse than that. She called an ambulance, and it turned out he has a tumor the size of a grapefruit. Inoperable. She said they told her he was in his final days—that he'd been lucky to make it this far. Now he's getting a ton of pain medication. They hired a nurse so he could die at home."

"Oh, Finny," Sylvan said, "it's so sad."

"It really is," Finny said. "I feel like I'm not built to handle this stuff."

"All you can do is what you're doing."

Finny shrugged, but just then an old woman in a large-brimmed hat pulled her Volvo wagon in front of Sylvan's Ford Taurus. She was going only about fifty miles per hour in the fast lane of Sunrise Highway, and Sylvan honked his horn and flashed his lights. But the display had no effect. Sylvan honked some more, but still no response. It was at this point that Sylvan jerked the car into the middle lane, tires screeching, and sped past the old woman who had clogged his lane. In the rearview mirror, Finny saw the old woman, who was wearing large plastic glasses with a librarian chain, lift her hand to give Sylvan the finger.

"Wench," Sylvan said.

In ten minutes they were stopped in front of MacArthur airport and Sylvan was helping Finny get her bag out of the trunk. He gave her a quick hug and said, "Good luck. I love you."

Mr. Henckel's bed had been set up in the living room of the little brown house, so that he could be next to his piano while he slept and woke. At the moment when Finny walked in, he was in a sleeping phase. Poplan was the only conscious member of the household. She greeted Finny with a long hug, explained that the nurse had gone out for the afternoon and that Earl was due to arrive in the evening. She brought Finny to the bedside, where Finny sat in a chair next to the pole on which the IV bag hung, dripping morphine into Mr. Henckel's vein.

Mr. Henckel lay in a square of late-afternoon sunlight that had pierced one of the tiny windows in the room. The light was so clear and soft that it set him off almost unnaturally from the rest of the room, which lay in a dull shade. He looked nearly as pale as his white bed sheets, and his face had an oily sheen to it. He was thinner than Finny remembered him from her last visit. She could see the cords in his neck. It struck her all of a sudden how old he'd gotten; she'd never thought about how old he was when she was a teenager. His hair, or what remained of it, was now a uniform steely gray, like an answer his body had settled on. He had the covers pulled up all the way to his chin, and the morphine must have been responsible for the content look on his face.

"He's been out of it because of the drugs," Poplan said to Finny. Her voice sounded weak, thinner than Finny had ever heard it. "Thank you for coming. He was asking about you before."

"How are you doing?" Finny asked Poplan.

"Exhausted," Poplan said. "This is a lot to take."

Finny reached over and gave Poplan's hand a squeeze, and they both smiled sadly at each other.

"Do you need anything?" Finny asked.

"Just your company," Poplan said. "How was your trip?"

Finny told her about her brother being cut off by the old woman with the glasses and the floppy hat, and Poplan laughed. They talked on about small things for a while, as Mr. Henckel napped. The light from the windows was fading, yet neither of them got up to turn on a switch. Mr. Henckel's eye-lids seemed held shut by the most tenuous pressure, and Finny felt as if the smallest movement might cause them to snap open like window shades. He was sweating now, his forehead wrinkling then falling slack. He seemed to be work-ing over something in his sleep.

"Is he in pain?" Finny said.

"Not for long," Poplan said. "Linda should be back soon."

At around seven Linda showed up, a large dark-skinned black woman with a pink scar over her left eye. She was dressed in hospital scrubs, her hair in braids. She asked Poplan how Mr. Henckel was doing. Poplan introduced Finny, and when Finny extended her hand, Linda gave her a hug. She told Finny about what she was doing for Mr. Henckel—mostly controlling his pain—and said she'd be happy to an-swer any questions Finny had. But Finny didn't have any. She decided to go for a walk while Linda adjusted Mr. Henckel's medicine and cleaned him up for the night.

Finny walked to the old vineyard. She took the familiar path, down the hill, across the road, past the bird pond that was too dark to see at this hour. She hadn't been back across this route since the summer when Earl left that first time, and now, as she walked between the vines that wrapped the wire trellis, she was struck by how small it all looked. She was a head taller than the green walls, and she could see all the way across the valley from where she stood. The countryside was quiet, the sky enormous, a gray-black ocean above. Lights were coming on in the farmhouses, like candles in a dark room. There is so much space in the world, Finny thought, hearing her own breath, looking across the wide valley, feeling a rush of loneliness like a cool breeze. She thought of that night years ago when she'd woken to the sound of pebbles tapping her win-dow, Earl's awful news, their sad goodbye. And the way that af-terward she was left by herself to bear it, as you finally are with all bad news, while the world spins in its well-worn circles.

She was getting cold. Night was dropping its curtain over the valley, and Finny worried she would have trouble finding her way back, it had been so long. So she started off toward the little brown house. She tugged her thin black sweater more tightly around her, the one she'd been wearing yesterday when she got to Judith's. It felt like so long ago.

Back at the house, Earl had arrived. He was sitting in the chair where Finny had sat, next to the IV drip. He got up and gave Finny a hug, thanked her for making the trip. He had a beard now, clipped short, and though he looked older, he was well-groomed and handsome in his way. His body had filled out in the years since Finny had last seen him, the youthful muscularity settling into a comfortable fleshiness—not fat, but solid. He seemed to stand straighter now in his checked sweater and faded khaki pants. He had the look of a tenured professor or a lawyer on his day off.

"It's so good to see you," he told Finny. "If only it wasn't such a miserable occasion."

"I know," Finny said. "It's a sad reunion."

They both sat down next to Poplan. Linda was in the kitchen, reading the Bible and humming to herself. Later she would go to sleep in Earl's bed, which Mr. Henckel had kept for him ever since he'd moved away. Poplan, Earl, and Finny stayed up through the night with Mr. Henckel as he slept in the living room. They'd switched on lamps, which provided only a dim light for the bedside. But it was enough. They could see Mr. Henckel with the sheet pulled up to his chin, looking small and scared as a child. Finny wanted to comfort him, to ease his sleep. They took turns holding the hand that wasn't hooked up to the IV, and when he woke briefly, they whispered comforting things to him, about how much they loved him, how wonderful their memories of him were.

Finny said she'd never forget her piano lessons, that he was the kindest teacher she'd ever had. She said she'd always be grateful for the way he'd welcomed her into his home. He mumbled something back about the coffeepot being warm for her. Earl talked about what a loving father Mr. Henckel had been, how close he'd always felt to him, how lucky he was to have been taken care of so well. He said he knew he was always loved, and he had such great respect for what his father had made of a difficult situation. Poplan simply said that her years with Mr. Henckel were the best and most meaningful of her life. She kissed him on his damp forehead and then wiped it with his handkerchief, the way Mr. Henckel used to after his confessions. They told him all the things they'd never found the right moment or taken the time to say. It was like a bedtime story for Mr. Henckel, as his eyelids began to close. Or like a suitcase they were packing for the journey ahead of him.

Toward morning he woke up. He seemed more lively and alert than he had during the night, though when he spoke, his speech was slurred. "Goff," he said.

"I'm sorry," Poplan said. "What?"

"Goff. Ee."

Earl understood. He went to the kitchen and prepared the coffee, setting the silver pot on the silver tray and then bringing it to the bedside. He poured the coffee into the china cups, and they each clinked their cup against Mr. Henckel's one last time. Mr. Henckel drank his thirstily. Finny distributed the milk and the sugar, stirring it with the little silver spoon, and they all enjoyed a brief coffee party together, like the old days, until Mr. Henckel lost his strength and spilled coffee on himself. Poplan was worried he'd been burnt, but he assured her he was fine, that coffee could never harm him.

"And one more. Thing," Mr. Henckel said, between heavy breaths, as if he'd just run up a flight of stairs. Finny could tell he was still dazed from the morphine, by the way his eyes wandered the room, yet the coffee seemed to have given him strength for this request.

"What is it?" Poplan asked him in her new, softer voice. "Can I get you something, sweetheart?"

Mr. Henckel shook his head slowly. He looked at Earl. "I wanna tell you," he said to his son, his tongue still sluggish. He swallowed to moisten his throat. "That I always thought. You and Finny were good for each other."

And with that, he fell asleep, for what would turn out to be the last time. In the final hours Poplan lay in bed with him, and held him as he slept.

Chapter **34**

Finny and Earl Have a Chance to Catch Up

Fortunately, Linda was there to take care of everything. She liked Poplan, and was happy to help. Poplan wasn't up to all the practical chores she normally would have taken charge of. Linda made the calls, arranged for the paperwork and talked to the funeral home. It ended up that she called Finny's old friends, the Haberdashers, and through the receiver Finny could hear when Mr. Haberdasher let loose a giant sneeze and his wife in her pickled voice yelled, "Holy Christ, you blew my head off!" Linda took the phone away from her ear for a second, then got back on and in a polite, assured way explained that Mr. Henckel was to be cremated.

Since Mr. Henckel's family had disowned him, and he hadn't talked to any of them for years, and his only friends were the kids he taught, they decided it was best not to have a formal service. They took the ashes back to the little brown house, and Finny played a few bars of a piece she remembered from her piano lessons. Earl read a page he'd written about his father's life, including Mr. Henckel's performing days and his time as a teacher. Poplan talked about how rich their life had been together, how she loved nothing more than to see him play the piano, how fulfilling their charity work had been. Poplan had informed Mr. Henckel's students about his death, and over the course of the afternoon, a number of them stopped by to pay their respects.

And then, because they wanted to lend some sense of finality to their ceremony, they decided to pour the ashes out of the bag, into the silver coffeepot. Earl did it, since he had the steadiest hands, and they listened to the sand raining on the bottom of the pot. Then Poplan said she would keep the pot on the piano, for as long as she stayed in the house. She didn't plan to be going anywhere soon. She would keep up the after-school program, and maybe go back to working at a school as well. Earl was going to stay with her for a few days, until she was ready to be on her own. Having Mr. Henckel's remains in the house with her, she said, would help her feel less lonely.

Earl offered to drive Finny to the airport in Mr. Henckel's car, a brown station wagon, though not the same one he had driven when Finny was a child. Finny had taken two days off work and couldn't afford to leave her kids with a sub any longer since it was the end of the school year. So she said goodbye to Poplan and that she hoped Poplan would come visit her in Boston when she felt up to it. They hugged, and Poplan thanked Finny for coming all this way to be with them.

"I'd always known you'd turn out to be a special person," Poplan said.

"I wouldn't have been anything without you and Mr. Henckel," Finny said.

Then she and Earl got into the car and started off toward the airport.

Finny and Earl hadn't said anything to each other about their lives for the entire three days they'd been together, since all their attention had been focused on Mr. Henckel, and now Finny experienced that old feeling of having too much to say to Earl, not knowing where to begin. Having spent such an intense couple of days with him, Finny didn't even feel angry or disappointed with Earl now; she simply wanted to talk, to open herself up to someone she could trust, who knew her. It was Wednesday evening, and she was booked on the last flight from BWI to Boston. She would get in around ten o'clock.

Earl steered them onto the paved tongue of the expressway ramp. He was saying something about Air France and American Airlines, how the food was better on one but the other was more punctual, but Finny couldn't still her mind for long enough to take it in. The car's wheels thumped little heartbeats over the grooves in the road. The stadium lights above the highway were lit, charging the night sky with an electric brightness. As they merged onto the road, Finny saw that it was crowded with the red and yellow cat eyes of other cars. The sheer number of other people was a surprise to Finny, after seeing so few people in Mr. Henckel's house, and Judith's before that. But here were other families, other lives, other stories. For a second, Finny was overwhelmed by the multitude of destinations, of paths that crossed and recrossed, journeys beginning or coming to an end.

"I wish we had more time to catch up," Earl said. His face had a raw, windburned look from all the crying he'd been doing the last couple days. "I know this just isn't the right time."

"I do, too," Finny said. "I mean, I wish we had a few minutes to chat."

"Are things going well?"

"Pretty well." She felt as if she should say something to lighten the mood between them, there'd been so much heaviness the last couple days, so she told Earl, "The other day one of my kids said he knew the 'three baddest words in the world.'"

"What are they?" Earl asked.

"*Crap, ass, sass,*" Finny said, "according to Gabe. I'm not sure how *sass* got in there."

Earl laughed. Finny could tell he was relieved to hear something funny. "Sass is not always a bad thing," he said, glancing at Finny. "It really could go either way."

"So do you think your mom will want to hear about your dad?" Finny asked Earl.

"Um," he said, and swallowed. "My mom passed away, Finny."

"I—" Finny began, but couldn't finish the thought. "I'm sorry, Earl. What happened?"

"She took pills," Earl said. "Last winter. It was all really sad. But it was a long time coming. She never really got her head above water. In the end, even having me there didn't make a difference. There was nothing I could do."

Why didn't you tell me? Finny almost asked Earl. But then she recalled sitting with her brother in the hospital cafeteria, after her mother died, and deciding not to share her own news with Earl. She couldn't blame him. It wasn't the kind of thing you called someone up to report when you hadn't seen the person in years.

So Finny said, "My mom died, too. Last summer. Heart disease."

"I'm really sorry," Earl said, glancing over at Finny again. She noticed his eyes had a way of creasing in the corners. She could tell he was sad for her. Earl never had to fake his sympathy. If anything, he felt too much.

"We're a pretty cheerful crowd," Finny said.

Earl let out a long breath. Again he seemed much older to Finny. "You know, I keep telling myself it's part of life," he said. "But that doesn't really help. It doesn't make it any easier." He shook his head. He seemed to be grieving over more than just his own losses.

"You never think about this part when you're younger," Finny said. "It's natural to ignore it. You're too caught up in the fun. But it's like you can't have one without the other."

"Beginnings and endings," Earl said.

But Finny felt they'd gone far enough down this road. "Anyway," she said, "are you planning to keep your mother's place, or did you decide to move?" She wanted to steer them away from these gloomy subjects.

"I'm going to move," Earl said. "The only reason I stayed was that I was finishing up some writing and editing. I actually have a book coming out."

"Wow. That's terrific news, Earl." She really was excited for him, knowing how hard he'd worked for it. "Did your dad know?"

Earl nodded, pressed his lips together. "He got to read the stories this year. He said some nice things." Earl's voice was flat as he reported this news about his life. Finny could tell he was depressed, and as always, her heart leapt toward him. She had to restrain herself from reaching out to touch him.

"It's not a huge deal or anything," Earl went on. "I won a contest. A university press is putting the collection out. Pittsburgh, actually. They're just going to print a couple thousand copies."

"Still. That's great." She put her hand on Earl's shoulder and squeezed. "I'm proud of you, Earl. I knew you'd do it one day. I'm sorry it comes at such a sad time, but you should feel good about this. What's the book called?"

"It's called *Calling Across the Years*," Earl said, flushing a little, the way he used to when he was younger. "I'm not crazy about the title. Especially now. It seems dramatic and silly to me. But I just wanted to capture the idea of moving across time. It's a line from one of the stories."

"I like the title a lot," Finny said. "It's pretty."

"You think so?"

"Yeah. But you remember our deal?"

Earl smiled. "Of course," he said. "A personal letter. I'll write it inside the front cover for you. As soon as the book comes out."

"I'll look forward to it."

And then Earl looked at Finny and said, "I have another piece of news. There just wasn't a good time for me to say it."

"What is it?" she said, watching the pavement stream beneath their headlights.

He turned back to the road. He opened his lips, then closed them, as if considering what to say. Then he told her, "I'm seeing someone, Finny. I mean, living with her."

"Oh," she heard herself say. She didn't know why, but the news struck her with an almost physical force. For some reason, she'd assumed Earl was moping around his Paris apartment by himself. And then she realized: she'd been waiting for him to ask her out, to say they should give it another try.

"Well, congratulations again," she said to Earl, though she knew her voice sounded odd, plastic.

"I didn't say anything at the house because it just didn't seem like the right time to talk about it. I know this is a bad way to end our visit, but I thought you'd want to know."

"I'm glad you told me."

"I met her while I was teaching a writing workshop in France," Earl continued. "She was a student." He blushed again. "Her name's Mavis. She's American. Ten years younger than me, to tell you the truth. She was studying abroad. We just kind of hit it off. She's living with me now. She would have come, but it would have been hard for us to afford the trip if we both took off work. Plus, I hadn't really talked to Dad about her. She's working as an assistant to a fairly well-known French scholar." Earl looked uncomfortable. She knew he felt like he needed to explain.

But she didn't want to hear any of that. She didn't want to put either of them through the discomfort of it. So she said, "Actually, I met someone, too. I'm really glad for you, Earl. We should do a double date sometime."

"Oh," Earl said, his mouth dropping open a little. "Oh. That's great." She could tell he was surprised by her news, that it hadn't been what he'd expected either. Yet he kept talking. "Mavis and I are hoping to move to a larger place in Paris, now that I'm done with the book. I have some fellowship money, and I've been working different jobs. Mavis can't leave Paris, because of her work. It's too good an opportunity for her. But she's hoping to come to New York with me this fall, when my book comes out. Maybe we can all hang out together then."

"Great," Finny said.

"What's your boyfriend's name?" Earl asked.

"Brad. Brad Miller. It sounds plain, I know, but he's a fascinating guy. He's traveled all over Europe." She felt that if she kept talking she could pave over the silence between them, the things they didn't say, the words Mr. Henckel had left them with. Finny didn't want to be alone in her head with these thoughts. If she kept talking, it wouldn't quite be real.

"I'm happy for you," Earl said. With an effort, he smiled; there was something hesitant and unconvincing in his manner. "Brad sounds really nice."

Their conversation was awkward for the rest of the ride. They jumped between topics, such as the weather in Paris versus Boston, Finny's teaching routine, the best ways to travel in the U.S. and in France, the relative merits of living in your own country versus moving abroad. They finally agreed that each experience was good in its own way, and felt comfortable leaving it at that.

Earl pulled up to the curb in the drop-off lane at BWI. Finny got out and took her bag from the back of the station wagon. She shut the door and was just planning to wave to Earl through the window, but he got out of the car and came over to her side. He put his arms around her, and they both hugged each other more tightly than they normally would have. She could tell there was so much left to say, but neither of them could figure out how to say it, to step across the gap between them. Finny felt herself begin to cry as Earl held her, and she swallowed back the hot ball in her throat. Neither of them seemed to want to let go. Only when several cars honked behind them did they loosen their grips on each other. As they came apart, Finny's lips brushed Earl's. She didn't know if it was his initiative or hers, but she saw that he noticed it. He had a startled expression on his face. It wasn't exactly what you'd call a kiss, though it felt like the beginning of one. Again, Earl seemed like he had something to say but was holding back.

She told Earl to let her know the dates he'd be in New York, and he promised he would. They exchanged email addresses. She said that she thought his dad was a great man, like a father to Finny, and she felt so sad about losing him. Earl thanked her, and said he would get that letter to her when the book came out in the fall. She said she couldn't wait.

Then they said goodbye.

Chapter **35**

Another First Date

It was easy to immerse herself in her life in Boston in the weeks after she'd left Baltimore. She caught up on her shopping and bill paying, her phone calls and emails. She got her hair cut, shorter than she'd ever had it before, almost boyish, though mussed in a hip way. Everyone at work said they liked it. And then there were the last weeks of school, the parent conferences and student reports. Through all this activity, Finny was successful at making the sad events of her time in Baltimore feel distant, like something she'd experienced a long time ago. She remembered a phrase from the first story Earl had shown her, when the narrator is describing the way he felt about his father, and he said that his dad was like an object in the rearview mirror. It was how so much of Finny's life felt now. She was young, but she felt old, like she'd lived a lot.

The only connection to her past now were the periodic calls she made to check in on Poplan. They didn't seem to have much news for each other, but somehow they were always able to fill up an hour on the phone. They could talk about anything—about something they saw on TV, or the books they were reading, or trips they would like to take. Finny felt so comfortable with Poplan that sometimes they could sit for a minute or two on the phone without saying anything, and it wasn't awkward. Poplan seemed more subdued now that Mr. Henckel had passed away. Finny kept telling her she should come up to Boston, but they never got around to planning it.

She hadn't heard from Judith since the weekend in the Hamptons, except for a brief email saying how sorry Judith was about Earl's dad, and that she hoped Finny would call her when she felt up to it. But in truth, Finny didn't feel up to it. She still couldn't shake the image of Judith in her nightgown coming out of Sylvan's room, the way Judith had looked at her in the hallway without saying anything, as if acknowledging both Finny's presence and how meaningless it was at the same time. Finny felt awful for how screwed up Judith's marriage was, but she also couldn't help thinking that Judith had brought it on herself.

As for Sylvan, Finny didn't get around to calling him either. As much as she would have hated to admit it, she'd lost respect for her brother after seeing him collapse under the weight of Judith's sexual advances. And she couldn't tell him that, how hurt she'd been by it. So she stayed away. She wrote emails that didn't say much.

The only notable event in the early part of summer was a call from Julie Fried, the editor Finny had worked under at *Doll's Apartment* magazine in New York. The ostensible purpose of the call was to say hi, see how Finny was doing, but after a minute of small talk Julie said, "Look, you know I can't do all this how-are-the-grandkids stuff. I just want to tell you we have a job for you, Finny. An editorial assistant position is opening up after Thanksgiving. You'd be on a track to full editor. We only do it with people we really like. I know it's not *The New Yorker*, but usually our people do pretty well. And by the way, the salary's a little better than last time we talked." Julie named a figure that wasn't as horrifyingly low as the previous one.

"It's not that I don't want to do it," Finny said. "It's just a little late for me to be starting over."

"Think about it, okay? Even though you're a hundred years old."

Finny laughed. "Thanks," she said, and hung up.

Only toward the end of July, a month after school had let out, two months after Mr. Henckel's death, did Finny begin to feel a little bored. Earl had never written about when he was coming to New York, and the long hot month of August stretched ahead of her like a sun-parched field. It was around this time that, going through her address book one evening, she came upon the card Brad Miller had placed in her hand the night he'd kissed her in front of Judith's vacation home.

Impulsively, she picked up the phone and dialed what she guessed was his cellphone, a 917 number. It rang five times, and Finny was on the point of hanging up when the line clicked on and she heard Brad say, "Brad Miller."

Did she really want to go through with this?

"Hello?" Brad said.

She knew that if she hung up now she could never call again, since her number would be in Brad's phone and the next time she called he would guess what had happened. But it was okay. She didn't need this.

And yet, against every good instinct, she found herself saying, "Hi, Brad? This is Finny Short, Judith's friend from—"

But he stopped her. "I'm so glad you called," he said. "I've been thinking about you."

It turned out Brad was coming to town that week for business. He and Finny made plans to meet on Friday night at a restaurant Brad wanted to try on Hampshire Street in Cambridge. He'd offered to pick Finny up at her apartment, but she assured him that the restaurant was a very short walk from her place and she liked getting the exercise.

Their reservation was for eight o'clock on Friday night, and Finny was running late. At seven-thirty she was still having trouble choosing her outfit. The blouse she'd originally planned to wear looked too low-cut when she put it on. So she switched to a vintage summer dress that showed off her legs, but then decided it was too formal for the occasion. So she went back to the blouse, which had a way of highlighting her shoulders and the plane of her chest. Since she didn't have boobs, she found she did best to accentuate her long, thin body. But then her hair didn't seem to do what she wanted it to. Her new style required her to comb it with her fingers, but it kept sticking up in back in a way that made it look like she'd just gotten out of bed. Maybe it was the humidity. In any case, she finally had to give up. She walked out the door at 7:56.

At the restaurant, Brad was already seated at their table. He was wearing a suit, without a tie. Like in Westhampton, Brad had the appearance of just having come from work. He looked a little pale and worn-out, and Finny figured it had been a long week for him. His forehead reflected the overhead lights as he studied the wine list, not seeing Finny as she approached the table. The top buttons of his shirt were undone once again, revealing a nest of chest hair. Finny couldn't help feeling a pulse of excitement—or was it anxiety?—at the sight of him.

When she was next to the table, she said hello. He got up and kissed her, then looked her up and down in the approving way he had that night on Long Island, like she was a car he was planning to purchase.

"I love your hair," he said as they were getting seated.

"Oh," Finny said. "Thanks. Actually, it was giving me all kinds of problems tonight. I'm sorry I'm late." She wondered if she'd given away too much by saying all this. Would he expect more if he knew she'd taken time to get ready for him?

But Brad simply smiled at Finny—he had a wide, pleasant smile that showed some teeth—and said, "If we were in New

York, you'd be early. Don't worry about it. I just figured I'd get our table. This place is so popular."

Finny looked around at the restaurant. It was a cute place. The dining room, where they were sitting, was designed simply, with wood paneling and floors made of some kind of varnished stone. The tables were packed tightly together, but Brad had gotten a booth near the back of the room, which gave them a bit more privacy. A long window to Finny's right offered a view of Hampshire Street, a quiet, mostly residential street. Only a few cars passed at this hour, and once in a while a couple or a small group on their way to a neighborhood bar. From the menu, it seemed the food was Middle Eastern, though the prices were much higher than what Finny would have expected for that type of food.

"Why don't we make things easy?" Brad said. "We can get the tasting menu and a nice bottle of wine. Then we don't have to make any decisions and we can enjoy each other's company."

"Or sit in agonizing silence," Finny said.

"Or that." Brad smiled.

In truth, she wouldn't have minded looking over the menu, which seemed interesting to her—cinnamon-scented pork, scallops wrapped in phyllo dough—but she agreed it was nice not to have to make decisions. She glanced at the price of the tasting menu—eighty-five dollars—and said a silent prayer that Brad had a generous expense account.

When the waitress arrived, Brad ordered for them. He then deliberated over the wine, whether to start with a Viognier or a Grüner Veltliner, two names Finny had never heard and that sounded vaguely like the names of exotic dancers.

Finny said, "I only usually have a glass, so get whatever you'd like. I'll have a lamp shade on my head in ten minutes either way."

"I don't see any lamp shades around," Brad said.

"I brought one."

Brad laughed. He settled on the Grüner, thanking the wait-ress for her help.

"So, what made you pick up the phone and call me all of a sudden?" Brad asked.

"Drugs," Finny said, and for a second Brad looked alarmed. "No. Actually, I'd been meaning to, but it's been a busy time." She didn't want to explain about Mr. Henckel, her trip to Baltimore, catching up at work. She figured Prince wouldn't have mentioned it. And furthermore, Finny felt de-tached from all that history tonight. Part of why she was in-terested in Brad was that she could be someone else, play a new role.

"Well, either way," Brad said, "I'm really excited to get to spend the evening with you." He reached across the table and squeezed her hand the way he had that night on Long Island, before he got into his car. They smiled at each other, and Finny felt again the flutter of anticipation Brad seemed to awaken in her.

The waitress came and poured their wine. Brad swirled it and sniffed it and tasted it. Then nodded his approval. Before the waitress left, he asked her, "Is this real bluestone?" point-ing at the floor.

"Yeah, they spent a fortune on it," she said.

"I had a feeling," Brad said. He had a way of letting con-versations hang like that, never stating his purpose, and the waitress hesitated a moment before leaving the table.

The food runner brought their first course, which was a miniature falafel made with spinach. Finny wrapped hers in the homemade pita bread and took a bite.

"Definitely better than Mamoun's," she joked.

"I should hope so," Brad said. "I've been reading such great reviews about this place."

She assured him it was a wonderful choice. They moved through a couple more tasty dishes: a salad with garlicky dressing, a peasant casserole with scalloped potatoes and spicy ground lamb, everything like miniature versions of less expensive dishes Finny had tried in other restaurants. They talked about their jobs and how nice Prince and Judith's place on Long Island was. Soon they'd finished the first bottle of wine. Brad ordered a second, with less discussion this time, then excused himself to use the bathroom.

When he came back, he looked refreshed. He seemed to have splashed cold water on his face, since his forehead was damp again. He still had the silvery half-moons under his eyes, but they were fainter. Finny admired his muscular arms, and the confident way he pushed his chest out when he walked.

"So," Brad said, "the important question is what we're going to do after this."

"I don't know," Finny said. "We could find an old lady to stick up. Or steal a car and go for a joy ride. Or just go for a walk or something. Your call."

"Let's keep thinking about it," Brad said. He'd nudged up closer to her under the table, and now she could feel his knee against hers. Suddenly his hand was there, too, and she felt him massaging her leg.

"Do you like that?" he said.

"My quads are a little tight since I played basketball the other day," Finny began, before realizing she didn't know what she was saying. "So it feels good."

"Good," Brad said, and flashed his wide smile. It was a corny gesture—the thought struck her that he was a silly man—but still, she couldn't help those tingly rushes of excitement rippling through her body when he touched her. She could feel herself getting warm, and the dampness between her legs. It was as if what she'd told Earl about her relationship with Brad were a kind of pact, and now it was simply a matter of going through with it.

Soon Brad excused himself again. He came back excited and bright-eyed, asking Finny if she'd thought more about what they'd do afterward. She said she hadn't. So they kept eating. And drinking. Brad went through more wine than she did, though Finny drank plenty. Maybe all the wine was the reason Brad kept getting up to use the bathroom. Finny counted that it was close to half a dozen trips by the time the shared dessert arrived—an enormous baked Alaska, its snowy peaks singed by a blowtorch. It was beautiful, but Finny was full.

"I think I'd have to sign a waiver to eat that," she told Brad.

"Then we'll just look at it," he said, and did that for a moment. Finny could tell he was drunk. He'd worked his hand farther up Finny's leg, even brushing his fingers along the zipper of her pants, testing. They'd turned down the lights in the restaurant, and since Finny and Brad were tucked so far back in the crowd, Finny knew no one was observing them. She put her hand on the inside of his leg, and felt that he had an erection.

He smiled at her and said, "Your place is close to here, right? What do you think about walking in that direction?"

"I might consider it," Finny said coyly. She felt like an actress reading a script.

It was just then that the waitress brought the check. Brad handed her his card without even looking at the bill.

"Well, keep considering," he said, and gave Finny's leg another squeeze. He got up from the table, straightening his pants to hide his excitement, then went to the bathroom.

When he got back, Finny said, "If you're doing anything interesting in there, let me know." She knew she was drunk, too, since normally she would never have made a comment like that.

"Maybe I will," Brad said. "Once we get to your place."

The waitress returned with the receipt for Brad to sign. She'd been quiet and somewhat cold the entire evening, but with the prospect of Brad adding a generous tip to the bill, she seemed to perk up.

"How did you all enjoy your flavors this evening?" she asked Finny and Brad.

It was an odd way to phrase the question, but they both answered that everything was great. Phenomenal even.

Back at Finny's apartment she barely got the door closed behind them before Brad had her against the wall, his hand on her breast, his erection poking her leg like an accusing finger. He'd dropped his messenger bag next to where they stood, on top of the row of shoes Finny kept by the door. As they kissed, he worked his other hand over her body, feeling her belly, her ass, her legs. He seemed warm from their walk outside, his forehead glistening. Finally, he inserted his hand into the waist of her pants, his fingers smoothing over the unmistakably wet patch on her underwear.

"I'm really turned on by you," he said.

Finny nodded. She felt his hand working into her underwear, then one of his fingers slipping inside her. She moaned. She couldn't help it. A flood of warmth rushed to her groin. She felt her hips begin to move with his in a gyrating motion, like an imitation of sex. His finger was gliding in and out, in and out.

"Where's your bed?" he said.

She tilted her head in the direction of her bedroom. She wasn't sure if she could speak, she was so turned on. She felt feverish. Buds of sweat had begun to bloom on her forehead. She put both her hands around his neck and let his finger thrust inside her.

"I want you so bad, Finny," he said. "It's painful."

She grabbed his shirt collar and gave it a tug. "Let's go," she said.

They slipped off their shoes, and she took him by the hand down the hallway. Their palms were hot and moist against each other. Finny could hear footsteps in the hallway above them, the Almeidas getting ready for bed. She snapped the light on in the kitchen so they wouldn't trip, and something about the sudden brightness, the cold linoleum on the pads of her bare feet, made her feel as if the act were already done, as if she were leading Brad to the front door, saying good night. She flipped off the light.

The bedroom was dim. Finny turned on some music she liked—Elliott Smith playing a solo concert with his acoustic guitar. The lights of the stereo cast the room in an electric blue glow. Brad pulled Finny to him, and for a minute they swayed together to the music like old lovers. She closed her eyes and imagined herself dancing in faraway places: Tokyo, Mexico, Paris.

Then Brad was laying her down on the beige comforter, his hands working over her, undressing her. He pulled her blouse over her head. He unfastened the clasp of her bra. He unbuttoned her pants and tugged them over her hips, revealing the small pair of black panties Finny had chosen for the occasion. He grinned at the sight of them. With one finger, he tugged on the lip of her panties, releasing the marshy scent of her arousal. He pulled the underwear down and pressed his nose into the thatch of her pubic hair.

"You're gorgeous," he said, just before she felt the tip of his tongue inserting itself where his finger had been. She shivered, convulsed. He was unbuttoning his own shirt, removing it. She heard the buttons tick against the floor when he tossed it off.

In a minute he was standing in his underwear, his chest shining in the blue light from her stereo. He had a nicely muscled body, some faint ridges along his abdomen, which was slightly bulged from all the food. The hair on his chest, which Finny noticed also grew more thinly on his upper arms and the top of his back, was the color of sawdust, and it looked softer than it had through the V of his open-necked shirt.

"Can you give me just one minute?" he said. "I don't know if you need to get ready or anything."

She knew he meant birth control. "I have condoms," she said.

"I'll be right back," he said.

He walked out into the dark kitchen, and she heard him knock into a chair and curse to himself. She laughed. She began to masturbate lightly, so that she'd still be ready for him when he returned.

In five minutes, he hadn't come back. She got up from the bed, put on her bra and underpants, and went into the kitchen, briefly flicking on the light so that she didn't knock into anything. She had goose bumps on her arms and legs. It was cool for summer, and Finny was always sensitive to temperature. She heard some clicking and unzipping in the bathroom, and noticed the line of light under the door. She was worried he might have gotten sick from all the wine, and thought that maybe she should check on him.

When she got into the hall, she noticed his messenger bag was not where he'd placed it before, on top of her shoes. He must have taken it with him into the bathroom, which was a strange thing. She was just about to knock on the bathroom door when she heard a long, decisive sniffing sound, like someone with a very bad cold. Then she heard the sound again. It was unmistakable. And it came to her all of a sudden why Brad had been making so many trips to the bathroom, what he had in the messenger bag.

She hurried back to the bedroom, stepping silently on the cold floor so that he wouldn't hear her, wouldn't know she'd been listening to him. She got back in bed, under the comforter, feeling cold all over. She'd lost her buzz from the alcohol, and with her drunkenness her ardor had also fled. She felt a rush of shame for how she'd acted. Like a horny teenager, she thought. So frivolous. It wasn't that Finny objected to sex, even casual sex; it was just the fact of getting it in this childish way, all the drinking and pawing at each other, the bribe of a fancy meal. And why Brad, who had probably snorted enough coke over the course of the evening to fund a Colombian cartel?

She got out of bed and started to dress. She no longer wanted to sleep with him, was even slightly repulsed by the idea. The springs had dried up. But how do you tell a man like Brad you've lost interest, once you've gone so far?

And the appearance of Brad at the bedroom door, his eyes glazed with lust and drugs, didn't make things any easier. Finny had put her pants and blouse back on, and had turned up the lights.

"What's the matter?" Brad said. His speech was rapid, quick as a drumroll.

"I just got cold," Finny said.

"I think I can help with that," he said, sitting down beside her, snuggling his hand into her crotch. "Can you get the lights, babe?" he asked, kissing her neck, swirling his tongue in her ear. It tickled, and she had to suppress the urge to laugh at him.

"Brad," she said.

He didn't respond.

"Brad."

"These lights are killing me, babe," he said.

"I'm not sure, Brad—"

But he pushed her back on the bed, straddling her. She knew that if she tried to wiggle free, his weight would keep her pinned to the mattress. Not that she tried. Not that she really meant to get him off her. He seemed encouraged by resistance anyway, and he smiled his wide smile at her. He planted a kiss on her lips. She could feel his nose pressing into her face, and when he pulled back, she saw blood in one of his nostrils. At first she had the irrational thought that it was hers, that he'd somehow cut her or bitten her. But then she realized it was his own blood, that nosebleeds were probably as common in his life as trips to the bathroom.

"You're bleeding," she told him weakly.

But he didn't seem to care. He'd opened the button of her pants and was tugging them down along with her underwear. Finny didn't even care anymore. She didn't see the point in resisting. She just wanted to get it over with as soon as possible so she could have the apartment to herself.

"Just use a condom," she told Brad.

While he was unbuckling his pants, she reached into a drawer by the bed and produced a condom for him. He tore the wrapper with his teeth and slid the rubber over his penis with remarkable swiftness. He was fairly large with an erection, and when he pushed into Finny, she gasped as if she'd been socked in the stomach. He began to move to the rhythm of the guitar music from the speakers, pushing in and pulling out of her. She felt a tingle at this familiar motion, and decided she would close her eyes. The bright light was bothering her anyway. But the spark never caught. She couldn't bring herself to enjoy him.

Soon she felt hot raindrops on her face. At first she thought it was his saliva, like from a rabid animal. But then she realized it must have been the blood from Brad's nose that was speckling her, and probably the comforter, too. She was thinking about how much a new comforter would cost, when he let out a long sigh, and she realized he'd finished. She heard applause from the CD.

"Oh," Brad said, breathing heavily. "Damn, that was good."

Finny pushed him off her, pulled up her pants, and went to the bathroom to pee. She wanted to get the feeling of his body out of her as soon as she could. And she wanted to get his actual body out of the apartment even sooner. When she was done peeing, she went to the sink and looked at her own face under the Hollywood bulbs of her bathroom mirror, her skin dotted with rust-colored beads of blood. She thought of the blissful expressions of couples in women's magazines, next to articles about hookups and sex moves. She thought of the way she used to model her rat's nest in front of the mirror when she was a child, and she laughed at herself—always her first reaction to pain—at how much had changed. She leaned down and turned on the faucet, splashing the blood off her face with water that was too hot and that ran in a pink stream into the drain.

When she came back, he was already dressed. He'd wiped the blood off his own face and had smoothed his hair. He was adjusting his belt, his shirt neatly tucked in. He was well aware of the fact that she wanted him to leave.

"Thanks," he said, coming over and kissing her on the cheek. "You were amazing."

He started toward the bedroom door. She knew she should have just let him go, but she couldn't help saying, "You were a fucking asshole."

He stopped. He turned around and looked at her. She could see how easily his lust turned to anger, like a train switching tracks. He breathed deeply, and his eyes widened.

But all he did was say to her, "You knew I didn't have any business in Boston, right? When I saw you, I knew I could have my dick in you in ten minutes."

Then he turned back around and walked out the bedroom door. Finny heard him picking up his messenger bag in the hall, putting on his shoes, and then the slam of the front door as he left the apartment.

Later that night, after she'd decided she couldn't sleep, Finny went into her study and turned on the computer. She checked her email, and saw that she had a message from Earl Henckel in her inbox:

Finny! I'm going to be in New York in September to do the reading for the book. It's at the Barnes & Noble on St. Mark's Place. I'll give you details when it gets closer, but I know the date is the 19th. I'm bringing Mavis, and I hope you can bring

Brad. Maybe we could all have dinner together afterward. Actu-
ally, it'll be kind of a celebration, since I have some news: Mavis
and I are planning to get married when we get back to Paris
after the reading. I know this is kind of sudden, but we've just
decided it ourselves. It's going to be a courthouse wedding, no
guests, since neither of us is into the idea of a big ceremony.
Anyway, I'm really looking forward to seeing you, Finny, and
will of course fill you in on all the details. And I'll have your
copy of the book all ready!

She saw by the time on his email—8:17 A.M., six hours
ahead of her—that he'd just written it. She knew that at this
very moment he was sitting in Mona's old apartment. She
imagined him with his laptop and a cup of coffee at the breakfast table in the room Finny had shared with him all those
years ago. It was Saturday morning, and sunlight was streaming through the little high window.

Chapter **36**

A Pleasant Evening

Finny, her brother's email began, *what are you up to? How have you been? I feel like you dropped off the face of the earth. I haven't talked to you in forever. Are you doing okay? Send me a smoke signal . . . . . . Sylvan*

She wrote back: *I'm doing fine, Sylvan. Thanks for your concern. It's been a tough summer since Mr. Henckel passed away. I just need some time to get moving again. I'll call you soon.*

But he wouldn't leave it at that. *We have to get together before summer's over,* he wrote. *I have two weeks with absolutely nothing to do. I was thinking I'd go up to New York one day. Why don't you come down?*

After her evening with Brad, Finny hadn't wanted to see anyone at all. She'd called Julie Fried and said thanks but she really couldn't make the move now. Julie would see very soon how big a mistake Finny was, and then Finny would be out of a job in the most expensive city in the country. Brilliant.

She couldn't talk to anyone—especially the people she was closest to—about what had happened with Brad. That's why she avoided Sylvan. And yet that evening occupied so much of her thoughts. Talking with Sylvan and not discussing it, she would have felt like she was lying. Plus, there was still the issue of Sylvan's affair with Judith. A nagging itch.

But when Finny didn't respond right away to her brother's email, he called her. And called her. And called her. Finally, in exasperation, she agreed to meet him one night for dinner in New York. He was bringing Mari, whom Finny hadn't seen since college.

In order to balance out the table, and so that Finny wouldn't be subjected to her brother's intense psychological scrutiny, she called Carter to ask if he'd be her date.

"I won't be expected to give you head, will I?" Carter asked.

"Only if I buy you dessert," Finny said, cringing at the memory of the untouched baked Alaska that had sat between her and Brad.

"Well then," Carter said, "in order to prevent such blatant exploitation, I propose we go to Garreth's restaurant. We'll be treated very well, and I'll receive enough free food that I won't be forced to compromise myself for a molten chocolate cake."

"Sounds good," Finny said.

"And by the way," Carter said, "I bring news from the front."

"Which front?"

"The silicone one."

"You really think Judith's boobs are fake?" Finny said.

"I was talking about Prince," Carter said.

So they all decided to meet at the restaurant where Garreth was a manager, in the bottom floor of a building off Washington Square Park. Finny took the bus down to have dinner with everyone, and then she planned to sleep on Carter and Garreth's couch, which Carter said was upholstered in a dog-hair fabric.

The restaurant was below street level, and when Finny walked into the bar, she could see pedestrians' legs scissoring across the large amber-tinted windows. The room had about a dozen small brass-topped tables in it, like in a French bistro. On the walls hung portraits of famous female movie stars—Greta Garbo, Marlene Dietrich, Carole Lombard—in an art deco style. There were also reproductions of famous paintings like Klimt's "The Kiss," made out of small tiles fit together into a mosaic. Only one table in the room was filled: two older women sharing a pot of tea. Carter had said it would be empty: summers were slow, and they were eating early. It was only six.

She found Garreth behind the large brass-railed bar with a synthetic marble counter. "He'll be here in one second," Garreth said about Carter. He had a pleasant, laid-back, almost sleepy way of talking, as if he'd known Finny for years. "I think he's buying cigarettes at the Duane Reade. He does that a lot since he quit smoking. By the way, I love your hair."

"I'm thinking of growing it out," Finny said.

"Why?"

"I'm not sure I like the guys it attracts. You excluded, of course."

Garreth smiled. "Well, let me grab you a drink while you're waiting."

"I'm not much of a drinker," Finny said.

"Which means you like fruity drinks," Garreth said. "Something you could get sitting under a beach umbrella in Tulum, right?"

"Sounds about right," Finny said, happy to see that Garreth had a sense of humor. She didn't think anyone could live with Carter without a sense of humor.

Garreth poured half a dozen ingredients into a shaker with ice, put the cap on, and then gave the whole thing a vigorous shake. He poured it into a chilled martini glass with a lime on the rim. The drink was a deep red, almost burgundy, color.

"What is it?" Finny asked.

"It's a goddamn travesty," Carter said from the doorway of the bar. The two women drinking tea looked in his direction, frowned, then went back to their tea. Carter was dressed in a bright yellow button-down shirt that reminded Finny of his yellow *Ship Shape* shirt. The color didn't sit particularly well on Carter. It made him look sallow, and a little puffy. "I don't even see how you can call that a martini," he went on about the drink, walking into the room.

"And what are you having?" Garreth asked Carter.

"Cranberry and soda," Carter grumbled.

Garreth poured Carter's drink into a martini glass, placing an inordinate amount of fruit—cherries and orange wedges, even a disk of green apple—on the rim. Then he passed the drink to Carter, who smelled richly of cigarette smoke.

"Very funny," Carter said. "I'm glad you take pleasure in the spectacle you've made of me. You're carting me around like your goddamn lobotomized grandmother."

"Just eat your orange and I might let you play with the soda gun," Garreth said.

Finny laughed, enjoying the coolheaded way Garreth responded to Carter's bluster.

In a few minutes Sylvan and Mari walked in. Carter got up from his bar stool and gave them both a kiss. Finny could tell her brother felt a little odd getting kissed by a man, but he bore it admirably. Only a slightly stiff expression on his face betrayed his discomfort. Mari, on the other hand, looked thrilled to see Carter.

"You look great!" she said to him.

"I look like Orson Welles at an all-you-can-eat buffet," Carter said. "But thank you for the thought."

Finny got up, and there were more hugs and greetings. Everyone said how much they liked Finny's short haircut. Carter introduced Garreth. The two women with the tea seemed irritated by all the commotion, and one of them began waving her finger for the check and calling, "Yoo-hoo, *yoo*-hoo," to Garreth.

"I love when they do that," Garreth whispered to Finny. "Don't ever get old."

She asked him how much she owed him for the drink, since it looked like Carter was heading to a table, and Garreth waved Finny off. "On me," he said, and went to attend to the tea women. "What can I do for you ladies?" he asked them, grinning, suddenly cheerful, and Finny could see why he made a good manager.

Carter picked out a table in the back corner, beneath the portrait of Marlene Dietrich. He and Sylvan sat on the cushioned bench that stretched all the way down the wall, and Finny and Mari took the chairs opposite them. They had the room to themselves. Soon the night bartender took over for Garreth, who had gone into the main dining room. Some rock music came on in the speakers above them, and a man's voice began to sing. Several appetizers arrived at the table before they'd even ordered: fresh guacamole and chips, fried calamari, a baked flat bread with sausage and cheese on it.

"He takes care of me," Carter said to Finny.

"I can tell," Finny said.

They all caught up for a few minutes about their lives. It was still bright outside the amber windows. Carter pointed out the flower arrangement he'd done for the window by the bar, which was full of sunflowers and purple lilacs, a cheerful summery look. The bartender was busy making drinks for the restaurant. The music cycled through a mix of eighties pop and jazz and soul. Finny noticed that Mari watched Sylvan when he talked, the way she'd watched Carter at Judith's party, where Finny had first met her. Mari barely took her eyes off Finny's brother, who seemed to enjoy the attention. When he talked about his work, she nodded and encouraged him. Finny thought it was sweet. And she knew her brother needed someone like that, who hung on his every word. Mari had grown into a plain-looking woman, with a wide, flat Midwestern face. She was, in fact, from Michigan, and she'd attended Columbia with Judith and Prince. She'd met Carter since he'd hung around the drama- and English-major crowd while he was acting and catering in the city. Mari had a straightforward, quiet, unadorned way of speaking about herself, and she wasn't vain at all. What a difference from Judith, Finny thought, and she wondered if that could be the reason her brother liked her. Because she was safe.

"So you'll be interested to know, Finny," Sylvan said as they were starting a bottle of wine, waiting for their entrées to come out, "that a friend of yours stopped by during my summer office hours."

"Who?" Finny said.

"You remember Dorrie Kibler?" Sylvan said.

"Really? Why did *she* come by?" Finny asked.

"I didn't even realize she was your roommate until we'd been talking for a minute, and I remembered you mentioning her. When I told her who I was, her mouth literally dropped open."

"Isn't there some sort of patient confidentiality agreement?" Carter asked. Finny realized he must have been seeing a shrink.

"Normally, yeah," Sylvan said. "But she didn't come in as a patient. She was just visiting the school, and she decided to drop by. She wanted to thank us. Or rather, to thank you, Finny."

"Thank *me*?" Finny said.

"She said she had lunch with you when she was pregnant, in college, and she admitted to you how scared she was. She said you were really supportive, and you listened to her, and didn't judge. It got her thinking that maybe that's what she needed—someone to listen. So she started coming to psych services at Stradler, not telling anyone. As you know, she had the baby. But maybe what she didn't tell you was that she ended up divorcing the guy she was with—Steven, I think—when she graduated. She's bringing the kid up on her own now. She got another degree in chemistry or something, and she's working on a big paper about proteins in mice. Anyway, she's doing well. She just wanted to say what a difference it made to have people who listened to her. That her life is much bigger than it ever would have been without that."

"Wow," Finny said. "Who would have thought? I assumed she'd be popping out little Steven Benches for the next twenty years."

"Those little moments can make a huge difference," Sylvan said, and Mari nodded. The music in the bar had switched over to a French singer with a light, breathy voice. It was pleasant, though it reminded Finny of her time in Paris, which always brought some sadness. Two college-age boys had come in and were sitting at the bar, talking to the bartender. One of them wore a corduroy hat and jacket and had some scruffy facial hair, and the other was wearing a full tuxedo with a cummerbund. They seemed to be the bartender's friends.

"Well," Carter said, "since we're on the topic of people leaving people, I have some news that I think this crowd will appreciate."

The food runner arrived with their plates and set them down in front of everyone. Finny had ordered a short rib dish. The meat had been braised in wine, and it was tender and rich and brightly flavored, better than anything she'd had during her eighty-five-dollar dinner with Brad. It put her in mind of the sorts of dinners she hoped to have from now on, the people she wanted to enjoy them with. "This is amazing," Finny said.

"See why I'm so fat?" Carter said.

"Anyway," Finny said, "you were saying?"

"Yes," Carter said, "I was saying. To make a long story short, Judith left Prince."

Sylvan's knife slipped out of his hand, clattering on his plate. They all turned toward him, and his cheeks flushed. "Sorry," he muttered. Mari patted his arm.

"Are you serious?" Finny said.

"She's camped out at the beach house," Carter went on. "Prince is at the apartment in the city. I think she's really serious about it. She says she's getting her stuff together to go back to school for English. She wants to get her Ph.D."

"I really can't believe it," Finny said. "I figured she'd be taking his abuse as long as Dorrie was having Steven Bench's babies." She noticed Sylvan had stopped chewing and was staring at Carter. Mari had a polite smile on her face. "What do Judith's parents think?" Finny asked.

"They're not happy," Carter said. "According to Judith, her mom isn't talking to her. And her dad is useless. He's always been. He tells Judith he'll talk to her mom, and then he promises her mom he won't talk to Judith. He's about as effective as a glass of cranberry juice."

Finny smiled at that. "So what was it? What made the change?"

"It was that weekend," Carter said. He turned to Mari and explained, "We witnessed the newest season of *Guiding Light* at Judith's house over Memorial Day weekend."

"I heard from Sylvan," Mari said, and Finny wondered exactly how much her brother had told her. She saw how dedicated Mari was to Sylvan, and she couldn't help feeling a little sorry for her, for the disappointments she was sure to face. Finny heard the boy in the tuxedo at the bar saying, "You really fucked me over," and the boy in the corduroy cackling at him, then coughing a rattly smoker's cough.

"Anyway," Carter said, "that fight and then the thing with the photos just pushed it over the top. They didn't talk to each other the rest of the weekend. Judith stayed in the room with me. By the way, thank you for leaving me in such comfortable circumstances, Finny Short."

"Finny had a lot to attend to," Sylvan said.

"I know, I know," Carter said. "I'm just joking. I'm really sorry about your friend, by the way."

"Thanks," Finny said.

"The whole weekend kind of opened her eyes," Carter said. "She told me she saw what she'd been missing in her life with Prince."

Sylvan looked at the table. He had the same stiff expression on his face as when Carter had kissed him.

"You should call her," Carter said to Finny. "I think it would mean a lot. I get the sense she's really trying to make amends. I can feel for her on that one. She wants to see you and Sylvan when she's back on her feet."

"Did you know any of this?" Finny asked Sylvan.

Sylvan shook his head. "It's new to me," he said.

Later, when they were finishing dinner and the light was fading outside the amber windows, Carter went into the dining room to talk to Garreth. Mari got up to use the bathroom. The boys had left the bartender alone again, and the music had switched back to some piano jazz.

"Sylvan," Finny said when she and her brother were alone. She knew she was a little drunk, but she also knew she had to talk to Sylvan now about Judith. "I saw Judith coming out of your room that night. It was late and I heard something in the hall—"

But her brother started shaking his head. "I had a feeling," he said. "Is that why you've been avoiding me?"

"No—" Finny started to say. But she couldn't say any more. Because of course he was right. He knew her too well.

"Listen," Sylvan said, and reached across the table to grab Finny's arm. He pulled her toward him, a little forcefully, and Finny almost yelled at him to stop. She could tell he was drunk, too, and she worried he would say something he'd regret. But when she leaned forward to speak, he cut her off. "You're totally wrong about what you think happened," he whispered. "I'm going to tell you the truth very quickly, before everyone gets back, and I don't want to say anything more about it. Judith came into my room and took off her clothes. She figured I'd jump in bed with her the second I saw her naked. And trust me, Finny, I wanted to. I know you don't want to hear this from your brother, but you don't know what it's like for a man to have a woman like Judith standing naked in front of him. It's painful. She started telling me all the kinky things she did with Prince, trying to get me excited. I could tell it was a power thing, like she wanted to prove the hold she still had over me. But I started to feel sorry for her, Finny. I saw how sad and desperate she was, and how much Prince had hurt her. And that's what kept me from sleeping with her. I just felt sad. I told her to leave. So she wrapped herself up and went. I didn't know she saw you. She wouldn't have told me that."

"Then why was she fighting with Prince in the morning?" Finny asked.

"Because he's an asshole. And because even someone as dumb as Prince can tell when his wife is flirting. He was a dick to me the rest of the weekend, and I ended up leaving early."

After saying this, Sylvan nodded quickly at Finny, as if to say, *You see?* He watched her, waiting for her reaction, and all of a sudden Finny felt an awful twang of guilt. She'd been wrong. She'd misjudged. Why hadn't she given Sylvan a chance to explain? It was as if she'd wanted to believe the worst about him. As if all her disappointments had colored her view of even the people she cared most about.

Sylvan didn't lie to Finny about how he'd felt, about how difficult it had been to resist Judith's magnetic sexuality. Finny knew it wouldn't have been fair to expect Sylvan not to be attracted to Judith. But Finny could see that her brother took pride in the fact that he'd been strong enough to know it was the wrong thing, that he cared enough for Mari, and for Judith, not to give in. Finny remembered the way Sylvan had sat there that morning when Judith had wept on the floor of the beach house, after Prince tossed the photos into the room. She understood now how angry he must have been at Judith for putting him in the position she had, for teasing him with what she knew was a long and deeply felt affection. He simply couldn't bring himself to go to her. Finny realized all that he had held in that morning, all that he'd suffered alone, and she wanted to tell him how sorry she was for doubting him. How much she loved and respected him.

But just then Mari came back from the bathroom. She saw Sylvan and Finny gathered close together, Sylvan's hand still gripping Finny's arm.

"Is everything okay?" Mari asked.

"I think so," Sylvan said, letting go of Finny and sitting back on the bench.

"It is," Finny said, watching her brother as she spoke. "We had a miscommunication about something. But I apologized to Sylvan. He knows I think I was wrong, and that I hope he'll forgive me."

Sylvan looked back and forth between Finny and Mari. He seemed dazed, as if the emotion of his confession had drained him.

"He will," Sylvan finally said, and took a slow breath. "He does."

Chapter **37**

The Reading

She was running late. The reading was set to begin at eight o'clock, and Finny was coming up the subway stairs at 8:02 by her watch. She was back to teaching, and she'd gotten out late today because one of the parents hadn't shown up to pick up a kid. So Finny missed her train. Then the next one was fifteen minutes delayed. She'd fixed herself up in the train bathroom, putting on her lipstick and doing her hair as the car wobbled and jostled her. It wasn't a perfect job, but it would have to do. Her hair had grown out a bit, and she didn't have to be so precise with it anymore.

Now there was a guy in front of Finny on the stairs taking forever. He had a green Mohawk, and the sides of his head were tattooed with some Chinese characters. He had piercings in the cartilage of his ears and the skin of his neck, and spacers that made the holes in his earlobes as large as quarters. When he turned, Finny could see he had a bull ring in his nose. She couldn't get around him because of the people coming the other way. Finally she said, "Excuse me, sir, I'm late." He looked back at her. He was a couple feet taller because he was higher on the stairs. He rolled his eyes and said, "I'm early." But Finny didn't have time to fight with him, so she simply ran around him and yelled back, "Do you know those Chinese letters spell *asshole*?"

"Bitch!" he yelled at Finny as she walked out of the station. She couldn't help chuckling.

Finny had figured out what she would say to Earl about Brad: out of town for the weekend, a business trip. As she walked past the bright shops of St. Mark's Place, the men with DVDs spread out on ragged quilts, the street punks and the drug dealers and the expensively dressed couples on their way to dinner at the latest Lower East Side gem, Finny prepared the smile she'd offer to Earl and to Mavis when she met them after the reading. It was a warm night, unusually humid for September, and Finny's skin felt prickly. She knew she was on the verge of breaking out in a sweat—one of those uncomfortable full-body sweats that leave the back of your shirt cold—and her anxiety over the coming meeting didn't help. What was there to worry about? She'd listen to a story, grab a bite to eat, and head back to her hotel. (She hadn't told her friends she'd be in town.) But still, each time she considered it, she felt a twitch of electricity in her chest.

At the Barnes & Noble she was directed upstairs for the reading. It was 8:18, and Finny worried she might have missed a good portion of it, but when she got there, she saw that a woman with black plastic-framed glasses was just finishing her introduction. She read a couple of nice quotes about Earl's book—probably from the back cover—and then asked everyone to welcome him. Finny sat down in the fourth row of folding chairs as Earl walked to the microphone that had been placed on top of the Barnes & Noble podium. There were only about twenty-five people in the audience, and the applause was polite, enthusiastic but not at all raucous. Finny wondered if the people gathered were friends of Earl's from when he'd been in New York. He'd mentioned that the only readings he was doing were this one and one he'd done earlier in the week at the University of Pittsburgh, where he'd won the contest.

Earl got up to the microphone and said that he was going to read from the first story he'd written in the collection, which was called "My Father the Collector." Finny was happy he'd chosen a familiar one. Earl even smiled at Finny when he read the title, since she was only about twenty feet from him. He seemed nervous, and a little shaky. She saw his hand tremble as he turned pages to find the story. He didn't talk as he did this, and the audience murmured to one another in the too-long pause. Earl still had his beard, but his hair was cut shorter and looked neater than it had in a while, like the way it was when he was a kid. At last, he found his place, and looked up at the audience. "Sorry," he said. "Here we go. 'My Father the Collector.'"

Immediately, when he began reading, his voice changed. It seemed deeper, less pinched, and he read at an easy, slow pace, pausing after the jokes as if he knew the audience would laugh. Which they did. Finny was taken aback by Earl's sudden confidence. The rhythm of the words he spoke seemed to calm him, and soon she wasn't hearing Earl anymore but Chris and his father. It's what Finny had always admired about Earl's writing: that ability to transform himself, to inhabit a character; that expansive sympathy.

As he read, Finny intermittently scanned the crowd, looking for Mavis. Finny had never seen a photo, but over the weeks since Earl had told Finny about Mavis, she'd developed a picture of her. She was short, olive-skinned, pretty in a serious, intellectual way. She wore glasses and dark clothes that were slightly too big for her, masking her body, which Finny even went as far as to imagine was nicely curved. (The opposite body type of Finny's long, limber frame.) But Finny didn't see this woman anywhere in the crowd. Most of the people were Earl's and Finny's age, except for a half dozen older listeners, probably retired people who regularly attended these readings. One pink-faced man with bifocals and hair as white as blank paper studied Earl intensely as he read, the man's mouth puckered and his forehead wrinkled, as if he were having trouble understanding what was being said.

There was a woman in the front row who also seemed to be paying particularly close attention. She was thin and fair-skinned, with dark hair, and she wore a plain blue turtleneck and black pants. She had her hair up in a loose bun. She smiled as Earl read, and Finny thought she had a pleasant, attractive face. Finny knew this was Mavis. No one else would have watched Earl so closely.

He was getting to the part at the end of the story when Chris goes back to his father's house, after his father died, and takes one more look around. Finny thought of those days she'd spent with Earl and Poplan as Mr. Henckel was dying, watching him sleep in the square of light from the little window. She didn't know if it was this or simply the story that made her eyes fill up when Earl said, "I knew my father was a great collector, and he could have hidden his findings anywhere." But Finny saw that the entire small audience was captivated, held up for a moment by the beauty of his words. She remembered the time Mr. Henckel had played the piano at the seafood joint in Baltimore and she'd witnessed the same thing, the way art can suspend you, the remarkable ability these men had to move people. For all the pain it had caused her, she considered herself lucky for having known Earl.

When the story was done, the woman who had introduced Earl came back up to the microphone and asked if anyone had any questions. There were a few questions about authors Earl liked reading, whether he'd gone to school for writing. He had a shy, somewhat awkward way of answering questions. He said *um* a lot. Clearly, the spell of the story had been broken.

But Earl was polite and unpretentious, and when the pink-faced man asked how he'd gotten the idea for the story he'd read, Earl said, "You know, I think all my stories are a combination of things I've lived through, feelings I've had, and then a bunch of stuff I think is probably funnier or more interesting or somehow more telling than what actually happened. So for example, with this story, I did grow up in a little brown house with my father. But my father was still alive at the time I wrote the piece. He'd never been a teacher's assistant. And we'd never tossed a chair down a hill together. Actually, he remarried very happily as soon as I left home. But I felt like I could talk best about some of my feelings about him by setting up the story this way. And I just thought it might be entertaining."

Earl seemed like he was going to leave it at that. He looked down at the book he'd read from, and smiled in a tight-lipped way. But then he looked back up at the man who'd asked the question and said, "I've always felt like there was a lot of loss in my life. Even before anyone I knew actually died. It probably wasn't much more than the normal bumps everyone gets, but for some reason they hit me harder. I think that's maybe the best reason I can give for why I wanted to become a writer—to be able to hold on to some things. I moved to France before I wrote this story, and I was away from both my father and a woman I loved very much, and though a lot of bad decisions came out of that time in my life, one good thing was this story. It captured for me that mix of happy memories and very painful regret." Earl nodded after he said this, like a punctuation mark, or as if to say that he'd gotten out exactly what he meant.

Then the reading was over. Everyone clapped again, and the introducer got up and said that people could get in line to have their copies signed. Earl sat behind a wide pine desk, and as the line filed forward, the introducer asked everyone for the spelling of their names, to make things easier for Earl. Since there were only a dozen people in line, Finny wasn't sure it was really necessary. When the woman asked Finny for her name, Finny said, "I'm an old friend. I'm pretty sure he knows how to spell my name."

When she got up to where Earl was sitting, she said, "You were wonderful."

He smiled at the sound of her voice, in the genuine, unrestrained way she'd always loved about him. "Thanks for coming," he said.

"I could tell everyone loved the story," Finny said.

"Half of them are my friends. They're paid to love it."

"No, really," Finny said. "I was crying at the end. It was beautiful."

"That means a lot to me, Finny." He reached across the table and touched her arm. "I've got your copy set aside. I'll give it to you later. I want to introduce you to some people."

Since Finny was the last in line, Earl got up from the table. He thanked the woman who had given the introduction, and she said he'd done a great job, that she'd expect him back when the next book came out.

"Whenever that is," Earl said.

"Whenever that is," the woman repeated, and shook his hand.

Earl walked over to the pink-faced man, who was reading Earl's book through the bottom of his bifocals. The book was a paperback with what Finny recognized as an inexpensive cover, a blurred photograph of a parrot in a cage on the front. Earl grabbed the man by the elbow and said, "John, this is my friend Finny. Finny, this is my agent and sometimes-friend, John."

The man laughed at this introduction, and patted Earl on the back. "You'll see what a good friend I am when that novel comes along."

"You're writing a novel?" Finny said to Earl.

"Allegedly," he said, and blushed the way he used to when he was a kid.

"It's damn good," John said. And then to Finny, "Make sure you keep up your friendship with Earl so he can buy you dinner when it comes out."

"Thanks," Earl said to his agent. "Thanks for coming, John. I really appreciate it."

"Of course," John said, and slapped Earl again on the back in a sportsmanlike way before telling Finny it was nice to meet her and then taking his leave.

Next, Earl brought Finny over to a man in a brown collared shirt, with dark eyes and curly hair that hung over his ears like an unpruned plant. The man had a light beard that grew down his neck, as if he hadn't shaved in a week. His hands were plunged in his pockets, jingling the coins and keys he kept there. He was standing next to the woman in the blue turtleneck. Finny thought it was nice how Mavis stood back and let Earl enjoy his evening in the spotlight.

"This is Paul Lilly," Earl said to Finny.

"I know you stayed at my place," Paul said, shaking Finny's hand, "but I don't think we ever got the chance to meet."

"It's a pleasure," Finny said. Paul's hand was damp from being stuck in the pockets of his wool pants. "And thanks for letting me stay over."

"This is Shana, Paul's girlfriend," Earl said, presenting the woman in the blue turtleneck. It took Finny several seconds to process what Earl had said, and so she stood there, probably with a blank look on her face, as Shana smiled and held out her hand. Shana. Not Mavis.

"Nice to meet you," Finny finally said, and shook hands.

"So, what are you up to?" Paul asked Earl.

"I'm going to catch up with Finny tonight, since we haven't gotten to do that in forever. But let's get lunch tomorrow. Are you guys still up for that?"

Paul and Shana said they were. They congratulated Earl, told him what a great reading it was, and then headed off, clutching their copies of *Calling Across the Years*.

"By the way, where's Brad?" Earl asked Finny.

Her lie flashed in her mind—business trip, out of town— and suddenly the whole story seemed foolish to her. She simply told Earl, "Things didn't work out with Brad. But it's for the best. Where's Mavis?"

"She couldn't make it," Earl said, pressing his lips together in a way that told Finny there'd been an argument about it. "Work again. She's very busy."

"Oh," Finny said. "That's too bad."

"But you'll still have dinner with me, right?" He looked at Finny hopefully.

"Only if you bring my copy."

"Deal," Earl said.

They decided to walk west, since Earl knew the neighborhoods better in that part of the Village. He only had a small messenger bag, and Finny just had her backpack with a change of clothes. Earl said he wanted to take Finny somewhere special. And then Finny said he was wrong about one thing: she was taking him.

"Like your agent said, you can treat when your novel comes out," Finny said.

"Listen," Earl said, "if you want to have dinner again with me in the next decade, I think you're safer not to place your hopes on my novel."

"John said it was great," Finny said. "I think he would know."

"What he liked was the part I sent him a year and a half ago, before my mom died. I haven't been able to write a word since."

"You will," Finny said, looking at him. "You just need time. You've been through a lot. Once you and Mavis settle somewhere new, I think it'll be what you need."

"Thanks," Earl said. "It's nice to hear that."

They were walking along the south side of Washington Square Park now. The arch, on Finny's right, was illuminated, and the cement pit in the middle of the park was full of people. There were hippies with dreadlocks strumming out-of-tune guitars and singing. There were crowds of skateboarders, and college students. There were the drug dealers in trench coats, riding bicycles, holding open the flaps of their jackets to display their merchandise to passersby. There were couples holding hands or kissing on park benches. There were the chess men along the southwest entrance to the park, sitting over their dirty boards, saying, "Want a game? Want a game?" Squirrels and rats scurried across the paths, or scampered into garbage bags. Since her time with Earl in the city, Finny had always had an affection for this part of New York.

"So where should we eat?" Earl said as they turned south on MacDougal, toward the noisy bars and falafel shops and pizza parlors, the music and the drunk people staggering out of restaurants.

"I don't know," Finny said. "What kind of food do you feel like?"

"Anything," Earl said. "To tell you the truth, I'm actually not that hungry yet. I was so nervous, I don't know how much my stomach can take. But I want to get you something good."

"You know," Finny said, "I'm not that hungry right now either. Why don't we walk and see how we feel?"

So they walked. They turned right and headed over to Sixth Avenue, walked north on Sixth past the IFC theater; the bright windows of the sex shops; the mannequins with breasts like torpedoes; the newsstands; the men holding brown paper bags of pornography, ducking into the entrance for the orange line. They turned left on Tenth, headed toward the river, past the bistros and coffee shops. It was still warm, and the streets were busy and well-lit from all the open stores. A stream of cars flowed past them.

"Oh," Earl said. "Here. Before I forget." He opened his bag and took out a copy of his book, handing it to Finny. "But promise me," he said, while his hand was still on the book, "that you won't look at what I wrote until we say good night."

"Why?" Finny said.

Earl still had his hand clamped over the book. "Because I'm shy, and I have a tendency to be corny. Looking over all these old stories stirred up a lot of memories. So please indulge me."

"All right," Finny said, and put the book in her backpack. "Anyway, what's Mavis so busy with at work?"

Earl looked down. They were stopped at a corner, next to a Starbucks, waiting for the light to change. There was a large brick building on the opposite corner, which Finny took to be a school. Its windows were dark.

"She's just very absorbed in her work," Earl said. "It's become kind of an issue between us."

The light changed, and they crossed the street, headed toward the school.

"Is everything okay?"

"Yeah," Earl said. He seemed to be thinking about something. Then he said it again. "Yeah. I was just very disappointed that she couldn't make it for this trip. This is a big moment in my life. It wasn't the way I expected it to happen. I'd hoped I'd have some big book deal, and we'd be rich. But it just didn't go like that. I got the sense that once she realized how small it was, she was disappointed."

"Earl," Finny said, and put her hand on his arm, "you should be proud of this. The stories I've read are some of the best I've ever seen, no matter how much you got paid for them. You can't let yourself worry about that stuff. You just need to write."

He was looking forward, and Finny took her hand from him. She wondered for a second why he wouldn't turn to her, but then she realized his eyes were wet.

"I'm sorry," he said. "I wanted us to have a nice evening together."

"This *is* nice," Finny said.

They were coming up on the water, and across from them was the West Side promenade, where joggers pounded across the brightly lit pavement, men and women on roller skates performed twirls and danced to unheard rhythms, homeless people pushed shopping carts and dug in the cluttered trash cans. They crossed the West Side Highway and sat down on a cement bench that wrapped a little swath of green garden, watching the people and the sloshing water, the gray clouds bunched like frosting on a cake, the distant lights of New Jersey. Finny put her backpack in her lap.

"Why didn't it work out with Brad?" Earl asked.

"He wasn't the right person for me," Finny said. "I was fooling myself into believing he was. But he wasn't."

"Why? What wasn't right?"

"Almost everything. He didn't care about me. He only thought about himself."

"What did you like about him in the first place?"

"I don't know," Finny said. "It's hard to say. I think maybe I just felt like I needed to find someone. Like it was time. But I don't think that anymore. I'll be okay by myself. In fact, I'm making a career move." She didn't know what made her say it, but the moment she did, she knew it was true. She'd call Julie in the morning.

"Move to what?" Earl asked.

"I worked at this women's magazine one summer. Not the typical kind, but sort of counter to that—a lot of pieces about how screwed up everyone is. My kind of thing. It was fun. I feel like I might have something to add."

"I think you'd have a lot to add."

"Thanks. I appreciate it."

Earl glanced at Finny, then back ahead of them, like a driver checking his rearview mirror. "Mavis is leaving me," he said. "She's moving in with the French scholar. Jean-Pierre. Like something out of *Les Mis*."

"Jesus," Finny said, looking at Earl. "I'm sorry."

"Like I said," Earl went on, "she needs something bigger than me."

"That's a dumb thing to say," Finny told Earl. "It sounds like this might be for the best."

Earl shrugged. They both looked at the water, the heavy clouds above it.

"You remember the old vineyard?" Finny asked him.

"Of course," Earl said.

"Well, that's where I went that night. When your dad was dying. Before I came and met you. I went back to the old vineyard."

"How was it?"

"Pretty much the same," Finny said. "Except for everything looked smaller. I think I like the memory better. Nothing's the same when you come back to it."

"I know," Earl said. "I like the memory, too."

Finny asked Earl what his plans were now that Mavis was moving out, and he said he wasn't sure, it was all up in the air, he'd have to see. He just wanted to settle somewhere and start writing again.

Then it seemed they ran out of things to say. They sat for a few more minutes, not talking, until Finny mentioned she was tired.

"It was a long day," she said. "I should probably get some sleep."

"Oh," Earl said, "sure. Sure. I don't want to keep you up. I know you're busy."

Finny didn't say anything to that. She saw that somewhere along the way it had been decided they wouldn't have dinner together, though neither of them mentioned it. The moment had simply passed.

Now Earl offered to walk Finny back to her hotel. But she said no, she was fine. The hotel was on the West Side, and she'd walk along the promenade, where it was safe on a warm evening. He protested, but she assured him she'd be okay by herself. She told him to call next time he was in the States.

"I will," he said.

Then they parted, only a hug as goodbye. Earl headed east, Finny north.

She was almost to the pier that stuck out like a tongue into the Hudson when she remembered Earl's book in her bag. She unzipped her backpack and took the book out to see what he'd written. But when she opened the book to the title page, where she'd expected he'd written, there was nothing there. It was blank. She flipped the page, and still there was nothing.

Then something fluttered out of the book. It was too quick for Finny to see it, but when she looked up from the book, she saw the object twirling and rocking in the breeze. She reached up and snatched it out of the air, held it up in the light from the overhead lamps.

She knew instantly what it was: a blue and silver feather, the one she'd stolen from the pond with the exotic birds, the one she'd given to Earl the day she'd met him, on the hillside near her old house. All of a sudden, like a warm gust of wind, his words came back to her: *I'll treasure it always*. At the time she thought he was being smart, sarcastic in the offhand way she herself had perfected. But she saw now that he was simply telling her the truth.

She turned and spotted Earl standing on the cement island next to the West Side Highway, waiting for the light to change. He had his hands in his pockets and was examining the sidewalk like he'd dropped something there. He hadn't seen her open the book, probably figured she'd wait until she got back to the hotel. She saw him step into the street, walking slowly, as if unsure where he was headed.

Without considering what she was doing Finny called out, "Earl!"

He turned, and when he saw her, he waved his arms over his head in his old way, like he was signaling an aircraft.

He started walking back toward her, and they met on the promenade, next to the metal railing by the water.

"The feather," she said, smiling, though as the words left her mouth, she was struck by a feeling that could have been either happiness or sadness, she wasn't sure. It swept over her like some dashing river, and for a moment she couldn't speak.

"I'm sorry," Earl said, standing in front of her, looking at her with an expression of such honest longing that Finny could do nothing but take him in her arms. He began to cry, and Finny smoothed his hair.

"I'm sorry for everything," he said. "For disappointing you. For not being better."

"I know," she said.

"I didn't know what I was doing."

"I don't either."

And then he kissed her. It was starting to rain, a late-summer mist, and Finny felt drops on her face.

Chapter **38**

A Final Look

The wedding took place the following summer, outside the little brown house. Finny got a week off work. She'd taken the editorial assistant job. Julie was going on leave in the fall to do some teaching, and another editor was stepping up to take her place, leaving a spot open that had been promised to Finny. Earl had agreed to stay in New York as long as Finny's work kept her there. She'd insisted on that before they started planning the wedding.

The ceremony was held in the open air, the reception in a tent, and while it was all very moving for those involved, it is perhaps in some respects true, to rephrase Stein, that a wedding is a wedding is a wedding. Finny wore a white dress, Earl a dark suit. As a gesture of forgiveness, Finny had asked Judith to be her maid of honor, and in the pale yellow dress they selected, Judith was nearly radiant enough to eclipse the couple in whose honor the ceremony was being held.

To her credit, though, Judith didn't seek this attention. She was much less aggressive in her approach to makeup and jewelry than she'd been, and the dress she wore was more conservative, if more elegant, than the direction in which her wardrobe was tending when Finny visited her on Long Island. Judith had been accepted as an English Ph.D. candidate at

Columbia—to everyone's surprise, considering her age—and was set to start in the fall. She talked about it as a second beginning. Money, of course, wasn't an issue for her. Her divorce from Prince was complete, and she came to the wedding alone. At the ceremony, Judith smiled and cried along with everyone else, and it seemed to Finny an especially significant development that Judith was happy to simply be one of the crowd.

Poplan took her job as best man very seriously. Earl had considered asking Paul Lilly to perform that role, but Earl and Finny decided in the end that they wanted to involve Poplan in a more intimate way in the proceedings. In accordance with tradition, Poplan donned the dark suit befitting a groomsman, as well as a purple silk tie—her favorite color—and seemed to lower her voice just slightly on the day of the wedding, so as to be more convincing in her role. After presenting the ring to Earl during the ceremony, Poplan proceeded to bow formally to Earl, and then to Finny and the priest, and then to the entire audience. Though Earl was puzzled by the gesture, and no one ever quite figured out the reason for it, Finny assumed it was made in the spirit of celebration, goodwill, and general love of Asian cultures. As Poplan had predicted, she'd stayed on in the brown house, expanding her charity work to include not only the after-school program but a day care and a weekend activities center. She spent nearly all her time with the children, and as a mark of her enduring love for and dedication to Mr. Henckel, she required all of the kids to learn how to perform a successful smile-frown.

Sylvan was of course in attendance as well, as a groomsman, and not at all offended that he didn't have a larger function in the ceremony. He knew that Earl was much closer to Poplan, and Sylvan was much less willing than Poplan to cross-dress, which dashed any hopes that he'd be the maid of honor. One surprise about Sylvan's attendance was that, like

Judith, he came alone. In one of the phone conversations that had become a weekly routine for Sylvan and Finny once again, Sylvan confirmed Finny's suspicion that, though he cared for Mari, he wasn't prepared to commit to her. Finny was sorry. She liked Mari, and thought she was a good person. Though she knew that these were not strong enough reasons for Sylvan to marry her. They'd broken up when Sylvan had moved out of Philadelphia to start his practice in Westchester, just outside New York City.

The other bridesmaid was Sarah Barksdale, Finny's friend from Stradler and the daughter of Finny's former principal. She also came to the wedding alone, never having gotten back together with Scott, the man she'd been engaged to briefly. Finny had debated for a long time over whether to invite the Old Yeller as well, since she held no particularly fond feelings for Mrs. Barksdale, and finally she decided to go ahead and do it. She left room for Mrs. Barksdale to bring a guest, assuming it would be her husband, though it turned out that Mrs. Barksdale's guest was a much larger and more imposing presence. Miss Filomena Simpkin came dressed in the most formal attire Finny had ever seen her wear: a great expanse of blue crêpe fabric that, with the many plungings and billowings it made over Miss Simpkin's generous form, had the appearance more of a rollicking sea than a party dress. Miss Simpkin also wore her signature white flower behind her ear.

It was only after the ceremony, when guests were lining up to offer their congratulations to Finny and Earl, that Finny had reason to feel the slightest pinch of regret over inviting this pair. She overheard Miss Simpkin say that Poplan's choice of wardrobe was "regrettable," and Mrs. Barksdale responded, "Once again, Miss Simpkin, you have proven your absolute unassailability in all matters of taste. I had entertained a similar thought myself but was unsure whether to verbalize it, until my suspicions were confirmed by your impeccable judgment. Many thanks, Miss Simpkin. Many thanks!"

Among the other members of the distinguished party, as Mr. Henckel would have put it, were the now-ancient Aunt Louise, who had to excuse herself periodically to call the cat-sitter; Earl's agent, John Goines, who had just sold Earl's first novel; Finny's boss, Julie Fried, and her partner, Amanda; and Dorrie Kibler with her fifteen-year-old son. Carter had brought Garreth along to the wedding. They had both lost weight, and during the reception Carter explained they were on a carb-free diet. "You don't know what it's like," Carter told Finny. "I dream of bread. I salivate when I pass an Italian restaurant. I'm like a pedophile walking by a kindergarten." Garreth shook his head. "His trick is, he goes through a pack of cigarettes like it's a box of Ding Dongs." Finny laughed, and left them to argue it out. She knew how crabby Carter could be when he was hungry.

A wedding always seems a hopeful occasion, and in many ways this one was, though it's probably only fair to mention that there was also some sadness under the tent beside the little brown house. Finny thought of her parents, both long buried now, and of the dinners they used to have where she teased her father and fed Raskal under the table. She thought of her father's burnt cooking, her mother sitting upright in the hospital bed and saying *You have to understand,* and Finny realizing, in that one moment, how much her mother regretted. She thought of Mona, adrift in a tide of sadness so deep and fierce she was never able to free herself. She thought of Mr. Henckel, gulping his coffee for the last time, his face drawn and pale, and the final words he'd offered Earl and Finny, his blessing.

All these ghosts were in the room with them that evening as they danced and laughed and drank. Along with the spoiled relationships and bad marriages and illnesses and be-trayals and failed friendships, the disappointments in work and love. As well as the questions: What made her call out to Earl that night on the promenade? Why did she accept his advances after she'd promised herself she never would? Was it simply affection? Or was the affection mixed with something else, something like pity or sentimentality? She would ask herself these questions again and again over the years, though never to a completely satisfying end. It was all too muddy, too stirred up with other things she felt. To know all the sources of love would be like knowing every stream that has fed an ocean.

Whatever her reasons, Finny understood there was more of it ahead of her, both the good and the bad, and the uncertainty. To leave her at this comfortable place is not to suggest that life stopped here, only that it paused for a moment to take a breath, before beginning again on its winding course.

There is only one further occurrence worth noting at this cheerful gathering, and that is the appearance, arranged by Poplan, of a genuine Irish fiddler. He came through the tent flaps, which were now tied open to let in the cool breeze. The sun was setting, and the light, in its final moments, had that wonderful clarity. The band stopped playing and the fiddler walked onto the stage. His hair was the color of a ripe tomato, and he had a spray of freckles across his nose and cheeks, like he'd been splashed with mud. He lifted the fiddle to his chin, raised the bow, paused dramatically for a moment, then began to play.

At first the crowd didn't know what to do. Most of them had never danced to an Irish fiddle before. But Sylvan helped the situation a little by pulling Judith onto the dance floor, spinning her out and then drawing her back to him, his arm around her waist, as if he didn't want to let her go.

And then Earl, with Finny's permission, held his hand out to Poplan, who took it eagerly, and ended up leading Earl onto the floor. Finny watched the two of them go. For a moment, they appeared much younger, like the people Finny had met all those years ago. There he was, the boy who'd caught her when the fence broke, and who'd helped her under the top rail. There was the woman who'd met Finny in the lobby of the Thorndon School, asking her if she'd washed her hands. They seemed to have shed the intervening years like so much bulky winter clothing.

The last image Finny would recall from the party, when she thought back about it many years later, was of Earl spinning Poplan on the dance floor. Finny saw her purple tie flapping in the breeze.

Acknowledgments

Many thanks to the organizations that supported me while I was writing this book: the Michener-Copernicus Society of America, the Hawthornden Fellowship, the Bookhampton Fellowship, the Sun Valley Writers' Conference, the Southampton Writers' Conference, and the Bogliasco Foundation.

I owe a huge debt of gratitude to a number of teachers and writers for their generosity, advice, and encouragement: Ethan Canin, Bob Shacochis, Elizabeth McCracken, Maxine Rodburg, Melissa Bank, and Betsy Bolton.

Thank you to Ayesha Pande, my inimitable agent, for your intelligence, guidance, and dedication; to Millicent Bennett for your peerless insights, energy, thoughtfulness, and humor; to Jill Schwartzman for so many great ideas, so much enthusiasm, and such valuable help in the final stages of this book; to Kate Medina for your wisdom and enormously meaningful support over the years; to Linda Swanson-Davies and *Glimmer Train* magazine; and to Jane von Mehren, Sally Marvin, Beth Pearson, Anne Watters, Kathleen McAuliffe, Lindsey Schwoeri, and the many people at Random House who have given their talents, care, and weekend hours to this book.

Thanks also to Connie Brothers, Lan Samantha Chang, Asali Solomon, Bob Reeves, Christian McLean, Adrienne Unger, Dan Salomon, Jan Zenisek, Deb West, and Marika Alzadon.

And for love and remarkable tolerance, my deepest gratitude to my family: Jim Kramon, Paula Kramon, Annie Kramon, Salli Snyder, Liz Harlan, Ellin Sarot, John Trieu, Sandy Hong, Brian Trieu, and, of course and always, Lynn Trieu.

PHOTO: © 2009 JOAN BEARD

JUSTIN KRAMON is a graduate of Swarthmore College and the Iowa Writers' Workshop. His work has appeared in *Glimmer Train, Story Quarterly, Fence, Boulevard,* and *TriQuarterly.* He has received honors for his fiction from the Michener-Copernicus Society of America, the Hawthornden International Writers' Fellowship, *The Best American Short Stories,* and the Bogliasco Foundation. Now twenty-nine years old, he lives in Philadelphia. You can find additional information about Kramon and his work, as well as the reading group guide for *Finny,* at his website: www.justinkramon.com.